VENDETTA

A Story of Love & Revenge Set in Venice

C. DE MELO

www.cdemelo.com
ISBN 978-0-9997878-8-5

AUTHOR NOTE

Public galleys and their precious cargo symbolized the Venetian economy of the late Middle Ages, and were integral to the financial prosperity of *La Serenissima*. Despite their success for almost two centuries, their activity began to decline at the onset of the sixteenth century. "The year 1569 marked the end of the system which had characterized medieval Venetian trade." Quote from the journal, *The 'Public' and the 'Private' in Sixteenth-Century Venice: From Medieval Economy to Early Modern State* by Claire Judde de Larivière (2012).

Veronica Franco (1546–1591) was one of the most celebrated courtesans of Venice. Sophisticated and witty, she belonged to several literary circles and became a well-known published poet within her lifetime. Historical texts allude to her fondness of pretty shoes. A bit of her writing is featured in this book.

Although a few of the characters and events mentioned are historically accurate, keep in mind that this is a work of fiction. Several artistic liberties have been taken by the author.

DEDICATION

THANK YOU, D.

"The best revenge is to be unlike him who performed the injury."

(Marcus Aurelius)

PROLOGUE
VENICE, 1570
FEAST OF THE ASCENSION

"There are two types of men in this world: those who speak much but do little, and those who speak little but do much."

Isabetta recalled her father's favorite phrase with heartache. Zanetto Bastian had been a man of few words and great deeds. As for Rocco, the mere thought of him evoked tears.

Gleeful cries of children broke her reverie and dragged her back to the present. Beyond their little heads, the *Bucintoro* gently cleaved the putrid water of the Grand Canal. Constructed in 1449, the oarless vessel was one of the oldest in the city's arsenal. Festoons of fragrant spring blossoms adorned the painted figure of *Justice* affixed to the prow. Embodying Venetian grandeur, the ship floated past colorful *palazzi* with the illustrious doge seated on board.

Venice would marry the sea today. The annual celebration drew thousands of onlookers, many as foreign as the Englishman at her side. A talented artist from London, he had spent the last several weeks procuring rare gemstones, brocades, and Oriental curios for his noble patrons. Tomorrow, he would meet with a dealer of antiquities to purchase ancient Greek texts.

Venice was an emporium in every sense of the word—an international bazaar draped in lush patterned velvets and glimmering jewels. Visitors often gaped in awe at the sumptuous displays of decadence, but Isabetta knew a different side of the city. One of lurking decay beneath the shiny veneer of sophistication.

The artist grabbed her hand. "Look!"

Countless pairs of eyes were glued to the doge as he stood from his gilded throne and tossed a gold wedding ring into the water. The centuries-old ritual of the *Sposalizio del Mare* symbolized the crucial relationship Venice fostered with the sea as a maritime republic. Cheers rang out and the sound mingled with the cries of gulls circling in the azure sky above.

Isabetta hid her disdain. How long would the city keep up this pretense in the face of dwindling power? The Dutch and Flemish were monopolizing the best sea routes and overtaking Venetian trade, just as the Portuguese and Spanish had done decades earlier.

The artist grinned. "Splendid, is it not?"

His accent amused her. "Indeed."

"We shall watch the great procession in the Piazza San Marco. I hear this year's parade of foreign treasures seized by the adventuring Venetians will be impressive. Afterward, we'll dine on oysters and fine wine. Does that please you, my pretty?"

She doubted there would be many 'seized treasures' on display, but smiled nonetheless. Having received a ruby pendant as payment for two portraits, the cheerful man felt like celebrating—and on a day such as this, who could blame him?

Although Isabetta enjoyed the artist's pleasant banter and generosity, she would not spend the night with him. She never fornicated with any of the men with whom Veronica Franco paired her because they only used her as a ruse—not that she judged them.

How could she?

Deception had become so entrenched in her daily life that it felt almost as natural as breathing. While the Englishman babbled on about Venetian wonders, her thoughts drifted to the only thing that mattered.

Vendetta.

Chapter 1
Venice
One Year Ago

"Your mother will be angry if she finds out."

Isabetta Bastian's honeyed eyes flickered to the stairwell leading to the bedchambers above them. "Only if you tell her."

The servant continued stirring the fish stew in the iron cauldron with a dour face. Barely thirty, Alba's premature gray hair and missing teeth rendered her haggish in the orange glow of the fire. "Signora Hortensa may wake up at any moment. Best if you abstain from mischief."

"Those draughts you mix up are so potent they could put a bull to sleep."

"Your father would never approve."

"He won't be back until suppertime."

Reaching for the salt, Alba said, "No."

"Pleeeeeeease?"

"Signorina Isabetta, your parents would have my head if they—"

"They'll never know."

"Fine. I'll give you the address but if you're caught…"

"I won't tell my parents I got it from you."

"Swear it."

"I swear."

"It will seem less suspicious if you pretend you're going to the market." Alba waited for Isabetta to pluck a basket from the shelf, then continued, "You must return before your mother wakes up."

"Don't worry, I'll be back long before then."

"You'd better. I have no desire to invent stories explaining your absence, especially when you're going to see—"

"Oh stop! *Everyone* goes there."

Before Alba could reply, Isabetta stepped outside into the burnished gold of late afternoon. She crossed the market square where the local fishmonger waved to her in greeting.

Pausing at his stall, she said, "*Buona sera*, Viaro."

Leathery brown skin crinkled around his eyes when he smiled. "Where are you off to at this late hour?"

"Running an errand for my mother," she lied, marveling at how easy it was to deceive people.

"How is she, by the way?"

"Better." Another lie.

"Glad to hear it."

"How is Miro? Have you received news?"

Viaro's eyes twinkled. "Last I heard he was fine. Won't be back for another fortnight." He glanced up at the sky and added, "Go on now, it will be dark soon."

Isabetta bade him farewell and continued on her way with hasty steps. Dozens of vessels of various shapes and sizes floated upon the liquid copper surface of the Grand Canal beneath the tangerine sky. Strolling along the quay, she absorbed the sensory pleasures of her *sestiere.* Laughing children frolicked in the street where neighbors exchanged snippets of gossip. Savory aromas permeated the air as servants and housewives prepared supper. She stopped before a modest house, rechecked the address, and made use of the iron knocker.

The door swung open abruptly, revealing a middle-aged woman in a violet silk gown. "Yes?"

Isabetta squared her shoulders. "Signora Immacolata?" At the woman's wary nod, she continued, "*Buona sera.* I would like to have my fortune read, please."

"Do you have money?"

"I do."

Immacolata ushered Isabetta into her tidy home, then took a seat at a table covered by a red Persian rug. Indicating an empty chair opposite her, she said, "Sit."

Isabetta did as instructed while admiring the collection of items upon the table's surface. Crystals sparkled within a green glass jar and there were smooth stones lined up in a row, each one bearing a strange emblem. A gleaming silver bowl brimmed with lemons and limes.

"How do you know about me and what I do?" Immacolata inquired with forced casualness.

The widow's accent was southern but Isabetta couldn't place it. Naples? Salerno? Basilicata? "Everyone in the *sestiere* knows about you, madam."

Somewhat pleased by this response, Immacolata reached for a deck of Tarot cards. Fanning them face-down on the table, she instructed, "Choose two."

Isabetta's hand trembled as she made her selection.

The widow picked up the first card and turned it over. *Four of Swords*. She flipped over the second card and paused warily. *Knight of Swords*.

"So many swords."

Licking her lips, the widow said nervously, "You must select one more card."

Isabetta made her final selection and then gasped in surprise when the woman swiped the card from her hand. "Wait, I didn't get to see it!"

Ignoring the protest, Immacolata took a guarded peek at the Tarot image and forced her expression to remain neutral. The sight of a skeleton toting a sickle held the power to strike terror into the hearts of the bravest men, let alone a tender soul who had yet to experience the world. "This isn't working. Perhaps it would be better if I read your palms, instead."

Isabetta reached across the table with both hands. The widow's brow furrowed as she carefully studied the map of lines embedded in the firm rosy flesh of each palm. What she saw made her recoil in horror. The innocent creature seated before her couldn't possibly deserve such a cruel fate...*or could she?* Either way, she wanted nothing to do with the girl.

"What do you see?" Isabetta demanded.

Immacolata stood, concluding the visit. "Nothing."

Isabetta remained seated. "You're lying—"

"Sometimes it's best not to know the future. It will prevent you from enjoying the present."

A sickening feeling settled into the pit of Isabetta's stomach. "Signora, I beg you…At least tell me *something* so I can prepare for what lies ahead."

Biting her lip in contemplation, she finally relented. "The most violent tempest can't keep the sun at bay forever. It's important for you to always keep that in mind."

Isabetta committed the words to memory as she placed a coin on the table.

Immacolata scooped it up. "Here, you can keep it. I don't want payment." Ushering the unwanted visitor outside, she added firmly, "Don't ever come here again."

"I'm sorry if I—"

The door slammed in Isabetta's face before she could finish the sentence. Staring at the iron knocker inches from her nose, she wondered what the widow had seen. Something upsetting, obviously. She hurried home in the early evening gloom with several questions churning in her head.

Alba frowned at Isabetta the moment she opened the door. "Took long enough, eh? Your mother is awake. Lucky for you she hasn't left her bedchamber." She rinsed out a ceramic pitcher, then filled it with ale from a small barrel. "How did it go with Donna Immacolata?"

"She told me the usual things fortunetellers say to girls."

Narrowing her eyes, Alba demanded, "Oh? Such as?"

"Ah…let's see. I'll wed a handsome prince and be rich one day. Pure nonsense."

Rolling her eyes, the servant shook her head in disapproval. "Coins are wasted on silly girls."

The door opened, startling both women into silence. Zanetto Bastian's gaze slid from his servant to his daughter.

"Hello Papa," Isabetta said before kissing his cheek.

Placing the hot fish stew on the table, Alba said, "Signora Hortensa is upstairs, sir. She had a coughing fit earlier."

Zanetto's brow creased in concern. "Another one?"

"Worse than last time," whispered the servant.

Footsteps on the landing above made the three of them turn around simultaneously.

Hortensa stood at the head of the stairs. Her doughy face, abnormally pale from prolonged illness, stretched into a tight smile. "I know you're talking about me."

Zanetto aided his wife downstairs, then led her to a chair. "How are you feeling, my dear?"

"A bit better."

"I came across Rosa and Cassandra while passing through Santa Croce. They send warm greetings to you and Isabetta."

"Did my sister tell you the news?"

"About your niece's betrothal to Petro Vendramin?" Zanetto waited for his wife to nod, then continued, "I think the entire *sestiere* knows by now. Rosa even mentioned the possibility of finding a husband for our daughter."

Isabetta rolled her eyes dramatically.

Hortensa held up a stubby finger in warning. *"Don't."*

Ignoring her mother, Isabetta said, "Cassandra has always been a spoiled brat—"

"Hush!"

"—and now that she's marrying into the Vendramin clan, she will become insufferable."

"Isabetta Bastian! You must learn to keep quiet in the presence of your betters."

"Just because Uncle Alzo is rich and can afford an expensive dowry doesn't make them better than us. Isn't that so, Papa?"

Before Zanetto could respond, Hortensa interjected, "Your aunt and cousin only want to help you. That merits gratitude, not complaint."

Unconvinced, Isabetta crossed her arms. "My cousin will no doubt try to marry me off to some fat old man with less money than Petro so there's no danger of her being upstaged."

Alba's muffled chuckle reached their ears.

Hortensa shot the servant a withering look before addressing her feisty daughter. "How can you say such things about your kin?" Zanetto laughed, evoking his wife's ire. "This is not funny, Husband. Isabetta is incorrigible."

"I know," he agreed cheerfully.

"You encourage her with your lax comportment, Zanetto.

No wonder she's unruly and—"

A string of hacking coughs caused everyone to fall silent.

Alba rushed forward with a cup and urged her mistress to partake of some water.

Zanetto took hold of Hortensa's hand. "Calm down, my love. Isabetta possesses a lively spirit but we've taught her well. When the time comes, she'll know how to conduct herself like a proper lady." To Isabetta, he added, "Isn't that right? Appease your mother's fears, I beseech you."

Adopting a meek demeanor, Isabetta assured, "Papa is right. Don't worry, Mother."

"See?" Zanetto reached into his pocket and extracted a letter. "Here, I have something that will cheer you. I meant to surprise everyone after supper but now is a good time. Rocco will be home soon."

Hortensa took the missive into her hands and kissed the parchment. In a gravelly voice, she said, "God be praised!"

***

Isabetta crept out of bed later that night while everyone slept. Tiptoeing down the hallway, she froze when her father stopped snoring. Ears perked, she waited in the ensuing silence. He mumbled something in his sleep before resuming his rhythmic breathing. Relieved, she continued to the narrow stairwell at the end of the hallway, then carefully climbed into the attic crawl space.

Thick layers of dust coated the beams of the slanted ceiling. Crouching low to avoid bumping her head, she shuffled to the highest window of their home. After unlocking the shutters, she threw them open to reveal a moonless night. A rush of icy wind blew into the space, causing gooseflesh to erupt along her arms and neck.

Positioning herself on the sill, she reached into the pocket of her dressing gown and extracted the telescope her father had gifted her last year. The delicate instrument was her most precious possession. Placing the viewing lens to her eye, she studied the endless expanse of black velvet. Venus gleamed like a polished diamond amid the twinkling stars; a steadfast beacon. She tried to discern what existed beyond her limited range of vision. Did God live there? Was He watching her right now? Was He angry that she was sneaking behind everyone's back to study the heavens? Worse still, did He know how much she envied her brother? The sobering thought made her pause. If God didn't want women to lead the same lives as men, then why create them with brains and passions? Why not make them dumb like domesticated beasts?

Clustered stars formed familiar patterns—the same ones used by fearless navigators to cross vast oceans. She had devoured several books throughout the years on the science of navigation, updated sea routes, and the wonders of the mysterious New World.

Isabetta's lips moved silently as she correctly identified each constellation and planet. Shifting the telescope slowly allowed her to focus on different patches of sky. She charted imaginary courses in her head, creating mental images as accurate and eloquent as her father's detailed maps. Dreaming of sailing made her feel alive and hopeful.

Maybe one day...

In that moment, nothing could steal her joy—not even Aunt Rosa's threat of marriage.

CHAPTER 2

Rocco Bastian's stomach growled noisily as he stepped onto the quay of Cannaregio, the second largest of Venice's six *sestieres*. Delicate shades of peach and rose stained the early morning sky. Hungry seagulls circled the boats of fishermen who were busily selling their fresh catches to vendors. He watched as one swooped down to steal a wriggling fish.

"Little bastard," he commented under his breath.

Tall and broad-shouldered, the robust twenty-one year old strode toward home with confident steps. He hadn't eaten a decent meal in over a month due to Venetian protocol. Incoming ships were forced to spend forty days in one of the lagoon's outer islands before being granted access into the city. The mandated *quarantena*, or quarantine, protected citizens from potential plagues and other illnesses from abroad.

Currently, he transported velvets and brocades from his Uncle Alzo's looms to Lisbon's port. Once the galley's cargo hold had been emptied of its contents, it would be refilled with precious Indian spices, curatives, and luxury goods. The demand for Venetian textiles by rich Portuguese nobles had afforded merchants like his father and uncle a profitable opportunity. Times were changing, however.

The expansion of trade routes throughout the world offered endless opportunities for those willing to take chances. Giant ships funded by savvy investors braved the great expanse of ocean to seek new lands and exotic items. The wealth of some ship captains rivaled that of the aristocracy. Rocco wanted to explore these options and make his own fortune, but his father insisted they continue trading exclusively with Portugal. Perhaps, *this time*, he could convince the stubborn old man.

He admired the façade of *Santa Maria del Giglio* as he veered onto his street. A pretty girl keeping pace alongside her beady-eyed chaperone dared to toss him a smile and he winked at her in return. The exchange cost her a sharp nudge in the ribs. It felt good to be home but apprehension overshadowed his joy. He hated being the harbinger of bad news.

***

"I'm home!"

Rocco's booming voice dissolved the cobwebs of sleep from Isabetta's eyes. The thump of his heavy satchel hitting the floor prompted her to scramble out of bed and dress in haste. She checked her reflection in the cracked mirror and ran the palms of her hands over her tousled hair before going downstairs.

Rocco's face beamed in pleasure at the sight of his little sister. "Betta!" Embracing her tightly, he spun her around and made her squeal in the process.

Hortensa clung to the railing on the upper landing. "Isabetta stop your screaming! Rocco, is that you?"

Bleary-eyed from sleep, Zanetto chased after his wife. "You shouldn't be out of bed."

Hortensa waved him away while slowly descending the stairs. "I want to greet my boy."

Rocco embraced his parents in turn once they had cleared the last step. "It's good to see you both. Mother, are you feeling any better?"

"Much," Hortensa lied.

Zanetto patted his son's back. "Hopefully, the food wasn't too bad during your quarantine."

"Barely palatable."

"You must be famished," Hortensa lamented while milling about the kitchen. "Alba! Wake up!"

"How is Alfonso?" Zanetto asked.

Rocco grimaced. "His condition has worsened considerably, I'm afraid. I doubt he'll survive the year. "

Hortensa crossed herself. "Poor man."

Alfonso Torres had spent the better part of his life distributing Venetian textiles to Portugal's most elite costumers. He also served as a reliable vendor since he procured cinnamon, nutmeg, cloves, and black pepper from India on his own ship. The convenient Bastian-Torres relationship had worked smoothly for over a decade.

Rocco cleared his throat. "Fernando is running the business alone now that his father's health has declined."

"Silvio is helping him, I assume," Zanetto concluded.

"Actually, no. The brothers have fought so much over how things should be run that they no longer speak to each other."

"Fernando is the eldest and heir. Silvio should support his decisions."

"In an ideal world that would be the case. Sadly, Fernando told his brother to seek his fortune elsewhere."

"I assumed things would continue as they always have."

"On the contrary. Fernando plans on sailing to Brazil in less than a month. Gold and gemstones are in high demand right now, as are rare woods."

Isabetta experienced a twinge of envy. "How exciting. I can only imagine the wonderful plants and animals he will encounter, and the strange costumes of the natives."

Hortensa glanced at her daughter and sighed. "Again with this foolish talk?"

Zanetto added, "Transatlantic journeys are fraught with danger, Isabetta. Vicious storms, hunger, disease—a ship is not a place for a young woman. The fragile female constitution cannot withstand such an onslaught."

"You forgot to mention the constant threat of pirates," Isabetta reminded him sarcastically.

Zanetto held up his finger. "Oh yes, the pirates."

Rocco cleared his throat to get their attention. "The Spanish are returning to Europe with galleons brimming with gold and silver from Mexico. They are also importing tropical fruits and rare woods that cost nearly as much as gemstones due to high demand. Fernando believes this will be the future of trade."

Alarmed, Hortensa interjected, "I don't want my son crossing the ocean! Zanetto, tell him."

"Your mother is right. It's dangerous and expensive." Rocco threw up his hands in frustration so Zanetto added, "The galley you now sail represents a lifetime of hard work and sacrifice. Need I remind you that I began working as a sailor thirty years ago on another man's ship?"

Having heard the story of his father's humble beginnings at least a hundred times, Rocco refrained from sighing. "No, sir."

Zanetto continued, "The *Tramonto* will be paid in full in a couple of years. I will transfer the vessel to your name at that time. Why can't you be happy with that?"

"I am grateful, but is it wrong to want to implement some of my own ideas in the family business? If you don't want me crossing the ocean, how about sailing to India? Obtaining spices directly from the source would increase our profits."

"A longer journey requires more supplies and higher wages for the crew. You must take into account both sides, my son."

Rocco hid his irritation by peeking into a cupboard in search of something to eat. He didn't want to deliver bad news on an empty stomach.

Seeing this, Hortensa shouted, "Alba! Wake up! I swear that woman could sleep through a cavalcade."

The effort provoked a coughing fit, so Isabetta poured some water into a cup. "Drink this, Mother."

Hortensa sought the nearest chair and took several tentative sips between coughs.

"You should get back to bed," Zanetto said, eyeing his wife with concern.

Ignoring him, Hortensa turned to her daughter. "Buy some fish for your brother, will you? Get some heads for stock too."

Isabetta grabbed a basket and dashed to Viaro's stall in the market. "*Buongiorno*. I'll take two fish heads and…" She scanned the display of slick fish and mollusks.

Lifting a gleaming fish tail, the grizzly old man suggested, "How about this fine mackerel? Caught half hour ago."

"Perfect," she replied, holding out the basket for him to drop the fish into it. "Rocco just arrived home and he's hungry."

"I'm sure I'll see him soon enough." Viaro's eyes lit up with glee. "My daughter is getting married next week to a fisherman. Fine lad. Son of my second cousin."

"How nice."

"Maybe the next wedding will be yours." A playful wink

followed the comment. "Miro is still unmarried. You'll never go hungry with a fisherman."

"Your son is a fine man but my goal is to be a spinster."

He laughed heartily as she paid him, then made to leave.

Isabetta's parents were still arguing with Rocco when she returned home. She knew her brother longed to spread his wings and fly, but their father kept him grounded. After all, Rocco carried the esteemed Bastian reputation on his shoulders. Luckily, he wasn't alone in this endeavor. The ordering, accounting, and correspondence between Venice and Lisbon were handled by "Beto," the bastardized version of "Betta," her childhood nickname. This tricky ruse was at the insistence of Zanetto himself, who didn't want anyone to know that his daughter ran the financial end of his successful enterprise.

Hortensa pointed to the cauldron within the hearth. Taking the hint, Isabetta went over and dropped the fish heads into the boiling water. A door in the corridor opened and closed. Alba padded into the kitchen while stifling a yawn.

Exasperated, Hortensa cried, "It's about time!"

"Welcome home, Signore Rocco," Alba said while tying an apron around her thin waist. "I didn't hear you come in."

Isabetta dumped the fresh mackerel onto a plate and Rocco eyed it appreciatively.

Hortensa glared at the servant with mock sternness. "Hurry up, you lazy bag of bones. My son is hungry."

While Alba cleaned the fish, Rocco made another attempt at reason. "Father, I understand if you don't want me sailing to the New World or to India, but I still think we should consider expanding our options to keep up with our competitors and these changing times."

Zanetto spread out his hands. "Why tamper with what works? What's taken me decades to achieve?"

Rocco looked to his sister. "Betta, what say you?"

Isabetta disappeared into the study and returned with an accounting ledger. Flipping it open, she ran her finger down a column of neatly written numbers. "We have maintained a steady, albeit stagnant, profit margin since the *Tramonto*'s maiden voyage twelve years ago. The last two years have shown a decline and I see this trend continuing. Father, you should listen to Rocco."

Zanetto made a sour face. "You *would* take your brother's side. You two think alike."

Isabetta bristled at the accusation. "Numbers don't lie."

"Luxury textiles are always in demand. We'll continue to export them as long as the Portuguese pay the asking price," Zanetto affirmed stubbornly.

Isabetta caught the look of worry that flashed across Rocco's face. What was he hiding?

Rocco leaned forward. "The number of weavers in Lisbon creating luxury fabrics grows daily. In time, their textile production will rival that of Venice and they won't need us."

Wanting to appease her distressed father, Isabetta said, "Smart distributors will gladly pay a bit more for top quality merchandise and honest dealings, both of which we provide."

Zanetto added, "Don't look so defeated, Rocco. I will consider your ideas if and when our velvets and brocades are no longer desired."

"It's a shame Silvio doesn't own his own ship, for he has good ideas," Rocco pressed, refusing to back down.

"Such as?"

"Selling textiles to distributors in Holland and Flanders."

Skeptical, Zanetto crossed his arms. "Humph."

Rocco continued, "Silvio will be in Venice soon to pursue some business ventures. I've invited him to come here and speak with us. You should hear what he has to say, Father."

"Whatever for? I've already told you that we're not changing how we do business."

It was time for Rocco to be brutally honest. "We have no choice. This was the last shipment of spices we will obtain from the Torres. As I've already said, Fernando plans to depart for Brazil and he won't be back any time soon."

"There are plenty of spice vendors in Portugal. I'm sure Alfonso can provide me with a few leads. I'll write to him at once," Zanetto said, unfazed.

"Alfonso can barely lift his head from the pillow, let alone respond to letters. There's more…" Rocco ran a nervous hand through his thick light brown hair. "Fernando refused to pay our asking price so I was forced to accept less money."

An unsettling silence fell over the room. Even Alba glanced over her shoulder at the family. Alfonso Torres had never before refused their price on a shipment. To hear that his son had done so was an insulting slap in the face.

Zanetto paled. *"What did you say?"*

"I was hoping you would be open to new ideas…I wanted to soften the blow. The truth is, Fernando gave me an ultimatum."

"An ultimatum?"

"That's right. Either we accept what he's willing to pay from now on—*once a year, not twice*—or we find someone else who better suits our needs."

More silence.

"The Torres-Bastian relationship is over," Zanetto quietly concluded, his expression one of utter disappointment.

Feeling pity for her father, Isabetta reached for his hand. "Don't worry, Papa. I'm sure we'll find a textile distributor and a spice vendor before the next journey."

Rocco shot his sister a dubious glance but said nothing.

Alba began frying the fish, filling the quiet kitchen with a pungent odor as the Bastian family contemplated their future.

CHAPTER 3

Clickety-clack, clickety-clack, clickety-clack.

The rhythmic sound of four looms in action reverberated throughout the large space. Alzo Cornetti strolled between the great wooden machines overseeing the work of his skilled weavers. Born and raised in the *sestiere* of Santa Croce, his *bottega dei tessuti*, or textile studio, produced some of the finest silks, velvets, and brocades in Venice. To be fair, he had inherited the bottega along with its excellent reputation from his late father.

Alzo stopped suddenly and lifted his hand, compelling one of the men to stop working. Peering at the thread, he frowned. "This shade is off. It needs more madder."

Venetian sumptuary laws governed textiles, colors, and furs. No color in Venice was more highly prized than red, the regal hue being favored by rich and poor alike. The two most requested shades were *scarlatto*, a warm tomato red, and *cremisino*, a cool blue-red. Given the decree that the *togas*, or robes of state, worn by the city officials should not to be a mournful color, Venetian looms produced leagues of red fabric in various textures to appeal to all classes and budgets.

Pausing at the next loom, Alzo nodded in approval. The design the weaver worked on involved threads of silver against a backdrop of black silk. The Portuguese court favored black garments but burgundy and deep red were also quite popular, especially when adorned with rich patterns. This particular design would go out with the next shipment on the *Tramonto*.

He was about to check another loom but a throbbing pain stopped him. The abrupt attack, concentrated at the base of his skull, had become a common occurrence since Cassandra's betrothal to Petro Vendramin. Although his wife had procured every headache remedy available, nothing helped.

A well-dressed man entered the shop so he smoothed the

distress from his face with practiced skill. Forcing a smile, he went over to his esteemed client. "Signore Paolo, this is an unexpected surprise. Where is Timoteo?"

Paolo Veronese, one of the city's most celebrated artists, smiled wryly. "Overseeing the work of a novice. Now that I've made him my senior apprentice, the lad feels he shouldn't be required to run my errands or pick up my orders."

"Neither should you, *Maestro*."

"I'm teaching him a lesson in humility. It's a fine morning and I could use a bit of fresh air anyway."

Alzo called out to one of his workers, who materialized with a wrapped parcel. His father had made a name for himself by weaving fine wool and canvas. Europe's distinguished artists needed the latter to produce portraits and bucolic landscapes for royal courts, and Cornetti looms produced some of the best.

Paolo extracted a few coins from his purse in order to pay for his order. "You should come and see the painting I'm working on now."

"I've already heard that it's another masterpiece."

"Yes," Paolo agreed, making no attempt at modesty.

"Alexander the Great, am I correct?"

Paolo nodded. "Along with the family of Darius III. You know where my studio is, don't you?"

"Who doesn't?"

"I have too much work—more than I can handle, in fact. My apprentices are painting day and night, and I still cannot finish my commissions."

"That is the price of success, my friend."

Gazing down at his paint-stained fingers, Paolo lamented, "See how worn they have become? I wish I could grow another set of hands. My physician prescribes arnica root ointment for the stiffness. To be young again would be a blessing."

Patting the artist consolingly on the back, Alzo accompanied him outside. "It's a shame we can't relive our youth."

"Indeed," Paolo muttered before shuffling down the street.

Alzo watched the old man thoughtfully, then caught sight of Zanetto Bastian rounding the corner. Waving, he called out,

"*Buongiorno*, my friend."

"*Buongiorno*...Is now a good time?" Zanetto asked once he had closed the gap between them.

"Collecting money is always a good time. Let's go in the back where it's quiet."

Zanetto tracked Alzo past the noisy looms and bolts of fabric to a snug room outfitted with a desk and chairs. Selecting a seat, he said, "Rosa and Cassandra are in good health, I hope."

Alzo settled behind the desk. "Fretting over wedding plans from dawn until dusk. How about your family? Rosa tells me Hortensa's condition has worsened."

"Unfortunately, her health shows no improvement."

"I'm sorry to hear it."

"We've tried everything the physicians have prescribed and yet..." Zanetto's eye reflected sadness as he trailed off.

"We will continue keeping her in our prayers."

"Thank you." Eager to get on with business, Zanetto placed a leather coin purse on the desk. "This is your share from our last journey. I warn you, there's a substantial amount missing."

Reaching for the money, Alzo frowned. "Why?"

"As you know, Alfonso is ill. His eldest, Fernando, has taken over the business and refused to pay the usual asking price."

"Does Alfonso know about this?"

"Yes, but the old man cannot remediate the situation. There's something else you should know. According to Rocco, the Portuguese are starting to produce their own textiles. Nothing compared to ours but—"

"Venetian weavers?" Alzo cut in, instantly alarmed.

Venetian silk merchants monitored their trade so cautiously that the majority of weavers were not allowed to leave the city. Secrets of production were jealously guarded. The thought of one of these advanced weavers moving out of Venice to ply their expert trade elsewhere struck fear and panic into the heart of every local cloth merchant.

"I'm not certain but I doubt it. Fernando is sailing to Brazil, which means I need to find another textile distributor and spice vendor in Portugal."

"How long will that take?"

"I don't know."

Cradling his head in his hands, Alzo cried, "No, no, no! This is most unwelcome news."

"Take heart, man…I'll find someone soon."

Alzo's head snapped up, his eyes wide with worry. "My God, what am I to do in the meantime?" Loosening the collar of his doublet, he swallow hard. "I don't feel well."

Zanetto stood and went over to the desk. "You've grown pale. Should I fetch the physician?"

Ignoring the question, Alzo continued in an urgent tone, "I was counting on that money."

"As I said—"

"You don't understand!"

Zanetto studied his partner with concern. Alzo's desperation signaled trouble. More precisely, *debt*. Production of top quality fabrics came at a steep price. A man could easily go bankrupt if profit margins weren't big enough to compensate for supply costs. Cassandra's upcoming marriage only worsened matters.

Alzo rubbed his throbbing temples. "Forgive me…It's been days since I've slept. Sales have been steadily plummeting. I cannot keep up, Zanetto."

"Do not despair—at least not yet. Alfonso's youngest son is coming to Venice to discuss some business prospects with Rocco. My son said Silvio is ambitious and has good ideas. Hopefully, we can recuperate our losses some other way."

"Isn't Silvio working with Fernando?"

"Not anymore. There's bad blood between the brothers." Zanetto hesitated, then added, "I assume the Vendramin family expects a sizeable dowry from you." He tactfully refrained from mentioning the wedding banquet, which would no doubt be decadent and cost a fortune.

Alzo's anxious gaze drifted to the thick accounting ledger as he nervously strummed his fingers upon the desk's surface. His eyes glazed over in a way that made Zanetto uneasy. "You have no idea…This wedding is going to kill me, I swear."

"It can't be that bad."

"Oh but it is...God help me."

Zanetto patted Alzo on the back in a gesture of comfort. "Your wife told me she intends to help Isabetta find a husband. I'm afraid I'll be in the same situation as you soon enough."

Alzo grimaced. "In that case, God help us both."

***

Hortensa shot her daughter a warning look before being consumed by a violent fit of coughing. Rosa and Cassandra had stopped by for a visit and Isabetta seemed ready to burst.

Rosa grew alarmed. "You sound worse now than you did the last time we were here. Do you remember our mother's posset recipe? Wine, milk, eggs—" The coughing grew louder and she pressed her palm to her sister's forehead. "You're not feverish."

Hortensa recoiled. "Stop fussing over me."

Retrieving her hand, Rosa said, "I'll send a servant to you with the recipe if I find it." Casting a pointed glance at her niece, she added, "At least you won't have to worry about Isabetta's future. That assurance alone should put you at ease and restore your health. Naturally, we must work on your daughter's appearance to make her more...*presentable*."

Cassandra placed a hand on Isabetta's arm. "Think of it, dear cousin. Both of us married to rich men with our very own servants to command."

Isabetta glanced down at Cassandra's soft ivory hand. Had the limp appendage ever performed a single chore? Gold rings adorned two of the plump fingers. She discreetly studied her own hands, which were slightly tanned and bore no jewelry.

Cassandra touched Isabetta's long bronze locks. "Your hair could use an herbal rinse to tame those unruly waves. I can teach you a few fashionable hairstyles too. As for your skin..." She winced. "I highly advise avoiding the sun to maintain a fair complexion. Otherwise, you might be mistaken for a peasant."

Rosa tapped her daughter's shoulder. "Don't be too harsh, Cassandra. Your cousin must help your aunt and doesn't have time for beauty treatments."

Isabetta stole a glance at her mother's forlorn face. Furious by her aunt's callousness, she announced, "Why bother with such frivolity? I don't want to marry."

"Don't want to marry?" Rosa repeated in a mocking tone. "Did you hear that, Hortensa?"

A derisive giggle escaped Cassandra's lips. "What will you do? Sail alongside Rocco?"

That's exactly what Isabetta wanted to do, but wisely refrained from making such a shocking confession. She had fallen in love with the *Tramonto* at first sight. Her interest in astronomy combined with her uncanny mathematical skills had prompted her father to demonstrate the usage of nautical instruments along with the rudimentary rules of sailing. These valuable lessons had been carefully recorded in her memory. As time passed, she had supplemented her knowledge through books. Last year, she had steered the galley to Torcello and back under Rocco's supervision. To this day, her father was ignorant of their escapade. The sheer exhilaration of standing at the helm with the wind on her face…

Mocking laughter jolted Isabetta back to the present. "I'm barely seventeen," she pointed out in the hope of dissuading her aunt and cousin.

Cassandra stopped giggling and shrugged. "What of it? I turned sixteen only last month."

Rosa added, "Respectable ages for marriage—unlike your scandalous neighbor whose mother married her off at twelve to that old man."

"Fourteen," Isabetta corrected.

"Twelve, fourteen, what does it matter? Veronica Franco is a whore raising bastard children without a husband. You should end your friendship with her lest it stain your own reputation."

"Aunt Rosa—"

Rosa's hand shot up in a gesture of impatience. "Do you honestly believe a respectable gentleman would marry the friend of such a degraded woman? Think of your future, will you? At least for your mother's sake."

Hortensa interjected, "In fairness, Veronica's marriage to Dr. Panizza ended badly due to her youth and inexperience. Marrying a young vivacious girl to a man old enough to be her great-grandfather had not been wise on the part of her parents."

Rosa sighed. "It doesn't change the fact that Veronica is a bad association for Isabetta—or any other decent young woman for that matter. Should she ever come knocking on your door while Cassandra and I are visiting, I shall not hesitate to send her away. I won't risk my daughter's unblemished reputation."

Isabetta bit back an angry retort. Secretly, she looked up to her neighbor. Twenty-four years old and highly intelligent, Veronica had worked hard to carve a place for herself in the world. She and her mother, Paola Fracassa, lived comfortably thanks to Veronica's name being added to the official catalog of the most honorable courtesans of Venice. This register displayed the names, addresses, and fees of the most sought-after women in the city.

"Veronica Franco has never stepped foot in this house," Hortensa assured in a raspy voice.

Rosa pursed her lips, then said, "I'm relieved to hear it."

"Veronica's father was a nobleman," Isabetta pointed out in her friend's defense.

"And her mother a whore, making Veronica a bastard," Rosa shot back. "How many children does that trollop have now? Two? Three? Each one conceived out of wedlock from her noble patrons. Expensive gowns and precious jewels will never change who or *what* she is."

It took most of Isabetta's self-control to remain silent.

"It's perfectly normal to be frightened," Cassandra said in a gentle tone while smoothing the plush rose velvet of her gown.

Isabetta quirked an eyebrow. "I'm not frightened."

"It seems to me that you are and fail to realize it. When my father announced my upcoming marriage, my first instinct was to rebel against him." When Rosa frowned, Cassandra instantly amended, "I admit, Mama, I was scared. Now, I consider myself extremely blessed. I'm looking forward to being Petro's wife."

Appeased, Rosa smiled indulgently. "Good girl."

Isabetta wanted to slap her cousin's smug face.

Hortensa reached for Rosa's hand. "Dearest sister, Zanetto and I would be grateful for any help you offer in finding a husband for our daughter. Isn't that right, Isabetta?"

Fuming inwardly, Isabetta dutifully nodded.

Satisfied, Rosa stood, thus concluding the visit. "I'm glad to see that my niece has *some* sense. Come along, Cassandra, we don't want to be late for your appointment with the seamstress."

"Father is creating a special wedding gown for me. It will be the most beautiful dress in the world!"

Isabetta watched as her cousin spun around like the foolish vain creature that she was.

Pinching her daughter's arm, Rosa snapped, "Stop that. You'll need to behave as a proper, dignified noblewoman once you're married. Twirling like a silly girl won't do. What would the servants think?"

Cassandra rubbed the sore flesh. "Yes, Mama."

Rosa's hard eyes swept over Isabetta disdainfully before she turned to Hortensa. "It would be good for Isabetta to be seen with us in public."

"Why?" Isabetta blurted without thinking, earning her a maternal look of reproof.

Rosa's eyebrow shot upward as she coolly regarded her niece. "To improve your image."

CHAPTER 4

Iseppo da Mosto sat in his study counting money. Of all the rooms in his home, the space where he conducted business contained the most expensive items. Silk tapestries, oil paintings set in ornate gilded frames, a teakwood table with inlaid wood, bookcases crammed with leather-bound tomes, and a chandelier crafted from red glass came together to impress potential investors. A finely woven Oriental carpet in shades of blue and green covered most of the terracotta floor, and a pair of giant yellow Chinese porcelain vases flanked the marble fireplace. Those who entered the room never failed to be impressed by the maritime merchant's stylish taste and apparent success.

Lamentably, the veneer of wealth was wearing thin. His last journey had proved less successful than the prior one, and declining profits were becoming disturbingly repetitious. Disastrous consequences loomed on the horizon if he didn't get things under control immediately. Running his index finger down the row of numbers in the accounting ledger, he felt a surge of anxiety mingled with frustration. More money needed to be produced—*fast*.

Polonia poked her head into the room. At the sight of her husband's angst, she inquired, "What ails you?"

Iseppo feigned a cheery smile. "Nothing, my darling."

"Are you feeling unwell?"

"I'm getting hungry. What's for dinner?"

"Roasted pork." Her eyes slid to the ledger on the desk. "Tell me what's wrong."

He hid his irritation while ignoring her comment. "Have the cook braise the pork in white wine. I prefer it that way."

She pinned him with a challenging look. "We're having money problems, aren't we? How bad is it? Be honest."

"Things are not as bad as they seem."

"Do you take me for a fool?"

"Times are changing and—"

"A curse on the Bastian family!"

Iseppo frowned. *Here we go again.* "You shouldn't say such things. Zanetto is a decent man."

"How can you think that? He stole everything from you—*from us.*"

He stood and rounded the desk to face his wife. "No, he was an honest worker who never stole a cent."

"While scheming behind your back, biding his time."

"Polonia *please.*" Seeing one of his servants, he snapped his fingers. "Bring me wine, girl."

Polonia watched the servant scurry to do her master's bidding. "I wish you would open your eyes, Iseppo."

"Not nearly as much as I wish you would stop this nonsense. We've always held the Bastian family in high esteem."

"*You* hold them in high esteem, not me."

"You're being unfair."

Crossing her arms, she glared at him. "Am I? Zanetto's sailing skills, his business savvy, and his connections are thanks to you. The Bevilacqua charge much more than your last textile vendor, whom Zanetto now utilizes—also thanks to you."

"Alzo Cornetti *is* Hortensa Bastian's brother-in-law. You didn't expect him to continue doing business with me once Zanetto purchased his own commercial galley, did you? As for the Bevilacqua, they're the oldest and most reputable textile manufacturer in Venice. Higher prices are to be expected."

"Why must you always defend Zanetto?"

Iseppo massaged his forehead in anticipation of a headache. "Dear Lord, grant me patience."

"Doesn't it bother you that Alfonso Torres favors him?"

"You'll be happy to learn that those days are over." Seeing his wife's puzzled frown, he explained, "Alfonso is on his deathbed. Fernando Torres is now in charge, and he has broken ties with the Bastians in favor of transatlantic trade."

She gaped at him. "How do you know this?"

"I bribe most of the sailors of this city in order to glean

information about my competitors."

Despite being impressed that her husband had taken this sly initiative, she said, "Your sources could be lying."

"Possibly, but then again, young lads nowadays don't know the meaning of loyalty. They'll betray their own mothers for money."

She crossed her arms. "So what do you intend to do?"

"Do?" he repeated with a scowl.

The servant returned with a silver chalice filled with wine. Iseppo dismissed the girl before indulging in a hearty sip. His wife's nagging would surely demand a second cup. Maybe even a third.

She continued in a haughty tone, "Are you going to sit back and do nothing? The Bastians *stole* what has taken you—*us*—a lifetime to build. If what those sailors told you is true, now is the time to strike."

Iseppo emptied the chalice before inquiring, "What do you propose, Polonia? Do you want me to kill the man for wanting to improve his lot in life?"

"What if I said yes?"

A string of soft curses escaped his lips before he said, "You're being most unreasonable. Zanetto worked hard, saved his money, and purchased his own vessel—I respect that kind of ambition in a man. Had I not inherited my father's ship, I would probably be working for someone else, and you would not be living in this fine house." He reached out to stroke the costly velvet of her gown. "You certainly wouldn't be wearing *this* or those expensive jewels around your neck."

Shifting away from his touch, she retorted, "I have looked through your ledgers, Iseppo. We are not doing as well as you would have me believe."

Balling his hands into fists, he bellowed, "How dare you come in here and go through my things?!"

Frightened by his anger, she took a step backward. "I have a right to know if my husband is in debt."

"*Everyone* in this city is in debt!"

"Don't be ridiculous. You know what I mean."

"What do you know about the business of men? Foolish woman! Your sole duties are the purchasing of foodstuffs, overseeing the servants, and the seamless running of this household. *Nothing more*." Putting his face close to hers, he added menacingly, "If I ever catch you snooping in my study, I will be forced to take disciplinary action. Am I clear?"

Polonia clenched her jaw and pressed her lips together to withhold an angry retort. She nodded once.

Gaining control over his ire, Iseppo leaned back and attempted to lighten the mood. "Good. I'm glad you have come to your senses. Tomorrow, we shall attend the concerto at the Palazzo Capodevin. Your friends will be there and you can show off your new gown." When she remained silent, he added, "Let's not quarrel. Things are not as bad as you think. Come now, don't be glum. Smile for your husband."

The corners of her lips rose a fraction of an inch.

"That's better. I need to work now," he said, heading toward the chair behind the desk.

Polonia glared at him before exiting the room. Stomping down the hallway, she could feel her blood boiling in her veins. If her stubborn husband refused to take action, then she would have to think of something to prevent their financial ruin. Her lady's maid emerged from another room and she seized the woman's arm. "Goretta, fetch my cloak. We're going out."

***

Cristofolo Trasontin stood at the window watching boats float across the greenish brown water of the Grand Canal. A flock of herons cried out to one another from a pewter sky that threatened rain. A distant rumble of thunder announced the oncoming storm.

Two young whores in ill-fitting threadbare gowns and fake paste jewels stood on the bridge waving at the brown-skinned men aboard a barge. Their attempt at elegance resulted in an overall pathetic shabbiness. Pretty, albeit tired looking, they possessed eyes that had seen too much too soon in life. A common trait among those practicing the oldest profession in the world.

One of the young sailors beat upon his shirtless chest to show off his muscular physique, which was no doubt the result of hauling heavy cargo. His companion held up a coin, earning him a generous view of the whore's deep cleavage. The veins of each round breast were expertly lined in blue and the rosy nipples, having been dipped in finely ground iridescent powder, caught the sparkle of the sun. Unlike wealthy courtesans who could afford to dip their nipples in gold dust, these two were forced to resort to ground fish scales.

The shrewd prostitute pointed in the direction of the Rialto *sestiere* where the city's whorehouses were located. The sailor nodded eagerly in response.

Cristofolo smiled wryly at the scene. Having availed himself of the voluptuous blonde on more than one occasion, he knew those generous breasts—and their slightly fishy smell too. Closing his eyes, he recalled the taste of the powder on his tongue and the scent of vetiver on the whore's supple skin. He could afford a better quality woman but he occasionally craved the depravity that only a *cortigiana di lume* could provide.

Two types of prostitutes were legally recognized in Venice. The *cortigiane di lume* had been servicing the lower classes and sailors in the Rialto for well over a century. They were strictly forbidden to ply their trade anywhere else in the city.

The *più honorate cortigiane*, on the other hand, were referred to as "courtesans" and never prostitutes. These highly educated women prided themselves on their intellect, as well as musical and literary talents. In addition to being sought after by the most prominent and wealthy members of Venetian society, many of them enjoyed international fame. Some of the best even entertained foreign royals.

Cristofolo had enjoyed his fair share of courtesans, not only in their beds but also as jolly companions during banquets and parties. Most of them possessed sharp wits, offering men a real challenge during political and philosophical debates. Their honed minds were tempered with honeyed words and warm humor in order not to come across as offensive. One could argue that Venetian courtesans had perfected the art of diplomacy so thoroughly that they could put many noble ambassadors to shame.

Only last week he had attended a banquet where Veronica Franco sat amid a group of gentlemen reciting the verses she had penned. Unsurprisingly, the respected courtesan belonged to prestigious literary circles where she participated in weekly discussions and contributed in editing anthologies of poetry. Veronica's colleague, Loretta Mino, had also been present at the event. Loretta, who had mastered the harpsichord by age ten, could perform mathematical equations in her head faster than any man he knew.

A painted carriage came to a halt below his window. Silk drapes hid him from view as he studied the attractive, impeccably dressed woman stepping out of the vehicle. Accompanied by her maid, she walked directly to his door. From his vantage point, he could see directly down the top of her snug bodice. A pair of firm ripe breasts pressed together within the fabric to create a tantalizing cleft.

How would those perky nipples taste in his mouth?

The wicked thought caused a stirring in his loins. Nearly fifty years of age, Cristofolo stood ramrod straight with a chiseled physique. Unlike his peers, who were either graying or balding, he boasted an abundant amount of brown hair. Only a few silver strands highlighted his temples. Compared to many his age, he appeared at least a good ten years younger.

Catching a glimpse of himself in the beveled mirror over the fireplace, he paused. Deep set blue eyes crinkled at the corners as he grinned. *You are indeed handsome,* the reflection communicated silently as he straightened his collar. Rugged features set off a full sensuous mouth and strong chin.

Humming a jaunty tune, he poured two glasses of wine from the sideboard. Ascending footsteps echoed upon the marble stairwell before a servant entered the room with his precious guest in tow. There was no denying the familial resemblance between them.

She ran into his open arms. *"Zio."*

Holding her close, he said, "Polonia, this is a delicious

surprise." He glared at the servant, who ducked out of the room and closed the door. Leaning back, he studied his niece's pretty face with slight concern. "Judging by your flushed cheeks and bright eyes, you're either furious with Iseppo or excited to see me. I'm hoping for the latter."

"My husband is a fool."

Offering her one of the wine glasses, he said, "Ah, so it's anger. I warned my brother against marrying you off to him, but you know as well as I do the sheer stubbornness of your father."

His older brother had been a thorn in everyone's side until he had the decency to die eight years ago. Cristofolo, sole heir to the family fortune, enjoyed his considerable wealth in blessed peace.

"Iseppo never listens to me," Polonia whined, her ringed fingers tapping the rim of the goblet.

"Darling, your husband is even older than I am. You're not yet thirty—still lovely and bursting with life. There's bound to be friction between the two of you. Go on, drink some wine. It will ease your anxiety." His eyes locked on her full lips as she took his advice. "Explain to me what Iseppo has done to make you so upset."

"He insults my intelligence by insisting that we are not in debt. I studied the accounting ledgers while he was out, so I know he's been lying to me for quite some time. I confronted him this afternoon and he threatened to discipline me if I ever again step foot in his study."

Although her desperate tone and glistening eyes worried him, the image of Polonia bent over Iseppo's knees and receiving a sound spanking on her bare bottom intrigued him. The mere thought of large red handprints on the firm twin mounds of flesh caused his manhood to twitch. "How bad is it?"

"Bad enough for me to come and ask for your help, dear uncle. You know I wouldn't do that unless it was absolutely necessary." She began to pace the room with frenzied steps. "I'm truly frightened and so is Iseppo, although he hides it."

His eyes tracked her movement through hooded lids. An errant brown curl escaped her neat coiffure and bounced with each step. "Calm yourself, Polonia. Carrying on like this will only make you feel worse."

She froze. "What if he's unable to recuperate his losses? What if we lose everything? The possibility of being poor makes me sick. Can you imagine me—*a Trasontin*—reduced to living and dressing like a commoner? How humiliating!"

Polonia was the only woman he knew whose arrogance and sense of entitlement matched his own. Undesirable traits to be sure, yet his chest swelled with pride nonetheless. How could he not indulge her? Give in to her every whim? After all, his blood ran in her veins.

She continued, "Profits have been plummeting ever since Zanetto Bastian stopped working for Iseppo to start his own shipping business."

"I get the impression that you dislike this man," he drawled, half amused by her vehemence.

Blue eyes flashed with rage. "God curse him and his family! That man stole my husband's main supplier and distributor."

Cristofolo marveled at her passion. Did she display such fervor in bed too? "*Stole* is a harsh word. You cannot fault an employee for following his employer's footsteps."

"You sound like Iseppo. Are you with or against me?"

"I am with you, but…" He shrugged. "What can I do?"

She bit her lower lip. "I don't know."

"What you need is a distraction." Clasping her hand, he led her to the window. Life bustled on the street below and the canal beyond. "Look there, in the gondola floating past the *campanile* of the cathedral, isn't that Signore Emilio's wife? That's the third time I've seen her with that young man, do you think—"

"Stop!"

He studied his niece's distraught face. Her refusal to indulge in gossip alarmed him. "You're serious about this."

"Yes! Haven't you been listening to me?" She licked her lips and placed a hand on his breastbone. "Forgive me, I didn't mean to be rude."

Caressing her cheek, he assured, "Forgiven."

"Let me ask you something. Are you aware that Alzo

Cornetti recently celebrated the betrothal of his only child, Cassandra, to Petro Vendramin?"

"Is that so? I would imagine the Vendramin family would have aimed higher, but then again Petro is the youngest son. What does this have to do with your situation?"

"I'm certain the dowry Alzo agreed to pay to have his daughter's name written in the city's prestigious Golden Book is worth a king's ransom. Therefore, he is most likely open to the idea of making some extra money."

Cristofolo narrowed his eyes. "You're probably right, but I still don't see the connection."

"Alzo's wife and Zanetto's wife are sisters. Alzo once provided Iseppo with merchandise for export."

"But he stopped once Zanetto started his business," he concluded as realization dawned on him.

"Correct. My husband has no choice but to buy textiles at a higher price from the Bevilacqua."

"Is your goal to lure Alzo away from Zanetto?"

Polonia moved to stand in front of her uncle in order to get a better view of the canal. It was indeed Signore Emilio's wife in the gondola sneaking off with her young lover. "I want more than that...The Bastians have recently received a hard blow. I'll spare you the details."

"Thank you," he drawled.

"In short, they must find a new distributor and vendor in Portugal before setting sail again this autumn. I want to take down that wretched family while they're weak."

God, she was ruthless. "Rather cruel, is it not?"

"What better time to strike than now?"

"I've never seen this side of you, Polonia."

Keeping her eyes focused on the black gondola, she whispered, "Are you disappointed with me?"

Setting his hands upon her shoulders, he inhaled the fragrant scent emanating from the soft skin at the nape of her neck. Fighting the urge to taste the smooth skin, he replied, "Never."

CHAPTER 5
JULY 1569

Silvio Torres sat in a gondola gaping in wonder at the majestic palazzos along the Grand Canal. Seafoam green, buttery yellow, burnt coral—each façade boasted a vivid hue. Ornate windows and gracefully twisted columns only added to the charm of these palatial homes. Some of the balcony doors were open to allow glimpses of sparkling chandeliers and frescoed ceilings. Luxury and beauty reigned supreme in the city where the streets were made of water. His head swiveled left and right, taking in the splendid sights with eager eyes. He had seen many lovely places in his twenty-two years, and his birth city of Lisbon was no exception.

But Venice...

The gondolier lifted an oar and allowed it to skim across the water's surface. "Venice is magic, is it not?"

Surprised that the Venetian had read his mind, Silvio nodded. "Such wealth, such beauty!"

The gondolier smiled proudly. "You are not the first passenger to express this sentiment about my city."

Silvio knew he wouldn't be the last, either. Ever since his release from quarantine that morning, he had done little else but admire the city. Reaching for a handkerchief to dab his damp brow, he struggled for air in the heat of mid-July.

They passed the *Riva degli Schiavoni*, an area slightly east of San Marco comprised mainly of Dalmatian ship builders, sailors, and sun-tanned boat rowers like the one steering the vessel in which he sat. Across the canal stood a palazzo with a stunning young woman fanning herself on the balcony.

"Is this your first time visiting our city, sir?"

Silvio continued to stare at the woman in awe. "Er...yes."

Glancing upward, the gondolier grinned. "Loretta Mino is among the costliest courtesans in Venice. You'll need a sultan's fortune to slip between the sheets with that one."

"Is that her palazzo?"

"No, it belongs to Signore Julio Hernandez, a noble Spaniard. One of several men currently infatuated with her."

"I see."

"Our courtesans are known throughout the European continent. Surely you've heard of them in Portugal?"

Silvio's face lit up in surprise. "How do you know I am Portuguese?"

"Venice is a city of foreigners, and I have transported men from as far as Cairo in my boat. In time, we learn the origin of various accents."

"In answer to your question, yes, I have heard a rumor or two about the prostitutes of Venice."

"Allow me to correct you, sir. There are *prostitutes* and there are *courtesans*."

"Are they not one in the same?"

"Not in Venice."

Silvio admired the Venetian's skill as he maneuvered the gondola away from the Grand Canal into a maze of watery back alleys. When they reached the quay of the Cannaregio, he stepped onto solid ground and extracted a coin from the leather purse at his waist. "Thank you."

The gondolier touched the brim of his felt cap after pocketing the money. "Good day to you, sir."

***

Tasked with purchasing food for the midday meal, Isabetta wandered through the stalls in the piazza. Although her mother had requested beef, the quantity of pepper and spices covering the slabs of discolored meat evoked suspicion. Edging away from the butcher's stall, she headed toward her friend, the old fishmonger. She made her selection and handed him some coins in exchange for a measure of gleaming sardines.

Viaro fixed his gaze on something in the piazza. "There goes a handsome fellow. Never saw him before." Turning his attention back to Isabetta, he teased, "A potential husband for you, eh?"

Without bothering to turn around, she demanded, "Why are you so eager to see me married?"

He shrugged. "Comely girls bear good-looking children."

Shaking her head in mock disdain, she teased, "Maybe I should purchase my seafood from Guglielmo across the way. At least he knows how to mind his own affairs."

"That old salty dog? Ha! My fish is much fresher." The fishmonger's gaze drifted again. "The lad looks Spanish to me. Maybe Greek."

Finally peeking over her shoulder, Isabetta noticed an attractive man in foreign garb. Short black hair framed an expressive face with wide set eyes.

Turning to his son, Viaro said, "What say you, Miro?"

Wiping his hands on a cloth, Miro glanced at the foreigner. "Portuguese, recently arrived."

Instantly alarmed, Isabetta said, "Are you sure?"

"I know of every ship that enters and exits our ports. A Portuguese *caravela* was freed from quarantine this morning." Changing the subject, Miro added, "Does your father need an extra hand for his next journey?"

Having spent the better part of his childhood on a fishing barge, Miro's sea legs were more reliable than his land legs. When the amicable young man wasn't working on merchant vessels, he was in the piazza helping his father sell fish.

Isabetta tore her eyes from the man she believed to be Silvio Torres in order to answer Miro's question. "I think so, yes. Rocco will let you know."

Viaro pointed. "That Portuguese fellow seems to be heading toward your house, Isabetta. Best if you hurry or some other girl will snag him."

***

Silvio arrived at a tidy house with a respectable entrance—not nearly as grand as a palazzo, but certainly not a shabby dwelling. The Bastian home reflected the modest wealth of a thriving sea merchant. Taking hold of the brass knocker, he announced his presence to those within.

Alba opened the door. "State your business, sir."

Her ugliness nearly made him flinch. "*Buongiorno*. My name is Silvio Torres and I'm a friend of Rocco Bastian."

Hortensa, who sat at the table drinking tea, said, "Please come in, Signore Silvio. We've been expecting you. My son went out with my husband but they should return soon."

Silvio entered the freshly swept interior and, at his hostess's insistence, took a seat at the table. Noticing the woman's pale lips and rheumy eyes, he concluded that she suffered from a serious malady. "Thank you, Signora Hortensa. It's nice to finally place a face to the name."

"Likewise. Is this your first time in Venice?"

"It is, and I find your city exquisite."

A strained smile hid her pain. "I'm happy to hear it. Alba, please serve our guest some spiced ale."

Alba filled a tankard and set it on the table.

Hortensa waited while Silvio took a sip, then said, "Zanetto and I were sorry to hear about your father's declining health."

"I'm sure Rocco mentioned that he won't live out the year."

"He did, yes. It must be difficult for you and your brother."

Silvio averted his gaze. "If my mother were alive, things would be much easier. Thankfully, we have good servants." Eager to change the subject, he looked around. "You said Rocco is out with your husband."

"That's right."

"Is your other son at home?" At Hortensa's blank stare, he prompted, "Roberto...*Beto*."

Her cheeks reddened. "Oh—ah, Beto isn't here."

"When will he be back?"

Alba and Hortensa exchanged worried glances.

He continued, "I feel like I know him personally after so many years of correspondence."

While Hortensa floundered for a suitable response, the door opened and Isabetta barged into the kitchen. "I purchased the freshest sardines, Mother. Oh, I see we have a guest."

Hortensa took in her daughter's staged performance, then said, "Isabetta, this is Signore Silvio Torres. I've just informed him that your *brothers* are not home."

Silvio's eyes roamed over Isabetta in obvious approval. "I didn't know Rocco had a sister."

Alba retrieved the basket of fish from Isabetta, who hastily improvised, "We're three in total. I'm the youngest."

"Well, it's a pleasure to meet you, Signorina."

She inclined her head at him, then took a seat. "Alba, pour me some ale, please."

Hortensa eyed her daughter pointedly. "Signore Silvio asked about Beto a moment before you arrived."

"He's away on business for my father," Isabetta lied.

"When will he be back?"

"Ah, I'm not certain..."

"Beto and I have much in common. When Fernando and I were working for our father, I performed the same duties as your brother—overseeing supplies, ordering stock and merchandise, checking the quality of goods...In short, we made everything run efficiently. We're both second sons too."

Isabetta ached to confess the truth to the handsome young man. Instead, she steered the conversation in a safe direction by asking him questions about his kingdom. Flattered by her attention, Silvio recounted the wonders of Portugal.

Zanetto and Rocco arrived a short while later.

Isabetta shot out of her chair and kissed her father's cheek. "Hello Papa. Look! Signore Silvio has finally arrived, but he's terribly disappointed that Beto is away on business."

Plastering a smile onto his face, Zanetto turned his attention to their guest. "Welcome, Silvio. It's good to see you."

Rocco offered Silvio a warm greeting.

The women retreated and the men settled around the table. Alba poured two more tankards of ale and set out a plate of cheese and savory biscuits. Before long, the men began discussing the various changes affecting Venetian trade.

Isabetta lingered in the background alongside her mother, gritting her teeth in irritation. She wanted to participate in their conversation rather than play the role of demure daughter. Silvio caught her eye and the corners of his full mouth lifted. She returned the gesture while admiring his grayish blue eyes.

Hortensa nudged her daughter while mouthing the words: *don't stare*.

Mortified, Isabetta gazed down at her feet.

Zanetto regarded Silvio with interest. "I want to ask our guest a rather impertinent question, if I may."

Silvio inclined his head in invitation. "Please speak freely, Signore Zanetto."

"Are you certain there is no reconciliation between you and your brother? Alfonso dedicated his life to building his business and reputation. Knowing him as I do, he must be distressed over this fraternal rift."

"He is, but Fernando and I have never been friends if truth be told. The mutual distrust that had sprouted between us during adolescence continued into manhood. My brother and I have very different personalities and hold opposing views on how things should be done. We could never foster a successful partnership."

Disappointed, Zanetto folded his hands and sighed.

Silvio continued, "I know this radical change has placed you and your son in an unpleasant predicament."

"Most unpleasant," Zanetto echoed.

"I wish I could help you, but my father's contacts have a vested interest in Fernando's latest business venture."

"Your brother has already departed for Brazil, correct?"

"Yes, and he's a fool for doing so."

Hearing this, Rocco expressed surprise but said nothing.

Zanetto leaned forward in his chair. "Why do you say that?"

Helping himself to a biscuit, Silvio explained, "The risk and expenditure of such a journey is needless when there is so much money to be made right here in Europe. I tried to advise him on exporting Venetian textiles to Flanders and Holland, but he ignored me."

Rocco interjected, "I told my father about Flanders and Holland. You also mentioned possible business opportunities here in Venice. Would you share your ideas with us?"

"Presently, I'm seeking to rent a warehouse in order to store the items I plan on purchasing during my visit."

"Items?" Zanetto repeated, curious.

"Mainly diluted dyes, used or damaged Indian silks that can be restored, and spices mixed with finely ground flour."

"Lower grade goods?"

"*Precisely*." When Zanetto and Rocco frowned quizzically, Silvio continued, "Ship merchants such as yourselves have dominated the market in luxury imports. You cater to an elite clientele with plenty of money to spend. In reality, most people cannot afford such high prices. I plan to sell my lower grade goods in the local markets."

"Catering to common people," Rocco concluded.

"Correct."

Zanetto scratched his head, perplexed. "How exactly will you make money? An inferior product demands a substantially lower price."

"My products will be cheaper but my customer base will be enormous in comparison to yours. I hope to set up a stall in every market square of Venice."

Isabetta listened in awe to the ambitious foreigner who stood to make a sizeable sum through sheer volume.

Rocco rubbed his chin pensively. "Your idea might work, my friend. You can sell almost anything in Venice if you present it properly to buyers. Once an item becomes fashionable, the demand inevitably increases."

"That is my hope, Rocco."

Zanetto inquired, "Where are you staying?"

Silvio reached for a second biscuit. "My intention is to rent a room in Santa Croce."

Hortensa scrunched up her face. "Public rooms are damp and drafty. You're welcome to stay here."

Zanetto added, "It would be our pleasure to host you."

Silvio looked from one to the other. "I don't wish to impose upon your family."

"We insist," Rocco stated firmly.

"In that case, I gratefully accept your hospitality."

Hortensa pulled Alba aside. "Air out the linens in the spare bedchamber. Dust the furniture too."

Isabetta remained quiet during supper that night as she stole furtive glances at Silvio. Every so often, her brother would shift his eyes in her direction. He grinned knowingly and the gesture made her cheeks burn with shame. Teasing would soon commence, no doubt, for he seldom missed an opportunity to laugh at her expense. Normally, she didn't mind since it was all in good fun. She feared her parents would take note of her newfound fascination with Silvio and disapprove.

Hortensa stood and tapped her daughter's arm at the meal's conclusion. "Come along, Isabetta. Let's leave the men to their talk. Goodnight gentlemen."

"Goodnight," Isabetta muttered reluctantly while daring a peek at Silvio. Her heart skipped when he gifted her a smile.

***

Silvio proved an ideal houseguest. On the second night, he brought the Bastian family a leg of lamb for supper as a show of gratitude for their hospitality. On the third evening, a flask of good wine. He purchased flowers, fruit tarts, and a ceramic pitcher as a gift for Hortensa. Polite and amicable, it was virtually impossible not to like the Portuguese man.

Isabetta awoke to the sound of heavy rain one gray morning. Thunder roared and lightning lit up the dim bedchamber. Scurrying to the window, she pressed her nose to the glass pane. She liked violent summer storms because they often produced breathtaking sunsets. Also, a good tempest served as a cleansing agent to rid the city of filth. Dressing hastily, she thought of Silvio. Perhaps the inclement weather would prevent him from venturing out today. Quietly, she stepped out into the hallway. Seeing the partially open door of the guest bedchamber, she paused and looked inside. Silvio sat by the window reading a book. He glanced up and smiled.

Fire consumed her on the spot. "Forgive me, I didn't mean to pry. The door was open so…"

"It's all right."

"Am I disturbing you?"

"No."

"May I ask what you're reading?" He held up the book so

she could see the title. "*The Imitation of Christ* by Thomas à Kempis. An interesting choice."

"I promised my father that I would finish it."

"Are you a pious man, Signore Silvio?"

"No, but he is. Are you religious, Signorina Isabetta?"

"I attend mass regularly."

Eyes twinkling with mischief, he said, "As a good Christian young lady should."

"Have you found the items you wished to purchase, sir?"

Setting the book on a table, he stood. "I've acquired a few things, but I'm considering my options and comparing prices. I must say, Venice is unlike any city I've ever seen. Exotic yet familiar, and quite colorful too." He moved to stand before her and studied her face intently. *"Beautiful."*

The last word spilled over her like a soft caress.

Taking a step closer, he lowered his voice. "I'm usually surrounded by men in this business. It's pleasant to see a lovely face. Neither your brothers nor your father ever mentioned you. I cannot help but wonder why."

"What's there to say about me? I spend most of my time at home with my mother." She added a little laugh for good measure, then wisely changed the subject. "I would love to learn a few words in your language."

Crossing his arms, he casually leaned his shoulder against the door frame. "What would you like to know?"

Distracted by the graceful yet masculine movement, she said, "Tell me the first thing that enters your head."

Gazing down at her through hooded lids, he purred, *"Tu es a estrela mais linda do ceu."*

Rocco's wry chuckle made the flirting couple jump apart. "Our guest has paid you quite the compliment, little sister."

Silvio's face turned scarlet. "Harmless fun, Rocco."

Isabetta tugged on her brother's sleeve. "Tell me."

Rocco shook his head. "It will only make you vain."

"I called you the prettiest star in the sky," Silvio readily confessed. "I meant no offense."

"None taken, my friend," Rocco said while patting Silvio's

back. "My father learned of an empty warehouse this morning."

Silvio's face lit up. "Where?"

"Let's find out, shall we?"

"Can I go too?" Isabetta inquired.

Rocco shook his head in response.

Isabetta watched the men walk away with a pang of regret, then went into her bedchamber and froze. "Mother?"

"Come inside and close the door." Hortensa waited until her daughter obeyed. "Have you no shame, girl?"

"What do you mean?"

"I expect you to conduct yourself respectably during our guest's stay." Hortensa's finger pointed accusingly. "You crept into a man's chamber—"

"I did no such thing! I merely paused by his open door."

"A highly inappropriate act for an unmarried girl."

"I was being friendly."

Someone knocked on the door downstairs, prompting both women to be quiet. Alba entered the bedchamber a moment later and handed her mistress a letter.

Hortensa studied the big wax seal before cracking it in two. Unfolding the parchment with eager fingers, she scanned the fancy script and grinned. "It's the invitation to Cassandra's wedding this Sunday."

Isabetta groaned. "Do I have to go?"

"You already know the answer to that question." Placing a hand on her hip, Hortensa speared her daughter with a stern look. "As for that other matter, don't be getting any ideas about Silvio Torres. I see how you look at him—we all do."

Blushing, Isabetta countered defensively, "You cannot deny that he is handsome."

"I'll grant you that, but he is not the man for you."

"Silvio possesses intelligence and ambition."

Hortensa cocked an eyebrow. "*Silvio*, is it?"

"Mother—"

"*Signore* Silvio is a second son with no inheritance. He has severed ties with the only man who could have aided him in creating a decent future. Without the support of Fernando, he is reduced to being a hustler scrounging a living in a foreign city."

Crossing her arms, Isabetta countered coolly, "I happen to think his ideas have potential."

"Selling diluted spices and cheap dyes? Don't be absurd."

"He wants to sell textiles to Flanders and Holland. It's only a matter of time before he obtains his own ship."

Going over to the vanity, Hortensa surveyed the items scattered upon its surface. "It took your father nearly twenty years to purchase the *Tramonto*. Do you know what my life was like as a sailor's wife before he became a merchant? There were times during the early days of our marriage when we barely had enough to eat. I lived in a constant state of agitation with two children to raise on his meager wages. Don't make the same mistake I did."

"You married Father for love."

"Yes, and it came with a high price. Love is a luxury, my child. Better to marry a rich man and never know hardship. Trust me." Hortensa picked up a small pot and sniffed it. "We need to get you a new batch of rouge."

Isabetta snatched the container from her mother's hand and set it down. "You're saying these things because Cassandra is marrying a rich man."

"I'm speaking the truth, you obstinate girl. Silvio Torres is penniless, whereas your cousin has promised to help you find a good husband. Consider yourself fortunate."

"Father can't afford the kind of dowry that attracts nobility."

"No, but we're not out of options yet."

Kneeling before the *cassone* in the corner, Hortensa began sifting through her daughter's clothing. The sturdy hope chest, filled with embroidered linens and dresses, sported a bucolic landscape on the outside cover. Inside, Cupid hovered over an amorous couple in a lush garden—an idyllic scene of love specifically created to inspire passion in a newlywed couple. The chest would accompany Isabetta to her future husband's home and remain at the foot of their nuptial bed.

Hortensa extracted a gown and inspected it with a keen eye. "You shall wear this dress on Sunday. There are successful men in this city—merchants like your father—who would be perfectly suitable for you."

"Silvio will be one of those men someday."

"*Someday*," Hortensa repeated pointedly before doubling over with chest pains.

Isabetta said nothing more as she retrieved the garment from her mother's hands and set it on the bed. "You should rest."

She put her mother to bed, then returned to her bedchamber. Eyeing the gown with contempt, she placed it back into the *cassone* with resignation.

Rocco and Zanetto returned for the midday meal a few hours later without Silvio.

Hortensa, feeling better after a nap, went downstairs to join them. "Where is Signore Silvio?"

Zanetto pulled out a chair for her, then sat by his wife. "He stayed behind to meet someone and sends along his apologies. He should be back by supper."

Rocco sat down. "Father, don't you find it odd that he never mentioned who he was meeting?"

Zanetto reached for the ale pitcher. "Not at all."

"I assumed he didn't know anyone in Venice," Isabetta mused aloud.

"Apparently, he does," Rocco said while tearing a loaf of bread in half with his big hands. "Didn't a message come for him the other day?"

Zanetto replied, "Yes, but I didn't wish to pry into the young man's private affairs so I made no comment. At least we found him a warehouse to let."

Hortensa reached for her cup. "That's good news. Did he mention how long he will be staying in Venice?"

"Another fortnight."

Isabetta's stomach did a little flip.

Silvio returned in time for supper that evening. Isabetta made sure to sit across from their guest, as she did every night since his arrival. To her consternation, he got better looking with each passing day. How was that possible?

At one point, Hortensa said, "Signore Silvio, my niece is

getting married this Sunday. As our guest, you are more than welcome to accompany us to the wedding celebration."

Although Isabetta had no desire to attend Cassandra's wedding, Silvio's presence would make it bearable. Almost enjoyable. "There will be dancing and merrymaking," she chimed, earning her an amused grin from Rocco and a disapproving glare from Hortensa.

Rocco added playfully, "My sister is stubborn and won't take no for an answer."

Silvio smiled apologetically. "Thank you for the invitation. As much as I would like to partake in such a joyous occasion with all of you, I'm leaving for Treviso on Friday."

Stricken, Isabetta exclaimed, "I thought you were going to stay another fortnight!"

"Isabetta! Signore Silvio can come and go as he pleases," Hortensa chided.

Silvio held Isabetta's gaze. "I've been tasked with visiting someone on my father's behalf and shall return to Venice on Tuesday. Be assured that I would have relished the opportunity to dance with you at the wedding, Signorina."

All eyes were glued to Isabetta's glowing face.

CHAPTER 6

"I'm *soooo* hot," Isabetta whined while fanning herself. Cassandra's miserable wedding simply had to fall on such a sweltering day.

Fluttering about her daughter's bedchamber, Hortensa said cheerfully, "Today may be the day you find a husband."

"Mother, you shouldn't go in your condition."

Hortensa pursed her lips. "I know what you're trying to do."

"This heat will only make you feel worse."

"Rosa would never forgive such an insult. We must go regardless of the heat."

"But you're not well."

"The tonics help. I'll have one before we go."

"They only provide temporary relief. Please, let's stay home together. What better excuse than illness?"

Sighing impatiently, Hortensa glanced over at Alba. "Get my daughter's gown, will you?"

Alba left the room and returned with the gown, which she had hung on a rope by the attic's open window. Sniffing the fabric, she made a face. "It's been airing out since yesterday morning but there's a lingering stench of must."

Hortensa waved her hand dismissively. "Nothing that a bit of rose water can't mask. My husband paid dearly for that measure of Cornetti silk. Hopefully, the dress will fulfill its obligation and turn the heads of eligible men. My daughter must look her very best today." When Isabetta groaned dramatically, she added, "Stop your nonsense. Hurry and get dressed or we'll be late. I'll see you downstairs."

Alba filled a basin with water. At the sight of Isabetta's pout, she smirked. "You heard your mother. Don't make my job any more difficult than it already is."

Isabetta ran a dampened cloth along the firm planes of her body before dabbing rose water on her skin. She then donned the dress and sat still at the vanity while the servant dragged a wooden comb through her long waves. She rarely gazed at her reflection but she had no choice as Alba worked on her hair. The green silk enhanced the golden flecks in her warm brown eyes, but her demure mouth seemed at odds with her expressive eyebrows.

Working the comb through at a tangle, Alba said, "You'll become as conceited as your cousin if you keep staring at yourself like that."

Isabetta lowered her gaze. "Don't worry. I don't have anything to be conceited about."

"That's where you're wrong. Why do you think Cassandra is always taunting you?"

"Because she's rich and I'm not."

"No…She's envious because you're ten times smarter and better looking." The servant paused to set down the comb. "Your parents would be pleased if you found a husband."

"*Relieved* would be a better description."

Alba plaited the hair with nimble fingers. "They want to find the right man for you."

"I don't want a man."

Snickering, Alba said, "No, you want to *be* a man."

"I wish I could change my sex."

"So you could sail your father's ship?"

"Why not? I've done it before."

"When?"

"With Rocco when we were alone. Don't tell anyone. He let me sail the *Tramonto* to Torcello. With a bit more practice, I could be as good as him someday. I know how to use every piece of equipment in the galley. Astrolabe, armillary sphere, compass—I can also chart a course and navigate according to the night sky."

Alba caught her young mistress's eye in the mirror and frowned in disapproval. "I won't reveal your secret, don't worry. But I will say this: you're much too old for this type of talk, Isabetta Bastian. It amused us when you were a little girl, but saying such things now verges on impertinence."

Miffed, Isabetta said nothing more as Alba shaped the thick braid into a coil and secured the style with ribbons.

"There," Alba said in satisfaction. "Pity Signore Silvio can't accompany your family today. It's *obvious* you're fond of him."

"That will be all, Alba."

The servant hid her amusement. "Have a merry time."

Zanetto spied his daughter descending the stairs and sighed. "We're going to a wedding not a funeral. For Heaven's sake, Isabetta. There's no need to look so glum."

She forced the corners of her mouth upward.

"That's better," he said before ushering his family outside. "We're going to be late if we don't hurry."

Isabetta spotted Veronica Franco heading down the street toward them. Accompanied by her maid, Malvina, the lavishly dressed courtesan stopped to greet the Bastian family. Hortensa responded politely, although her expression remained cool. Zanetto and Rocco inclined their heads and pressed onward.

Isabetta deliberately lagged behind. "It's good to see you, Veronica. How is your mother?"

"Quite well, thank you. You look fetching today. May I ask where you're going?"

"My cousin's wedding."

Veronica whispered, "Cassandra?"

"Yes."

"I'm sure you'll have a wonderful time."

A giggle escaped Isabetta's lips, causing Hortensa to retrace her steps and grip her daughter's arm. "Come along, we don't want to be late. Good day to you, Signora Veronica."

"Good day," Veronica replied with a saccharine smile.

Once they were out of earshot, Hortensa leaned close to Isabetta. "Remember what your aunt said about ruining your reputation with bad associations."

"Greeting our neighbor is a display of good manners."

"That's not what people will think if they see you."

"Who cares what small-minded people think?" She yelped when her mother tugged on her earlobe.

"I care, and so should you."

Isabetta let the matter drop.

The Bastian family strolled the short distance to the church where the wedding would take place. Hortensa greeted her sister with an embrace before she and her family took their places amid the other guests. The bride soon entered the church and everyone fell silent. Cut from the finest brocade with detailed patterning in gold thread, Cassandra's gown publicly announced her family's wealth while advertising her father's livelihood.

"She may as well wear a sign around her neck promoting Cornetti fabrics," Isabetta muttered.

Hortensa's eyes darted nervously to make sure no one had overheard the rude comment. "Behave, will you? I bet those pearls around the bride's neck were a gift from Petro. Wouldn't you like to have jewels like that?'

Rather than reply, Isabetta silently eyed her young cousin as she stood beside the groom—a man almost twice her age with thinning hair and a slight paunch. Petro wasn't ugly, but he certainly wasn't the dashing hero of female daydreams.

A high price for exquisite pearls.

Innocent but not ignorant as to what transpired in the marital bed, she wondered if Cassandra would enjoy the feel of her husband's spindly hands on her body when he claimed her maidenhead. Silvio's face shimmered into focus in her mind.

What would the intimate act feel like with him?

Chastising herself for the wicked thought, she lifted her gaze to the domed ceiling where an ancient mosaic of Christ and his apostles presided over the congregated people below.

Isabetta nearly fell asleep during the drawn-out ceremony. She was almost relieved when her family joined the guests making their way to the Cornetti household afterward. Painted pastel blue, the house stood three stories tall with woven tapestries and frescoes adorning the interior walls. Beef pies seasoned with costly black pepper were displayed on a buffet table beside a tray piled high with oysters. Other delicious items included delicate soufflés, aged cheeses, an array of stewed and fried vegetables, and a suckling pig.

Isabetta ate to her heart's content and drank plenty of wine. She was about to select a piece of marzipan when Hortensa materialized at her side. A bit of extra rouge had aided in mimicking the appearance of health, but failed to mask the pain reflected in her eyes. "Mother, are you unwell? You look exceedingly pale. Maybe I should accompany you home."

"I feel perfectly fine." Prompting her daughter away from the buffet table, she warned, "You'll get fat if you continue to stuff yourself. That dress is already tight. One more bite and you'll tear the seam. Step away from the buffet table lest you scare potential suitors. Gluttons are expensive to maintain."

"You're right, Mother."

Isabetta reached for the piece of marzipan and popped it into her mouth the moment her mother's back was turned. Not daring to chew the treat, she allowed the sugary almond paste to melt on her tongue.

People applauded the bride and groom as they danced together. Isabetta positioned herself where she could study the couple discreetly. She pitied her cousin, who had been sold to the highest bidder like a prized calf. Cassandra's nubile body would be forced to produce heirs—as many as her husband desired. In exchange, she would enjoy a dull life of comfort and ease. Dressed in lush fabrics and jewels, to be showcased like a doll before her husband's family and peers.

Isabetta shuddered in disgust. Spinsterhood was preferable to mindless breeding. Resisting the temptation to snatch another piece of marzipan, she distracted herself by admiring a group of dancers who seemed to glide effortlessly across the marble floor. Someone gripped her hand at the onset of a new melody.

Breathless and flushed, Cassandra cried, "You haven't yet congratulated me!"

Isabetta forced a smile. "Felicitations."

The bride's eyes roamed over her cousin's gown. "I remember when Uncle Zanetto purchased that silk from my father. How long ago was that? Three, four years?"

Gritting her teeth, Isabetta overlooked the barb. "Three."

"What do you think of my new dress?"

"Your father has truly outdone himself."

"I know." Cassandra cast a glance at her new husband while fingering the glimmering white orbs at her throat. "I love my new pearls too. A wedding gift from Petro."

"He has excellent taste." Isabetta's eyes scanned the room in boredom. "I assume you're happy."

"I am indeed. Petro makes me laugh. When you get married, you must select a man with a sense of humor."

"I'll keep that in mind."

"Petro's family villa is located in Mestre. He owns vast amounts of land in the countryside and several vineyards. Our families get along well together, which is important."

"That's wonderful," Isabetta said flatly. She wanted to run out the door screaming.

"Poor Petro lost his mother last year so I won't have a mother-in-law to contend with—a blessing in disguise, don't you agree? Remember our old friend Cornelia? Her mother-in-law drove her mad." Cassandra tugged on her cousin's hand. "I love this melody. Dance with me."

"I don't think—"

"You cannot refuse a bride on her wedding day."

Isabetta relented and joined the dancing couples. The girls spun around and tapped their feet in tune to the music. They were soon giggling the way they had done as children—long before social status and wealth mattered in life.

Cassandra spun to a halt, then placed a hand to her chest. "Oh dear! I can barely breathe. I'm thirsty."

"Me too."

They wandered away from the dancers toward the buffet table. A servant poured white wine into two goblets.

Cassandra said, "This wine is from my husband's vineyards. Tell me what you think."

Isabetta took a sip. "Very good."

"I'll gift a few bottles to your family."

"I'm certain my parents would like that, thank you."

Cassandra stared at her cousin for a long time, her face serious. "I see sadness in your eyes, but try not be envious of me. You'll be happily married someday if God wills it." Ignoring Isabetta's stunned expression, she focused on something across the room. "Do not despair, for your luck may be changing sooner than you think. My father is introducing a potential suitor to your father as we speak."

Isabetta followed her cousin's gaze. Sure enough, a slender mature man with a pinched face and crop of graying curls stood between her uncle and her father. A murmured expletive escaped her lips.

Cocking her head to the side, Cassandra demanded, "Didn't you know that Alessio Innocenti would be here?"

"Who?"

"Widower, rich banker, and rather attractive, don't you think? Aunt Hortensa requested an introduction. My mother convinced my father to speak with him on your behalf. I'm surprised your parents didn't tell you."

Isabetta spotted her mother across the room speaking with a group of ladies. *Traitor.*

Cassandra grinned mischievously. "Oh look! The men are glancing our way, which means Signore Alessio is asking questions about you. Quick, pinch your cheeks and bite your lips to heighten their color."

"I have to go."

"Isabetta, wait!"

Ignoring her cousin's plea, Isabetta cut through a group of people and darted outside to the spacious courtyard. A short passageway covered with bougainvillea provided plenty of fragrant shade in which to hide. The floral tunnel led to a walled garden at the far end of the property. Crouching by a potted lemon tree, she tried to slow her racing heart. When no one exited the house in search of her, she wandered toward a cluster of tall rose bushes. Potential suitors be damned.

Stifled giggles followed by heavy breathing made her stop in her tracks. She moved toward the sound with silent footsteps. Branches and vines bursting with summer blossoms formed a verdant wall of latticework, thus hiding the identities of the amorous pair.

"I've missed you so much."

"Shhh...someone might hear us."

"Tell me you love me."

"You know I do, Lucia."

"Wait! I hear something."

"It's your imagination...I'm almost done."

"Rocco..."

Isabetta went rigid. Carefully, she stuck her fingers through a thicket of leaves and created a space big enough for her to peek through. Placing her eye near the small opening, she saw her brother in the arms of a woman with dark hair and big hazel eyes. Squatting low to the ground, she tried to block the sound of their lovemaking by covering her ears.

"Rocco! Oh my love..."

Grimacing, Isabetta retraced her steps as hastily as possible. She slipped into the house and headed toward the first servant she saw. "Wine, please."

Blurring the memory of what she had witnessed outside took precedence over hiding from men. Rocco had never mentioned a woman named Lucia. Who was she?

"There you are."

Isabetta whipped around. "Mother!"

"Your father and uncle have been looking for you."

"I was out in the courtyard—"

"With whom?"

"No one…I was getting some air."

Hortensa's eyes bulged in outrage. "You shouldn't be roaming outside unchaperoned like a wildling. Do you know how easily you can lose your chaste reputation? There are drunken men about the place."

"What about Rocco?" Isabetta shot back angrily. "Are you searching for him as well?"

"Rocco is a *man*."

"Doesn't he have a reputation to maintain?"

"Your brother's reputation is impeccable. You will remain by my side, young lady."

Isabetta seethed inwardly.

A page returned with the wine Isabetta had requested but Hortensa shooed him away. "You've had enough wine for one night. Besides, your wits need to be sharp. Ah, here comes your father now. For the love of God, smile."

The trio of men who had sought her earlier were heading straight toward them. Isabetta groaned, earning her a sharp poke in the ribs.

"Turn around and be polite," Hortensa instructed through clenched teeth. "Do not ruin this chance."

Isabetta plastered a smile to her face. The blue eyed man between her father and uncle did not return the gesture. Instead, he looked at her from head to toe in the same manner one would assess a race horse.

"Isabetta, there you are," Zanetto said in a pleasant tone laced with warning. "Signore Alessio Innocenti, I present to you my daughter."

Alessio inclined his head before peering down his arrogant nose. "It's a pleasure to make your acquaintance, Signorina."

Isabetta curtsied to the well-dressed man while taking note of the huge sapphire on his pinky finger. "You are Tuscan, sir."

A crease appeared between his fine brows. "You recognize the accent. Perhaps I am not the first Tuscan you've met?"

Instantly suspicious, she noted. Possibly jealous and possessive too. "You are the first, sir, but I live in a city of foreigners. One learns to decipher accents at a young age."

"Clever *and* comely." He waited for Isabetta to appear dutifully modest by his bland compliment. "I was born in Pistoia but lived in Florence for most of my life before moving to Venice. Have you ever been to Florence?"

"No, but I hear the artwork is sublime."

Finally, he offered her a genuine smile. "An apt description. Maybe someday you will see it for yourself."

"I would like that."

Hope lit up his features. "Would you?"

The underlying meaning of the question was clear. Wishing to put him off, she said casually, "Who wouldn't? In fact, I would love to see the entire world."

His smile vanished. "The world is a big place, Signorina Isabetta. Surely, you can't be serious."

She pretended not to notice her father's threatening glare. "Aren't you curious about the mysterious lands that exist beyond the great ocean?"

"I've been too busy fulfilling my familial obligations, which leaves little time for such grandiose fantasies."

"That's a shame, sir."

Alessio's gaze hardened. "As the eldest son, it is my responsibility to carry on my father's legacy. My wife died three months ago, leaving me with two sons to raise."

Looking for a young wife to dump them upon. "I'm sorry for your loss, Signore Alessio."

The Tuscan shrugged. "Death is a part of life."

"And life is short, which is why I wouldn't squander my time fulfilling duties if I were you."

Zanetto and Hortensa stared at their daughter aghast.

Alessio cast an uneasy glance at Alzo, who finally stepped in to remediate the situation. "My niece has a vivid imagination and tends to be rather outspoken."

Zanetto amended, "Pay no mind to her childish chatter. Isabetta still has much to learn. I'm guilty of indulging my daughter and it doesn't help that my son fills her head with stories of his sea voyages."

"I understand perfectly, gentlemen," Alessio assured.

Zanetto glanced at Isabetta, who stood watching the men with a wry smile playing about her lips. *Damn the girl.* "As her father, I can assure you that she's a dutiful daughter—obedient, chaste, and goodhearted."

"I don't doubt it, Signore Zanetto," Alessio conceded good-naturedly. "Let me ask your daughter a question. Signorina, do you wish to enjoy the freedoms of men?"

"What if I said yes?"

Hortensa whispered, "Comport yourself."

Alessio cleared his throat. "No need to chastise her honesty, madam. It's an excellent and rare character trait these days. Isabetta's vivaciousness is refreshing."

Hortensa's face fell in disappointment.

Alessio bowed gallantly over Isabetta's hand. "I bid you a good evening. It's been a pleasure."

"Likewise, sir."

Zanetto's stoic expression spoke volumes.

Alessio's eyes darted around the room and settled upon a timid young lady glued to an old matron. He looked pointedly at Alzo. "We're done here."

Hortensa and Zanetto blushed with embarrassment as Alzo led the Tuscan to another potential wife.

Zanetto shot his daughter a menacing look.

"You have shamed us," Hortensa whispered before stomping off with her husband.

Despite their anger, Isabetta sagged with relief when her parents left her alone. Having dodged the danger of becoming a stepmother called for a celebration. Where had that page gone with her wine? In her search for libations, she noticed the doe-eyed Lucia discreetly inject herself into a circle of guests. A corpulent man in a red doublet materialized beside her almost immediately. Urging her away from the others, he led her to a corner where they were soon engaged in a heated discussion. Rocco strode into the room a moment later and scowled at the sight of the arguing couple.

Isabetta grabbed two chalices from a tray and veered toward her brother. "Wine, Rocco?"

He reluctantly tore his gaze from Lucia and accepted the vessel. "Why aren't you dancing, Betta?"

"I would much rather know who that woman is."

"Which woman?"

"The pretty one you were staring at just now."

Rocco's cheeks reddened. "Do you mean Signora Lucia?"

"I do. Who is that man?"

"Giorgio Fosetti, her husband. Why do you ask?"

Lucia was married! "I like her gown," Isabetta improvised.

"Signore Giorgio often does business with our uncle. I'm surprised Cassandra hasn't introduced you to his wife."

"Our cousin is too busy showing off her gown and pearls."

Rolling her eyes, she added sarcastically, "Besides, I've had enough introductions for one day."

Chuckling, he said, "Ah, so you've met Alessio Innocenti."

"You knew?"

He almost recoiled from the accusation in her tone. "Father told me this morning after the ceremony. Signore Alessio can provide you with a comfortable life in Tuscany."

"He's seeking a nanny for his two sons."

"At least you wouldn't be bored." She made a face and he frowned. "You cannot remain a little girl forever."

"*Little girl?* Is that what you think I am?"

"No, but you've been spoiled by Father."

"I would trade places with you in the blink of an eye."

Rocco shook his head disdainfully, then drank deeply from the chalice. "Do you think my life is easy, Betta?"

"You are *free* whereas I am not."

His eyes drifted to where Lucia and Giorgio were angrily gesticulating. "None of us are free, little sister."

"At least our parents aren't trying to match you up with some old ninny."

"You could do much worse than Alessio Innocenti. Our uncle says he's a decent man with a good reputation. We aren't members of nobility so you can't afford to be overly choosy."

"Marriage is a life sentence. People should be very selective of their prison mate." When he only sighed, she added, "I don't want to marry anyone. I want to sail the *Tramonto* with you."

He regarded her thoughtfully. "You have no idea of the dangers lurking at sea. Hunger, exhaustion, scurvy, mutiny—not to mention violent storms and the constant threat of pirates and foreign plagues."

"You sound like Papa! Is it so wrong to pine for adventure?"

"God has cursed you with too much wit and boldness. You see the world through brightly colored veils."

"That's not it at all, Rocco."

"No? Enlighten me," he said before drinking more wine.

"I understand the potential beyond what is afforded me. What's more, I see a world filled with possibilities, whereas

Mother and Father—*and you*—only see a husband and babies in my future."

Although his patience had reached its limit, he made one more attempt at reason. "There are no female ship captains."

"I could be the first."

Rocco's eyes and mouth hardened simultaneously, making his face almost intimidating. Enough was enough. "Don't be naïve, Betta. The crewmen would ravage you in an instant."

Taken aback, she countered, "I can defend myself. You taught me how to use a knife and sword, remember?"

"Maybe I was wrong to indulge you. It's made you lose your sense of propriety."

She touched his arm. "Please don't say that."

"I love you, but the time has come for you to grow up and assume some responsibility. You need to marry and start your own family." Seeing that he had offended her, he amended, "I'm only trying to—"

"Stop. You've said enough."

They grew silent when they spotted their father walking toward them with purpose.

Zanetto eyed each of his grown children with a twinge of suspicion. "Where is your Uncle Alzo? I haven't seen him since that disastrous introduction."

Isabetta averted her gaze at his jibe.

"I don't know," Rocco replied.

"It's late. We need to be up early tomorrow to meet with an investor but I don't wish to leave the party without thanking our host." Zanetto spotted his wife saying farewell to her sister. "No matter, I'll stop by Alzo's bottega tomorrow. Go on you two, say your goodbyes."

Isabetta watched her father walk away, then noticed Rocco scowling at something. Following his gaze, she saw Giorgio clasping his wife's wrist and pulling her across the room toward the door. Lucia's pleading eyes met Rocco's for an instant before she and her husband exited the palazzo.

CHAPTER 7

Wandering the streets after sunset was unwise so the Bastian family made their way home via gondola beneath the starry sky. Despite the glares Isabetta received from her parents as they huddled together in the narrow vessel, no one dared to speak in the presence of the gondolier. Venetians who wished to preserve their good reputations knew not to provide fodder for potential gossipmongers.

Isabetta admired her surroundings with hungry eyes. Rarely did she see Venice at night, and it was nothing short of spectacular. Torches along the canal illuminated the façades of various palazzos. Doors and windows were thrown open to cool the inhabitants within. Some of these homes were fully lit up and she peeked into these interiors with voyeuristic enjoyment. A group of dancers spun on a giant black and white chessboard floor, elegant guests dined in a plush banquet hall, and a beautiful couple kissed on a carved travertine balcony. Excitement and mystery lurked behind every corner of the city, and this was as close as she would ever get to it. Her existence seemed suddenly bland in comparison.

You'll see Silvio soon enough.

The thought cheered her instantly. Silvio was handsome, charming, clever…Thanks to him, she was enjoying the best summer of her life.

A gondola going in the opposite direction floated by them. Seated within was a richly dressed man and his veiled female companion. Both wore black eye masks to hide their identities.

Intrigued, Isabetta stared at the mysterious couple. Who were they? Where were they going? Was she a courtesan? A mistress of someone important? Maybe they had been invited to one of the elegant palazzos where a late dinner, music, and dancing awaited them. What she wouldn't give to experience the thrill of such an evening!

The gondolier steered the vessel toward the Cannaregio dock where they alighted onto the quay.

Zanetto fell into step with his daughter once the gondola had melted into the night. "You disappointed me tonight, Isabetta. Alessio Innocenti could have given you the kind of life that I've always wanted to give your mother."

"I'm sure he could, but—"

"Do you think you can do better? Is that it?" He searched her face in the moonlight. "I hate to say it but your arrogance is unwarranted."

"It's not arrogance, Papa, I swear. I would much prefer to continue running the Bastian business than be a common wife."

"When I die, Rocco will inherit my ship and my clients—*not you*. Do you understand?"

His sobering words made her falter. "I'll be just as happy working for Rocco. You know he's not good with numbers."

"That's not the point!" Pinching the bridge of his nose, he sighed. "Your mother and I know what's best for you."

Isabetta didn't reply. It was late, she was tired, and there was always tomorrow to speak of this matter.

They entered the square where Viaro the fishmonger would be selling his wares at dawn. Rocco and Zanetto rounded the corner onto the narrow street leading to their home. Only a few flickering torches offered light, making the familiar route seem almost sinister.

Hortensa cast a sidelong glance at her daughter. "Signore Alessio could have been the answer to our prayers. Such an opportunity may not present itself again."

"An answer to your prayers, not mine."

"You stubborn girl, when will you—" Hortensa froze when she noticed that her husband and son had stopped short. Placing a hand on Isabetta's arm, she urged her daughter to be still.

Isabetta craned her neck and saw a cloaked figure wearing a *bauta* standing in front of her father and brother. The white oval masks were worn by most during the Carnival season, but only the nobility wore them year round. Like the couple in the gondola, this man did not wish to be identified.

"Take cover," Zanetto called out to his wife and daughter as he sprang in front of his son. A small explosion tore through the silent night and he went down like a stone.

Isabetta faltered, her eyes glued to the intricately designed ivory-handle of the pistol in the stranger's hand. A plume of bluish smoke rose from the weapon's nozzle.

Ivory...smoke...pistol...

The man hissed a curse and stared at her from behind the mask. An odd buzzing began inside her head. Rocco lurched at the stranger and a scuffle ensued. Muffled gasps came from somewhere nearby but she couldn't pinpoint the source since the sound blended with the murderer's retreating footsteps. The buzzing noise intensified...Was this a dream? Had she fallen asleep inside the gondola?

Jolted from her stupor by her mother's high-pitched cry, Isabetta noticed Rocco sprawled on the cobblestones. The wooden hilt of a knife stuck out of his inner thigh. She watched in horror as he pulled out the blade with unsteady fingers. Blood flowed from the wound at an alarming rate.

Hortensa kneeled beside her son's body. "Help! Help! Someone call for the barber-surgeon!"

Isabetta crawled to where her father lay motionless and placed a hand on his chest. Wet heat permeated the fabric of his garment, coating her fingers in a dark slick liquid. *Blood.* A scream bubbled up in her throat and burst from her lips.

Shutters were thrown open above their heads. A woman's shrill voice called out for the *Signori di Notti*, the guards who kept order in the night.

Rocco groaned and looked at his sister through half-closed lids. "Care for...*Mother*."

Hortensa gripped her son's shoulders. "Rocco!"

Roused from their peaceful slumber, bleary-eyed residents of the Cannaregio surrounded them with candles held aloft.

"Two men, dead!"

"Go and fetch the physician!"

"Right outside our door!"

"Lord help us..."

Zanetto stirred and took hold of Isabetta's wrist. Colorless lips moved, prompting her to lean closer. "Live your life..."

Heartbroken and angry, she vowed, "I'm going to find out who did this, Papa. I swear to you before God that I will avenge you and Rocco."

Impending death prevented him from protesting. Revenge would not save him now, and he certainly didn't want his beloved daughter wasting her time and energy. A weariness unlike any he had ever known seized him and he closed his eyes. Forever.

Sensing that her father's soul had fled his body, Isabetta fell upon his chest and wept until she succumbed to the numbing comfort of darkness.

***

Merry birdsong and sunshine greeted Isabetta when she opened her eyes on Monday morning. She sat up and winced due to her throbbing head.

Alba appeared and forced her back down onto the pillow. "Better if you rest, Signorina. You've suffered a bad shock—"

Bewildered, Isabetta glanced around the room. "How did I get here? Where is my mother?"

"Signora Hortensa is still sleeping, thank God. The state that poor woman was in…" Alba trailed off, her eyes watering. "She thought she had lost you too. The *Signori di Notti* carried you home in a dead faint."

Last night's memory crashed down upon Isabetta with the force of a tempest. Throwing back the covers, she swung her legs off the edge of the bed and almost fell over.

Alba's face twisted in worry. "Please get back into bed."

"Help me get dressed."

"Signorina—"

"Now."

The servant pursed her lips in disapproval, then reluctantly helped her young mistress bathe and dress.

Isabetta's body shook throughout the process, her face waxen. Overwhelming nausea made her head swim. Gripping the bedpost, she doubled over and heaved a few times. A ceramic chamber pot was quickly placed beneath her chin. She vomited and then plopped onto the edge of the bed. Placing her head in her hands, she wept. A knock on the door made her sniff and look up. "Have you sent for my aunt?"

"Not yet."

They went downstairs and Alba opened the door.

Veronica stood outside wearing a concerned expression. Pushing past the servant, she hugged Isabetta. "The whole sestiere is talking about it…Mother and I are sickened by this news. We share your grief."

"A man accosted us out of nowhere—it happened so fast."

"Santa Madonna."

"I feel as if I'm in a nightmare and I can't wake up."

"Here, sit down." Turning to Alba, Veronica demanded, "Where is Signora Hortensa?"

The servant glanced upward. "Sleeping."

Isabetta refused to sit. "Fetch my cloak, Alba."

Concerned, Veronica inquired, "Where are you going?"

"I must go to the magistrate at once."

"I'm certain an official will come by your house to speak with you and your mother."

"I need to relay what happened yesterday while the memory is fresh in my head. My mother is in no condition to speak with anyone right now."

"As you wish." Casting a fleeting glance at Alba, Veronica added, "I'll go with her."

Alba shot the courtesan a look of gratitude before going upstairs to retrieve her mistress's cloak.

Veronica and Isabetta crossed the city via a maze of streets. The latter was received by an official and shown into an antechamber. Between ragged breaths and bouts of tears, she described the brutal murders with as much detail as she could recall. The burly man took notes and never glanced up.

At length, he studied her face. "From what you've described, the murderer's intention was to kill your brother and your father intervened. Tell me, did Rocco Bastian have enemies?" When Isabetta failed to reply, he prompted, *"Signorina?"*

"Rocco was respected and well-liked by everyone."

Was.

The word caused a sharp prickle of pain.

Eyeing her skeptically, he repeated, *"Everyone?"*

"I don't know a single person who would wish him harm. I'm hoping you can solve this mystery, sir."

"We will do our best."

His tone implied dismissal so Isabetta nodded slightly and said nothing more.

Veronica led her dazed friend outside. They walked in silence for a while before she said, "I cannot fathom the pain and frustration you're experiencing, but you must be strong for your mother's sake. Otherwise, her fragile health may not withstand this tragic blow."

"I know."

Veronica only spoke again once they were outside Isabetta's door. "My mother and I are here for you if you need us. I must go now but I'll check on you later."

"Thank you," Isabetta said before going inside.

Alba stood by the hearth, relieved to see her mistress safely home. "I'm making porridge. You should eat."

Isabetta pulled out a chair and sat at the table with a heavy sigh. "Dispatch a messenger to my Aunt Rosa informing her of the calamity that has befallen our household. Here, take these coins and find a boy who can run fast."

Alba placed the iron cauldron with the bubbling porridge on the terracotta floor to cool. After pocketing the money, she exited the house.

Floorboards creaked above Isabetta's head. "Mother?"

When no answer came, she ran upstairs. White-gold sunlight poured from the hallway window behind her mother, casting her in deep shadow. The ghost-like silhouette moved forward with tentative steps, swaying slightly.

"Zanetto?"

"Mother, you should go back to bed."

Hortensa's face crumpled like that of a child denied a treat. "Zanetto! Rocco! God has forsaken us…Why?"

Gathering every ounce of strength, Isabetta put on a brave face. "I've already spoken to the magistrate this morning. They will find the monster who did this and he will be brought to justice. I'll make sure of that."

"Santa Madonna."

Spent from grief and illness, Hortensa slumped against the banister. Isabetta helped her mother back to bed, then dragged herself downstairs to the kitchen to mix another poppy infused draught. After making sure her mother drank it, she returned to the kitchen to think.

Alba returned after having completed her task. Seeing the porridge still in the cauldron, she inquired, "Shall I…?"

"Don't bother. I have no appetite."

"You should at least take some broth. Getting sick will only make matters worse. I'll mix you a draught so you can rest."

Sleeping would ease the pain. "Yes."

Isabetta consumed a bit of the broth and the draught. Alba helped her somnolent mistress upstairs and put her to bed.

Rocco held Lucia in his arms and kissed her amid a sea of sunflowers. Butterflies with gossamer wings fluttered around them as the sun shone behind puffy white clouds. Lucia broke free from the embrace and ran, giggling as she peeked over her shoulder. Laughing heartily, Rocco began chasing her…

Isabetta woke up smiling, then remembered that Rocco was gone forever. The memory of her brother's pale corpse made her shiver from head to toe. He had been so full of life and vitality; big and strong and handsome—

God could have saved them.

Instead, He allowed two good men to be slaughtered like pigs in the street. Overcome by seething anger, her thoughts verged on blasphemous.

Someone knocked on the door below and Isabetta strained her ears to listen. Rosa's shrill voice floated up the stairwell and she braced herself for the encounter.

***

Haggard from grief, the Bastian women accepted the condolences of mourners after the priest had concluded the funeral service. Curatives had done little to ease Hortensa's pain, and the sight of the coffins being lowered into the earth had caused her to swoon at one point. Rosa stood between her sister and newlywed daughter. Petro was away on business.

Tumultuous clouds scuttled across a precarious slate blue sky. The threat of rain hung heavily in the humid morning air, prompting the gravediggers to work fast. Zanetto and Rocco had been dressed in their finest clothing before being laid to eternal rest.

Isabetta shuddered at the ominous sound of metal shovels slicing through dirt. Despite the heat, she felt cold. She did her best to control her roiling emotions as a Greek sea captain by the name of Basil Anastas stepped forward from the group of mourners to pay his respects. Having lived in Venice for nearly thirty years, the swarthy bearded man knew almost everyone in the shipping business.

Taking one of Isabetta's delicate hands into his big rough one, he grimaced sadly. "The people in this *sestiere* admired your father and brother—especially me."

"I appreciate that, Signore Basil. I'm still trying to make sense of it…But I'm at a loss."

"Zanetto and I spoke as recently as last week. He was upset after having received troubling news from your uncle. Life is so unpredictable." Casting a glance at Hortensa, he added, "My wife sends warm regards. She's home caring for our youngest, who has fever. We'll both pray for you and your mother."

Isabetta gripped his hand tightly. "Wait. What news did my father receive from my uncle?"

"He told me that Alzo Cornetti will be providing only half the measure of textiles from now on."

Hiding her surprise, she pressed, "Did my father say why?"

"Your uncle is going to start exporting to the Flemish."

Her eyes darted to where Alzo stood speaking with a group of men. "I know Rocco was keen on trading with Flanders and Holland, but neither he nor my father had solidified this plan of action. They would never have apprised my uncle without first arriving at a decision." She refrained from adding that she knew everything that transpired within the Bastian shipping business.

At this, he shook his head slightly. "You misunderstand me. Alzo is doing business with someone else now, which I suspect also angered Zanetto."

"What?"

"Forgive me," he offered awkwardly. "I assumed you and your mother knew. Perhaps I should not have said anything."

Releasing his hand, she assured, "You did well to tell me."

Basil shuffled off in order to allow others a chance to pay their respects. Isabetta tried to calm her racing thoughts as Iseppo da Mosta and his wife came forward. The merchant's eyes reflected genuine sorrow whereas Polonia, dressed in costly patterned gown, showed no hint of emotion. Isabetta took in her decadent garment and wondered if the woman felt relief now that her husband's biggest competitor was dead.

Polonia stopped to speak with Hortensa while Iseppo placed a gentle hand on Isabetta's shoulder. "My sympathy on your loss, Isabetta. I'm deeply distraught by this tragedy."

"Signore Iseppo, thank you for coming."

"Fine men, both of them. Crime is the scourge of every city and robberies happen frequently. Thieves normally don't kill their victims after stealing their money and jewels, however."

"Thieves? We weren't robbed."

Confused, he looked over at Polonia. "My wife overheard people talking, and they said you and your family were accosted by an armed thief while returning home late at night."

"We were indeed accosted by an armed man wearing a *bauta* while returning from my cousin's wedding. He shot my father and stabbed Rocco, then ran away without stealing anything—my mother and I were wearing our best jewels too." A thief would have availed himself of them, for they were fashioned from silver and gold.

Iseppo eyed her warily. "Are you suggesting someone killed your father and brother *deliberately*?"

Memories of that fateful night pierced her heart. "That's exactly what I am affirming."

Polonia stepped between them and took her husband's arm.

"Others wish to pay their condolences, my dear." To Isabetta, she added, "We were shocked by the news, and feel so badly for you and your mother. We'll pay for a sung mass, won't we, Iseppo? Please send word if there is anything you need."

Isabetta stared at the retreating couple until the sound of soft female weeping drew her attention. She traced the sound to a veiled woman standing off to the side. Intricate black lace failed to fully conceal a familiar profile. Confronting the lone figure, she said, "You knew my brother well, didn't you?"

"Pardon me?"

"You were at my cousin's wedding celebration on Sunday."

"Ah yes, Cassandra…I was there with my husband."

"*And* Rocco.

"I don't know—"

Isabetta's fingers curled around Lucia's upper arm. Without a word, she led the woman away from the others. Stopping behind the wide girth of an oak trunk, she whispered, "Jealous husbands often commit unthinkable crimes."

"Let go of me!"

"I saw you and my brother together in the garden."

Lucia finally confessed, "I loved him."

"Did your husband know about you and Rocco?"

"No."

"Are you certain?"

Lucia dabbed at her swollen eyes with a lace handkerchief. "I'm almost certain, yes. Rocco was more than my lover—he was my savior, my friend. He didn't deserve to die."

"Neither did my father."

"The world is a miserable place."

"How long were you and Rocco…?"

"Two years."

"The murderer aimed his pistol *directly* at my brother. Clearly an act of revenge."

"If Giorgio did know about my adultery, I doubt he would care. He doesn't love me. Whenever he's in residence, which is rare, he spends most nights in the house of his mistress. That doesn't count the whores he entertains whenever he's abroad."

"If your husband didn't care or love you, as you so claim, why was he angry when he saw you coming in from the courtyard? Don't bother denying it because Rocco and I saw you two arguing. Your husband seemed quite jealous."

"That wasn't jealousy, I assure you. Giorgio couldn't find me, then he saw me coming in from the garden alone. What you saw was me being interrogated."

"What did you tell him?"

"I needed to use the privy and aided an old woman who felt unwell. He believed me."

"Are you certain of this?"

"Yes." She paused as fresh tears ran down her cheeks. "Rocco was my life, Signorina Isabetta. *My life*."

At that, Lucia turned on her heel and ran off.

Paola and Veronica, who had remained several feet away from the rest of the mourners due to their low social status, wore somber black gowns and waist-length veils over their faces. Jewels glimmered at their throats beneath the sheer dark fabric. Fat raindrops began falling from the sky, prompting Rosa to lead Hortensa to the awaiting carriage. Only when the mourners dispersed did the courtesans approach Isabetta.

Veronica touched her friend's arm. "You can count on my mother and I for anything you need. Our servants have already prepared a large quantity of food for your household. There is enough to last a few days."

"That's very kind but Alba has been—"

Paola lifted a jeweled finger to stop Isabetta's protest. "I saw your servant this morning. She doesn't look well."

Isabetta glanced at Alba's slight frame. "She's been caring for us ceaselessly since this nightmare began. Your consideration and generosity is most appreciated."

"Today, Alba will take some much needed rest."

Paola slipped her hand into the crook of her daughter's elbow. "Come along, Veronica, before we get drenched."

Rosa and Alzo accompanied Hortensa and Isabetta home. Alba set out the food that Veronica's servants had thoughtfully prepared while they took their seats around the table. By now, the rain was falling hard. Someone knocked on the door and Alba paused to open it.

Silvio bounded into the room while running a hand through his wet hair. Dripping wet, he said breathlessly, "Greetings everyone." Eyeing the succulent ham and bitter greens on the table, he added cheerfully, "I've arrived just in time, it seems."

Chapter 8

Silvio faltered in the face of everyone's stony silence. Only when he noticed their mourning garments did his jolliness fade to dust. "What's going on here?" Alba pulled out a chair for him and he sat down. When no one replied, he looked around. "Where's Rocco and Signore Zanetto?"

Hortensa replied flatly, "They are both dead."

Silvio's face blanched as the woman fell into a fit of tears. His eyes sought Isabetta, who apprised him of the dire situation. Crossing himself, he uttered a silent prayer before offering words of comfort to the Bastian women.

Alzo cleared his throat and stared directly at Hortensa. "I hate to bring this up so soon but you must think of your future. With Zanetto and Rocco gone…"

Rosa said, "My husband is right. You and Isabetta need to consider your next step."

Hortensa's eyes, reddened and swollen from countless tears, began to water once more.

Alzo heaved a sigh. "Zanetto had debts—"

Furious that he would bring up this topic now, Isabetta interjected, "Father was up to date on every payment."

"How would you know?"

"I know more than you think, Uncle Alzo. Would you mind explaining to me why you're providing only half the normal order of fabrics?"

"Who told you this?"

"Basil Anastas, who spoke to my father only last week."

Alzo cast a fleeting glance at Silvio, then replied, "Zanetto told me the Torres-Bastian relationship was over, so I had no choice but to invest elsewhere."

Narrowing her eyes, Isabetta concluded, "In other words, you chose to abandon us in our time of need."

Rosa leaned forward. "Isabetta, your impertinence—"

"Be quiet, Aunt Rosa."

Rosa gasped. "Hortensa, say something to calm your daughter. She is overly distraught."

Isabetta pierced her aunt with a sharp look. "*I said* be quiet. My conversation with your husband has nothing to do with you. As for my mother, can't you see that she is devastated? For once in your self-absorbed pampered life, concentrate on someone other than yourself."

Rosa's mouth formed an "O" but she remained silent.

Alzo scowled at Isabetta. "Not only are you rude to my wife, you're meddling in the affairs of men. We shall overlook this atrocious behavior since you've suffered a shock—"

"Who is the recipient of the other half?" Isabetta demanded without preamble.

"What does it matter to you?"

"For your information, I do *all* of the accounting in this household. That includes the family business."

Alzo flinched in surprise. "Hortensa, is this true?"

Hortensa heaved a shuddering breath. "It is."

Alzo studied his niece with renewed interest. "I had always assumed either Rocco or Zanetto kept the books."

"That's been my responsibility for years." Casting a fleeting glance at Silvio, Isabetta added, "I also do the ordering, oversee the quality of our products, and take inventory of the foodstuffs on board prior to departure."

Silvio frowned. "I thought Beto did all of those things."

Rosa frowned too. "Who is Beto?"

"Hortensa's other son," he replied.

Alzo and Rosa looked at each other in confusion before turning their gazes to Hortensa.

Isabetta confessed quietly, "I am Beto."

Everyone turned their heads to stare at her.

Finally, Silvio asked, "*You?* You pretended to be a man?"

Isabetta averted her eyes. "Yes."

Rosa leaned toward her sister and whispered, "Did you know about this?"

Hortensa nodded, her eyes dull.

Alzo said, "I can hardly believe what I'm hearing. How long have you been maintaining this farce?"

"Papa's eyes faded several years ago and he could no longer read the ledgers. Rocco isn't good with numbers. I possess talent for arithmetic so they both agreed that I should handle the accounting. Papa thought it best for the business to give the impression that I was male, so my childhood nickname *Betta* became *Beto*." Alzo's incredulity prompted Isabetta to add, "Why do you look at me like that? Have I ever made any errors in my calculations? Given you reason for complaint?"

"No, but that doesn't mean I approve of this shameful charade. On the contrary, I find it deplorable."

"A *harmless* charade, Uncle Alzo. For the sake of our family business, nothing more."

"There is still the problem of debt. Your father owes quite a bit on the *Tramonto*."

"I'm aware of that, but very few sea merchants in Venice own their ships outright."

"Iseppo da Mosta does."

"He is the exception not the rule." Cocking her head to the side, Isabetta studied her uncle intently. "You groveled back to Iseppo, didn't you? Don't bother replying because I can see the answer on your face. No matter. The galley should be paid off in the next year or two. I shall continue with the payments."

Alzo's expression turned frosty as he placed his elbows on the table. "How do you intend to do that?"

"The *Tramonto* is scheduled to set sail for Portugal at the onset of October—with or without the full order of Cornetti textiles. I'll pay the next installment from my profits."

Alzo's eyebrows shot upward. *"You?"*

Isabetta bristled. "Who else? Have I not proved myself sound of mind and capable until now?"

"Isabetta, you are a clever girl but—"

"I'm more than merely a 'clever girl.' I keep abreast of our profits and losses, know our customer preferences, and I'm familiar with the inner workings of the galley. Don't worry, I'll select a good captain."

Rosa gasped in shock whereas Silvio watched Isabetta with keen interest. Hortensa kept her eyes closed as she pulled ragged breaths into her weak lungs.

Alzo shook his head disdainfully. "The days of your father indulging you are over, Isabetta Bastian."

Isabetta's eyes flashed. "I have no choice but to continue where Papa and Rocco have left off. How else are we supposed to maintain our household—or do you expect Mother and me to starve to death?"

"How dare you?"

"She's too upset to reason with you, Alzo. Let's talk of this another day," Rosa chided with an apologetic glance aimed at her grieving sister.

Alzo's eyes were glued to Isabetta's face as he lifted a hand to silence his wife. "Now is the best time. Isabetta must face the reality of her current predicament."

"I'm well aware of my predicament," Isabetta snapped.

"Are you? It doesn't seem that way to me. Let me put it in simple terms so that you can understand. No man in this city will conduct business with a woman—unless he's negotiating the price for a prostitute."

The harshness of his words dragged Hortensa from her stupor. "Alzo, you are speaking with my daughter!"

"Forgive me, Hortensa, for I know this is a difficult time. I care for you both, which is the reason for my brutal honesty. Zanetto and Rocco are gone forever. Isabetta can no longer continue carrying on as this fictional *Beto*."

Silvio cleared his throat. "May I be of assistance? I'm happy to negotiate on Isabetta's behalf."

Alzo shook his head. "With all due respect, Signore Silvio, I am her uncle. It is my duty to intercede on behalf of the Bastian family affairs from now on, not yours."

Silvio inclined his head. "I meant no disrespect."

"None taken."

Isabetta's rage simmered like molten lava beneath her deceptively cool exterior as she stared at her uncle.

Alzo leaned back in the chair nonplussed. "I have already

been approached by a few investors—"

"Vultures!"

He continued as if his niece hadn't spoken. "They are interested in purchasing the *Tramonto* and I'm certain I can obtain a decent price. That should sustain you and your mother for a long time until we can figure out something else."

Pounding the table with her fist, Isabetta ground out, "The *Tramonto* is not for sale!"

Searing her with a withering glare, Alzo countered, "I am going to do what is best for you and your mother regardless of your childish tantrums."

Rosa turned to Hortensa and said, "The best thing she can do at this point is marry."

Isabetta shot out of her chair so abruptly that it fell backward with a loud crash. Eyeing everyone in turn, she pressed her lips together to keep from cursing and then stormed out of the room.

***

Hortensa took to her bed the day after the funeral. Unwilling to eat, she did little more than cough, cry, and sleep thanks to Alba's continuous administration of strong herbaceous brews laced with sedatives.

Two *vigili* came to the house shortly after midday. Alba granted the men entrance while Isabetta was in the process of descending the stairs.

One of the officers said, "This was the home of Zanetto and Rocco Bastian, correct?"

That word again. *Was*.

"Yes," Isabetta replied, clearing the last step and placing her hand on the banister for support. She spied Silvio seated at the table reading a book.

"Is Signora Hortensa Bastian at home?"

"My mother is unwell and resting upstairs. I am Isabetta Bastian. Do you have information regarding the murder of my father and brother?"

Exchanging a glance with his companion, he replied, "We believe we have found the man who did it."

Hearing these words caused Isabetta's knees to buckle.

Silvio rushed to her side and guided her to a chair.

The officer waited for Alba to give her mistress some water, then inquired, "Were you aware of your brother's illicit relationship with Giorgio Fosetti's wife, Lucia?"

Nodding, Isabetta replied, "I found out about it at my cousin's wedding, which was on the night of Rocco's death. Signora Lucia came to his funeral yesterday."

"We know. That's what triggered the confrontation leading to her death."

"What?"

"We arrested Giorgio Fosetti this morning. According to one of their servants, he confronted his wife about her affair with Rocco when she returned home. He was livid that she had attended the funeral service, for it signaled to the world that he had been made a cuckold."

"Signore Giorgio knew about her adultery?"

"You sound surprised," the officer observed.

"I spoke to Signora Lucia yesterday on the matter and she assured me that her husband had no knowledge of her romantic liaison with Rocco."

"Their servant said that her master was in possession of an intercepted love letter signed with a letter *R*. Lucia supposedly laughed in her husband's face and flung insults at him."

Perplexed, Isabetta said, "She was inconsolable yesterday—I can't imagine her behaving like that."

"She probably went mad with grief. The servant said that's when Giorgio gave in to his rage."

With a heavy heart, Isabetta recalled her happy dream featuring the two lovers. "How did she die?"

"Giorgio struck his wife in the head with an iron poker. Terrified for her own life, the servant fled the scene. She came to us this morning to denounce her employer."

Lucia's pretty face loomed in Isabetta's mind. "Dear God."

"We believe Giorgio killed your father in error since he is known for his bad aim. In fact, it seems his peers openly joke about this embarrassing trait. Two noblemen have confirmed that he is seldom invited on hunting trips."

Isabetta shook her head. "No, that's not what happened. The pistol was aimed *directly* at Rocco and my father got shot pushing my brother out of harm's way. The murderer appeared to be much taller than Signore Giorgio too."

"How do you know? Did you ever meet Giorgio Fosetti?"

"I saw him at the wedding celebration on Sunday." She also witnessed the pair leaving the palazzo before her family did. Could Giorgio Fosetti have lain in wait for Rocco with murderous intent?

The other officer, who had been silent until now, made a face. "Signorina Isabetta, with all due respect, you suffered a shock that night. Your memory is unreliable."

His partner added, "You reported the man wore a mask."

"He did, but—"

"It was dark, perhaps you didn't see things clearly."

"I know what I saw," she insisted in a cool tone.

"We believe Giorgio wanted to kill Rocco in order to salvage his reputation. His wife's infidelity served as motive. Who else would have reason to kill your brother?"

"Has he confessed to the crime?"

"No, or rather, *not yet*."

Isabetta studied each man in turn. "I assume you are keeping this matter private for the sake of my late father's good name and the legacy of his business."

"We are."

"This is ridiculous…absolutely, ridi—" Unable to finish the sentence, Isabetta turned her face away to hide her emotional breakdown from their eyes.

Silvio took the officers aside and spoke quietly with them. After a moment, they left the house.

"Alba, would you make some chamomile tea for your mistress?" Silvio said before sitting beside Isabetta and placing a comforting hand on her shoulder. "At least they caught the man and he will pay for his sins."

"Of all the women in Venice, Rocco chose Lucia Fosetti to satisfy his lust. Stupid man!"

Hortensa appeared at the head of the stairs. "Isabetta? Who

was at the door?"

"Only a beggar demanding bread." Lowering her voice, Isabetta motioned to Alba and instructed, "Put my mother back in bed, will you? Don't say a word about the officers."

The servant abandoned the tea and went upstairs.

Silvio asked, "You're not going to tell your mother?"

"She would be devastated. Mortified too."

"What if she discovers the truth?"

"Why not prolong that feeling for as long as possible?"

"I concede to your point."

Alba descended the stairs and said, "She is not well."

Isabetta and Silvio exchanged worried looks and ran upstairs. An alarming amount of blood had escaped Hortensa's lips during a coughing fit, compelling Isabetta to dispatch an urgent message to her aunt.

Rosa sent her personal physician to the Bastian home, but it did little good. In fact, he made the patient worse through copious bloodletting. In the days that followed, Hortensa's intense grief slowly ate away at her already deteriorating health.

Concern for her mother prompted Isabetta to pay a visit to Veronica. A servant showed her inside the courtesan's palazzo and bade her to wait. Boasting tapestries, paintings, and quality furnishings, it wasn't as big as many of the noble homes along the Grand Canal, but it was stylish and comfortable nonetheless.

One look at Isabetta's face and Veronica grew alarmed. "Is everything all right?"

"Mother isn't getting any better and I don't know what to do. Aunt Rosa's physician proved useless. I came here hoping you could help me since you know so many people in the city. Can you recommend someone?"

"My maid, Malvina, is a wise woman. She aids me and other courtesans in the city when we require certain *services*." She waited for Isabetta to nod in understanding at her meaning. "Malvina knows about the human body, especially women's bodies. She will examine your mother and, hopefully, devise a cure. I'm expected at the doge's palazzo this afternoon for an event, otherwise I would accompany my servant."

Isabetta gripped Veronica's hand. "Thank you."

"I'll come by later to check on you and your mother. Wait here while I summon Malvina."

The quiet mulatta with knowing black eyes followed Isabetta back to her home.

Hortensa recoiled at the sight of the exotic woman nearing her bed. "Who are you?"

"Greetings, Signora Hortensa. My name is Malvina. My mistress, Veronica Franco, sent me here to help you."

Isabetta added, "You remember Malvina, don't you?"

Hortensa mumbled incoherently.

Malvina sat on the edge of the bed and placed her head on Hortensa's chest. "Take a deep breath for me."

Still drowsy from the last draught she had consumed, Hortensa complied. Malvina listened for a long time before examining the sick woman's eyes, ears, throat, and even her tongue. Grim-faced, the servant exited the bedchamber and motioned to Isabetta.

Once they were far enough away from Hortensa's bedchamber, the wise woman whispered, "I'm sorry to tell you this, but the sickness is deeply embedded in her lungs. The only thing I can do for your mother is make her comfortable by easing the pain."

Isabetta's lower lip began to quiver. "There's no cure?"

"She will have good days and bad days. There will be times when you think she is healed, but don't be fooled. This may go on for a few months." Malvina's eyes expressed empathy as she continued, "The truth is this: her breathing will become ever more difficult until she can breathe no more."

"Cristo Santo."

The mulatta's black eyes gleamed as she patted Isabetta's arm in a comforting gesture. "I'll return in a little while with some medicine."

Silvio emerged from the guestroom the instant he heard Malvina's retreating footsteps. Taking Isabetta into his arms, he said, "I heard everything. I'm sorry."

She clung to him as a drowning man would hang on to a

floating piece of wood after a shipwreck. Sensing her distress, he pulled her closer and held her tightly.

Malvina's strange, foul-smelling remedies helped Hortensa significantly. She kept to her bed the next morning, going outside for a bit of air after the midday meal, and then reading a book in the afternoon. Isabetta sat with her mother while Alba prepared supper.

Hortensa said, "I am worried about you."

"You should be worried about yourself, Mother, not me. I'm in fine health."

"Close the door, will you?"

"Can't this wait until morning?"

"No."

Isabetta moved away from the bed to close the door.

Hortensa sighed wearily. "I'm going to die soon."

"Mother please—"

"—and you must be prepared for it."

"You'll get better."

"I saw Malvina's face when she left the room to speak with you, so there's no need to lie. I won't be here much longer and my dying wish is to know that you'll be safe in my absence. The world is a cruel place, my child."

Reaching for her mother's hand, Isabetta said, "You and Papa taught me well."

"Did we?"

"Yes. Get some sleep and stop worrying about me."

Droopy lids closed and Hortensa began to snore. Saddened by the brief exchange, Isabetta vacated the room. Reorganizing her father's study would provide some distraction, so she set her hand to the task.

Silvio eventually appeared in the doorway. "May I help?"

Setting down the stack of books, she nodded. They worked together in companionable silence, going through drawers full of scrolls and sheets.

After a while, Isabetta said, "I want to ask you something."

When she hesitated, he prompted, "I think our friendship has arrived at the point where you can be honest with me."

"Are you going to tell your father about Beto?"

"You've been through enough, Isabetta. I have no desire to add to your burden so put your mind at ease. My father need not know your family's secret."

"Thank you for sparing me the humiliation." She turned to place the books on the shelf. Self-conscious of his eyes on her, she stopped. "What will you tell him?"

"Exactly what I was told—Beto was on a business trip during my stay in Venice." Walking over to where she stood, he asked, "Does that please you?"

"It does, thank you."

Searching her face, he admitted, "I care about you."

"I care about you too," she confessed, heart fluttering.

They stared at each other.

A combination of panic and excitement seized her when he tilted his head and leaned closer. Her first kiss proved sweet. She sighed and hooked her arms around his neck as her soul lifted slightly from its earthbound state. A loud gasp coming from the direction of the doorway caused them to break apart.

Alba stood scowling at them. In her hand was a lit candle to ward off the late afternoon gloom. "Signorina, this conduct is most unbecoming. As for you, Signore Silvio, you are older and wiser than my innocent mistress. You should know better, sir."

"You are absolutely correct, Alba. My apologies to both of you," he conceded with a formal bow.

The servant afforded him a dubious look. "Humph. Supper is almost ready."

Alba went about her business and left the couple to their soft giggles. It was the first time Isabetta laughed since the funeral.

"It's a relief to see your spirits lifted," Silvio said softly before kissing her again without a shred of remorse.

***

Challenging days of caring for Hortensa were punctuated by Rosa's frequent visits. The obnoxious woman did little else but criticize Isabetta's efforts. First she complained that her niece had sought the help of a whore's servant, then she declared Malvina's curatives useless. She made Alba toss out a cauldron of perfectly good broth after claiming it had been brewed incorrectly. When she hinted that her niece was 'too distracted by the handsome houseguest' to properly care for Hortensa, Isabetta finally confronted her aunt.

"How can you say such a thing, Aunt Rosa? Do you not see me working continuously? Have I not gone out to procure every remedy possible? I am completely dedicated to my mother yet you deny it because of Silvio Torres. It's not fair."

Rosa shrugged almost sheepishly. "A comely young man and a girl of marriageable age residing together in the same household is unseemly."

Thankfully, Silvio had gone out earlier and wasn't present to overhear them. "You make it sound so...*sordid.* This tragedy happened during Signore Silvio's stay. Thank God he was here, for I don't know what my mother and I would have done without his help during this difficult time. And we are not *residing together*. May I remind you that my mother is in a sickbed and Alba lives under this roof too?"

"Calm yourself," Rosa advised curtly.

"Complaining about everything isn't helpful. I'm doing the best I can under harrowing circumstances." Although she didn't wish for her aunt to see her cry, that's exactly what happened.

Softening in the face of her niece's grief, Rosa relented. "I don't mean to be harsh with you, Isabetta...I'm scared for my sister and don't want her to die."

"I'm scared too."

With that, the two women embraced. Rarely had they ever expressed affection toward each other.

Rosa pulled away first. "There, there. Take a deep breath. Your mother will get better soon."

"No, she won't. Malvina said the illness is deep in her lungs, so it's only a matter of time."

"What does that foreign heathen know?"

"She is a wise woman, a healer."

Rosa made a derisive sound. "Where she's from they rely on pagan gods and magic. We Christians rely on the one true God and the divine power of prayer."

Isabetta made no reply. It sufficed that they had finally made peace. Maybe now her aunt would stop tormenting her with negativity.

***

News of Giorgio Fosetti's execution reached Isabetta's ears via the market vendors. After weeks in prison awaiting trial, he had been found guilty and sentenced to death. He was neither noble nor well-connected, but his wife claimed kinship to a baron in Trieste who demanded justice. What's more, Giorgio's insurmountable debts came as a shock to many who believed him to be wealthy. The condemned man went to the gallows swearing to God and all the saints that he had not killed Rocco and Zanetto Bastian.

That night, as Silvio and Isabetta supped together, she said, "Do you think my mother will ever find out about Giorgio Fosetti? Everyone is talking about it."

He made a face. "I doubt it. Gossipmongers are always seeking new scandals to disperse."

"I hope you're right."

They played cards after the meal. During the game, Isabetta stole several furtive glances at her attractive companion. His departure date loomed close on the horizon, and she lived each precious day dreading the moment when she would be forced to say goodbye.

That day came upon her too soon.

On the evening prior to Silvio setting sail, they ate a quiet dinner under Alba's watchful gaze. Both remained seated by the fire after supper. Hortensa had tasked Alba with chaperoning, but the somnolent servant fell asleep in her chair. The couple admired the red glow of firelight while sipping hot mulled wine.

Isabetta relished the sound of the crackling flames mingled with howling wind outside. "I wish you didn't have to leave."

"I don't want to go." Silvio gently caressed her cheek. "I've grown fond of you in the short time I've been here."

"I feel the same way about you. Even Alba has grown to like you, and she seldom likes anyone."

He stared longingly at her mouth before claiming her lips.

Not wanting him to go tomorrow, Isabetta held him tightly.

Reluctantly, he pulled away. "I'll be back soon."

Breathless, she asked, "When?"

"Now that I've found a warehouse to let, I need to fill it. I hope to sail to India shortly after my return to Portugal, then be back in Venice by February or March."

"I'll miss you."

"I'll miss you too." He kissed the tip of her nose. "I'm planning on asking your mother's permission to write you. Does that please you?"

"Very much."

"I'm going to say something you may not like…I believe Alzo Cornetti is right. You need to think of your mother's future as well as your own."

"Are you suggesting that I get married?"

"Eventually, yes. Impersonating a man might work for a little while longer without the protection of your father and brother, but sooner or later someone will discover the truth about Beto Bastian. As your uncle correctly pointed out, no one will want to deal with a woman."

A deep furrow marred Isabetta's brow. "I need some time to think on this matter."

Satisfied, he stood. "Do that. Now I must bid you goodnight because I need to get some sleep."

She also stood. "Sweet dreams."

"If you're in them they will be."

She giggled softly at his flirtatious words.

Alba woke up with a start. "What's going on here?"

"Nothing," Isabetta assured with a straight face.

"Goodnight," Silvio said to both women.

Isabetta slept fitfully that night and sat at the table with a heavy heart the next morning. A lump in her throat prevented her from breaking her fast.

Hortensa had made the effort to rise early in order to bid farewell to their guest. She cast several pointed looks at Silvio as he solemnly chewed on a piece of buttered bread.

At length, he rose from the chair. "Alas, it's getting late and

I must go. Signora Hortensa, thank you for your hospitality."

Hortensa smiled at him. "Thank you for your support during our difficult time."

"I only did my duty, madam." He paused. "There is a matter I wish to discuss with you before I depart, if I may."

Hortensa nodded warily, her gaze piercing.

"I would like to write to your daughter, if you don't mind. I had intended to ask permission of your husband…" He trailed off rather than stating the obvious.

"You may write to Isabetta but be aware that I'll be reading the correspondence on both ends."

Silvio inclined his head at her words. "I expect no less from a virtuous and chaste woman such as yourself. My intentions are honorable, I promise."

"Godspeed, Signore Silvio, and safe travels," Hortensa said primly before moving toward the back of the room and pretending to examine a candlestick.

Isabetta accompanied Silvio to the door. "I'll pray for God to watch over you every day. I look forward to your letters."

He boldly kissed her hand, then whispered, "Think of me often, for I will be thinking of you."

Consumed by sadness, Isabetta watched him go. He turned and waved before ducking into a side street. For the first time in her life she entertained the notion of marriage and it didn't seem distasteful. Playing the role of wife to a man like Silvio Torres would be worth the trouble.

The instant Isabetta closed the door, Hortensa said, "I would have preferred that you marry a wealthy man like Alessio Innocenti but that opportunity is lost. My sister informed me that he's already asked for the hand of another young lady."

"I cannot say that I'm disappointed."

"Silly, silly girl," Hortensa muttered before heaving her heavy, tired body up the stairs.

Chapter 9

Hortensa and Alba sat by candlelight mending hems and darning stockings after supper one evening. The steady pitter-patter of rain against the roof did little to soothe their frazzled nerves. They glanced occasionally at Isabetta, who sat at the table calculating figures amid stacks of accounting ledgers.

Isabetta massaged the back of her stiff neck. "I'm done."

"Well," Hortensa demanded.

"We're fine—*for now*. We have a bit of money set aside."

"How long will it maintain us?"

"A few months. Don't worry, Mother."

"We should sell the galley."

"And then what? Once we've spent the money from the sale we'll be right back where we are now. It would be a temporary solution, not a permanent one."

"Your uncle has a string of wealthy men interested in your father's business and the vessel."

"Didn't you hear what I've just said?"

"Watch your tone."

Although Isabetta was quickly losing her patience, she attempted another tactic. "The *Tramonto* is my only connection to Papa and Rocco. Our only means of income too."

Hortensa set aside her sewing with a heavy sigh. "We wouldn't be in this dire predicament if you were married. We're facing starvation because of your stubbornness."

"We are not facing starvation."

"Not yet."

"Silvio loves me—"

"Marrying him won't help us! The man has nothing!"

Isabetta left the room in the midst of her mother's hysterical fit and sought sanctuary in the study. Closing the door, she uttered a brief prayer to God for strength and guidance. How would she ward off the debt collectors? Food needed to be salted and dried for the winter months. She had no choice but to purchase supplies on credit, and to do that the *Tramonto* would need to sail as scheduled in October.

***

Blessed September breezes banished the remains of August heat from the city. Silvio's much-anticipated letter arrived mid-month on a foggy morning.

Hortensa read the letter, then handed it over to her daughter. "It contains favorable news."

Isabetta scanned the missive while smiling.

Dear Isabetta,

I hope this letter finds you well and your mother's health greatly improved. In a few weeks, I will depart for India on a merchant ship captained by Denis Amaral. Given his reputation and amicable manner, I informed the captain of your situation. He relayed my words to his father in Lisbon, and Senhor Norberto Amaral has agreed to distribute your uncle's textiles and sell you his spices at a fair price. He awaits your confirmation at the address below. I hope this news lifts your spirits. You are constantly in my thoughts and prayers. Warmest regards to your mother.

Yours, Silvio

She took note of the Lisbon address at the bottom of the page. "That's one problem solved."

"I've given the matter considerable thought. Although part of me still believes that selling the ship would be the best course of action, I concede to your point. It would only fix things temporarily. Furthermore, Rocco believed that trading with Flanders and Holland would be profitable, so maybe we can plan on that for next year. Let this autumn be the galley's final journey to Portugal."

Relieved, Isabetta exhaled deeply. "Thank you, Mother."

"Before you get excited, I have some stipulations. I've spoken with your uncle." At the sight of her daughter's crestfallen face, Hortensa amended, "Listen to me, will you? Alzo believes you should speak with Iseppo da Mosta."

"Whatever for?"

"To join forces with him next year."

A silent beat passed as Isabetta struggled to remain calm. "Let me see if I understand correctly…Alzo halves our order and now he wants to diminish our profits?"

"Don't be a fool."

"Forgive me for saying this, but you are the fool if you think Iseppo won't take advantage of two women alone in the world. He will cheat us for certain."

"Watch your tongue! Iseppo da Mosta is an honest man with as fine a reputation as your father."

"I doubt that very much, Mother. I'm going to notify Signore Norberto of our estimated arrival in Lisbon. I trust Silvio's judgement more than my uncle's counsel."

Hortensa shook her head in irritation. "Headstrong, just like your father."

"I'll take that as a compliment." Isabetta's gaze drifted to the window. "I need some fresh air. I'll be back soon."

"You're going out alone?"

"Please get some rest," Isabetta said before slipping outside.

Butchers and cheese vendors called out from their stalls as she picked her way through the crowded square. She made a beeline to the port where the anchored *Tramonto* bobbed gently upon the water. It would need to be treated and stocked with supplies before the journey.

Investors were needed as well. First, she would approach the ones with whom they had been doing business for years. Hopefully, the deaths of her father and brother wouldn't dissuade them. Nearly everyone in Venice was involved in some kind of trade—from the doge himself to priests, peasants, and nobility. Anyone with a bit of money could lend it on a merchant venture, much like a gambler at the gaming tables. No merchant guild existed in Venice so it was a free for all.

Rocco had once told her about a man from Sicily who transported ground-up mummies from Egypt. The powder was sold as a medicinal curative for certain ailments. In short, the Venetian laws—or lack thereof—worked in her favor. Given the rampant charlatanry in the city, surely an honest woman with a functioning brain could make some money. A large sum was required to pay the crewmen, purchase supplies, and obtain the stock to sell. Captains didn't come cheap either. How could she lower her costs to compensate for her uncle's shorted order? Gears within her head began to spin with ideas.

Supper that evening proved a quiet affair with each woman lost in her own thoughts. Isabetta pretended to go to bed early, then waited for Alba and her mother to fall asleep. Tiptoeing to Rocco's bedchamber, she mentally prepared herself for what she was about to do. His scent engulfed her the moment she opened his clothing chest. Longing and heartache followed as she cautiously rummaged through the neatly folded garments. After selecting a few pieces from the bottom of the receptacle, she made certain the items at the top appeared as if they were never disturbed.

Shirts, breeches, and doublets that Rocco had outgrown during adolescence would serve her well. Once she had stuffed the stolen items into a burlap sack, she fished out a strand of multicolored glass beads from her jewelry box. Straining her ears for her mother's snore, she descended the stairwell and exited the house. Her steps were sure and swift as they carried her into the next sestiere.

She passed a tavern where the voices of men singing could be heard within. Candlelight spilled from greasy mullioned windows to create faded yellow diamond patterns on the street. An alley flanking the establishment reeked of urine and vomit, causing her to wrinkle her nose in disgust. She rounded a corner and stopped at the house of Donna Rita. A candle flickered in the window and she spied the seamstress working within the pool of light.

Rather than use the iron knocker, she rasped softly on the door. "Donna Rita, open up."

A stout woman with sharp eyes stood in the open doorway an instant later. "What in God's name?"

Isabetta pushed past the seamstress and invaded the tidy home. Baskets of colored thread and bolts of fabric were crammed into the small space. Various shelves along the wall held stacks of folded clothing waiting to be claimed by patrons.

Placing the burlap sack on the table, Isabetta said, "I'm sorry for the late hour."

"Couldn't you have waited until tomorrow?"

"I have an unusual request and it must be done swiftly."

"No request is too difficult for a skilled seamstress if you have payment."

Isabetta held out the sparkling glass beads. "I don't have money. My cousin gave me this for my sixteenth birthday. It's from Murano and the tiny beads separating the glass ones are fashioned from pure silver."

Donna Rita made a face as she examined the necklace against the candle's flame. "Silver, eh? *Va bene.* Let's see what you have in that sack." Isabetta removed the garments and she flinched. "Men's clothes?"

"I need them fitted to my body."

"Humph. What are you up to, girl?"

"I cannot tell you, but you must swear not to breathe a word of this to anyone."

"None of my business anyway. Never been one to gossip." Rita shuffled to get her measuring string. "Stand up straight and hold out your arms. If you need a pair of men's boots, my nephew is a *calzolaio*."

"Thank you, Donna Rita."

In a matter of days, Isabetta possessed three men's shirts cut from bleached linen, two fine doublets, two pairs of breeches, and a pair of sturdy leather boots that she purchased on credit.

***

Isabetta made her way to Viaro's stall in the mellow gold of a late September morning. Only one thing had to be done before the *Tramonto* could depart for Portugal.

After exchanging pleasantries with the fishmonger, she asked, "Is your son here today?"

"Ah, so it's Miro you seek." Her cheeks burned at his insinuation and Viaro chuckled. "He's behind you."

She turned around to see Miro heading toward the stall with a basket full of gleaming fish, many of which were still squirming. Sunshine sparkled on the water in the background and some of the rays kissed the dark curls on his head. No sooner had he dumped the fish into one of the empty crates than several women came over to negotiate prices with Viaro.

Miro smiled at Isabetta. *"Buongiorno."*

She returned the gesture. "Do you have a moment to spare? There's a matter I wish to discuss with you."

Setting down the basket, he gave her his full attention. Viaro cast a glance their way and grinned knowingly.

She pulled Miro aside. "The *Tramonto* will set sail on the first of October. I need someone I can trust on board the ship."

"That's less than a week away."

"I should have come to you sooner, but I've been busy purchasing foodstuffs and supplies."

After giving her a measured look, he demanded, "Are you attempting to run your father's business by yourself?"

"What if I am?" When he didn't respond, she added, "I'll pay you a fair wage."

"It's not the money I'm worried about."

"There you are, Signorina Isabetta."

They both turned to see Alba staring at them. "Your mother woke up early today and grew worried when you weren't in your bed. She sent me out to look for you."

"I wanted to buy fresh fish for our midday meal."

"Where's your basket?"

Glancing down at her empty hands, Isabetta hid her mounting irritation. "I forgot it." Urging Miro away from the meddlesome servant, she whispered, "I need your answer now."

"Are you sure you know what you're doing?"

"Trust me."

"Very well." She breathed a sigh of relief and he continued, "I'll be on the *Tramonto* at dawn October first."

"Thank you, Miro."

Alba waited for Miro to walk away then gripped Isabetta's arm. "Tell me what you're really doing here."

"I told you..."

"Oh stop with that nonsense. You're not buying fish. What

have you got brewing in that pot of yours?"

Isabetta looked around to make sure no one stood within earshot. "I'm going to sail the *Tramonto* to Portugal."

The servant's eyes became as wide as saucers. "Have you gone mad? What you're proposing is dangerous."

"Captains are expensive, Alba. The more money I can save, the better. Supplies need to be purchased for winter and debts have to be paid."

Alba scowled. "This is most unwise, Signorina Isabetta."

"Starving is unwise. A debt collector at our door is unwise. Losing our home is unwise. Captaining the galley to prevent our financial ruin *is* wise."

"Your mother will be sick with grief."

"She'll be very angry indeed, which is why *you* must keep this secret. You'll need to comfort and care for her while I'm gone." When Alba regarded her dubiously, she firmly assured, "There's no need for you or my mother to worry. I'll be accompanied by Miro, who is an experienced seaman. He has worked with Rocco on the galley many times and knows the vessel well. Also, I'll be disguised as a man."

Looking upward, the servant whispered, "God help us. This is reckless and foolish—even for you, Isabetta Bastian."

"Not a word, Alba. Please, I'm begging you. I'm doing this to save us from financial ruin. It's a short journey so I won't be gone for too long."

"I don't know if I can go along with this…"

"If you betray my trust, I will never forgive you." Her words resulted in a protracted stare from the servant.

Finally, Alba said, "I won't say anything to your mother but let it be known that I do not approve of this dangerous plan. *Not one bit.*"

"Duly noted."

CHAPTER 10

A frigid drizzle announced the first of October. Isabetta rose long before dawn and dressed in haste. Thanks to Donna Rita's talent with needle and thread, Rocco's black suede doublet fit her perfectly. She had taken care to bind her breasts before donning the heavy garment. After knotting and tucking her hair into Rocco's plumed cap, she fastened the silver clasp on her dark cloak and studied her reflection in the mirror. She looked like an effeminate young man—a passable male.

Moving quietly, she packed her leather satchel with the rest of the men's clothing and her father's trusted compass. Yesterday, Miro had supervised the loading of merchandise onto the ship, as well as stocking the *Tramonto* with lemons, laying hens, barley, salted fish, barrels of fresh water, ale, cider, and diluted wine.

She went downstairs and placed the letter she had written last night on the table where her mother would see it later on. Hoisting the satchel over her shoulder, she left the house surreptitiously so as not to awaken anyone. Her heart beat so rapidly that she could barely breathe. Sheathed at her waist was Rocco's wicked stiletto, which he had carried on his person on every voyage. Although he had taught her how to use the weapon, she hoped the need would never arise to do so.

Making her way to the *Tramonto* in the predawn gloom, she practiced speaking in a low voice. Her footsteps quickened when the galley's masts came into view. Men milled about on the ship making last minute preparations. Stepping aboard the vessel, she watched with a keen eye as they readied themselves for the journey.

Miro stared at Isabetta in disbelief as she closed the gap between them. He was about to protest when she gripped his wrist tightly. "As of today, my name is Beto."

His eyes widened. "What are you doing here?"

"Isn't it obvious? I'm coming with you."

"This was not part of the original plan."

"What do you mean?"

A few crewmen stopped working and turned their attention on them. Isabetta shifted her body to block their curious stares.

Angry, Miro whispered, "You can't come with us. The men won't like it. *I don't like it.* You failed to mention this part of your *scheme* when you spoke to me at the market."

"I know the names of each man on this ship yet none of them know me. They've never seen my face. Have you not noticed that I am dressed as you are? Like a man?"

"Yes, but—"

"I won't get seasick."

"That's the least of my fears, Isabetta. It could become dangerous if the men discover your little secret. Do I need to spell it out for you?"

Discreetly, she pushed aside her cloak to reveal the stiletto. "I can defend myself, don't worry."

"Signore Zanetto and Rocco would never approve."

She placed her lips to his ear. "It's *my* galley."

Miro was about to protest when the sound of horse hooves on the quay captured their attention. A gentleman clad in expensive clothing sat in the saddle staring at them through the rising mist. Reddish gold clouds along the horizon created a garish background to his imposing silhouette.

"Who is that?" Isabetta demanded.

Miro replied, "I have no idea."

Two *vigili* and a tall man in a long black coat appeared beside the horse. The latter came onboard and began shouting orders to the crew. Isabetta noticed that he carried on his person not one but three weapons: a pistol, a sword, and a dagger. Three scars marred his face and the skin possessed a leathery texture. A seaman for certain.

Isabetta stepped in the intruder's path. "Who are you?"

The man sneered. "Out of my way, lad."

Isabetta turned to Miro and demanded loudly, "Do you know this arrogant fool?"

Before Miro could reply, the man said, "I am Captain Rizo Santino and I was hired to take this ship to Lisbon. Now, show some proper respect before I haul your carcass overboard."

Fear coursed through her veins, turning her blood to ice. Despite this, she held her ground. "Apparently, there has been a misunderstanding."

Rizo's dark brows came together in a menacing frown as he placed his hand on the hilt of his sword. "The last man who dared to confront me lost an eye."

Tilting her chin, she shot back, "Save your threats, sir. As of right now, you are dismissed."

Having overheard the exchange, the man in the saddle said in a booming voice, "I'm afraid I won't allow that."

Isabetta spun around to glare at him. "And you are?"

"Cristofolo Trasontin." Pointing to Rizo, he added, "And that is the captain I've hired to sail this ship. Who, in God's name, are *you*?"

She squared her shoulders. "Beto Bastian, rightful owner of this galley."

"As far as I know, the late Zanetto Bastian had sired only two children. A son who is dead and a daughter. How exactly do you lay claim to this vessel?"

Isabetta faltered. How did this stranger know so much about her family? "I…I…"

Miro met Isabetta's panicked eyes and placed an arm around her shoulders. "This is Zanetto Bastian's nephew and I can vouch for his character."

She almost sagged in relief.

Cristofolo quirked an eyebrow. "What's your name?"

"Miro Fiore. I've worked on this galley and many others in Venice. I've known Beto and his family my entire life."

Isabetta finally found her voice as well as her courage. "That's right. Uncle Zanetto hired Miro on many occasions as an extra hand on deck. Cousin Rocco captained the ship. I ran the Bastian business and did the accounting."

"Well, *boy*," Cristofolo said, emphasizing the word to imply his superiority. "I've paid off your uncle's debt."

Stunned, she blurted, "You can't do that!"

A wry chuckle mocked her outrage. "I can—and I did."

The *vigili* moved forward on the quay and stared pointedly at Isabetta. Head swaying, she staggered against the nearest mast for support.

Cristofolo's expression grew serious. "I have every right to keep this galley as collateral until I am repaid in full—*if* I'm repaid, that is. The details are listed in a legal contract drawn up by Zanetto Bastian's banker and solicitor. What's more, I can use the property as I please."

Legal contract? What was happening here? The officers stepped onto the deck, took hold of Isabetta's arms, and forced her off the vessel.

Cristofolo urged his horse forward with a cold smile on his lips. "Unless you have a sack of money to deliver into my hands, I must insist that you leave here. My men have work to do and you're presence is distracting them."

He motioned to the *vigili*, who gave Isabetta a slight shove. Some of the crewmen jeered and laughed. Feeling utterly humiliated, she wanted nothing more than to pierce the cruel man's heart with her deadly stiletto. Sensing her ire, Cristofolo smirked and then rode off without a backward glance.

***

Isabetta stood on the dock watching the *Tramonto* glide into the liquid gold of a morning sunrise. Miro stared at her from the stern with apologetic eyes. She remained rooted to the spot until the galley became a pinpoint on the horizon. Defeated, she hung her head and made her way home with heavy steps. Pausing outside the door, she drew in a deep breath before going into the house to face her mother's wrath.

Hortensa sat slumped in a chair with the letter in her hand. At the sight of her daughter in Rocco's altered clothing, she shrieked. A mixture of relief and fury settled upon her features. "Isabetta Bastian! Thank God you've come to your senses. What were you thinking?"

"Mother, I can explain—"

"Your letter explained enough! Are you trying to disgrace

your brother's memory? What would your father say to this madness? Not to mention dragging others into your scheme. Miro will certainly relay the story to his father, and soon everyone in our sestiere will know what has transpired."

Isabetta dropped her satchel on the floor and sagged against the wall. "I'm sorry, I didn't mean to hurt you. Winter is coming and the larder is nearly empty. You need medicines too. We can't afford the exorbitant cost of a captain's salary so I decided to remedy the matter myself."

"Have you lost your wits? The shame of it!"

Isabetta gritted her teeth. "*Shameful* is Uncle Alzo putting me in this predicament by cheating us."

Shock dawned on Hortensa's face. "The men kicked you off the galley, didn't they?"

"Did you hear what I said, Mother? You should direct your anger at your brother-in-law, not me." Isabetta considered mentioning Cristofolo Trasontin, then thought better of it. News of the galley being seized would only cause more devastation.

"Stop blaming Alzo for your lack of scruples. How could you run away and *abandon* me in my precarious condition?"

Spreading out her hands in supplication, Isabetta countered, "I didn't run away or abandon you. I would never do such a thing. Alba and Rosa would have kept you company during my brief absence."

Ignoring her daughter's attempt at reason, Hortensa shook her head in disgust. "Who would ever marry such a girl? Unruly and foolish, that's what you are!"

Alba gently intervened, "Signora, you'll make yourself sick if you keep carrying on like this."

Hortensa stood on shaky legs. "Look at her, Alba! Dressed in her brother's clothes and impersonating a man. Have you ever seen such a horrid sight? Why did God curse me with such a child? She is an abomination!"

"Signora, you should sit."

Waving away Alba's advice, Hortensa placed her palms on the table top and heaved a shuddering sigh. "What if someone recognized Isabetta in the street? The city is full of people at this hour. The shame of it! Oh Lord...I can't show my face in church anymore..."

"Please, Signora," Alba interjected, truly worried by the way the color suddenly drained from her mistress's face.

Hortensa continued her tirade, undeterred. "How could she be so reckless? Stupid, selfish girl!"

Isabetta covered her ears with her hands. "Stop!"

Balling her meaty hands into fists, Hortensa shuffled across the room and began hitting her daughter.

Isabetta deflected the blows by raising her arms and crossing them in front of her face. "You're hurting me!"

Hortensa continued to administer blows until every ounce of energy drained from her body. At length, she backed away, arms limp at her sides. "Damn you, Isabetta Bastian. You cause me nothing but grief. It should have been you that got killed that night, not my precious son." Ragged breaths edged the hateful words, and her face became grayish-white. Clutching her chest in pain, she cried, *"Santa Madonna!"* Her eyes rolled into the back of her head as she collapsed onto the floor with a dull thud.

***

According to the physician, Hortensa's death was due to a bad heart. Losing her husband and son simultaneously had taken a tremendous toll on her troubled mind and ailing body.

Rosa insisted on making the funeral arrangements and Isabetta made no protest. Dazed and grief-stricken, she attended the funeral clad in a cloak of guilt and shame. Had she not attempted to captain the *Tramonto*, her mother would still be alive. She barely acknowledged the mourners as they murmured the same words as last time.

Last time...

How could God have allowed such a calamity? Three deaths in a matter of months. Her entire family was gone. How much more pain could she endure? Would she ever rekindle her faith?

Veronica and Paola accompanied her home after the funeral and remained for the midday meal, which their servants had prepared. Refusing to 'break bread with harlots,' Rosa went home with her husband. Isabetta was relieved, for she had no desire to be in their insufferable company.

A crate of salted cod and a sack of spelt arrived at the house a few days later. The accompanying letter sported a wax seal with a "V" stamped on it.

Cousin Isabetta,

I didn't wish to broach the subject at the funeral, but I'm well aware of your difficult financial situation. Petro's cousin, Donata, is already serving as my lady's maid. Our household could use another servant, however. My father has already made an arrangement with Petro on your behalf. You will be paid a decent wage for your services. I will be expecting you at my home on Monday. Also, I'm sending you a crate of salted fish and a sack of spelt.

Affectionately, Cassandra

Going to the hearth, Isabetta crumpled the sheet and tossed it into the fire.

Alba placed a steaming bowl of porridge on the table. "Who sent the gift?"

"My cousin."

"You seem vexed. Do you not think it a kind gesture?"

"I resent her pity."

"Pride won't fill our bellies. Best to eat the porridge while it's hot. You'll need your strength if you plan on resolving things this morning."

Isabetta wandered to the window and gazed out at the street. "Cassandra offered me a servant position."

"Given your ability with numbers, you could easily overtake the steward's job."

"I'll wager my cousin would rather see me on my hands and knees scrubbing the floor. What am I going to do? I have no desire to work for Cassandra."

"Take heart, she's only trying to help."

"No parents, no dowry. I can barely afford to keep us fed, let alone continue to pay your wages."

Panicked, Alba said, "I'll find some more work. The laundresses can always use an extra set of hands. Please don't put me out, Signorina. I have nowhere else to go."

"Calm yourself, Alba. I would never put you out." Isabetta sat down at the table and picked up her spoon. Running the tip of the utensil through the hot lumpy porridge, she mused, "I need to think." She ate mindlessly, her thoughts like acrobats tumbling over one another. She stood after a few spoonfuls. "I'm going."

"I'll accompany you."

"No, stay here."

Blue skies did little to lift Isabetta's foul mood as she set out to Ernesto Fosco's office. He had served as their banker and solicitor for many years.

Ernesto glanced up from the pages of a ledger and froze at the sight of Isabetta. A wiry man with a narrow face, he peered at her with curiosity. "Can I help you?"

"I need to speak with you, sir."

Shifting his gaze over her shoulder, he expected someone else to enter the room. "Are you alone?"

"I am."

Grimacing, he turned his attention back to the ledger. "As you can see, Signorina, I'm a busy man."

She slipped into his office and closed the door. "My name is Isabetta Bastian."

Realization dawned on him. "Zanetto's daughter?"

"Correct."

Clearing his throat, he stood as a gesture of respect. "I was very sorry to hear the news about your father and brother. I'm glad they caught the murderer and punished him." Reclaiming his seat, he added, "Please, sit. What can I do for you today?"

She perched on the wooden chair set before his desk. "I'm here to discuss the *Tramonto.* A man by the name of Cristofolo Trasontin paid off the balance my father owed."

"Given that the galley's owner and rightful heir are both deceased, I had no other recourse than to accept an investor's generous offer."

"Our payments were up to date, sir. The galley should have gone to his widow but my mother has recently expired. As Rocco's sister, I am the next in line to inherit."

"I'm sorry, Signorina, but I didn't even know of your existence. I only knew of one heir to the property; Rocco."

Having dealt mainly with her father and occasionally Rocco, Isabetta knew he spoke the truth. "I realize that, but isn't there anything you can do to rectify the situation? The *Tramonto* is my only means of income."

"At this point, no. A contract was signed and it's legally binding." At the sight of Isabetta's glistening eyes he amended, "There *is* a clause in the agreement…"

Somewhat hopeful, she sniffed. "What clause?"

"If you pay Signore Cristofolo the money he invested plus interest within the allotted time, the galley may be transferred to your name. Assuming you can prove that you are Zanetto Bastian's legal child."

Relief washed over her. "I can prove it, yes."

"Very well. You have nine months."

"Nine months?" Groaning, she placed a palm to her forehead. "That's not nearly enough time!"

Ernesto spread out his hands. "I'm sorry, but the situation is out of my control. Interest is thirty percent."

"If I don't pay the remaining balance on the *Tramonto* plus thirty percent interest by next June, Cristofolo Trasontin becomes the galley's legal owner?"

"Correct."

She took a deep breath to calm herself. "How did he come to you in the first place? Who is this man? My father never mentioned his name."

"I don't know."

A wave of hot rage cascaded over her body. "How could you have negotiated this deal without so much as sending us notification? You claim you didn't know of my existence, I'll grant you that, but what of Zanetto Bastian's widow? You could have at least sent word to my mother."

Ernesto shrugged apologetically. "I didn't want to miss out on the opportunity presented to me by a wealthy investor. Surely, you can understand that, Signorina. I'm a businessman, after all."

Without a word, she got up and left.

On the way home, she stopped to purchase fish heads. She and Alba had been consuming large quantities of fish stock. Unsurprisingly, they were losing the much-needed weight required to keep them healthy throughout the harsh winter. Viaro often threw in an extra head for the same price and she gratefully accepted his charity with a touch of shame. The food sent by Cassandra would feed them for only so long.

Rounding a corner, she paused at the fountain where the Cannaregio laundresses washed linens. Raw red hands busily scrubbed and wrung out bedsheets and shirts. Water spilled from the fabric, the droplets sparkling like diamonds in the sunshine. In winter, the battered skin would undoubtedly crack and bleed. Could she work as a laundress? She tried to imagine herself alongside the other women, her rough wet hands numb with cold, the brittle nails, the exhaustion...

Isabetta turned to go, abandoning both the scene and the idea. Employment opportunities for women were few, and this was especially true for desperate women with no male protectors. Sobered by the harsh reality of her plight, she thought of Cassandra's letter. The prospect of working as a servant in her cousin's household held far more appeal than washing the soiled garments of strangers.

CHAPTER 11

Wind shaped the mist into fanciful curlicues over the Grand Canal's surface as the ferry floated toward Mestre. Once it reached the dock, Isabetta alighted the vessel and hastened to Petro Vendramin's villa. The yellow ochre structure sat atop a gentle slope dominating the pristine landscape. Boxed hedges and cypress trees surrounded the gracious home, and a Roman statue eaten away by the elements stood like a sentinel at the main gate.

A servant spied Isabetta bounding up the path that led to the front door, so she ran inside to alert her mistress. Cassandra appeared on the stoop a moment later in a celery green gown with emeralds glittering at her throat. "Hurry, come in! You must be frozen. It's cold today."

Isabetta credited her cousin for the personal greeting, for it lessened the bite of humiliation. "I'm a bit chilled."

Cassandra led the way through an elegant room where frescoes graced the ceiling and a multicolored glass chandelier hung from its center. Seeing Isabetta pause to admire the latter, she said, "My parents gifted me the chandelier as a wedding present. Lovely, isn't it?"

"Your home is quite grand," Isabetta said, her eyes darting around the space.

"Yes, it is. Let's get you warmed up, shall we?"

They went into the kitchen where a sullen woman in an undyed smock and white apron busied herself around the biggest hearth Isabetta had ever seen. A long table laden with vegetables, fruits, and ceramic bowls stood in the center of the large room.

Cassandra pushed two chairs near the fire, then snapped her fingers. "Pina, make us some tea."

Pina's eyes swept disdainfully over Isabetta before setting water to boil in an iron kettle.

Leaning close to Isabetta, Cassandra said, "Father doesn't want you to think of this position as charity. We expect you to earn your keep in order for you to preserve your dignity." She cast a glance at the servant before lowering her voice. "He is trying to find someone who will marry you without a dowry."

"You're probably thinking that I should have married the Tuscan when I had the chance."

Cassandra sighed theatrically. "You never listen, do you? I've always known you to be a willful girl. Parents *do* know best. Look at me." Lifting her hands she indicated the space around them. "I'm the lady of this fine house with servants to command. You could have had the same privilege."

"You're right, I must now pay the price for my foolishness." Isabetta almost choked on the words.

Appeased, Cassandra smoothed the fabric of her skirt. "What's done is done, I suppose. We cannot change the past. The only thing you can do at this point is place your trust in my family and accept our advice next time."

Pina set two steaming cups on the table, then moved to the opposite end of the room.

Isabetta blew on her tea. "I'm not sure what duties you had in mind for me, but your father can attest to my excellent mathematical and accounting skills."

Cassandra laughed slightly. "Yes, he informed me of your little adventure as Beto Bastian."

Miffed, Isabetta retorted, "I hardly call running a successful shipping business for years a 'little adventure.' "

Slowly sipping her tea, Cassandra regarded her cousin with amusement over the rim of the porcelain cup.

Isabetta continued in a humbler tone, "What I mean to say is…my accuracy with numbers will be useful to you."

"We already employ a chamberlain *and* a steward to manage Petro's lands, vineyards, and sheep." Setting down the teacup, Cassandra added airily, "As I mentioned in my letter, Donata is my lady's maid."

"I see. What sort of work will I be doing, exactly?"

Cassandra's eyes drifted to the dour servant. "Pina is my

cook and oversees the scullery maids. You will be aiding her with the daily cooking and some light cleaning. I realize traveling back and forth between Venice and Mestre will tax your strength. You're more than welcome to stay here at the villa with us. We have the space."

A smile touched Isabetta's lips. At least she would be treated like family. "That is most kind, thank you."

"Room and board will be deducted from your monthly wages, of course."

Isabetta's smile disappeared. "I prefer to come by boat."

"Every day? Won't you be too tired to work?"

Fighting the urge to curse her selfish cousin and leave this wretched place forever, Isabetta assured, "I'm hardy and hale. No need for you to worry."

Cassandra stood. "Very well. I'll leave you with Pina, who will instruct you on what's to be done today. Think of this as your home."

I would sooner think of Hell as home.

Seething with resentment, Isabetta watched her cousin go. Rearranging her face into a friendly mask, she approached the servant. "Hello Pina. My name is—"

"I know who you are." Pointing to a bowl of carrots without looking up from her task, Pina continued, "Peel those. There is an apron hanging on the peg over there."

Isabetta tied the apron around her waist and began peeling carrots with the edge of a knife. Her attempts at friendly banter were met with disapproving looks from the priggish servant who continually doled out chores. The remainder of the morning was spent peeling vegetables, cleaning fish, and baking a savory pie. By the time she scrubbed the kitchen table clean the noonday church bells were ringing in the city.

"Here," Pina said, holding out the pie wrapped in cloth. "Careful, it's hot. Hurry up and serve the master and his wife before it cools."

Isabetta carried the freshly baked pie to the table. Pina tracked her steps with a bowl of boiled vegetables.

Petro sat at the head. "Isabetta, welcome."

"Thank you, Signore Petro."

Seated at her husband's right hand, Cassandra inquired, "How are you settling in?"

"Well enough," Isabetta replied awkwardly as she served her new employers. "I hope you like the fish pie."

"It looks delicious," Petro said appreciatively, his eyes on her breasts rather than the slice of pie.

Isabetta tracked Pina into the kitchen where they prepared a fruit plate to cleanse the palate. The servant instructed her on how to make lovely decorations with the colorful cut-up pieces. At the meal's conclusion they quickly cleared the plates.

Isabetta was about to bring out the arrangement of fruit when Pina stopped her. "Place the plate by Signora Cassandra, not her husband."

She did as she was told and returned to the kitchen. Pina cast a glance in her direction but kept her expression stoic as she doled out more chores. They worked in silence throughout the afternoon.

Isabetta almost collapsed from exhaustion after riding the last ferry home. Placing her elbows on the table she rested her chin in her hands. "I'm famished."

"You look tired too," Alba commented, setting a plate of comforting spelt soup before her mistress.

"This smells wonderful."

"I began working as a laundress today. Four times a week in the afternoons. The extra money paid for a pair of chicken feet and a neck to make the broth for the soup."

Isabetta smiled before indulging in a taste. "Thank you, Alba. It's delicious."

"How was your first day of work in Signora Cassandra's house? I pictured you in an elegant study surrounded by books and working on ledgers."

"Nothing could be further from the truth. My cousin has me working in the kitchen with an ogre named Pina."

"The kitchen?" Alba shrieked in surprise.

"Petro already employs a chamberlain and a steward, and the position of lady's maid is also filled, so I'll be doing domestic chores."

Alba broke off a piece of stale bread, chewed, then swallowed. "The kitchen is the best place to be in a wealthy household. At least you'll be able to eat well."

"I helped Pina bake a nice fish pie and she forbade me from tasting it after the meal had been served. Apparently, we cannot partake of any leftovers because Cassandra wants it fed to the pigs instead of slop. She believes it makes the ham taste better."

"Pina should have allowed you to eat. You are in your cousin's home, after all."

Isabetta laughed without humor. "Do you know what Cassandra told me? She said that I could live in the villa, but room and board would be deducted from my salary."

Alba's eyes widened in surprise. "I'm sorry to hear this, Signorina. I would have expected a bit more kindness from her, especially now that she is so wealthy."

Isabetta shrugged and continued eating. "She has always been a vain, self-absorbed creature."

"God doesn't sleep," Alba said at length.

"Really? Seems to me He's been sleeping for a long time." Pushing the empty bowl aside, Isabetta stood and stretched. "I'm going to bed."

"Things will get better, you'll see."

Isabetta made no reply as she ascended the stairs. She stripped, got into bed, and fell asleep immediately.

She woke up early and hurried to the villa in Mestre in the gray light of dawn. Still tired from the day before, she stifled yawns while helping the scullery maids to sweep and scrub the floors downstairs. She then prepared the midday meal with Pina in the kitchen.

"After you help me serve the meal, go and wash those linens," Pina instructed, jabbing a thumb over her shoulder.

Isabetta cast a glance at the pile of kitchen cloths and aprons to be laundered before carrying a platter of oysters to Cassandra and Petro. Plastering a smile on her face, she held the tray while her employers served themselves. Once they had finished, she returned to the kitchen and popped an oyster into her mouth when Pina wasn't looking. She savored its briny flavor as she lugged the dirty laundry to the fountain out back. Humming a tune, she spent the better part of the afternoon scrubbing the stained fabrics until they were clean.

A dark-haired young woman in a blue silk gown neared Isabetta as she was hanging the items to dry. Dangling a scrap of fabric from her elegant fingertips, she drawled, "Signora Cassandra wants you to wash this at once. It is fragile and expensive so be careful."

"You must be Donata."

"Indeed I am."

"Could you please ask my cous—"

"*Signora* Cassandra," Donata corrected icily while eyeing Isabetta's humble garments with disdain. "While you are working under this roof, you will address our employers with the respect they deserve. Petro is my cousin and I refer to him as *Signore*." Her impertinent gaze settled on Isabetta's hands, which were reddened from hard work. A mocking smile curved the young woman's lips before she turned on her heel and retreated into the house.

Isabetta trembled with indignation. Fuming silently, she finished the chore and went home. The next day was similar to the one before, and the tedious routine continued throughout the week. Opening her eyes on Sunday morning, she stared at the wood-beamed ceiling of her bedchamber. A spider busily spun a web in the corner and she marveled at the tiny creature's industriousness. Church bells rang in the distance rousing worshippers from their warm beds. Relieved that she didn't have to work on the holy day, she stretched lazily.

Alba entered the bedchamber with a small basin of water and a cloth. "It's a clear day. You might want to take advantage of the good weather."

Once she had washed her face, armpits, and chest, Isabetta announced, "I'm going to church today."

"Would you like me to accompany you?"

"I want to go alone."

She set off for *Santa Maria dei Miracoli*. Listening drowsily to Holy Mass, she thought of her father and brother. Were they in Heaven watching her in that moment? She waited for the majority of the parishioners to leave before slipping into a tiny chapel illuminated by sputtering candles. A statue of the Blessed Virgin stood on a cracked altar. Chipped paint and waxy smoke stains marred the figure's sweet face. Sinking to her knees, she desperately begged Mary for a miracle. She also uttered a prayer to God for good measure.

***

November rains drenched the city. Cold, soggy days merged together in an endless sequence of unpleasant domestic chores. Isabetta woke early, worked hard, and slept poorly from Monday through Saturday. Sundays were reserved for God. Life became dull and increasingly difficult. Although tiredness seeped into the marrow of her bones, she preferred the distraction of physical labor to the ever-expanding hopelessness taking root within her mind. There were days when she didn't feel like eating or talking, and the world around her lacked luster. Sometimes, she wished she could simply stay in bed.

Death would at least offer a respite.

The alarming thought came to her one day while she worked in the garden. Pina had given her the choice of killing a chicken and dressing the bird in the warm kitchen, or clearing the yard of fallen leaves. Despite the bitter cold, she had chosen the latter in order to get away from the cranky servant.

"Isabetta."

Startled, she looked up to see the master of the house striding toward her with purpose.

Stopping inches from her face, Petro admonished, "You'll catch your death out here." Taking one of her frigid hands, he rubbed it vigorously between his own. "You are frozen! I pay a gardener to do this kind of work."

Embarrassed by the intimacy of the gesture, she tried to reclaim her hand. "I didn't want to kill the chicken..."

Mischief sparkled in his eyes. "Pina is up to her old tricks again, I see. Come along."

"I'll be fine—"

"Nonsense." He led her to one of the side doors of the villa. "My wife would be angry if you got sick."

The door revealed a dimly lit corridor that ended at a wall where one could turn left into the house. Petro veered right, which led to yet another door allowing access to the small lead and glass structure attached to the main villa.

With a sweep of his hand, he explained, "Welcome to our *limonaia*, where we grow oranges and lemons."

She had seen it from the outside while cleaning the yard. Potted citrus trees fought for room to spread out their branches in the crammed space. Lichen covered most of the uneven terracotta tiles beneath her feet.

Isabetta was about to tiptoe around the plants to examine the other side of the greenhouse when Petro took hold of her arm. "Careful, lest you slip."

"Thank you."

Fingers tightened around her flesh as he regarded her intently. "Do you like working in my home?"

"Yes, sir."

Eyeing her intently, he said softly, "You're a pretty thing."

This felt terribly wrong so she tried to side-step past him. "I should get back to work now."

Slamming her back against one of the glass walls, he cupped her jaw and claimed her mouth roughly. Too stunned to move, Isabetta endured the onslaught for a few seconds before struggling to free herself from his grip.

"Your skin is so soft," he said while using his weight to keep her pinned in place.

Icy dampness penetrated the fabric covering her spine. Could someone see them from the yard? What about the house? "Don't...please stop!"

"Calm yourself."

To her horror, he lifted her skirt. "No!"

He nipped her ear. "Don't be a fool. Give in, and you may find a coin in your apron pocket later."

Isabetta brought her head forward sharply, hitting the bridge of his nose.

Covering the injured appendage with both hands, he muttered an expletive. The distraction afforded her the opportunity to lift her knee and hit him between the legs, just as Rocco had taught her years ago. Petro cursed again before bending over and cradling his crotch. She ran into the house and almost collided head-on with Donata.

Skidding to a halt, she offered, "Sorry."

The imperious lady's maid eyed her with suspicion. "You're flushed and disheveled. What were you doing?"

Casting a furtive glance over her shoulder, Isabetta replied breathlessly, "Gathering fallen leaves."

"Look at you! The hem of your garment is filthy. You can't run around the villa like a peasant."

Balling her hands into fists, Isabetta resisted the urge to strike the snob. "I'm on my way to the kitchen."

"You should have gone through the garden entrance instead of the main house," Donata shot back before examining one of her neatly trimmed fingernails. "My mistress was looking for you earlier. She wishes to speak with you."

"Where is she?"

"In her bedchamber. Go on, what are you waiting for?"

Isabetta felt the heat of Donata's contemptuous stare burning into her back as she ascended the marble stairwell. She found her cousin clad in a satin dressing gown sorting through a pile of fine garments on the bed.

"There you are, Isabetta! I'm going through some of the dresses I've outgrown." Patting her thickening midsection, Cassandra added cheerfully, "Petro feeds me quite well."

Isabetta studied her cousin's thickening arms and expanding jowls with discretion. "Are you with child?"

"I never thought of that! Wouldn't it be wonderful? I'm certain Petro and I will make beautiful babies." Indicating the pile of dresses, she added, "I've set three aside for you."

Isabetta blinked in disbelief. *"For me?"*

"You're the only one scrawny enough to fit into them. I would have gifted them to Donata but she is petite. You, on the other hand, are almost as tall as a man."

Isabetta took the jibe in stride as her gaze caressed the costly fabrics. "They're gorgeous."

Cassandra's chest puffed with pride. "Woven from my father's looms. Do you want them?'

"I've never worn anything like this," Isabetta said while running her hand along a measure of soft velvet.

"Here's your chance."

"Of course I want them."

Cassandra grinned indulgently. "They're yours."

Resisting the urge to cry from gratitude, Isabetta held one of the gowns against her body. "Thank you so much."

Heavy footsteps in the corridor made both women look expectantly at the open door.

Petro entered the room, his tight gaze drifting from Isabetta to his wife. "What's going on here?"

Cassandra batted her eyelashes. "Nothing, my darling. I'm going through some of my old gowns. Isabetta has agreed to take a few off my hands since they no longer fit me." Rubbing her belly, she added, "Who knows? Your son may be growing inside of me as we speak."

"My happiness would be complete. I'll summon the midwife to confirm your suspicion." Turning to Isabetta, he added coolly, "I'm sure the gowns will look fetching on you, *Cousin* Isabetta. My wife's taste is impeccable."

Cassandra went over to him and placed a hand on his arm. "I married you, didn't I?"

Laughing a bit nervously, he agreed, "You most certainly did. I need to go into the city to take care of some business. I bid you ladies good afternoon."

"I'll have Donata fold these and make a parcel for you to take home this evening," Cassandra said in a tone of dismissal.

Isabetta left the bedchamber with light steps. Cassandra probably felt bad for making her own cousin work so hard. Could Aunt Rosa have put in a good word too? Three new gowns! Such a lavish and thoughtful gift.

"Where have you been?" Pina snapped the moment she entered the kitchen.

Isabetta pierced the insufferable woman with a haughty look. "Upstairs with *my cousin*, if you must know. Signora Cassandra had been searching for me while I was working outside."

Pina grunted something unintelligible. Pointing out the window, she said, "You failed to pick up the leaves. Go and finish, then come back and help me start supper."

Isabetta did as she was told, then spent the remainder of the afternoon basting a chicken on the spit. She stepped onto the last ferry of the evening with the parcel tucked beneath her arm. A shudder of revulsion snaked through her as she recalled the scent of Petro's skin and the taste of his lips. Of one thing she was sure: there would never be a repeat performance.

Alba greeted her warmly when she got home, then asked, "What have you got there?"

"My fat cousin gifted me three gowns that she has outgrown, can you believe it?"

Touching the expensive fabric, the servant whispered, "They must be worth a small fortune."

"No doubt. I'm going to try them on."

"What about supper?"

"I'll eat later."

Cassandra had been correct when she described Isabetta as 'scrawny' because the garments hung on her.

"Once you flesh out, they'll fit perfectly," Alba offered after lacing up a bodice. "As for your cousin…if she's not careful, she'll become corpulent. Husbands don't like fat wives."

"Cassandra is idle and does nothing all day but eat rich foods. I suggested that she may be with child."

"Fat and pregnant is what she is expected to be. I wouldn't be surprised if Signore Petro has a mistress."

Refusing to relive the disturbing scene that had transpired earlier, Isabetta shrugged in response. No need to trouble Alba with it. Running her palms down her torso, she felt her ribcage. How much weight had she lost since her mother's funeral? The chipped mirror revealed the hollowness of her pale cheeks. Gone was the healthy rosy glow that had once graced them.

"Don't be sad, Signorina. You are still comely."

Isabetta's eyes flickered to Alba's face in the mirror before returning to her own reflection. If things didn't improve soon, she would eventually resemble the emaciated servant. The mere thought prompted her to massage an herbal salve into her skin and pinch her cheeks to redden them. She would have to start eating better soon. Fish broth wasn't enough to maintain her body now that so much work was being demanded of it.

***

The remainder of the week proved uneventful. Petro kept his distance and her cousin gave in to moodiness after the midwife had determined that she was not pregnant. Cassandra's surliness caused Donata and Pina to treat Isabetta worse than usual.

On Sunday, Alba suggested tentatively, "Shall we go to the market today? The cloth merchant is in San Marco, the one who sells exotic fabrics and trimmings from the Orient."

The spider that lived in the bedchamber crawled along a wooden beam and Isabetta watched the insect from the comfort of her bed. "I think I'll stay in today."

Wringing her hands worriedly, Alba pleaded, "You barely smile these days. Make an effort for both our sakes, please."

"What's there to smile about? Maybe you should go alone for you'll find my company as sour as spoilt milk."

"Nonsense. Please, Signorina."

Heaving a sigh, Isabetta relented. "If you insist…"

Relieved, Alba opened the window shutters to allow sunlight into the room. "It will lift our spirits. Get up so I can help you dress."

Chilly air greeted them when they stepped outside. Thankfully, the sun's rays were hot enough to keep them warm as they made their way toward San Marco. Once a month, the lively market sold an array of products and drew great crowds. Some of the vendors sold rugs from China and ivory trinkets from Africa.

"Silvio will have his spice stalls in markets like these," Isabetta mused aloud. "Imagine the money he will make."

"I hope you're right."

Painted prostitutes sauntered along the edges of the *piazza*. Balancing on their high-heeled *chopins*, they captured the attention of many. Venetian law required them to stand a head above chaste women so they could be easily detected. Gaudy dresses and fake jewelry made them appear crass, yet their plump figures suggested a rich diet. Evidence of their success.

Isabetta studied these women, who were paid to endure the carnal lusts of men. Did they enjoy it? She thought of Veronica, who wore real diamonds and expensive gowns. Did *she* enjoy it? While courtesans did not stalk the streets like common whores, they provided the same services. Did the city's poor men behave any differently than the rich ones when they were stripped naked in bed?

She pondered these questions while watching the prostitutes in action. Moving in a calculated manner, the experienced women engaged in direct eye contact with men, their smiles loaded with insinuation and promise. The recipients of their exaggerated female prowess seemed mesmerized, causing her to arrive at a startling conclusion.

Certain women were capable of exerting power over men.

"Look at this array of ribbons," Alba said, cutting into the thoughts of her mistress. Moving closer to the stall, she added, "These green ones would bring out the color of your eyes."

"I've no money for such frills."

The vendor in the next stall over coaxed potential patrons with promises of best quality for price. A striking woman went over and fingered a length of intricate lace.

Covering her head with the hood of her cloak, Isabetta nudged Alba. "Quick, turn around!"

"What's wrong?"

Isabetta waited for her servant to obey, then replied, "Iseppo da Mosta's wife is standing right over there."

Alba craned her neck to take a peek as a well-dressed man placed an arm around Polonia's shoulders. "Who is that man?"

Incredulous, Isabetta replied, "Cristofolo Trasontin, the man who seized the *Tramonto*."

"What is he doing with Signora Polonia?"

"Excellent question."

Isabetta and Alba watched as the pair began whispering and giggling like two lovers. Polonia's boldness verged on shocking since most women wouldn't dare parade their husband's cuckoldry in public.

Snapping his fingers at the vendor, Cristofolo eyed the lace. "How much?"

Polonia made a perfunctory attempt at preventing him from purchasing the expensive gift. Ignoring her protests, he paid the exorbitant price without flinching.

She kissed his cheek. "Thank you, Uncle Cristofolo."

"Anything for you, my sweet girl," he said, caressing her cheek while gazing deeply into her eyes.

Isabetta gaped at them from within the shadow of her hood.

Uncle?

Alzo possessed plenty of flaws, but at least he had never touched her in such a...*familiar* manner. The way Cristofolo regarded his niece transformed the seemingly innocent gesture into something odd. Something forbidden.

"You're upset, Signorina," Alba observed, interrupting the sinful thought. "Let's go in this direction."

Isabetta allowed the servant to lead her to another vendor. Something was wrong, and she couldn't shake off the feeling for the remainder of the day.

The drudgery of servant life recommenced on Monday morning. Isabetta scrubbed floors, emptied slop buckets, and chopped vegetables in a state of dazed confusion. Try as she might, she could not stop thinking about what she had witnessed at the market.

Pina said, "Roll up those sleeves. Time to bake bread."

Kneading dough allowed Isabetta's mind to drift. Cristofolo wouldn't have known about the *Tramonto* unless someone had told him. Who else but Polonia's husband, Iseppo? The ship merchant was known to be savvy and wouldn't waste such an opportunity as his rival's death to further his own interests.

"Watch what you're doing, girl," Pina snapped.

Isabetta glanced down at the overworked dough.

The servant took over the job of kneading and barked, "Add more wood to the fire."

Shaking the flour from her hands, Isabetta went over to the kindling basket. One piece of wood bore a sharp point at the junction where it had been snapped from a branch. She entertained the notion of spearing Pina with it. Working like a slave for a pittance surely wouldn't provide the huge sum needed by June of next year. Seized by overwhelming frustration, she wiped at her stinging eyes and threw the wood into the fire. Tomorrow the servants would collect their salaries. The letter Cassandra had sent in October stated fair wages, but she had never mentioned a number. Isabetta had never thought to ask. They were family, after all.

The servants arrived at the villa earlier than usual the next day to be paid. Isabetta found her cousin speaking with Pina in the kitchen and approached her almost shyly.

"*Buongiorno*, Signora Cassandra."

Cassandra inclined her head and said, "Isabetta."

To Isabetta's dismay, she continued the conversation with the servant. After several minutes, her cousin made to leave.

Isabetta went after her. "May I have a word with you?"

Cassandra nodded and followed her cousin to the corner of the kitchen. Eyes gleaming with excitement, she asked, "Are you going to tell me a secret? Or share a tidbit of gossip from Venice?"

"Neither." When Cassandra only stared askance, Isabetta added, "Am I not to be paid today?"

"I've already paid you," Cassandra replied glibly. "Father has instructed me to deduct the monetary worth of those gowns from your wages."

Stricken, Isabetta gaped at her cousin in disbelief. "I was expecting that money. I have debts to pay."

A hand flew to Cassandra's chest as though she had taken offense. "The fabrics alone are worth a fortune! Far more than a mere servant's wage. Besides, having something decent to wear will improve your chances of finding a suitor. Do you think you'll snatch a gentleman while wearing rags?"

Isabetta gritted her teeth, then said in the meekest tone she could muster, "The gowns are magnificent and I appreciate your generosity, but I can't pay off my father's debt with brocade and velvet. I need money."

Cassandra gasped. "If I didn't know any better, I'd say you're being ungrateful. Your current position in my household was my mother's idea, you know. She's the closest thing you have to a mother and she wants the best for you—as I do."

Forcing down a mouthful of angry retorts, Isabetta said primly, "Forgive me if I spoke out of turn."

"Don't worry. You'll pay your debt in time. *Trust me*."

Fighting against an onslaught of tears, Isabetta nodded and went over to Pina to be instructed on what needed to be done. Resentment pulsated throughout her body as she scrubbed the outer walkway. A string of silent curses paraded through her mind. How could Cassandra be so clueless? So out of touch with reality?

***

On Sunday, Isabetta wrapped herself in warm wools and set off for the *Basilica di San Marco*. Her goal was to confront Iseppo da Mosta after Holy Mass, assuming he and his wife would be in attendance. They lived nearby, and almost everyone went to church on Sunday to see and be seen. She doubted Polonia ever missed the chance to advertise her husband's profession.

Cloying incense accosted Isabetta's nose as she entered the massive cathedral. Patterned velvets peeked from beneath opulent fur-lined capes and gemstones glittered in the dim candlelight. The city's wealthiest worshippers were on display.

She selected a seat toward the back where she could observe the scene yet remain virtually unnoticed. Her simple garments didn't draw anyone's attention, and she kept her veiled head low. To her surprise, Basil Anastas took a seat in the pew across the way. Beside him sat a hideous-looking adolescent. The Greek sea captain not only recognized her, he caught her eye and nodded in a friendly gesture, prompting her to do the same.

She was in luck, for Iseppo and Polonia strode into the

church with their heads held high. Decked out in costly garments, they strutted down the nave like a pair of peacocks to claim a seat upfront with the other prominent citizens of Venice.

Throughout the service Isabetta kept her gaze focused on the ostentatious pair. She had planned on confronting them both after the concluding prayer but Basil intervened.

"Greetings, Signorina Isabetta. How are you?" he inquired, his wizened eyes crinkling at the corners.

"Well enough, thank you. How are you and your family, Signore Basil?"

"Fine, thank God. My wife is pregnant again."

Isabetta cast a fleeting glance at Iseppo. "Felicitations! This is your sixth child, correct?"

"Seventh."

"You are blessed."

"I am indeed."

Basil placed his arm around his companion's shoulder. "I am spending time with my nephew today. My sister and her husband live in this sestiere. This here is Adonis."

Adonis smiled, exposing crooked teeth. *"Buongiorno."*

Isabetta inclined her head at the homely young man whose ironic name mocked the ancient male god known for his beauty.

Noticing that her eyes kept darting to where Iseppo stood, Basil said, "I heard about his wife's uncle seizing your galley."

Now he had her full attention. "From whom?"

"This is a city full of secrets and yet nothing stays hidden for long. People talk, Signorina Isabetta."

"I have until June to pay the total amount plus interest if I wish to reclaim the *Tramonto*."

Wincing, he said, "Not much time, is it?"

"No, and I blame Iseppo da Mosta for my dire predicament."

Basil seemed puzzled. "Why?"

"Who else would have alerted Cristofolo of the situation? It seems they are now partners in my demise."

"Those types of investments are common enough, I daresay. Bankers don't want to lose money. I'm sure this wasn't done as a personal attack against you. Iseppo and I have known each other for years, and I can vouch that he's a good, honest man." When Isabetta displayed skepticism, he added, "I doubt Iseppo approached Cristofolo with the idea. Those two *hate* each other. They wouldn't sit at the same table for a meal let alone venture into business together."

This revelation threw her off balance. "Are you sure?"

"Yes, I am. Many people are aware of their mutual contempt. Polonia adores her uncle and spends much time with him, but you'll never see Iseppo out with those two." Adonis mumbled something in Basil's ear, and he added, "For what it's worth, I'm sorry for your troubles. If there's anything I can do to help, let me know. You must excuse me, for my sister is expecting us. Enjoy your Sunday."

"Likewise, thank you."

He moved to go, then stopped and retraced his steps. "Take heart, Signorina Isabetta. You're a good soul and certainly don't deserve this plight. God has a plan for each one of us and everything in life happens for a reason. The future may seem dark, but the light will shine through at some point. Try not to worry too much."

Easier said than done. "I appreciate your kindness, sir."

Offering her a smile and a nod, he retreated.

Casting a measured look at Iseppo da Mosta, she decided not to confront him.

CHAPTER 12

Isabetta stood outside emptying the slop bucket and spotted movement from the corner of her eye. Swiveling her head, she spied Donata and Petro kissing inside the *limonaia.* Her lip curled in disgust because they were in the exact same spot where he had attempted to seduce her weeks ago.

Shifting her body behind the wide girth of an ancient cypress tree, she was allotted a clear view of the couple without being seen. Anger flared when Petro pinned his cousin against the wall and lifted her skirt. Isabetta waited for the young woman to fight him off as she had, but that didn't happen. Instead, Donata eagerly responded to his advances and even pulled him closer. How many coins would find their way into the pretty maid's pocket?

Isabetta dropped her gaze to the wooden bucket in her hand. The slimy residue within it gave off a rank odor, summoning the bile to her throat. Donata's willingness toward immorality made her immune to such disgusting chores. The lady's maid pranced around the villa in fine silk while performing menial tasks for her mistress. Had Petro deliberately chosen his cousin for this reason? How long had they been fornicating behind Cassandra's back? Turning her attention back to the couple, Isabetta glimpsed Petro adjusting his breeches while his lover smoothed her skirt with the palms of her hands. Donata kissed her cousin's lips before disappearing into the house.

Petro exited the greenhouse through the exterior door that led to the yard. Seeing this, Isabetta cursed under her breath and rushed toward the herb garden.

He caught up with her. "What are you doing here?"

Maintaining her distance, she lifted the bucket. "Pina instructed me to empty this and pick some rosemary."

His eyes settled on the swell of her breasts. "Get to it."

Under his watchful gaze, she yanked a handful of rosemary

before retreating to the kitchen with hasty steps.

Pina cast a sour look in her direction before placing a small pot to boil in the hearth. "Took long enough. You won't last in this household if you keep dragging your feet like that."

Picking up a knife, Isabetta began to chop shallots. "Pina, are Donata and Petro first cousins like me and Cassandra?"

"Why do you ask?"

"Curiosity."

"They are *second* cousins."

Pina's tone implied something else, but the stoic servant was quickly absorbed in another chore before any more information could be extracted.

Isabetta returned home later that evening in deep thought. She rejected Alba's supper under the pretense of going straight to bed. That night, she couldn't sleep. For some reason, her uncle's harsh words during his last visit rang in her ears. *'No man in the city will conduct business with a woman—unless he's negotiating the price for a prostitute.'* The dark tunnel that was now her life kept stretching longer and longer with no glimmer of light at the end.

The next day dawned rainy and cold. Exhausted from lack of sleep, Isabetta left for work in a foul mood. Her head ached and her throat felt sore.

Pina greeted her with a grunt. "The outside walkway needs to be scrubbed down."

Isabetta said nothing as she filled a bucket with water and soap, then grabbed a brush. She picked up the heavy bucket and carried it with difficulty across the floor. Lost in thought, she almost collided with her cousin.

Cassandra recoiled, then immediately examined the front of her gown. "Isabetta, watch where you're going!"

Feeling despised and degraded, Isabetta offered, "Sorry."

Huffing in irritation, Cassandra went over to Pina in order to discuss the week's menu.

***

December blew through the city with such ferocious winds that it caused the rain to slant sideways. Ferry rides to and from

Mestre proved increasingly difficult in the inclement weather. Cassandra talked of little else except Christmas during those bleak wintry days. Petro had insisted on hosting several dinners and even a banquet with music and entertainment.

Isabetta continued to lose weight as her spirit plummeted further into despair. She had naïvely hoped that Cassandra would at least allow her to attend one of the events as a guest, but an invitation never came.

One afternoon, Cassandra burst into the kitchen in a fine gown of blue and gold brocade. She was humming a tune and stopped. "Your expression says it all, Isabetta. I was about to ask if you like my new gown. My father created this design last month especially for me."

"It's gorgeous," Isabetta replied honestly.

Cassandra spun around once, then floated out of the kitchen in a haze of excitement.

Pina's amused gaze rested on Isabetta. "Donata never gets invited to the parties, so neither will you."

Isabetta glared at the woman before selecting another turnip from a basket. The *Tramonto* would be returning any day now. Hopefully, her share of the profit would at least purchase food staples and maybe, if she was lucky, some of it would go toward paying off the debt she owed.

Sunday morning bells rang throughout the city calling the good citizens of Venice to church. Isabetta tried to banish the noise by burrowing deeper into her pillow.

Alba appeared in the doorway. "It's getting late. Shall I help you dress? The sun is shining."

Rather than reply, Isabetta pulled the sheets over her head and fell asleep again. The concerned servant remained rooted to the spot for a long time before receding into the hallway.

An hour passed before Alba ventured into her mistress's bedchamber once more. "Are you sick, Signorina?"

Opening one eye, Isabetta groaned. "You should find yourself a husband and leave this wretched house."

"What are you saying?"

"My life is unbearable. I toil from dawn to dusk for a selfish creature, and I have no chance to improve my situation."

A long beat passed before Alba said, "I'll be back shortly."

Isabetta stared at the ceiling, unconcerned. The spider web was gone, which meant the insect had either died or moved to another part of the house. Footsteps ascended the stairs some time later, followed by a knock on the door. "Leave me, Alba!"

"Greetings, my friend," Veronica said gaily, slipping into the bedchamber and closing the door behind her.

"Veronica, forgive me. I thought it was Alba."

"Your servant went over to my home to fetch me."

"She shouldn't have inconvenienced you," Isabetta said while sitting up in bed.

"I'm glad she did. To be honest, my mother and I have been quite worried. We haven't seen or heard from you since your mother's funeral. You haven't accepted our dinner invitations."

Shame tinted Isabetta's cheeks. "I wasn't trying to be rude. My life has changed drastically, you see…"

"Ever since you began working for your cousin?"

"Alba told you."

"Your servant revealed nothing since I already knew. Don't look so surprised. Courtesans know most of what goes on in the city. I'm also aware that Petro Vendramin seduced you—or at least that's what he bragged. I doubted the story's veracity."

Isabetta's mouth fell open. "He tried but failed. I fought him off by kicking him in his...*you know*."

Veronica threw her head back and laughed. "Well done!"

"I can't believe he would lie about me like that."

"Drunk men love to talk at parties. Petro once described you as a *scrumptious morsel*. Luckily, he never revealed your name and only referred to you as 'my wife's cousin.' "

Isabetta rubbed her throbbing temples. "Does he ever speak of his wife's lady's maid, who also happens to be his cousin?"

"Donata? Oh yes. He refers to her as his *sweet little trollop*."

Were all men vile? "What else do you know?"

Pulling up a chair, Veronica sat by the bed and regarded her young friend earnestly. "Well, I know that Cristofolo Trasontin is plotting to snatch the *Tramonto* from under your nose. He boasted about his recent acquisition to one of my clients."

Cringing from the disturbing revelation, Isabetta asked, "Do you know him well?"

One side of the courtesan's mouth curved up. "*Intimately*, although the old rogue hasn't visited me in quite some time. Most of my colleagues know him too."

"What sort of man is he?"

"Wealthy, aloof, cynical…Oddly enough, despite being selfish he is known to be generous. Even witty at times."

"Dangerous?"

"I wouldn't go that far, although I suppose any man can be dangerous if provoked. Cristofolo is a lifelong bachelor who keeps to himself. He has a voracious appetite for women but avoids romantic entanglements." Changing the subject, Veronica said, "Working for Cassandra has taken a toll on you."

It wasn't a question. "I toil from sunup to sundown in order to amass the money needed to pay back the debt I now owe to Cristofolo. Maybe it's useless. Maybe I'm a fool."

"Fate has been unkind to you lately but don't give up hope." Veronica rubbed her lower back and winced. The movement revealed her slightly protruding belly.

Isabetta's gaze locked on the subtle swell beneath the velvet gown. "Are you…?"

"Pregnant again? Yes."

"Who is the father?"

"I am sworn to secrecy since his wife is overly-jealous. I'll only reveal that he is obscenely rich and important. He has no heirs and desires a lovechild from me. I stand to make a small fortune from this service, especially if I bear a son." She paused, grinning. "You seem shocked."

"Excuse my ignorance. I didn't realize that you…"

"Life as a courtesan doesn't merely consist of pretty dresses and banquets. I grant men access to my body, my time, my mind…and in this case, my womb."

"It can't be worse than emptying stinky slop buckets and scrubbing walkways on wintry days." Holding up her chapped hands, Isabetta added, "Look at them."

"Malvina makes the best hand cream. I'll give you some. Your hands will be softer than before." Frowning slightly, she observed, "I'm surprised your cousin has you doing such taxing chores in the first place."

At this, Isabetta laughed mirthlessly. "Do you want to know what's worse? Cassandra paid me in fabric the first month I worked for her, can you believe it? She gave me her cast-offs because she's grown fat, then deducted the dresses from my wages. I can barely keep Alba and I fed, let alone repay debts."

After a long pause, Veronica inquired, "How much is the *Tramonto* worth to you?"

"That galley is my father's legacy. It's the one thing I have left from my family, and my only chance at making a decent living. I'll do anything to get it back."

Going to the door, Veronica ordered, "Get dressed and come over when you're done. Together, we'll sort this out."

No sooner had she left than Alba entered the room. "Shall I help you bathe and dress?"

Scowling, Isabetta accused, "You've been eavesdropping." Not a hint of regret could be seen in the servant's eyes as she nodded. "I should be angry with you."

Yanking the bedcover off her mistress, Alba corrected, "You should be *grateful*. If anyone can help you in this city, it's Veronica Franco."

Veronica and Paola greeted Isabetta warmly a little while later. Over tea and cake, mother and daughter regaled their young guest with funny stories and racy gossip. Names were kept strictly confidential since the vast majority of their male clientele were important and powerful. Isabetta soon found herself laughing, which served as a remedy for her soul.

Paola eventually excused herself when a gentleman arrived wishing to make an appointment.

"It's good to hear you laugh again," Veronica commented when they were alone. Peeking out the window, she pointed. "Do you see that ugly old man? Mother will schedule him to come sometime this week. He is one of my wealthiest clients and pays dearly for my time. I will be expected to pleasure him in every way he desires."

Studying the corpulent man with pock-marked skin, Isabetta wrinkled her nose. "As distasteful as I'm sure it will be, I would still prefer to be in your shoes than in mine. You have no financial worries, which is no small thing."

"True, but…" Veronica spread out her hands to indicate the room. "Look around you. Much of the money I make is spent on everything you see. In addition to expensive clothing, which is needed to maintain our prestigious images as courtesans, our homes must reflect our success. Quality wine and sweetmeats are served to my clients even if they come for a brief visit. Dinners are costly affairs where we offer a spread of fine foods and wines. We spend a fortune on luxuries to make our clients feel special. Thankfully, the pockets of my patrons are deep and my mother is a shrewd businesswoman."

Isabetta's lips curved. "It seems Signora Paola and I have much in common when it comes to accounting and procuring the best prices for supplies."

"In that sense, yes. As you've probably heard, my mother was a famous courtesan in her day. She trained me to have the same high standards. My job requires a strong stomach and stamina, as well as a resilient character. It is no secret that we are shunned by the chaste wives and godly women of Venice."

"True, but you are embraced by the most powerful members of society. Surely, that accounts for something."

"While we're young and desirable, yes. Once the wrinkles show and the flesh sags, we lose popularity with those of the opposite sex. Thank God for my children, for they will be my only company in old age."

A deep furrow formed across Isabetta's forehead at hearing the sobering words. She hadn't thought of that.

The courtesan stood. "I want to show you my new dress."

Isabetta followed her host upstairs, then paused to admire Veronica's boudoir. *Pleasure den* would serve as a better description for the spacious chamber. From the rose-gold silk canopy over the bed complimenting the courtesan's skin to the costly objects of beauty on display—everything in the decadent room was designed to seduce. Naked cherubs frolicked amid cottony clouds above their heads, while sinuous nubile figures danced along the wall. The painter had molded the youthful supple bodies in an idealized manner in order to stir passion.

Isabetta's eyes were drawn to an armoire fitted with glass doors and several shelves. On display was the most expansive collection of shoes she had ever seen. Red, green, yellow, blue, and even leather shoes painted with flowers were lined up to delight the eyes. Some had silver buckles, others gold.

The courtesan smiled sheepishly. "As you can see, I have a penchant for pretty shoes."

"Do you wear *all* of them?"

"Each and every one."

Throughout the decorated walls were strategically placed gilded mirrors reflecting various angles of the bed. Isabetta's face warmed as she imagined the acts performed in this room. Off to the side were richly upholstered chairs and a chaise longue offering views of the narrow canal that ran behind the house. A table held a crystal decanter of wine that sparkled in the sunshine.

"This is an incredible room," Isabetta said, pausing to study the group of painted young men and women in varying stages of undress on the wall. The eyes of these life-sized frescoed figures seemed to follow her wherever she moved.

"Lord knows the amount we paid to decorate it. This is where I entertain my clients, so everything must be perfect." Lifting the lid of a big *cassone*, Veronica extracted a gorgeous plum damask gown adorned with seed pearls. Holding it up to her body, she said, "A gift from a French duke."

Isabetta went over and touched the soft fabric. "It's divine. The neckline is stitched with gold thread."

"I can't even imagine the cost. I won't be able to fit into it for much longer with this little one growing inside of me."

"Am I wrong to assume that you won't get as many clients during your pregnancy?"

"I won't be as busy, but there are a few men who enjoy the ripe lushness of a pregnant woman."

"Such strange creatures."

"Men?"

Isabetta nodded. "Although, I know so little about them aside from my brother and father."

"*And* Silvio…."

"We've exchanged sweet words and a few kisses."

"Nothing more?" When Isabetta shook her head, Veronica chuckled in a knowing manner. "You're blushing! No wonder you're the protagonist of Petro Vendramin's fantasies. You have what most women in this city lack—*purity*."

"Unfortunately, it doesn't pay to be pure."

Veronica's eyes gleamed wickedly. "Oh but it does, my dear. With your face and figure, you could earn a small fortune in a single night."

Isabetta refrained from cringing so as not to cause offense. "How many men would I need to bed?"

"One."

"One?"

Taking Isabetta's hand, Veronica led her to the balcony where a gondola glided silently beneath them. "Believe it or not, there are those who would pay a lot of money for the pleasure of claiming your maidenhead."

Scandalized yet fascinated, Isabetta said, "Truly?"

"Truly…Would you consider it?"

"I would."

"What about Silvio? Do you love him?"

*Silvio…*A pang of guilt shot through Isabetta. "We are corresponding and our intention is to wed. If I were to…If I actually did sell my virginity, he could never know."

"No, he could not." Veronica said nothing more as she watched Isabetta ponder the ramifications of her suggestion.

"What constitutes a 'small fortune' in your world? Do you think I could make enough to pay my debts?"

"Maybe not quite all that you owe, but close. I know how much Cristofolo paid to cover your father's debt on the galley."

Biting her lip, Isabetta thought hard on the matter. "I would be selling my body—*my flesh*, not my heart."

"Correct."
"I'll do it."
Veronica smiled encouragingly. "Very well. We need to do some work first. I can't present you to the public just yet."
"I'm willing to learn if you'll teach me."
"Can you read?"
"Fairly well."
"Which books have you read?"
"Aside from prayer books, almost everything I've read pertains to navigation and the shipping business."
Veronica led her friend away from the view. "So you know nothing of history, philosophy, poetry?"
"Very little, I'm afraid."
The courtesan paused to run her fingers along the strings of a magnificent gilded harp. "How about music? Do you play any instruments?"
"No."
Veronica went over to the book shelf and selected a few books. Setting them on the table, she asked, "Do you know what the difference is between me and the whores of the Castelletto?"
Isabetta knew that the Venetian government had established a system of legalized prostitution in that specific area. Illicit brothels abounded, the most successful being run by savvy women with solid business sense. Debit and credit were used to purchase all kinds of goods in the city, including sex. This system often served to keep prostitutes subservient to their masters and mistresses. Courtesans, the city's greatest luxury items, were openly tolerated as a means of avoiding attacks against the good wives and noble daughters of Venice. Also, the taxes generated by the brothels were enough to fund several warships. In response to the question, she said, "Your fine clothing and manners?"
"Noble wives possess both in abundance, yet their husbands still seek me out. It takes much more than that to get a prince to fall in love with you."
"You entertain men with music and poetry too."
"Many noble wives are accomplished musicians, some can

sing and even recite poetry. That's still not enough."

"I don't know the answer. What's your secret?"

"My intellectual capacity and my ability to converse with men. I can offer valuable insight on societal issues, politics, and business. Men fall hopelessly in love with clever women, but you need to temper your intelligence with wit and humility. Otherwise, they will feel intimidated."

"I think I understand."

Smiling, Veronica went over to the mirror to pat her hair into place. "Men are contradictory creatures. For example, they love the Virgin Mary yet come here to lose themselves in my arms. In some ways, you'll need to be both saint and sinner."

"Rocco once told me that I should be sweet and docile."

"Men want submissive wives to bear their sons but in reality they crave a challenge. Your most powerful asset—the greatest aphrodisiac in the world—is your mind. The art of seduction requires *this*." Veronica met her friend's eyes in the mirror's reflection, then tapped the side of her head. "Therein lies the difference between obtaining a man's lust and his love. The latter keeps him coming back for more."

Isabetta's face fell in disappointment. "It would take me years to learn what you know!"

Moving away from the vanity, the courtesan laughed. "I don't know everything, silly girl. I must keep up with current affairs in order to engage in lively debates. I study philosophy books in order to quote Aristotle, Plato, and Socrates. Just the other day a nobleman brought up *Meditations* by Marcus Aurelius. Knowing that I would see him again, I read as much as I could beforehand." Leafing through one of the books on the table, she added, "Here it is, the words of a wise emperor. Your first reading assignment. People nurture the misconception that we courtesans spend most of our time on our backs. Nothing is further from the truth."

Isabetta clutched the book to her chest. "I could read one hundred books and I'll never be like you."

"Don't be glum, Isabetta. There is one thing you have that I do not, and it holds more value than anything I can provide."

"What would that be?"

"I've already told you—*virginity*. Why do you think noble daughters are closeted in their homes? They can't step foot outside without being closely chaperoned. Given the constant male preoccupation with paternity, virgins are valuable commodities on the marriage market. A whisper of impropriety can ruin a girl's reputation forever."

"Will you schedule me for an appointment here?" Spreading out her hands in supplication, Isabetta confessed, "I haven't the faintest idea how one sells their virginity."

"And why would you? You're in the shipping business," Veronica countered with a grin. "Traditionally, a courtesan will take on a protégé and train her, then put the word out that she is ready to be presented to the public. In your case, it would be a *deflowering*. I will plan a wonderful party for my best patrons, which means my wealthiest. You will be presented to the men, then you will leave before the bidding starts."

"Good God, it's like auctioning a horse!"

"An expensive horse swathed in brocade and jewels."

Isabetta couldn't help laughing at the analogy. "There's only one thing that worries me. I don't wish to be recognized by anyone. I don't want Silvio to ever find out."

"Let down your hair, will you?"

Pulling at her hair ribbons, Isabetta allowed her hair to cascade over her shoulders.

Veronica toyed with a few bronze strands. "Henna rinses would redden your hair, setting off your golden brown eyes. Expert application of cosmetics would render you a bit older...I think we can change your appearance a bit."

"I'll need to use an alias too."

The courtesan squinted in thought. "Right. Let's think of a new name for you. Since virgins are venerated, I'll introduce you as Venerada. What do you think?"

"Venerada," Isabetta repeated dubiously.

Veronica picked up a gold earring from a dresser and lifted it toward a sunbeam. The deep yellow metal flashed. "Venerada d'Oro since you'll require a surname."

"Venerated Gold?"

"It suits you."

Isabetta's eyes slid to the jewel-encrusted silver statue of the Virgin Mary on the bedside table. A symbol of Veronica's corrupted faith and wealth, an icon lacking true veneration. "You know best, I suppose."

"I do. What's more, no protégé of mine scrubs floors or empties slop buckets. *Venerada* will cease performing such distasteful tasks at once." The panic in her friend's face prompted her to add, "Trust me."

"I do trust you, Veronica."

"Good. I insist that you remain and dine with us tonight. My mother and I will teach you how to eat."

"But I already know how to eat."

"Not like a courtesan."

***

"There is nothing more powerful than a desired woman. Competition and rivalry among men only raises your value in their eyes." Veronica snapped her fingers and two servants materialized from behind a painted screen to place food and wine on the table. "Let's pretend you're my escort," she said, lifting her goblet. Gazing at Isabetta through hooded lids, she smiled slightly, took a sip, and then slowly licked her lips. The movements were slow and deliberate. *Sensuous*.

"You are captivating," Isabetta murmured.

"That's why my daughter receives so many requests and gifts from admirers," Paola said with pride.

Inclining her head at the compliments, Veronica reached for a sliver of cheese. Her other hand rested gently on her bodice to draw attention to her breasts with the index finger resting in the shadowy cleft. "Everything you do must allude to the art of love and the promise of passion. Each movement should cause a stirring in a man's loins. You are building his hunger for later when the two of you will be alone."

Paola indicated Isabetta's goblet. "Now, you try it."

Isabetta reached for the wine and did her best to copy Veronica's movements. She burst out laughing, partly because she felt ridiculous and partly from nerves.

"You will improve with practice," Veronica assured with a dazzling smile. "I shall expect you and Alba here tomorrow afternoon so that we can dye your hair. Malvina will teach your servant a few simple tricks to aid in your beauty ablutions. Bring one of Cassandra's cast-offs with you."

"Why?"

"It's a surprise."

Isabetta left Veronica's house with a different perspective on life—one that offered a solution to her problems. Reaching the door of her home, she heard a man's voice from within. Who would pay her a visit at such a late hour? She found Miro seated at the table and Alba pouring him a tankard of ale.

He stood. "Greetings, Isabetta."

"Miro, welcome back. When did you arrive?"

Reclaiming his seat, he replied, "A moment ago."

"The journey? How was it?"

"Well enough."

"The *Tramonto*?"

"The ship is in fine shape. I oversaw the unloading after we were released from quarantine."

"Good. Tell me everything." She listened intently to his detailed description of the journey, which had gone well with neither crewmen nor cargo lost at sea. "I'm relieved that you and the galley are home."

Miro extracted a small pouch of money from the pocket of his wool cape. "This is yours."

Bouncing the pouch in her palm, she surmised, "Feels light." She spilled the contents on the table and frowned. "If we're splitting the profit three ways, then I am owed more than this."

Miro sheepishly removed a document from his cape that bore a *T* on the red wax seal. "Signore Cristofolo instructed me to hand deliver this to Beto Bastian."

Isabetta expected to read a full report, instead she saw several rows of numbers. It took her a moment to realize that the document was an itemized bill.

Miro pointed to the sum listed at the bottom of the sheet.

"He said *that* is your share."

"This is absurd."

"Signore Iseppo expressed the same sentiment and tried to dissuade Cristofolo, but it was to no avail. In fact, Cristofolo said—"

She held up her hands to silence him. "Wait. Iseppo?"

Miro nodded. "Signore Cristofolo met with him and your uncle to sort out the money."

Isabetta's hands flew to her temples as she processed his words. "Basil Anastas assured me that Iseppo da Mosta and Cristofolo Trasontin are at odds. Those two loathe each other."

"They do, but Polonia has a vested interest in the *Tramonto* since she's the one who convinced her uncle to—"

"Is everyone in this city out to ruin me?"

"I'm sorry, Isabetta. I truly am…Are you all right?"

"I'm fine."

Isabetta was far from fine, however. She was tired of people looking at her with pity in their eyes—tired of her tedious life, her bad luck, of everything and everyone. Fiery rage bubbled beneath the surface of her skin, threatening to burn her alive. Deep within her core something snapped, and the fragments scattered in different directions. She was no longer whole.

Meeting Miro's gaze, she said calmly, "I can't go to the warehouse, so I am trusting you to be my eyes and ears."

He nodded slowly, his expression troubled. "I've already sent a message to the doge's palazzo. Is there anything else you need me to do for you?"

"No. Have you been paid?"

Reluctantly, he shook his head. Isabetta stared at him while cursing Cristofolo, Alzo, and Iseppo to the rotten depths of Hell. Scooping the coins from the table, she refilled the small pouch and tossed it at him. "Here, take it."

Shaking his head, he countered, "I can't accept this."

"You've earned those wages, my friend."

"I cannot leave you with nothing."

"Don't worry. I have recently come into a considerable sum of money." Ignoring Alba's quizzical look, she continued, "I'm sorry the amount is less than you were promised, but I'll compensate you soon enough. You have my word."

Miro stood and pocketed the money. "It's more than enough, Isabetta." He went to the door, then stopped. "Let me know if I can be of further assistance. You know where to find me."

She offered him a tight smile. "Goodnight."

The moment he left the house, Alba said, "I don't want to pry into your business—"

"That makes two of us."

"What money are you speaking of?"

"From this day forth, I ask that you not meddle in my affairs. It's best if you don't know what I'm doing."

The servant wrung her hands nervously, debating whether or not to press the matter. Finally, she ventured, "Signore Cristofolo—"

"Hush, Alba. Don't speak his name to me right now. My hatred for that man is such that I would kill him if I had the chance. Polonia too."

Lowering her head, Alba retreated to the farthest end of the kitchen. As she scrubbed one of the pots, her eyes frequently drifted to her mistress. Isabetta sat staring at the wall for a long time before heaving her body upstairs.

CHAPTER 13

Isabetta and her servant made their way to Veronica's home the next afternoon, as instructed.

"Aren't you going to send word to your cousin?" Alba inquired, the words mingling with the sound of their shoes clicking against the cobblestones.

"I hate Mestre, I hate that villa, I hate Petro, but most of all, I hate Cassandra. Why should I tell her anything?"

Alba remained prudently silent in the face of her mistress's caustic reply.

Isabetta added, "My aunt will come sniffing around here soon enough."

A sad sigh escaped the servant's lips. Life was slowly embittering the sweet girl she had helped Hortensa raise. Isabetta's anger and resentment seeped from her body like pus from an infected boil. Gone was the carefree, happy girl she once knew. "Are you going to work for Veronica Franco?"

"In a way, yes."

"As a lady's maid?"

"Something far more profitable." Before Alba could protest, Isabetta whipped around and stuck a forefinger in the servant's face. "Don't you dare say another word or bring my deceased parents into the conversation. I have been used and abused by people I once trusted. I'm not a little girl anymore, so let me do what needs to be done in peace."

Alba nodded slowly, her face crestfallen. "I'm only sorry that it has come to this."

Pausing at the palazzo's entrance, Isabetta reached for the iron knocker. "So am I, Alba."

They were led upstairs into the boudoir, where Veronica and Malvina awaited them.

Polite greetings were exchanged, then Veronica examined the garment Alba carried in her arms. "This gown is lovely. It will be perfect for the occasion this evening."

Isabetta watched as Malvina took the gown and laid it on the bed. "What occasion? Is that the surprise you mentioned?"

"No questions yet. We have much to do. First, your hair. Alba, will you help Malvina, please?"

The servants went off to prepare the henna rinse, and then they applied it to Isabetta's hair. As they waited for the color to permeate the strands, Malvina applied a mask of milk, herbs, and honey. Next, the mulatta filed down Isabetta's brittle, uneven nails. A soothing, emollient cream was applied to the dry hands and cuticles.

Veronica came over to examine the hair color. "This is going to look wonderful, Isabetta. Once we rinse out the henna, we'll give you a bath with fragrant oils."

Isabetta had never been so pampered. The bath made her skin smell and feel wonderful. As for her hair, the deep reddish hue showcased her creamy golden skin.

"Have a seat at the vanity." Veronica paused to address Malvina. "Do your best work. Alba, pay attention."

Malvina began deftly coiling the tresses to create an elegant coiffure. Tucking a small feather in the braided bun for a touch of flare, she said, "There."

Isabetta gasped at her reflection in the mirror. "I don't even recognize myself."

"You're sure to impress my guests."

Turning around, Isabetta repeated, *"Guests?"*

"Two of my oldest clients are coming to dine with us this evening. Gossipy old men who know everyone in Venice. I will introduce you as my protégé. Malvina, escort Alba out and alert me when Signore Osvaldo and Count Guglielmo arrive."

Alba cast a worried glance over her shoulder as Malvina led her to the door.

"Something is missing." Veronica extracted a simple topaz pendant from a jewelry box. Fastening it around Isabetta's throat, she added, "Much better."

Isabetta touched the gemstone with her fingertips. "What if I say or do something wrong?"

"Don't worry. Your only duty tonight is to look good and exude grace. Be demure. Speak only when spoken to and as little as possible. I will signal when it is time for you to smile sweetly, bid the gentlemen goodnight, and go home."

Malvina poked her head into the room several minutes later. "They're here."

Slowly, they descended the stairwell and entered the elegant marbled foyer where two ostentatiously dressed old men stood gawking.

Veronica kissed each man on the cheek. "Count Guglielmo, Signore Osvaldo, welcome! It's lovely to see you again. Thank you for accepting my invitation on such short notice." The men's eyes kept darting to Isabetta, prompting her to step aside. "May I introduce my new protégé? Venerada d'Oro will be joining us this evening. She is the natural daughter of a certain nobleman in Milan of great importance."

Isabetta shot Veronica a look of disbelief. *Natural child* was the terminology used to describe a noble bastard.

Osvaldo demanded, "Whose daughter?"

Veronica patted his arm. "You know how privacy is important in our line of work. We cannot reveal his name. Suffice it to say that she comes from one of the *finest* families."

Isabetta felt as vulnerable as a cornered hen being eyed by two hungry foxes. The men grinned lecherously and undressed her with their eyes before offering gallant bows.

"Are you hungry, my lords?" Veronica inquired,

"Famished," said Osvaldo with his eyes still on Isabetta.

"My cook prepared oysters and *branzino*, your favorite."

Guglielmo said irritably, "Ugh. I despise seafood."

Veronica gave him an indulgent look. "Which is why *you* will be served roasted pheasant with chestnut stuffing."

"How did you know that is my favorite dish?" Guglielmo demanded, instantly placated.

"I sent my servant to speak with your cook."

"Sneaky girl," he teased, lightly tapping Veronica's bottom as they entered the well-appointed dining room.

Everyone took their seats and the men were about to ply

Isabetta with questions when Veronica held up her hand. "My good lords, I beg your patience. I have instructed Venerada to remain silent tonight so that she may learn from me."

"Are we to only gaze upon her?" Osvaldo protested.

"Yes," Veronica replied matter-of-factly. "Drink her youthful beauty until you've had your fill, but remember that she is inexperienced and of a tender age. This is her first time in public, and I have chosen you two gentlemen to be the first men she meets during her training."

Osvaldo's gaze slid to Guglielmo and he muttered under his breath, "I'd like to be the first man."

The other man teetered at the sexual innuendo.

"You can be, my lord," Veronica said, pouncing upon the opportunity. "Venerada is as immaculate as Mary when she first received the message from the Angel Gabriel." The men stared at Isabetta with calculating expressions as she added, "She will be making her official public debut very soon. I'm counting on you both to help me spread the word throughout the city."

Once the men agreed, Veronica motioned to a servant who emerged from behind a screen to serve dinner. She took a few perfunctory nibbles in order to politely accompany her guests, who ate ravenously. Isabetta wanted to stuff herself with the delicious food but refrained from doing so. Instead, she copied everything the sophisticated courtesan did.

The men spoke and laughed loudly, whereas Veronica's mellow tone remained soothing and pleasant. They dictated the topics and she obliged them with intelligent conversation sprinkled with humor. Isabetta committed as much as she could to memory, making a mental note to practice when she returned home. Once the men had enjoyed their fill of food and wine, they began to make suggestive comments. Osvaldo took Veronica's hand and kissed it whereas Guglielmo stared at Isabetta.

Veronica stood and so did the male guests. "Alas, it is time for my friend to retire. We wish you a good evening, Venerada."

Isabetta inclined her head at Veronica, then offered the men the most sensational smile she could muster. "Thank you for a wonderful evening, my lords."

Isabetta's heart raced as she walked to the door under the male scrutiny. Peeking over her shoulder, she caught Veronica's encouraging wink.

***

A message arrived from the Vendramin household two days later demanding to know if Isabetta had taken ill. Under Alba's watchful eye, Isabetta penned a response.

Dear Cassandra,

Forgive me for not having written sooner. I have found employment as a lady's maid in my sestiere, and won't be returning to my post in Mestre. Thank you for everything.

Your cousin, Isabetta

Alba, who could read somewhat well, inquired, "Why thank her? That girl did nothing for you."

"I don't want my uncle or aunt delving into my business. Heaven forbid if they discover what I'm really doing."

"Sooner or later they'll find out you're working with Veronica Franco and draw the inevitable conclusion."

"I shall tell them that I'm serving as her lady's maid."

"I suppose that's believable."

As predicted, Rosa showed up at the Bastian house the following week. She gaped at her niece in shock and cried, "What on earth have you done to your hair?"

Employing her new manners and docile tone, Isabetta patted the neat coiffure created earlier by Alba and gave a little laugh. "An experiment. Lovely, isn't it?" Before her aunt could formulate an answer, she indicated a chair with a graceful flick of the wrist. "Won't you sit down, Aunt Rosa? Your visit is such a pleasant surprise. Alba, please make some tea."

Rosa's curious eyes roamed over Isabetta. "You look exceedingly well. I recognize that dress."

Isabetta spun in a circle. "You should."

"Ah, yes, that's one of the gowns my daughter gifted you. She is such a generous young woman."

"How is Cassandra?"

"She is the very reason why I'm here. Your cousin informed

me that you're working as a lady's maid. Who is your new employer?"

"Aunt Rosa, your concern for me is heartwarming."

Flustered by the unexpected compliment, Rosa pretended to smooth the wrinkles from her skirt. "Well, I owe it to my deceased sister to keep an eye on you."

"I work for Veronica Franco."

Alarmed, Rosa declared, "I knew it was a matter of time before you caved to her influence."

"Whatever do you mean?"

"Stop playing coy with me, girl. Red is the color of harlots," Rosa said, staring pointedly at her niece's hair.

"Really, Aunt Rosa, I thought you were above such nonsense. Veronica wanted to test a new hair dye and I readily volunteered. Plenty of respectable noble women apply henna or walnut shells to alter the shade of their locks."

Alba laid out the cups for tea, thus providing a much needed distraction.

Rosa sighed dramatically. "Cassandra was offended that you would abandon your post so abruptly."

"Oh? I'm sorry she feels that way. Veronica offered a *much* higher wage and she needed me immediately, so I couldn't let the opportunity pass."

"What about marriage? You will taint your reputation if you continue working for that whore."

"Silvio Torres has declared his sentiment and procured my mother's permission to write prior to his departure." Leaning forward, Isabetta dropped her voice and added, "I believe most men would prefer to wed a lady's maid to a scullery maid."

Rosa bristled. "You weren't a scullery maid." When her niece gaped incredulously, she amended, "We tried to help you and you repay us by working for a whore."

"With all due respect, have you ever scrubbed a floor on your hands and knees? Emptied the revolting contents of a slop bucket? Gutted a slimy fish? I would much prefer working for a famous courtesan than go back to that."

"You make it sound as if Cassandra mistreated you."

Isabetta eyed her aunt coolly and remained silent.

Miffed, Rosa continued, "My daughter opened her home and offered a dignified means of making a living. Yet you sit here implying that she has done you wrong."

"I'm not the one implying that, Aunt Rosa. *You are.*"

Alba set the steaming pot of tea on the table along with some stale biscuits.

Rosa stood. "I'm afraid I cannot stay for tea."

Opening the door for her aunt to leave, Isabetta said, "Pity. Send my regards to Uncle Alzo."

With their unwanted guest gone, the women relaxed.

Alba blew out a long breath, then sat down in Rosa's vacated seat. She poured out two cups of tea and pushed one across the table to her mistress. "Piece of work, that one."

Isabetta blew on the hot tea before indulging in a cautious sip. "Hopefully, Rosa and Cassandra will leave me alone. I can't risk either of them discovering what Veronica and I are planning. They would ruin everything."

***

"A bidding war is happening right now in Venice. I've already received impressive offers from three distinguished gentlemen," Veronica said excitedly while removing the lid from a porcelain rouge pot.

Isabetta blinked in surprise in the mirror's reflection. "A bidding war?"

The courtesan nodded, then gently dabbed a bit of rouge on her friend's cheek. "Osvaldo and Guglielmo must have sung your praises far and wide. Consider them your first admirers! We must organize the banquet at once."

Veronica was in the process of giving her protégée a lesson in cosmetic application and paused to reassess.

Isabetta's expression became somewhat troubled. "This is really happening…"

The courtesan held out the pot. "Yes, and it's too late to back out now. My reputation is at stake. Here, do the other cheek like I taught you."

Isabetta applied the creamy red substance to her skin and

blended it carefully in a circular motion. "I have no intention of doing so, but there *is* a stipulation…Cristofolo Trasontin must win the bid." Worry eclipsed the initial shock on Veronica's face, so she explained, "I've been pondering the matter for days. The thought of him inadvertently helping me regain the *Tramonto* brings me immense satisfaction."

"I see…"

Setting down the rouge pot, Isabetta admitted, "Do you know what would be even better? If I could make him fall in love with me—Venerada. Maybe even become his mistress."

"I thought you loved Silvio."

"I do…Silvio is in India and hasn't written to me in many weeks. Maybe his affection for me has waned. In the meantime, I can siphon much-needed money from Cristofolo."

"And break his heart when you're done?"

"Ideally, yes. If I could crush that man and make him suffer as much as he's made me suffer, I would be content."

Wandering away from the vanity, Veronica surmised, "A brilliant vendetta, indeed." She pretended to study something outside the window in order to hide her concerned face.

Isabetta rose from the chair and went over to where the courtesan stood. "Will you help me?"

"If that's what you truly want, I'll do everything within my power to make it happen."

Squaring her shoulders, Isabetta declared, "It's more than what I want, *it's what I need*."

"Very well." Going over to the desk, Veronica sat down and procured a clean sheet of parchment.

Isabetta followed her. "What are you doing?"

Dipping the quill into a pot of ink, the courtesan replied, "We're going to require the aid of a third person."

CHAPTER 14

Isabetta followed Veronica into a large salon, and froze. Elegantly painted doors on the opposite wall were thrown back to allow a glimpse of the rose marble fountain in the courtyard. Creamy flesh accentuated by rosy buttocks and flushed cheeks accosted her eyes when she studied the walls of the chamber. A wrap-around fresco depicted life-sized adults indulging in various forms of erotic acts, juxtaposed against an orchard with trees heavily laden with ripe fruit. Cupid dominated the ceiling as he hovered above the mortals with a love arrow clasped in his chubby fist. Her gaze dropped from the ceiling to a massive gilded desk. A gorgeous woman leaned her hip against the incredible piece of furniture and crossed her arms.

"Take your time," Loretta Mino purred to Isabetta, her luminous dark eyes twinkling with amusement.

Veronica took her colleague's hands into her own before kissing both cheeks. "Thank you for receiving us, Loretta."

"It's always a pleasure to see you, my dear. Your note said it was urgent."

Embarrassed at having been caught gawking, Isabetta lingered in the background to study the famous courtesan. Loretta's burgundy gown flaunted an extremely low neckline—so low that her nipples rested on top of the bodice's edge. A light coating of gold dust made them appear enticing against a flawless powdered white décolletage with veins delicately lined in blue. Blonde curls framed an oval face with dimples.

Motioning for Isabetta to come closer, Veronica said, "This is my protégé, Venerada d'Oro."

Loretta examined her young visitor with renewed interest, her sharp eyes taking in every detail. "So *this* is the girl Count Guglielmo has been taking about. How old are you?"

"Seventeen," Isabetta replied.

Veronica said, "The last three auctions you've hosted here

were highly successful. I'm hoping you can accommodate us."

A catlike smile stretched across Loretta's face. "Anything is possible for a fee."

Veronica leaned closer and dropped her voice. "In that case, I'll request a stipulation: Cristofolo Trasontin *must* win the bid. Naturally, I will pay extra for your assistance."

Surprised, Loretta's eyes darted to where Isabetta stood. "Before I agree to anything, I need to know why."

Having already invented a ruse, Veronica explained, "Venerada has admired the handsome bachelor from afar for years. The fact that he is obscenely wealthy and a devilish rake reveals her sharp sense of business, don't you think?"

"Impressive foresight. Cristofolo's conquest will no doubt inspire other men to taste the sweet fruit. A winning strategy. Very well. I'll help you because we've known each other a long time, but this conversation remains within these walls."

"That goes without saying, my friend."

"Venerada must never speak of this to anyone. I don't want to be accused of not playing by the rules."

Spearing Isabetta with a pointed look, Veronica said, "Trust me, she will not. You have my word."

"I will take that as a guarantee."

Veronica bade Loretta farewell before ushering Isabetta toward the door. The two of them walked for several minutes without speaking.

Isabetta finally said, "Thank you."

"I hope you know what you're doing," Veronica stated with eyes focused straight ahead.

"Why do you say that?"

"I am risking much to help you."

"I will repay you someday for your kindness, I promise."

The courtesan slowed her steps. "There's no need for that. It's a pleasure to be able to assist you. There are a few lessons I still have to teach you before the banquet, but today will be your last day of instruction. Have you been practicing?"

"Often."

Two men with shabby clothes and missing teeth leered at

them from inside a tavern. They hastened their pace and went straight up to Veronica's boudoir when they arrived at her palazzo. Malvina whispered something into her mistress's ear while handing her a note.

Veronica went over to her desk. "I need to reply to a message at once. Would you excuse me for a moment?"

Isabetta nodded in response. Several books were scattered atop a table so she went over to examine their titles. She picked up a journal with a posy of daffodils drawn meticulously upon the cover. "Did you draw this?"

Glancing up from the letter she was writing, Veronica admitted, "I'm afraid so. Not very good, is it?"

"I think it's charming."

"There are more sketches inside, along with a few verses I've been working on."

"You don't mind if I look?"

"Not at all."

Isabetta leafed through the book, then paused to admire the sketch of a fat lap dog with ribbons tied at the ears. Her eyes dropped to the bottom of the page where a few lines were scrawled in Veronica's neat penmanship.

"So sweet and delicious do I become, when I am in bed with a man who, I sense, loves and enjoys me, that the pleasure I bring excels all delight, so the knot of love, however tight it seemed before, is tied tighter still."

Blushing at the intimate nature of the words, she continued flipping through pages to another drawing of a bowl of fruit. Individual fruits followed—apple, pear, fig, then more text.

"We danced our youth in a dreamed of city, Venice, paradise, proud and pretty. We lived for love and lust and beauty. Pleasure then our only duty. Floating them twixt heaven and Earth and drunk on plenty's blessed mirth. We thought ourselves eternal then, our glory sealed by God's own pen. But paradise, we found is always frail, against man's fear will always fail. "

The poem struck Isabetta as deeply profound, for nothing remained forever in this world. No matter how wealthy, young, beautiful, healthy—we returned to dust in the end. Life, which at times seemed overwhelming, passed quickly. The sobering thought, although melancholy, served to stiffen her resolve to change her current situation for the better while she still had the strength, beauty, and resolve to do so.

Sketches of fanciful shoes filled the next three pages, then she came upon another poem.

"When we too are armed and trained, we can convince men that we have hands, feet, and a heart like yours; and although we may be delicate and soft, some men who are delicate are also strong; and others, coarse and harsh, are cowards. Women have not yet realized this, for if they should decide to do so, they would be able to fight you until death; and to prove that I speak the truth, amongst so many women, I will be the first to act, setting an example for them to follow."

Veronica summoned her maid to take the sealed letter and give it to a messenger.

When Malvina retreated, Isabetta pointed to the passage and said, "This is my favorite thus far."

The courtesan wandered over to where Isabetta stood and peered down at the words. "I read that aloud at a dinner party recently. One of the guests, an English earl, said the poem aptly described his queen."

"It is said that Queen Elizabeth is a formidable woman, but I think this poem describes you too."

Flattered, Veronica grinned. "Me?"

"I've always admired your independence and tenacity."

"That's sweet of you to say, thank you."

Changing the subject, Isabetta inquired, "Do you think Loretta will convince Cristofolo to bid on me?"

"Most likely, yes. Loretta's opinions are valued in high social circles. If she praises you, wealthy men will want you, including Cristofolo."

"Good."

"Keep in mind that he has bedded many beautiful women. Remember what I've told you: good looks will only get you so far. The superficial aspects of attracting a man is easy. Keeping him interested is the hard part. With a man like Cristofolo, you will need more than mere wit and humor. Let him know that you have an opinion of your own. Disagree with him on occasion. If you value yourself, he will value you too."

Isabetta wandered to the window and gazed upon the water. "Are you implying that I should argue with him?"

"Men have nagging wives and mothers to contend with at home, so you don't want to remind them of either one."

"How do I disagree without being disagreeable?"

"Be calm, composed, and accommodating *most* of the time. Challenge him in the same manner a man would; with conviction, logic, and reason. Never confront him with anger or pettiness or—worst of all—jealousy." Veronica took the journal from her friend's hands and set it down on a table. "There's a matter I wish to discuss with you."

"You sound serious."

Veronica led Isabetta to the bed and urged her to sit on the edge. "This *is* serious. Your naïveté makes you vulnerable so I feel compelled to act as the voice of experience on your behalf. Please know that I'm only trying to save you from heartache."

A sad smile touched Isabetta's lips. "You're a bit late."

Rubbing her friend's arm consolingly, Veronica offered, "I know, and I'm sorry you've suffered. I don't usually dole out unsolicited advice but I believe it is for your own good."

"I will always value your counsel," Isabetta assured while covering her friend's hand with her own.

"Then take my words to heart. One should have no trace of doubt when it comes to revenge. Deliberately wreaking havoc upon the lives of others is a terrible thing. If you later discover that you were mistaken, the damage is irreversible and you will be forced to live with the guilt. You must be sure, Isabetta."

***

"You're not eating your porridge," Alba observed while removing a kettle from the fire. "Is it not to your liking?"

Pushing the grayish mush with the edge of her spoon, Isabetta replied, "I'm not hungry."

"You'll need your strength for tonight."

Groaning in response to the arch comment, Isabetta stood. Her eyes picked out the dust motes floating in a ray of sunlight. The morning appeared clear and bright beyond the window panes. "I'm going out."

"Shall I go with you?"

Isabetta shook her head. "I need to be alone."

Alba fetched her mistress's cloak, then said, "You can always back out of this, Signorina."

"Too late," Isabetta countered before exiting the house.

Shivering in the icy air, she pulled the edges of her cloak together for extra warmth. Submerged in deep thought, she went directly to the small chapel around the corner and lit a candle for each of her deceased family members. Kneeling on the cold damp floor, she also prayed forgiveness for the sin she was about to commit. Could her parents be watching her from Heaven? If so, they must be disappointed at the level to which she had stooped. She was about to leave the sacred space, but then remembered Silvio. Only two viable reasons could explain his extended silence. Either he was suffering from illness in India or he was basking in the arms of another woman. Uttering a quick prayer to keep him safe, she hoped it wasn't the latter. Rising to her feet, she crossed herself and exited the chapel.

Despite the early hour, she went straight to Veronica's palazzo, as previously instructed.

The courtesan received her with an encouraging smile. "Are you ready for tonight?"

"I'm frightened."

"You *should* be scared, you're a virgin. Men will sense your fear and pay dearly to savor it in private. You will be presented to the gentlemen at six-o-clock and the bidding will start the moment you exit the room." To Malvina hovering in the background Veronica said, "Fetch my cloak, we need to go. Loretta is expecting us."

"Now? It's not yet noon. I didn't think we were going to Signora Loretta's house this early."

"There's much to do." Fastening the clasp of her cloak, Veronica studied Isabetta's face. "Have you been crying?"

Isabetta averted her gaze. "I've been praying."

"Forgiveness for the sin of fornication?" At Isabetta's reluctant nod, she continued, "Age and experience will lighten the burden of an unclean conscience due to immorality. Trust me on this. Let's make haste, shall we?"

Looking down at her simple dress, Isabetta protested, "Wait, what will I wear tonight? One of Cassandra's gowns?"

"Everything you need is already at Loretta's palazzo."

The women hastened toward their destination beneath a moody sky. Tumultuous clouds scuttled across the horizon, mirroring Isabetta's mood.

You can always back out of this, Signorina...

Alba's words earlier were still echoing throughout her head. Casting a sidelong glance at Veronica, she silently chastised herself. The time for vacillating had long ended and there was no way to go but forward.

Upon arrival, they were ushered inside by a discreet servant. Loretta appeared a moment later in a lovely dress of plum brocade. After greeting her guests in turn, she said, "My best chamber has been prepared. A special supper of aphrodisiacal foods and excellent wine will be sent up for Venerada and her gentleman companion to enjoy." Looking pointedly at Isabetta, she added, "Remember, your actions this evening will reflect upon the reputations of myself and Veronica. I implore you to act accordingly."

Solemn-faced, Isabetta nodded. "I will."

Loretta gave her a curt nod. "Do you have any questions?"

Isabetta bit her lip. "Will it hurt?"

Veronica and Loretta exchanged glances before the latter replied, "Belladonna will spare you the discomfort."

"Is there anything else I should know?"

Touching Isabetta's cheek, Loretta said, "Dear girl, the less you know the better where *that* is concerned. The reason men are willing to pay such a high price for a virgin is because they want to be the teachers. Otherwise, they would have scheduled an evening with myself or your mentor." Dropping her hand, she added, "Think of yourself as unexplored territory—like a field covered with newly fallen snow, pristine and untouched."

"Should I think of Signore Cristofolo as Marco Polo?"

The courtesans laughed in unison.

Loretta said, "Correct. Let's take some refreshment now. Afterward, we'll prepare Venerada."

The women retreated into a charming room decorated in shades of green with a round table set for three. There, they enjoyed a light meal of fish and vegetables with diluted white wine. When they had finished, Loretta led the way upstairs where two servants awaited within a spectacular bedchamber hung with plush velvets and silks. The room shimmered with gold and various shades of vermillion. A chandelier highlighted the center of a gilded coffered ceiling, and suggestive paintings in ornate frames lined the walls. Mirrors were strategically placed above and beyond the bed for amorous couples to watch themselves while performing carnal acts.

"Venerada, you are blushing!" Loretta observed.

The servants giggled in turn as they helped Isabetta undress. Using dry linen cloths, they rubbed her naked body vigorously to slough off the dead skin to make it soft. Isabetta caught a glimpse of her sore red body in one of the many full-length mirrors. A sheet was placed atop a long narrow table and she was made to recline on it. Both servants lathered their hands with scented oil and proceeded to massage every inch of exposed skin.

Isabetta sighed deeply, enjoying the feel of their strong hands as they kneaded her tense muscles.

Veronica approached the table. "Feels divine, doesn't it?"

"Mmm, yes," Isabetta whispered with her eyes closed. "This is what the Queen of Sheba must have felt like before being brought before King Solomon."

"You know your Bible stories."

"A few."

Veronica retreated with a smile. The servants continued kneading Isabetta's firm flesh for several minutes before making her flip over to repeat the process on her back.

Would sex feel this good?

Isabetta flinched at the unbidden thought. How could she entertain the possibility of pleasure with a man whom she despised? One of the servants began rubbing her shoulders, which made her eyes heavy. The edges of the world soon melted to black under their relaxing ministrations.

"Venerada."

Wiping the drool that had pooled on her lower lip, Isabetta opened her eyes. Had she fallen asleep? She sat up groggily.

Loretta stood in the center of the room holding a simple ivory gown patterned with a hint of silver thread. "Time to get dressed. How do you feel?"

"I feel wonderful."

The servants washed the excess oil from her body with perfumed water before drying the glowing skin with a clean towel. Next came the dress, which fit like a glove. A low neckline made her breasts appear full and ripe without exposing too much.

Isabetta studied her reflection in the mirror. "I almost look like a bride."

Veronica said, "That's the whole point."

Loretta added, *"Virgo intacta."*

Red locks were combed and piled into a mass of curls with a few tendrils to caress the nape of Isabetta's soft neck. Perfume was applied to her throat, earlobes, and cleavage. Cosmetics were used sparingly to provide a pretty flush to cheeks and lips. Finished with their duties, the servants exited the room with quiet efficiency. Loretta and Veronica remained to evaluate the finished product.

"I am lacking jewels," Isabetta commented.

"You must look innocent and pure at your presentation, thus the simple style of the gown and lack of adornment. It is customary for the gentleman to offer a token after he deflowers you—an *expensive* token. Think of yourself as a fresh canvas ready to receive whatever gift he bestows," Veronica explained.

"A simple strand of pearls is the most common gift for virgins, which will be yours to keep," Loretta added as she pressed a tiny glass vial of murky liquid into Isabetta's hand.

"Here, this is a precaution against pregnancy. You must drink it after he falls asleep."

Veronica opened the door of the bedchamber. "It is time."

Isabetta glanced at the twilight sky outside the bedroom window. Streaks of violet and gray adorned a deep orange sky with glittering stars. She spied the planet Venus high above, shining like a flawless diamond.

Venus, goddess of love.

The trio descended the stairs and turned onto a long corridor with a door at the end of it. Loretta placed her hand on the latch and pushed. Male voices and laughter ceased when she breezed into the room and dazzled the men with her smile.

Veronica followed suit, leading Isabetta by the hand. "Good evening, gentlemen. It is my pleasure to present my protégé, Venerada d'Oro." She paused to allow the men to visually drink their fill of the virgin. "As you can clearly see, she is both beautiful and graceful. I've enjoyed many conversations with Signorina Venerada and can attest to her wit and cleverness. A fine companion for anyone desirous of a delightful evening."

Isabetta offered the men a deep curtsy. The searing heat of male stares on her throat, hands, and lips made her feel self-conscious. Some even whispered naughty things to one another. Despite her best efforts to stay calm, she trembled beneath their collective scrutiny. This seemed to please them.

"Dolce vergine."

"Bellissima."

"Signora Veronica, a word..."

Men crowded around Veronica and Loretta, some whispering in their ears while others discreetly handed them slips of folded parchment containing huge sums.

Scanning the room through lowered lashes, Isabetta spotted Cristofolo leaning against the wall with his arms crossed. Stone-faced and silent, he pinned her with a steely stare that caused her face to burn. Rather than look away, she held his gaze like a stunned deer trapped by a hunter. Something in his eyes shifted, darkened. Struck by panic, she prayed to God that he didn't recognize her.

"Does she speak?"

The question came from an elderly gentleman wearing a sapphire blue cape trimmed with mink. Grateful for the much-needed distraction, Isabetta said shyly, "Yes sir, I can speak."

His eyes lit up. "Can you sing, my lovely?"

"If it pleases you."

Loretta placed an arm around Isabetta. "Venerada can be a songbird for one of you lucky gentlemen. Right now, she must bid you goodnight."

Isabetta curtsied low again, eyes demurely focused on the floor before flickering a glance at Cristofolo one last time. He continued to stare at her with the same neutral expression on his chiseled face.

Veronica put her lips to Isabetta's ear. "Loretta will take you upstairs now. I am going home after the men have placed a final bid. Come to my house tomorrow morning. Good luck."

Once they were inside the lavish bedchamber, Loretta noticed Isabetta's unsteady hands. "Are you nervous?"

"I am."

"Good." The courtesan went to the vanity, uncorked a dark brown bottle and handed it to Isabetta. "Belladonna. You need to put it *inside*. I'll hold up your skirt."

"What does it do?"

"You'll find out soon enough."

Isabetta coated her finger with the plant extract and then inserted it into her most private part. A tingling sensation radiated throughout the delicate skin. It would numb the pain.

Loretta replaced the bottle on the vanity. "Cristofolo will be here soon. I bid you a pleasant evening, Venerada."

"Thank you for everything, Signora Loretta."

"No, thank *you*. These events fill my pockets," the courtesan said with a wink. Crossing the room, she came to a stop at the door. "A word of advice…it's obvious by the way you stared at him downstairs that you are in love. Cristofolo's appetite for women is insatiable, but he isn't the type of man to offer his heart. If you want to be successful in this business, you should mimic his strategy."

Isabetta watched Loretta leave with a pang of regret. Overwhelmed by fear and helplessness, her whole body shook. The bravado and confidence she had expressed to Veronica about seeking revenge suddenly dissipated. In the light of her current reality those words seemed foolish. Childish. Did she really think she could go through with this? How could she possibly allow Cristofolo Trasontin near her, let alone grant him access to her body as if he were a bridegroom? What had she been thinking?

This is madness.

Heavy male footsteps on the stairs made her freeze in terror. The sound grew louder, which meant that he was drawing closer. Thump, thump, thump…

Panicked, Isabetta's eyes darted around the room. There was nowhere to hide! Her gaze settled on the window and she ran toward it with determined steps.

CHAPTER 15

Cristofolo barged into the room without a perfunctory knock. Isabetta stiffened while keeping her back to him. She heard the door close, then the soft click of the key being turned inside the lock. Tearing her gaze from the comforting scene outside the window, she slowly spun around to face him.

You can do this, Isabetta. Remember what Veronica taught you. Think of him as a challenge; a puzzle to solve.

The wolf closed in, his cunning eyes summing up the lamb he was about to slaughter. She took in her enemy's face and the fine quality of his clothing with begrudging approval. The man was undoubtedly attractive and exuded confidence. Also, he smelled like fresh lemons wrapped in leather. Thankfully, there was no hint of recognition in his eyes as he brought her knuckles to his lips.

"*Buona sera*, Venerada. A fitting name, given that you'll be venerated by me tonight."

Voice as smooth as plush velvet. Charming too. "May I offer you some wine, sir?"

Tossing his cloak over a chair, he replied, "Please."

Despite her shaky hands, she managed to pour wine into two chalices without spilling a drop.

He touched the rim of his vessel to her own. "To us."

Isabetta took a sip. "Is the wine to your liking, sir?"

His eyes swept over her body. "*Everything* is to my liking. Let us do away with formality, shall we? I prefer that you call me Cristofolo."

"Cristofolo," she repeated softly.

His hand reached out to play with one of the loose tendrils of her hair, then dropped to caress her neck. "There is much talk about you in the city. Is it true that you were born in Milan?"

"Yes."

"A noble bastard."

Lowering her eyes, she nodded.

"I know many people in Milan. Who is your father?"

"I have been instructed never to reveal his name."

"I see," he murmured, his finger tracing a course from her clavicle to the shadowy cleft between her breasts. "You look like a princess."

"Thank you," she said, trying to suppress a shudder.

"Are you cold?"

She met his gaze. "Only anxious, sir."

Cocking an eyebrow, he laughed suggestively. "Have you ever been kissed, Venerada?"

"Only once, by a boy…it was a chaste kiss."

Cristofolo grinned slyly before leaning in and claiming Isabetta's mouth in a hard, demanding kiss. His lips felt dry and hot against her own, which were surely bruising under the vicious onslaught. An exploratory tongue invaded her mouth and she resisted the urge to recoil.

Pulling away, he regarded her through hooded lids, his eyes dilated with excitement. "*That* was a man's kiss." He kissed her jaw, then said, "I'll have you now."

Surprised, she faltered.

A corner of his mouth lifted upward at her discomfiture. "Were you expecting pleasantries and idle chatter, my girl? Do you take me for some young foppish courtier?"

"N-no sir."

Cristofolo drained the chalice, then began unbuttoning the front of his doublet. Isabetta set down her drink and took over the task with inexperienced fingers. Pleased by her bold initiative, he covered her hands with his own. "Like this…"

He removed his boots and breeches, leaving only his long linen shirt. Thankfully, it covered his nakedness.

"Your turn," he urged devilishly.

Faltering, Isabetta only stared at him. Without a word, he began to untie the laces of her bodice. Pushing the fabric off her shoulders, his eyes caressed her flawless décolletage before roughly devouring her throat with his mouth.

"Your skin is so sweet," he muttered before licking her neck and causing her to shiver from head to toe.

Cristofolo's hands groped her breasts and his lips moved from her neck to her nipple. A moan escaped her lips when he began suckling each one in turn. Growling, he continued to remove her garments with deft speed. The animalistic sound intimidated Isabetta, who couldn't stop her body from betraying her mind. When she stood naked, he stepped back to admire her body. She watched in awe as the hem of his shirt billowed forward to accommodate his growing member.

"Do you like what you see, Venerada?" he asked before removing his shirt and fully exposing himself. He laughed heartily at her shocked expression. "You look as frightened as the doe I hunted a few weeks ago. I pierced her heart with an arrow."

She took an involuntary step backward, for his words were laced with sadistic pleasure. Whatever was about to take place, and wherever he intended to insert that horrid thing, she knew it would be painful. He laughed again, relishing her fearful expression.

Challenge him in the same manner that a man would, with conviction, logic, reason...

Her chin tilted defiantly. "If you're trying to scare me, it's not working. I am not afraid of you."

"A brave virgin, how delightful. What other surprises do you have in store for me tonight?"

"Do you like frightening women before bedding them?"

Shards of ice glinted within the depths of his blue eyes. "What if I said yes?"

Knots formed in her belly. "Then I say do your worst."

Circling her like a giant cat, he mocked, "Such valiance from one so young."

"A weary spirit lurks within this body, Cristofolo."

Closing the gap between them, he stared down into her face. Isabetta couldn't resist drowning in the azure pools, and what she found there made her shiver.

Smiling cruelly, his hand circled her slender throat. "Still feeling brave?"

She licked her lips slowly. *"It is not death that a man should fear, but he should fear never beginning to live."*

Fondling her breast, he said, "Marcus Aurelius…I doubt you lack fear of death."

"Being dead inside is far more terrifying," she replied breathlessly, her nipple pebbling at his touch.

"Why?"

Rather than respond, she averted her eyes.

"You've suffered, child. I can see that," he said, his other hand cupping her face almost roughly.

She managed to surprise him by nuzzling her cheek against his palm. "Can you make the pain go away?"

Staring at her intently, he said hoarsely, "You're asking the wrong person."

"I beg to differ."

Eyes narrowed, he demanded, "Do I know you?"

Panic, thick and bitter, caused her mouth to go completely dry. "No…but I know you."

Suspicion coated his stare. "Who are you?"

"Just a girl who admires you from afar."

"Just a girl, eh?" He gently stroked her most intimate part and her knees almost buckled. "Oh how ready you are for me."

"Cristofolo…*please stop*."

At that, he chuckled and leaned in to nip her ear. "*Stop?* Why should I stop when your body is begging for mine? Besides, I paid a fortune for you."

Isabetta heard his breath hitch in his throat before being swept up in his arms and carried to the bed. He then devoured every inch of her body with his mouth and bejeweled hands before kneeling between her legs.

"Don't hurt me," she whispered.

Rather than reply, he chuckled. To her surprise, he began slowly, his eyes almost kind as they gazed into her own. Once he had claimed her maidenhead, however, he behaved selfishly. She endured the discomfort as he took his satisfaction. True to Loretta's words, the belladonna had numbed the pain.

Hearing her sigh in relief at the act's conclusion, he said,

"You are worth every cent but we are far from done, my darling. I'm famished. Summon our supper. We shall eat and continue our love play afterward."

Cristofolo got up and strode to the opposite side of the room to remove something from the pocket of his cloak.

Isabetta marveled at his lack of self-consciousness. Would she ever be able to strut across a room devoid of clothing and act as cavalier as he?

Holding up a string of pearls, he retraced his steps to the bed. "A gift for you."

Cassandra's bridal pearls came to mind. Like her cousin, she had paid the price for expensive jewels.

"How lovely," she said as he fastened the necklace around her neck. "Thank you."

***

Isabetta woke up the next morning feeling sore and bruised. A stream of milky sunshine revealed Cristofolo's sleeping face in profile. He had availed himself of her body several times before finally falling asleep at dawn. That he could perform in such a vigorous manner at his age was nothing short of astonishing. The illicit acts they had committed were seared into her memory forever.

Dear Lord...

How could she ever face Silvio?

Two servants crept into the room. Standing at the foot of the bed, they motioned for Isabetta to get up and follow them. She moved cautiously so as not to awaken Cristofolo. Crumpled sheets bore the blood of her virginity mingled with stains of spilled wine. Would he relish such a sight? Probably.

One of the servants covered Isabetta's nakedness with a silk robe, then gingerly plucked a rose from a flower arrangement in a nearby vase. Tiptoeing to the bed, she placed the flower on the empty pillow beside Cristofolo's head. The other servant lifted the tray containing the remnants of last night's supper and went to the door. They ushered Isabetta into an adjoining room containing simple furnishings. There, they helped her wash the traces of *man* from her body.

Loretta eventually appeared holding a small ceramic pot. "*Buongiorno* Venerada. I assume it went well last night?"

"Signore Cristofolo seemed pleased."

"Excellent. Did you take the contents of the vial?"

"After he fell asleep, as you instructed."

Loretta lifted the lid of what appeared to be congealed oil. "A salve to ease the swelling and prevent bruising. Apply it liberally during the next few days." The courtesan's eyes went to Isabetta's throat. "Judging by the size and color of those pearls, I'm certain he'll want to see you again."

"I hope you're right."

"Veronica is expecting you so I'll bid you farewell."

After Loretta had gone, Isabetta dressed in the gown she had arrived in yesterday. She stepped out into the hazy light of a crisp morning feeling different…*corrupted.* Burdened with the weight of carnal knowledge, her steps were sluggish and uncertain. Cristofolo's desire had overwhelmed her, and she felt sore in unimaginable places. Pulling the hood of her cloak low over her eyes, she went straight to Veronica's home.

The courtesan greeted her protégé, then handed her a leather coin purse. "I've already deducted Loretta's fee and my own."

Marveling at the substantial weight of coins, Isabetta smiled.

Going over to a nearby table, she grasped a crystal decanter of red wine. "How was your first encounter with Cristofolo?"

"I'm not certain since I have no reference."

"Was he charming and polite, at least?"

"I suppose so."

"Did he hurt you?"

"Not really. He was even tender at times."

"That's surprising since he's not the sentimental type." Veronica poured a bit of wine into two glasses and held out one to her friend. "There's something you should know…Cristofolo Trasontin was the highest bidder last night."

Isabetta blinked in disbelief. "You're joking."

"So intent was he on claiming you for himself that he took me aside and promised to double the amount of anyone who dared to outbid him."

Panicked, Isabetta began reliving the events of last night. "He demanded to know who I was, so I told him I'm only an admirer…do you think he suspects?"

"I doubt it, but even if he does there's no legal obligation for you to return the money you've earned." Pausing to adjust one of the gold rings on her finger, Veronica prompted, "Describe his comportment."

"Polite, passionate—he gave me these pearls."

Veronica examined the jewels with a keen eye. "A fine gift from a man smitten with Venerada d'Oro. If it makes you feel better, I didn't detect any suspicion on his part."

"This makes no sense. Why would he want me?"

Pointing across the room, the courtesan replied, "Stand in front of that mirror. You'll see a pretty girl with intelligent eyes, pure as freshly fallen snow."

Averting her gaze, Isabetta murmured, "Not anymore."

"Well, your mind and spirit are still pure. Cristofolo boasts about never having married, but I'm willing to wager he craves love like any other man. As for his aloofness…those who display callousness are oftentimes the most vulnerable inside. He'll be contacting me in order to see Venerada again."

"I hope you're right."

Veronica smiled. "It seems your plan to have him fall in love with you is off to a promising start." Wandering to the desk, she picked up a small book. "How would you like to make some more money in the meantime?"

Although she cringed inwardly, Isabetta did her best not to let it show. "Selling my virginity to one man for one night was something I did out of necessity."

"You won't have to engage in any physical intimacy." Placing the book back on the desk, the courtesan touched her pregnant belly. "Given my current condition and lack of work, I could schedule appointments for you, and keep a small percentage for my services as your mentor."

"What exactly is required of me?"

Veronica's grin was catlike. "Signore Rinaldo Alberti needs an escort for a banquet next Friday. The man hosting the formal affair is a powerful aristocrat, so Venice's most important people will be there—including the doge. Cristofolo will also be present. I think it's a wonderful opportunity for you to make him jealous. If you want money to start pouring in, he must make you his official mistress." Veronica pulled aside a curtain to purvey the scene outside. Her eyes tracked four men in a gondola as she continued, "You'll be required to spend the night in Signore Rinaldo's palazzo after the party, but he won't lay a finger on you. In the morning, you must make a big production of leaving his home. Make sure many people see you as you pretend not to be seen."

Isabetta's face twisted quizzically. "Why the charade?"

"Rinaldo's parents are extremely religious. It would kill them to know that their only son is a sodomite with a voracious appetite for male youths. There are other men like him who hire courtesans to improve their image in society while masking their true nature. I could arrange for you to be their escorts as the need arises. It won't be steady work, but it will provide some extra money."

Silvio's face shimmered into focus in Isabetta's mind. A pang of guilt accompanied the image. He would never approve of her working as a courtesan, even if it meant entertaining sodomites. "I'll do it."

Veronica refilled their cups with wine. "Wonderful. I want you to accompany me to dinner at an old friend's house this evening. Cristofolo will be there, and it will be good for him to see you immediately after last night. I intend to parade you before him in the days leading to the banquet next Friday. We have less than two weeks to make him long for your exclusive company, so you must do *exactly* as I say."

Isabetta finished her wine, then went home feeling hopeful and inebriated.

Alba eyed her mistress with relief as she entered the door. "I barely slept last night from worry."

A hard thump was accompanied by a merry jingle when Isabetta tossed the purse on the table.

Wide-eyed, the servant said, "Virginity is expensive."

"Do you want to know a secret?" The words had come out slurred and Isabetta giggled.

Taking a step closer, Alba sniffed the air. "Signorina, are you drunk? It's not yet noon."

"Do you want to know the secret or not?" At the servant's wary nod, she continued, "That's Cristofolo's money."

Alba's face paled. "Are you saying that *he* is the man with whom you spent the night?"

Isabetta nodded triumphantly. "And I planned it that way." At Alba's horrified expression, she added, "I'm going to make him pay dearly for what he's done to me and my family."

The servant was about to say something, then stopped.

Isabetta continued, "I know what you must be thinking. Don't worry. I know what I'm doing."

Milling about the kitchen to appear busy, Alba muttered under her breath, "You're a grown woman. Far be it from me to tell you what to do. I'll make you some tea and porridge."

"I'm not hungry. I'm going upstairs to take off this gown."

The servant wiped her hands on a dish rag and moved to follow her mistress. "I'll help you."

"No!" The last thing Isabetta wanted was for Alba to see her body ridden with Cristofolo's love bites and bruises. In a softer tone, she added, "I can manage alone. I must meet Veronica this evening. Wake me up at six."

Alba receded into the kitchen, her face etched with concern. "As you wish."

CHAPTER 16

Dressing her mistress's hair as Malvina had taught her, Alba inquired, "Will you be out all night, Signorina?"

"I don't know. No need to wait up for me."

Isabetta left the house in a plain black cloak for warmth and Veronica let her borrow a fur-lined cape. Together, they made their way to a noble home.

"Did I mention this is a literary group?" Veronica commented as they entered the cozy salon together. "I belong to several of them in the city."

"Will I be required to read anything?" Isabetta inquired while admiring the shelves of books on the opposite wall.

"No. Stay close to me, speak little, and listen much."

A life-sized portrait of a man in a suit of armor dominated the room. Beside the massive frame stood a group of gentlemen holding sheets of parchment. One of them was Cristofolo, who happened to glance up and catch Veronica's eye.

Pretending to remove a bit of lint from her protégé's cloak, Veronica whispered, "Cristofolo has spotted us and is now coming our way. Be polite but brief."

"Good evening ladies," he said with a gallant bow.

Aware of his burning gaze, Isabetta kept her eyes downcast as they exchanged formal pleasantries. It seemed odd to her that they would speak thusly after having been so intimate.

Turning to Veronica, Cristofolo inquired, "May I ask you something?"

"Certainly."

"Is it true you were the neighbor of Zanetto Bastian, the man who was brutally murdered along with his son?"

Hearing this, Isabetta nearly swooned.

Veronica's eyes flickered briefly to her friend's white face. "Yes…Everyone in our *sestiere* was shocked."

"Indeed. Did you know the family?"

Perspiration broke out on Isabetta's forehead.

"Not very well. Why do you ask?"

"I'm trying to gather information on a certain Beto Bastian. Did you ever meet him?"

Isabetta stared so intently at Cristofolo that Veronica shifted slightly to hide her from his view. "No."

He scratched his head, bemused. "Funny."

"What's funny?" Isabetta interjected.

Deep blue eyes narrowed as he swiveled his head in Isabetta's direction. "Do you know Beto?" When she shook her head nervously, he explained, "The man is a mystery. One person told me he is Zanetto's second son, another person said he is Zanetto's nephew, and a third assured me that there is no Beto. I don't know who to believe."

Tucking her hand into the crook of his elbow, Veronica led him away from Isabetta. "I'm afraid I can't help you, Signore Cristofolo." She added cheerfully, "Oh look, there's Rosalina! I've been wanting to introduce her to Venerada. Would you please excuse us?"

Cristofolo stepped aside, his eyes tracking Isabetta as they retreated to the other side of the room.

The courtesan tugged her rattled friend toward her voluptuous colleague who revealed large white teeth when she smiled. Introductions were made, and the trio chatted of mundane things while Isabetta gathered her wits.

A moment later, Veronica guided Isabetta toward a pair of cushioned chairs. "Compose yourself, please."

A pair of gentlemen paused to greet Veronica and she introduced Venerada. Isabetta played her role convincingly but her head spun with jumbled thoughts. She had stood beside Miro on the galley when he had lied to Cristofolo about Beto being Zanetto's nephew, but who were the other two people? More importantly, why was Cristofolo trying to gather information on Beto Bastian?

The assembled group began taking turns reading passages of prose, and Veronica was invited to read one of her own poems. Isabetta forced herself to pay attention. Since her mentor had instructed her to ignore Cristofolo, she never allowed her gaze to drift in his direction. He, on the other hand, eyed her like a hawk stalking a rabbit in the field.

Curious to meet the new Milanese courtesan everyone had been talking about recently, several men tried to engage Isabetta in conversation during the buffet dinner afterward. Charming and polite, she said little and never left Veronica's side. One man brought her a chalice of wine in the hope of currying her favor, but she tactfully declined. Another offered to accompany her onto the balcony for some air and she invented a pretense in order to refuse him.

Veronica whispered, "See? The more you reject them, the more they will swarm around you like bees to honey. Cristofolo has been watching you all evening. Did you ignore him?"

"Yes."

"Good. Be sure to grant him only one look before you go."

Isabetta went to the door and looked over her shoulder at Cristofolo. Their eyes met for the span of a heartbeat and the corners of his lips twitched slightly.

***

Viaro bared his crooked teeth in a wide grin when he saw Isabetta approaching his stall. "*Buongiorno*! It's been a while since I've seen your pretty face at the market. How are you?"

"I'm doing very well, thank you."

"I can see that. Your radiant beauty competes with the sun this fine morning."

Blushing from his extravagant compliment, she nodded and then asked, "Is Miro here today?"

"He is on a fishing barge and won't return for another week. I can relay a message, if you'd like." Chuckling jovially, he added, "My son is still unmarried you know…"

Accustomed to his teasing, she smiled. "The women of Venice must be blind to pass up such a fine opportunity." Eager to change the subject, she said, "Those mackerels are calling to me. I'll take two and…oh, some of these mussels." As Viaro placed the seafood in her basket, she added, "I want to thank you for all those extra fish heads."

"It was nothing," he said with a dismissive wave of his hand.

She placed several coins into his palm. "It was *everything*."

Viaro gaped at the amount of money. "I can't take this…It's far more than what those fish heads were worth."

Backing away from the stall, she smiled. "I know."

"I'll tell Miro to call on you when he returns," he cried to her retreating form.

In the days leading up to the banquet, Veronica insisted that her protégé accompany her to various social events. Isabetta's favorite topics sparked the interest of several influential men, for she knew about trade, luxury goods, geography, navigation, and astronomy. Cristofolo often lingered nearby within earshot whenever she spoke to other gentlemen. Although he pretended to be disinterested, she knew he listened to her every word.

Veronica guarded her protégé possessively, never allowing anyone to get close. When men tried to woo Isabetta, the savvy courtesan would explain that she was 'already reserved for the evening' or 'still in training,' which were blatant lies. Men, who were prone to desiring what they could not have, pursued Isabetta with ardent devotion.

On the rare occasions Isabetta spoke with Cristofolo, she balanced aloofness with charm and resisted his advances. This confused him, for she had already confessed to being his admirer. Veronica implemented these strategies in the hope that the nobleman would eventually become mad with desire for her young friend.

A full moon graced the sky on the Friday when the banquet was set to take place. Isabetta presented herself at Veronica's house in a brocade gown flaunting intricate gold embroidery. It was the loveliest of the three gowns her cousin had given her.

"You look splendid," Veronica exclaimed, turning Isabetta slightly to examine the back of her head. "Alba did a fine job of dressing your hair too. I see you're wearing the pearls Cristofolo gifted you. Excellent."

"I'm happy you approve." Admiring Veronica's diaphanous blue silk gown, she added, "You look gorgeous."

"It arrived today. A gift from someone special. Come, we

must hurry because Loretta is expecting us. We will travel to the banquet together since our host expects a grand entrance."

"How exciting."

"This is one of those times when it's fun to be a courtesan."

They made their way to the nearest dock and a gondolier came over speedily while wearing a toothy smile. Once they had settled into the vessel, he pushed off from the quay.

Veronica said softly, "You'll draw the eyes of many, I'm sure. Don't stray from Rinaldo unless he is occupied in conversation and desires privacy. Be charming and pleasant to everyone, including other courtesans, but don't flirt with any man except the one who has paid for your company."

Putting her lips to Veronica's ear, Isabetta said, "What about Cristofolo? Should I continue to ignore him?"

"Deprive a man for too long and he'll lose interest. We've teased him enough. Tonight you may give him encouragement but be discreet."

Two gentlemen in a nearby gondola called out to them in greeting. Veronica smiled and nudged Isabetta to do the same. Dazzled by their beauty, they plied the women with outrageous compliments.

Loretta spied them from the window and came outside an instant later. Isabetta gaped at the woman, for she looked like a goddess in a gown of silver and gold. Once she had taken her seat, the gondolier steered the gondola to a glittering white marble palazzo on the Grand Canal.

Isabetta pondered her life while the two courtesans whispered to each other. Months had passed since she rode in a gondola with her family on the night of Cassandra's wedding. She remembered the mysterious masked couple in the other vessel gliding past them in the night. She had wondered what kind of exciting evening awaited them. Now, here she was going to a grand banquet presided by none other than the doge himself! Scanning the candlelit vessels around her and the palazzos beyond, she felt as if she were in a dream.

"Is Venerada excited?"

Isabetta turned to Loretta, who had asked the question.

"Nervous would be a better description."

Patting her protégé's hand, Veronica said, "There's nothing to be afraid of, my dear. You've been doing so well since the night of the auction."

Loretta added, "Every gentleman I've entertained this week has mentioned your name. You have a long list of admirers."

"Has Cristofolo been bragging about his conquest?" Veronica inquired, amused.

Loretta shook her head slowly. "On the contrary. He's been unusually quiet, leaving several men perplexed."

Veronica's face expressed surprise.

Isabetta wasn't sure how to interpret this tidbit of information. Roiling emotions were temporarily set aside as they neared the palazzo's private dock. Music floated on the breeze and a spattering of men stood on the balcony eagerly watching their approach. One wore the clerical robes of a bishop. The nobleman beside him threw roses at the trio of beautiful women as they alighted the gondola and ascended the steps to the front entrance. Some of the men broke out in light applause.

To Isabetta's astonishment, the bishop took Loretta's hand and kissed her lips with obvious familiarity. She discreetly waved goodbye to her female companions and allowed herself to be led toward a group of noble guests.

A burly, rosy-cheeked gentleman with a cheerful face and curled black mustachios bent over Veronica's hand. "You get lovelier each time I see you."

Veronica stroked his cheek affectionately. "You are kind, my lord." She gestured to Isabetta. "Rinaldo Alberti, I present Venerada d'Oro."

Isabetta offered him a graceful curtsy. "My lord."

Rinaldo brought her knuckles to his lips. "Another lovely flower has been added to our garden in Venice."

He led Isabetta toward a stairwell, but not before she caught sight of a handsome nobleman taking Veronica's hand and leading her away. Could he be the father of the child growing in the courtesan's womb?

"I've heard much about you, Signorina Venerada."

"Favorable things, I hope."

"A protégé of Veronica Franco is destined to be the topic of conversation in every Venetian salon. Has she shared her poetry with you?"

"She has, and I find it moving."

"Already showing your good taste. Come along, let's join the others. I hope you're hungry," he said as they headed toward a sweeping marble staircase.

Upstairs, a sumptuous feast was underway. Seated at the head of the long table was the guest of honor, the doge, Alvise Mocenigo. Musicians played in the corner of a richly decorated dining room boasting an enormous red chandelier. Rinaldo pulled out one of the upholstered chairs for Isabetta, then claimed the seat beside her. A silver bowl brimmed with luscious fruit and she plucked a grape. Smiling, she placed it to his lips and he took the juicy orb between his teeth. Raucous stories circulated and boisterous laughter exploded.

Loretta and the bishop sat nearest to their noble host—an elderly gentleman wearing rubies and diamonds on his gnarled fingers. Flanked by two pretty courtesans, the old man seemed to be enjoying himself.

"Can you sing?" Rinaldo inquired.

Isabetta winced as she selected another perfect grape. "No."

"Play the lute?" When she shook her head, he frowned in bemusement. "Surely, you can recite poetry."

Isabetta had already memorized a special poem for this event. "*That* request I can accommodate. I beg your patience, sir. This is my first banquet."

"Don't fret." Leaning over, he put his lips to her ear. "I'm sure Veronica explained the situation."

She popped another grape into his mouth and nodded.

Rinaldo smiled as he chewed, then swallowed. Snapping his fingers, he said, "Lords, ladies, your attention, please. My lovely companion, Venerada d'Oro, is the newest addition to our collection of Venetian beauties. I have asked her to recite a bit of poetry, if it pleases you."

The guests responded with an encouraging round of applause. Isabetta took a steadying breath and stood. Veronica, who lingered in the doorway beyond with her companion, gave a nod of approval. Cristofolo, arriving fashionably late, discreetly entered the room and claimed a vacant seat across from Rinaldo.

Angling her body away from his view and toward the host, Isabetta cleared her throat. *"Love is fire that burns without being seen. It is a wound that hurts and does not feel. It is discontented contentment. It is pain that unravels without hurting. It is not wanting more than wanting well. It is a lonely walk among people. It is never content to be content. It is a care that you gain in losing yourself. It is wanting to be bound by will. It is to serve those who win, the winner; have someone kill us, loyalty. But how can cause your favor, in human hearts friendship, if so contrary to itself is the same love?"*

Cristofolo stared intently at Isabetta as she reclaimed her seat with downcast eyes.

The doge lifted his chalice. "Well done, Signorina. I am fond of Luís de Camões. Why did you select a Portuguese poet instead of an Italian one?"

"I wanted to be original." In truth, she knew the doge loved a certain spiced sweet wine made by a group of Portuguese monks in a monastery outside of Lisbon. The delicious elixir was not only costly but rare.

Alvise grinned. "You've succeeded in your goal. A toast to Venerada d'Oro and her continued success."

Rinaldo leaned over to her and said, "Praise from the doge's lips on your first banquet. You deserve a prize."

He selected a fig from the silver bowl and placed it to her mouth. Rather than eat only the tasty morsel, she deliberately encompassed the tip of his finger with her mouth and gently bit down on it. This caused a stir among the men, who couldn't tear their eyes away from the fresh young courtesan.

Rinaldo placed his moistened finger on her bottom lip. "Aren't you the little vixen?"

"I enjoyed your poem immensely."

Isabetta feigned surprised as she looked across the table. "Signore Cristofolo. It's a pleasure to see you."

"The pleasure is mine, I assure you." His metallic eyes darted to her companion and she glimpsed jealousy in them. "I take it you are well, Signore Rinaldo."

"As you can see, I couldn't be better," Rinaldo retorted while placing an arm around Isabetta's waist. "Venerada is a most agreeable and comely lady, don't you think?"

"Oh *I know* she is."

Cristofolo's confident affirmation made Isabetta's face burn, for it publicly declared the intimacy they had shared. As Veronica had predicted, teasing him was now paying off.

Rinaldo inclined his head and said nothing more. Cristofolo leaned back in his chair, his eyes adhered to her face. They shared a meaningful look before she turned her attention to the man at her side.

A group of courtesans stood and sang for everyone's entertainment. Veronica recited some of her own verses after their stellar performance. Isabetta clapped her hands, smiling at her talented friend. A mature, richly dressed man leaned over to whisper in Rinaldo's ear.

He nodded and stood. "Venerada, would you please excuse me for a moment?"

"Certainly."

"Don't stray too far," he warned before the other man led him away from the table and into an adjoining room.

Grateful for the respite, Isabetta stood and wandered around the large room. She admired paintings and sculptures, then stepped onto one of several balconies. Venice was pure magic at night. Mellow light spilled from many windows and torches lit up the pastel façades of neighboring palazzos. The Grand Canal resembled glittering obsidian beneath the silvery light of the moon. Gondolas and boats flitted past, their oars making soft splashing sounds against the water's surface.

"Venerada."

At the sound of his voice, she turned around slowly to face him. It was the first time she had allowed him to get her alone.

"Cristofolo."

Tracing the curve of her cheek with a gentle finger, he said, "You're lovelier today than when we first met. How is this possible?"

"Was I not to your liking before?"

"You misunderstand me."

A caustic laugh escaped her lips. "Do I?"

"Have you no sweet words for me?"

"A handsome and sophisticated man like yourself can have any woman he wants in Venice. Why flatter me falsely?"

Taken aback by her harshness, he quipped, "I have no need to flatter you, given that you are for sale."

"My point precisely, *sir*."

His eyes narrowed suspiciously. "It seems you have no shortage of endearments for Rinaldo."

Bitterness laced his words. *Good.* "Are you jealous?"

"Should I be?"

Recalling Veronica's advice to temper her words with honey, she said softly, "You said it yourself; I am nothing more than a woman for hire."

"Sharp-tongued little shrew."

Pretending to be hurt, she made to move past him. "Would you please excuse me?"

He grabbed her arm. "Don't go. *Please…*" When she stared at him expectantly, he confessed, "I haven't stopped thinking about you since our night together."

"If I hone my tongue and make it even sharper, who knows? You may very well fall in love with me," she teased playfully, earning his smile.

Pulling her closer, he lowered his head and claimed her lips. She kissed him back without restraint. His eyes caressed her features when they broke apart. "Have you been with any other men since…?"

"Of course I have."

Gazing deeply into her eyes, he whispered, "Liar."

She lowered her head. "No one has touched me since you."

"So the rumors are true."

She noted the wonder in his voice. "What rumors?"

"Veronica has not allowed anyone near you despite implying otherwise. One of my peers offered her a large sum for your company and she declined it. Why the farce?" When she refused to answer, he surmised, "I suppose that will change tonight. Rinaldo is known to be a womanizer."

"What do you care?"

"Would it surprise you to know that I *do* care?"

They stood eye to eye, perfectly still and silent, assessing each other. She wanted to ask him about his interest in Beto Bastian, but that would be folly. Although she hated to admit it, part of her was attracted to Cristofolo Trasontin. He posed a challenge and—as perverse as it was—she found it thrilling. Had her mother been correct? Possibly, for she was indeed behaving like a shameful, foolish, unruly girl…

She led him to the farthest corner of the balcony and whispered, "Rinaldo is a sodomite."

Cristofolo's eyes widened in surprise. "You jest."

Shaking her head, she confessed, "The reason Veronica hasn't let anyone near me is because I refuse to bed other men."

His eyes narrowed. "What game are you playing?"

"There's no game, I swear. Please don't repeat what I've told you or else Veronica will be angry with me."

"You're rather naïve to be her protégé. The first rule of being a courtesan is discretion. Never give away secrets."

"I told *you*, Cristofolo. I would never tell anyone else."

This prompted him to quirk an eyebrow at her. "Are you saying that you trust me?"

"Yes."

"Why would you trust an old rogue like me?" When she failed to respond, he took firm hold of her chin. "Answer me."

"Isn't it obvious?"

"You claimed to admire me."

"It's the truth. You're not a frivolous young fool like many of the men here tonight. You're *different*."

He smiled drily. "That's a polite way to call me old."

"Now it is you who misunderstands me. I see you as a highly

sophisticated man of the world. An icon of impeccable taste, wit, and intelligence. I could learn much from you." Boldly slipping her arms around his neck she added, "I find you desirable and…"

When she trailed off, he prompted, "And?"

"Intimidating."

Not expecting to hear that, he demanded, "How so?"

"I don't want to get my heart broken." Disbelief colored his features but before he could protest, she pressed her soft lips to his. When the kiss turned urgent, she gently pushed him away. "I should go back inside."

His ragged breathing betrayed his desire. "Wait. When will I see you again?"

Isabetta deliberately ignored his question as she ducked into the palazzo.

Peering past her shoulder at the shadowy figure on the balcony, Rinaldo said, "There you are, Venerada. Who were you talking to out there?"

"No one of importance. Come, Signore Rinaldo. I think more wine is in order."

Offering his arm, he said, "I believe you're right."

Isabetta danced and made merry until the wee hours. At the evening's conclusion, Rinaldo took her to his palazzo where a boy in a costly gown of copper satin awaited his lover's return. The transvestite glared at Isabetta before summoning a servant to take her upstairs to a guest chamber. Hand in hand, the men disappeared into another room and closed the door behind them.

Isabetta was shown into a comfortable room that smelled faintly of vetiver mingled with lavender. Exhausted from the night's revelry, she fell asleep almost instantly.

CHAPTER 17

Isabetta awoke to the sound of church bells and the sun high in the sky. Noontime. Her head throbbed from overindulging in wine and her feet sported a small blister from exuberant dancing. Veronica had warned against drinking at parties, 'Take tiny sips and consume as little as possible lest you lose your wits and your good looks.' A wave of nausea made her sit up and reach for the chamber pot. Only a few dry heaves, nothing more. She needed some bread to settle her stomach.

Veronica had given her a black lace eye mask, so she put it on and stared at her reflection in the mirror. Satisfied that her identity was protected, she dressed in haste and tiptoed downstairs. Many people saw her emerge from Rinaldo's home in a hooded cloak that she had deliberately left open to reveal her party gown and scandalous cleavage. Curious eyes tracked her steps as she made her way to the Cannaregio. Old women gossiped, men leered, and youths snickered. Maintaining a brisk pace, she went directly to Veronica's palazzo. The courtesan greeted her the moment she was shown into the boudoir.

"A messenger just dropped this off," Veronica said gleefully while holding up a piece of parchment. "What did you say to Cristofolo last night?"

"Why do you ask?"

"He wants to see you tonight."

"So soon?"

"That's what I thought too." Peering at her young friend, Veronica demanded, "Too much wine last night?"

"Does it show?"

"You'll learn not to do that again. Malvina, we need your remedy."

The mulatta applied a cool cream that felt almost minty against the delicate skin surrounding the eyes. "What is this?"

"One of Malvina's herbal concoctions to ease swelling.

She'll make a tonic for you to settle your stomach." Holding out the note, Veronica added, "You'll want to look and feel your very best this evening."

"Why, where is he taking me?" Isabetta accepted the missive and her eyes scanned the masculine penmanship. "Cristofolo has invited me to supper."

"*In his home*." When Isabetta stared blankly, the courtesan continued, "Only two women have ever dined at that man's table or slept in his bed. Both were official mistresses."

"I thought you said he was a whoremonger."

"Courtesans and prostitutes are *never* invited to stay under his roof. For Cristofolo to make such an exception is quite telling of his admiration for you."

"He kissed me last night, then asked if I had been with any other men. I lied at first, then confessed the truth."

Veronica's hand flew to her chest. "That he even asked that question astounds me!"

"Did I do the right thing?"

"Absolutely."

Isabetta left her friend's home in a pensive state. Once she had bathed and changed into a plain gown, she spent the remainder of the afternoon doing some accounting and paying off a few of the smaller debts she owed for supplies and foodstuffs. Afterward, she took a nap.

"Are you going out again tonight?" Alba inquired when she saw Isabetta airing out a fine gown. "You look tired. Maybe you should stay home and rest."

"Cristofolo has invited me to dine in his home and I may spend the night there."

The servant wrung her hands. "What are you doing?"

"I told you. I want to become his mistress and extract as much money as I can from him."

"At the risk of your immortal soul?"

"God doesn't care. Do you think I would be in this predicament if He did?"

"What about Silvio Torres?"

Isabetta's eyes hardened. "I haven't heard from him in

months. Help me get ready and speak of this matter no more."

Defeated, Alba nodded and set her hand to the task.

That night, Isabetta presented herself at Cristofolo's stately home. A servant led her up a marble stairwell to a huge study. Books and artwork lined the walls and she gazed upon the collection, impressed by his eclectic taste.

Cristofolo waved away the servant before greeting Isabetta with a gentle kiss. "I've been looking forward to this moment all day."

"Honestly, I didn't expect to see you so soon."

"I wanted to bring you home with me last night after our conversation on the balcony." His fingertips skimmed across the skin of her neck. "So young and soft…How can I resist?"

"I'm flattered, sir."

"And I'm famished," he growled before pulling her close and devouring her throat.

"Wait," she whispered.

"You're right," he said, pulling away. "Let's dine first. I pine for your words as well as your body."

Accepting his proffered arm, she kept pace with him as he led her to a charming round dining room. Yellow damask walls punctuated by life-size Roman sculptures embraced a circular dining table. Expensive porcelain and silver graced its surface and gleamed in the candlelight.

"A marvelous room," Isabetta exclaimed, spinning slowly in a circle to admire the statues.

"King Arthur intrigued me as a boy, thus the round table. It pleases me that you like it." He placed his hands upon her shoulders and brushed his lips against the nape of her neck, causing her to shiver. "Please, sit."

The man possessed magic fingers and lips that caused her body to betray her mind. She loathed him, yet craved him physically, which only served to humiliate her.

"My niece came by to visit me today," he said before bringing a silver chalice to his lips. "Aside from you, she is the only woman who occupies my thoughts."

"Once again you flatter me. That I occupy a space beside a

cherished family member warms my heart. I've done nothing to merit such esteem."

"You have awakened something within me that has lain dormant for a long time," he revealed in a low voice.

Servants came out with their dinner, prompting him to act in a reserved manner. They spoke of mundane things over braised beef and a soufflé as light as air.

He visibly relaxed when they were alone again. "I want to know more about you and your past."

"There isn't much. I was placed in a convent at the age of eight. My childhood was difficult so I don't speak of it." The sad story was invented by Veronica.

"Illicit children are often rejected."

"Yes," she agreed, focusing on her plate. "My mother is dead, which is why I am forced to live this life."

"It explains the pain I see in the depths of your eyes."

Isabetta shifted uncomfortably in her chair. Although he was referring to her fictitious past, his words were too painful. *Too accurate*. Before she realized it, a tear slid down her face and she quickly wiped it away.

"Don't hide your tears, dear Venerada. You are a tender soul and your father is a fool for not acknowledging you publicly. I would be proud to have you as my daughter."

His words struck a chord, for it afforded the chance to veer the conversation away from her. "Do you have any children?"

"No."

"Why not?"

"I never married."

"Marriage frightens most men, I think."

He laughed lightly. "Well, yes."

The wine flowed freely, serving to loosen their lips and inhibitions. Cristofolo asked many questions and demanded to know Isabetta's thoughts on several current problems facing Venice. She provided him with well-thought answers. In truth, she found his company fascinating.

At the meal's conclusion, he declared, "You please me, Venerada. You are a credit to the weaker sex."

She bristled. "The word 'weaker' is a bit insulting."

"Fair enough. Weak in physical attributes but strong of mind. Does that suit you?"

"A marked improvement."

His eyes twinkled. "There is no guile in you, is there? It's as though you're made of glass, transparent. You know nothing of this world, do you?"

"I confess, I am young and have much to learn."

Peering at her thoughtfully, he rested his chin on his fist. "Your mind is a fresh canvas and I would relish the opportunity to be the artist who paints upon it."

"I'll gladly provide you with the brushes."

At that, he laughed. Suddenly, he rose from the chair and offered his hand. "Will you come upstairs with me?"

Isabetta was struck by the fact that he asked rather than commanded. To her own astonishment, she replied honestly, "With pleasure."

Grasping his hand, she followed him to a lavishly styled bedchamber. There, he tempered his lust with gentleness and gazed into her eyes during the act. Who was this man? Certainly not the same one who had lain with her during the deflowering.

Confused, Isabetta found herself pretending less and enjoying more. Her breaths came out in small gasps as he coaxed her body to respond to his caresses. What was he doing? She had never felt anything like this. Mounting pleasure led to an explosive climax that consumed her in a cocoon of bliss.

"Oh God!"

The ecstatic cry had burst through her lips. One look at his cocky grin in the moonlight suggested that he was more than satisfied with the result of his handiwork as a lover.

Her powerful reaction to his lovemaking not only terrified her, it disgusted her. She hated herself for betraying the memory of her slain father and brother, and she hated her traitorous body too. What did her behavior say about her character?

"Venerada..."

His ecstatic cry flung her back to the present. Shuddering in her embrace, he murmured endearments while kissing her neck.

Pinned under his weight, she traced the line of his spine with her fingertips. The skin felt hot and firm.

"Stay the night. I want to see your face when I awaken in the morning," he murmured, already sleepy from his powerful sexual release.

She nodded and kissed his cheek. When he finally shifted to his side, she smiled and cried in the darkened room. Joy and horror.

***

After that night, Isabetta escorted Cristofolo to many social events. Dinners, parties, concertos…it soon became a blur of expensive gowns, jewels, and lush feasts. She would spend the night in his home and share his bed with frequency. His bedchamber became a sacred place where he was the teacher and she, the student. There, she discovered the wonders of her own body and the depths of her passion.

Days soon turned to weeks, prompting him to make an arrangement with Veronica to see her protégé exclusively, even paying extra for that privilege. Although the ice had melted from the eaves and the days were growing longer, he had yet to claim her as an official mistress.

"Do you think he'll ask me soon?" Isabetta inquired of Veronica one afternoon.

The courtesan rubbed her ripe belly thoughtfully while gazing at early spring buds blooming on a branch outside her window. "I believe so. In the meantime, be patient. You're making a decent amount of money, are you not?"

"More than decent."

Veronica winked. "So am I. Tomorrow you are going to Loretta's birthday celebration with him, correct?"

"I am, are you going too?"

"No. The baby has been restless within me and the physician advised rest for a few days. Give Loretta a kiss for me."

Loretta's raucous party lasted until dawn. Isabetta and Cristofolo danced through the night, then made love in a gondola while the gondolier pretended not to notice. Exhausted, he did not insist that she come upstairs with him once they arrived at his palazzo. The morning sun had already risen, so she bade him a good rest before the vessel set off for the Cannaregio. Sleep in her own bed was all she wanted.

Alba was sweeping the kitchen floor when her mistress entered the house. "Are you all right, Signorina?"

Isabetta groaned in response and headed to the stairwell.

Pointing to the table, the servant said, "A letter arrived for you yesterday while you were out with Signore Cristofolo. Can I make you something to eat? Some tea?"

Isabetta swiped the letter from the table before slowly ascending the stairs. "No, thank you."

Alba watched her go with a pained expression. "Please try and rest so you don't become ill."

Once inside her room, Isabetta sank onto the bed and broke the wax seal. Her lip quivered as she read the words.

My dearest Isabetta,

I arrived in Portugal only a few days ago to find your letters awaiting me. My deepest condolences on the death of your mother. She was a fine woman and a devout Christian, so I know she is watching over you from Heaven.

My trip to India proved successful, despite having contracted a terrible fever that forced me to remain much longer than I had anticipated. Thankfully, my health is now fully restored. My father, on the other hand, has survived longer than expected, but his condition has taken a turn for the worst. My selfish brother is too busy to care for him, so it is up to me.

I plan on departing for Venice as soon as I am able to do so. My arms ache to hold you and my lips crave your honeyed kisses. Please write to me, for I long to read your tender words.

Faithfully Yours, Silvio

"Faithfully," she whispered. Overwhelmed by guilt and shame, she let the letter fall from her fingertips to the floor. Placing her face into the pillow, she wept bitter tears.

Chapter 18
April 1570

"I want you *here*."

Cristofolo's declaration came after a night of intense lovemaking, which Isabetta shamelessly enjoyed despite having received written confirmation of Silvio's fidelity. How wanton she had become. *How wicked.* "I *am* here."

Morning light spilled across the white sheets, highlighting only half his face. "I am claiming you, my precious Venerada, as my official mistress. Do you accept?"

This was the moment she had been waiting for, but Veronica had taught her never to appear eager. "I am happy to carry on as we have thus far. I know how you appreciate your freedom as a bachelor. Are you certain this is what you want?"

Leaning up on his elbow to gaze down at her face, he replied, "I've never been more certain of anything in my life…I am not happy unless you are completely mine."

"In that case, nothing would please me more than to be exclusively yours, my darling."

Her reply earned her an ardent kiss before he declared, "No other man shall touch you henceforth. I will send a message to Veronica at once, and pay whatever fee she imposes to cover her losses. You will no longer be in her employ. You'll need to fetch your things. I'll send a servant." Realization lit up his features and he added, "I don't even know where you live."

"My modest home is in the Dorsoduro," she lied.

Her ability to utter fabrications had improved tenfold since becoming Cristofolo's lover. At times, the line between Isabetta Bastian and Venerada d'Oro blurred to the point that she no longer recognized her reflection in the mirror.

Who are you?

She continued, "Please let me go home to make my own arrangements. I'll need at least a few days to pack and settle some of my affairs."

Throwing off the covers, he made to get out of bed. "Very well, sweetheart. I have a meeting this morning with an old friend. I'll summon a carriage for you."

Isabetta watched him stride across the room naked. Accustomed to his body, she stared without reservations. She, too, rose from the bed devoid of clothing. No longer the blushing maiden, she went over and kissed his shoulder.

Chuckling at her flirtation, he caressed her breast. "Perhaps there is a little time…?"

She nodded breathlessly as he pushed her toward the big canopied bed. Together, they fell onto the soft feather mattress.

Later, Isabetta rode home in silent contemplation.

Deep pockets. Tramonto. He is your enemy...

***

"Rumors are spreading throughout the city," Polonia said crisply after greeting her uncle with a kiss on the cheek.

Cristofolo pulled away and shivered. "You are chilled. No mild spring this year, it seems. Come inside and warm yourself by the fire."

She entered the room and held her cold hands toward the hearth. "Did you hear what I said?"

He went over to the sideboard and poured some wine into a pair of chalices. "Rumors, yes. Since when do you pay attention to gossip?"

Arranging her face to appear amused, she said with forced levity, "When it's about you being in love."

He chuckled derisively. "People do like to talk."

Accepting the chalice, she tried to capture his gaze but he resisted. "I think you're avoiding my question."

"It sounded more like an accusation."

"They say you have a new mistress, *a courtesan*."

"They?" At his niece's level stare, he continued, "Venerada is different."

She studied him with a mixture of astonishment and disapproval. "*Venerada?* A bizarre name for a whore."

"There's no need to be petty," he snapped before taking a

long sip of wine. He would need more than one drink for this dreaded and inevitable conversation.

A gush of cynical laughter escaped Polonia's painted lips. "Uncle, I'm surprised! It's not like you to be so gullible." Sensing that she had caused him offense, she set down her chalice and embraced him. "Don't sulk. I'm only worried."

Pushing her away, he confessed, "I care about her. A bit of respect on your part would be appreciated."

"Respect a whore?"

"Is she not a woman like you?"

The situation was worse than she had imagined. "That is where you are quite mistaken."

He drained the remainder of his drink, then proclaimed, "My days of being a carefree rake are over."

Polonia staggered to the nearest chair and placed her hands upon the back of it to steady herself. "You can't possibly be considering marriage to this…this slut…*are you*?"

Cristofolo was surprised to see that his chalice was already empty. Thoughts racing, he poured himself more wine. "Please sit and allow me to explain." He waited until she had done so to proceed. "Venerada d'Oro was training to be a courtesan under Veronica Franco, who happens to be an accomplished writer and poet. She is well-known in the literary world, and admired both here and abroad."

Scoffing, she demanded, "Are you implying that she's a respectable courtesan?"

"Actually, yes. Her protégé made her debut and I…" He trailed off, not wishing to mention the auction. His niece didn't need to know about the sordid world of men. "I claimed her maidenhead. She is a woman of quality, I assure you. Her father is a nobleman in Milan."

Polonia stared at him stonily. "Who is her father?"

"Courtesans never reveal that sort of information."

"Rather convenient, no?"

"It wouldn't matter to me if she had been born of a fishwife." Seeing his niece's shocked expression, he commented, "Every woman starts out as a virgin—even courtesans. She hasn't been with any other man except me. Also, she never had the chance to work as a courtesan in the true sense of the word. She became my lover almost immediately after I deflowered her."

"I see. Exclusivity must cost a fortune these days."

"My purse is lighter, I won't deny it. She was—*is*—worth every cent. Truth is, I feel young again. Full of energy and joy."

"I'm glad she brings you such pleasure, Cristofolo," Polonia commented, her voice and expression as icy as the unusually cold wind beating against the window panes.

"Are you? Because you don't appear to be."

She wandered to where he stood and placed a tentative hand on his arm. "Forgive me if I've given you that impression."

Although his niece reminded him of a snake in that instant, he brought her knuckles to his lips. "That's better." Changing the subject, he asked, "Iseppo is doing well, I hope."

She shrugged. "Well enough."

"And you?"

"I miss my dear, sweet, generous, attentive uncle," she said, gently caressing his cheek. There was no mistaking the venom in her words or the flirtation in her voice.

"I haven't gone anywhere, my dear."

She pouted. "You're barely home these days, and you don't reply as quickly to my messages as you once did."

"Venerada keeps me occupied," he admitted, waggling his eyebrows suggestively.

"How old is this woman?"

"Nearly eighteen."

"She's a child!"

"A young woman," he corrected in a warning tone.

How could she ever compete with Venerada's firm young flesh and perky breasts? The thought made her pause in self-reflection. *Compete?*

"Polonia, are you all right? You've grown pale."

Shaking her head to clear it of sinful thoughts, she asked, "Aside from spending a fortune to have Venerada to yourself, do you buy her pretty things?"

His eyes twinkled mischievously. "If I didn't know any

better, I would think you're jealous of my mistress."

Slipping her arms around his neck, she said, "Maybe I am."

It was wrong to desire his own flesh and blood, but in that instance he wanted nothing more than to taste her lips. "In that case, I would tell you to look inside that vase over there."

She squealed in delight. "A surprise? For me?"

Although the gift had been planted for Venerada, his niece needed to be appeased and reassured of his undying affection. "I knew you were coming here today. You sent a message, remember?"

Crossing the room, she carefully picked up the large green vase from the table and gently shook it. Something jostled within so she reached inside. Admiring the lovely aquamarine pendant dangling from a silver chain, she grinned.

Her childishness charmed him. "Do you like it?"

She ran over to him and gave his lips a quick peck. "Yes! I want to wear it now." A delicious shiver snaked its way down her spine as his fingers brushed against the delicate skin of her nape while fastening the clasp.

Placing his hands on her shoulders, he spun her around to face him. "No woman will ever come between us. You are my flesh and blood, Polonia. You come first and foremost in my life and in my heart. *Remember that.*"

Feeling sheepish for having doubted her beloved uncle, she lamented, "I wish I could meet her but…"

Cristofolo nodded in understanding. No self-respecting woman would allow a courtesan into her home, let alone attend a social event where they were present.

Polonia would find a way to see Venerada d'Oro with her own eyes and judge the greedy trollop accordingly.

***

"Alba! Come help me dress."

Poking her head into the room, the servant inquired, "Another party?"

"Yes."

"Will you be home tonight?"

"I've already told you that I'm going to live with him."

Alba's face became a mask of disapproval. "This has gone well beyond what you had planned. Your parents and brother must be turning in their graves!"

"So help me God, if you keep badgering me like this I will put you out." Isabetta sighed wearily, regretting her sharp retort. "Forgive me. I do have a plan. I know what I'm doing and I need you to trust me."

"As you wish."

"Please fetch the gown Cristofolo gifted me last week."

The sumptuous red velvet dress was promptly extracted from the *cassone*. Alba eyed the garment with disdain. Signora Hortensa would never have approved of such a low neckline. Risking a glance at Isabetta's face, she saw that it looked haggard. Whatever she did with that horrid man was consuming her from the inside out.

Isabetta applied a bit of extra rouge to make up for her sallowness. She wanted nothing more than to crawl beneath the covers of her bed and sleep, but Cristofolo insisted that they dine at the home of his acquaintance. She didn't care for the shifty-eyed man the first time they met, but she had no choice but to plaster a smile to her face and act like the perfect companion.

That evening, Isabetta and her lover sat side by side at a table groaning beneath the weight of platters heaping with roasted meats. She plied him with wine throughout the meal, keeping his vessel filled to the brim. Hopefully, he would be too tired to make love at the night's conclusion so she could get some much needed sleep.

Cristofolo puffed out his chest proudly when Isabetta kissed him. Glimpsing envy in the eyes of his peers brought him immense satisfaction. The pretty young girl who doted on her mature lover with the utmost loyalty was the talk of Venice.

The dinner party soon took a turn toward debauchery, as these events were prone to do. Isabetta had expected as much from their odious host.

"You own my whole heart," Cristofolo suddenly confessed, slurring his words.

Servants moved about the room, clearing away empty plates and the carcasses of various animals. Platters of fruits, nuts, and sweetmeats were set out for the merry guests.

"Here, have more wine," she said, refilling his chalice.

"Have I complimented you on your gown?"

Laughing, she said, "You gifted it to me, remember?"

Having overheard their conversation, their inebriated host studied the gown and interjected, "Cornetti's work."

Cristofolo nodded. "You have a keen eye, my friend. Almost every noble whose name is in the *Libro d'Oro* wears garments cut from my partner's fabrics."

Isabetta eyed each man in turn with veiled disgust. Sealed within the "Golden Book" Cristofolo mentioned were the names of the city's wealthiest and noblest families. A *Libro d'Argento* or "Silver Book" existed for rich merchants and lesser nobles. Her uncle's name was inscribed in the latter, as were the Bevilacqua and other high-end luxury producers.

Feigning ignorance, she said, "Your *partner*?"

Cristofolo explained, "I export Alzo Cornetti's textiles."

"Ah…I didn't know you dabbled in maritime trade."

"Venetian fabrics are in high demand," croaked the host. Lifting his chalice, he added, "Almost as much as our women!"

Male laughter accompanied his crude comment.

Cristofolo lifted his chalice, wine sloshing onto the bleached white linen tablecloth. "A toast to Venetian women!"

The men in the room drank to that while the courtesans pretended to be flattered by their drunken proclamations.

Cristofolo leaned over and whispered, "A toast to you, my gorgeous and perfect Venerada."

She stroked his cheek. "I'm far from perfect."

"You're perfect for me…Venus personified."

Isabetta kissed his lips, then ventured, "Would you fancy another partner in your shipping venture?"

The question sobered him instantly. "Why do you ask? Does one of Veronica's wealthy clients wish to make an investment?"

"No…I do."

His eyebrows rose. "You?"

Cheeks burning with anger, she tried to appear coy. "I have a bit of money saved..."

Chuckling, he tapped her nose playfully as one would a child's. "What do you know about business, anyway? I already have one headstrong woman to contend with as a partner, I don't need another. Save your money, sweetheart."

Pretending to be jealous, she asked, "Who is the headstrong woman in your life? The one you refer to as your *partner*."

"Beware, she's a feisty one," their host interjected.

Pleased by her jealousy, Cristofolo drew her close. "There's no need for you to worry, dearest. The woman is my niece, Polonia, wife of a well-known shipping merchant. She is the one who convinced me to export textiles to Lisbon. My ship returned from Portugal in December and it will sail to Flanders in June. She has a head for numbers and business. A rare talent in women, who much prefer to spend money than to make it."

Isabetta wanted to throw the contents of her chalice in his face when he referred to the *Tramonto* as his property. Between the money she made from the auction and the jewels she had pawned—gifts from her lover—she almost had enough to reclaim the galley. She needed to be patient a little while longer. "Your niece sounds impressive. A savvy woman, indeed."

Eyeing her slyly, he nodded. "She's jealous of you too."

Isabetta's hand flew to her chest. "*Of me?* Why?"

Inevitably, his eyes were drawn to her cleavage. "I've doted on her since birth. Polonia is accustomed to having my full attention and hates sharing me with anyone."

"Do you love her very much?"

Dipping his finger in the shadowy cleft, he stroked the side of her breast. "She means the world to me."

"Is she charming and elegant like her uncle?"

"She is that and so much more..."

Glimpsing the lust in his eyes only confirmed her suspicion. Isabetta wasn't certain if the pair had indulged in an incestuous relationship, but she wouldn't be surprised if they had. "My heart is broken. Shattered to bits."

"Can't a man love two women?" At the sight of her surprised

expression, he amended, "You need not worry, my sweet."

Isabetta melted against him when he nuzzled her neck. A few couples were engaged in love play at the table, and one courtesan cried out in mock outrage when her companion pinched her nipple.

Whenever she was in Cristofolo's arms, Silvio came to mind. Ever since receiving his letter, her Portuguese suitor had presided over her thoughts and dreams. She hated playing the role of harlot, but her secret life was both profitable and informative. Tonight, she confirmed that Polonia had been the impetus behind Cristofolo's actions. *She* had convinced her uncle to pay Zanetto Bastian's debt. *She* had devised the plan to confiscate the galley. *She*, not him.

Did Polonia convince Alzo to join in on their scheme?

Cristofolo's groan interrupted her train of thought. She made no move to stop his hand from creeping beneath her skirt. The smell of wine on his breath overwhelmed her as he plied kisses on her throat. While his fingers worked their way up her thigh, she swore she heard him whisper '*Polonia.*'

***

Isabetta paid Veronica a visit the next morning to apprise her friend of what she had learned from Cristofolo.

"It's no secret that Polonia holds tremendous influence over her uncle. Cristofolo has no children of his own, so his niece has been spoiled since birth."

"I once spied them together in the market. Had I not known of their kinship, I would have assumed they were lovers."

Veronica smirked as she rubbed a bit of lotion into her hands. "You're not the first to notice. Everyone speculates on their relationship, which borders on obscene at times."

"Polonia is to blame for the current state of my life. She's the reason why I'm cavorting with her uncle, why I had to sell my virginity, and why I had to suffer working for my cousin." Isabetta paced the room wearing a mask of fury. "There is nothing I want more than to wreak havoc in that woman's life. I want her to suffer as much as I have—perhaps even more."

Her friend's determined face compelled Veronica to ask,

"Isn't it enough that you're siphoning money from Cristofolo? The man has fallen in love with you, and he will surely be devastated when you break it off with him."

"I certainly hope so," Isabetta replied vehemently, her eyes narrowed into two slits. "In answer to your question, no. It's not enough. I want revenge."

"Believe me when I say the best revenge is to live well."

"I will live better after I've ruined them both."

After a moment of quiet reflection, Veronica went over to a bookshelf and selected a book. "If you are intent on this goal, then allow me to provide you with a bit of inspiration. Have you ever heard of Queen Eleanor of Aquitaine?"

Isabetta froze. "No."

"She's a fascinating woman from the twelfth century who was crowned queen twice—first France, then England. At one point in her extraordinary life, she led a female crusade to Antioch where her handsome uncle, Raymond of Poitiers, ruled as prince. She had gone to him in anticipation of her husband's arrival. According to some historians, and more than a few witnesses, the lovely Eleanor and her uncle were rumored to have indulged in an *inappropriate liaison*."

Enthralled by the story, Isabetta asked, "Incest?"

Waving a ringed hand, Veronica replied, "Some argue it's only speculation, yet Eleanor's husband, King Louis VII of France, became incensed when he arrived in Antioch. He went as far as accusing his wife of engaging in a romantic dalliance with her own kin. He wouldn't slander his own queen if the story didn't hold some truth."

"Why are you telling me this?"

Veronica placed the book in her friend's hand. "Why do you think?" She paused to let her words sink in. "I still believe you should marry the Portuguese young man, put the past behind you, and enjoy your life. If you decide against that sage course of action, then your strategy should be solid. After all, a hunter takes aim with intention to kill."

CHAPTER 19

Isabetta read the biography of Eleanor of Aquitaine with keen interest. Veronica had been correct about the woman being an interesting person. Courageous and brazen too. The French queen, having grown weary of her dullard husband, divorced Louis to marry the young and handsome English upstart, Henry. They had five sons and three became kings.

Before taking any further action against Polonia or Cristofolo, Isabetta needed to know the extent of Iseppo da Mosta's involvement in this treacherous affair.

Cristofolo mentioned that he would be accompanying his niece to see a mutual friend in the afternoon, so Isabetta seized the opportunity to visit Iseppo. She donned a plain gown and hid her red hair beneath a modest linen coif before donning her cloak. Mentally rehearsing what she would say to him, she made her way to the merchant's home. A servant led her into his sumptuous study where she was received with a blend of surprise and courtesy.

"Thank you for seeing me, sir."

Iseppo motioned to a chair. "Don't thank me, child. You may not believe this but I think of you often. Poor Zanetto and Rocco are never far from my thoughts, or your mother for that matter. How are you?"

She sat down and folded her bare hands in her lap. "I appreciate your sentiment, Signore Iseppo. I know you're a busy man so I'll be brief. I've come here in search of the truth. Was it your idea or Signora Polonia's to pay off my father's debt and seize the *Tramonto*?"

Caught off guard by the blunt question, he cleared his throat. "With all due respect, what difference does it make?"

"It makes a difference to me. Given what I've endured these last several months, I'm owed an explanation for the tragedy that is now my life."

Iseppo regarded the solemn girl, then heaved a sigh. "My wife spoke to her uncle without my knowledge. Cristofolo then went immediately to Alzo Cornetti since Polonia mentioned that he and I had conducted business together in the past. Both men came to me *after* having reached an agreement."

"You were never consulted?"

"No. Cristofolo and I avoid each other whenever possible. Our mutual contempt spans decades. Polonia insisted that I go along with their plan, and when my wife sets her mind on something there is no dissuading the woman. She also had the full support of Cristofolo and Alzo, which meant that I would be risking economic losses if I resisted." Isabetta's icy glare made him wince inwardly, so he amended, "If it's any consolation to you, I haven't enjoyed a peaceful night of rest since agreeing to their idea."

"It does not console me in the slightest."

Stung by her retort, he offered, "I'll have you know that I got into a vicious argument with Cristofolo over the interest he added to your debt. Initially, I believed he would give you a fair chance to gain back the *Tramonto* but I see now that I was wrong. My wife is behind his belligerence, I'm afraid. She is as greedy and ruthless as my late father-in-law. I'm truly sorry, Isabetta."

Trembling from head to foot, she stood. "Thank you for your time and honesty, Signore Iseppo."

"Wait." Spreading out his hands in supplication, he demanded, "How can I make this up to you?"

She went to the door and turned the latch. "You cannot."

Iseppo's candid words reverberated inside her head as she exited the house. He would no doubt suffer in the aftermath of whatever punishment she devised for Polonia and Cristofolo. Deep down, she believed the merchant to be a good man who wanted to do the right thing, yet failed miserably.

As far as Alzo Cornetti was concerned, he could have easily rejected the idea. At the very least, he could have reported the intentions of Cristofolo and Polonia so that she and her mother could have prepared themselves when the time came. Instead, he put greed before family. An unforgiveable offense.

Isabetta tossed and turned in Cristofolo's bed later that night. While her lover slept soundly after their tender embraces, she conjured ways in which to trap him and Polonia. Every idea was carefully scrutinized. There was no room for error.

A hunter takes aim with intention to kill…

***

Fierce wind made Silvio's eyes water as he headed toward the Cannaregio. Today was the first of May and quite chilly. At least he was no longer in quarantine and would soon be kissing the lips of his beloved Isabetta. Turning the corner, he caught sight of her house and his heart thrummed with anticipation.

Alba greeted him at the door. "Signore Silvio! We weren't expecting you."

"Didn't your mistress get my last letter?"

"No, sir."

He entered the house without invitation and dropped his satchel on the floor. Ignoring her question, he demanded, "Where is your mistress?"

Although the servant knew the answer to the question, she shrugged nervously. "I don't know."

"Do you mind if I sit and wait?"

"Suit yourself."

"Do you have any idea when she will return?"

The door opened suddenly and Isabetta burst into the room. "Dear God, that man is—" She stopped short at the sight of Silvio and immediately drew the edges of her cloak closely together to hide her low-cut gown from view.

He stood. "Isabetta."

"Silvio…why didn't you notify me of your arrival?"

"I did, I sent a letter a fortnight before my departure from Lisbon. Your servant informed me that it never arrived."

She forced a smile. "It's good to see you again."

"I've missed you more than you can imagine." Lifting her gloved hand to his lips, he sniffed the soft leather and frowned slightly. "Perfumed gloves?"

"Ah…Rocco bought them for me." The expensive gloves

had actually been a gift from Cristofolo, whose bed she had vacated less than an hour ago.

"An extravagant gift for a sister." His gaze shifted. "And your hair. It's so...*red.* Why did you change it?"

She patted her messy coiffure, which had been haphazardly constructed by her own hands while her lover nibbled her ear. "I've been working as a lady's maid these last few months. My mistress wanted to try the apothecary's newest concoction on my head before applying it to her own. Do you like it?"

"I prefer your natural color." His eyes focused on her face. "Are you required to wear cosmetics too?"

Isabetta wore the remnants of last night's rouge and lip paint. Most of the latter had been kissed and licked off her lips. *Dear God...*"Sometimes."

A flash of skin from her plunging bodice compelled him to inquire, "May I ask where you've been?"

"Church." Ignoring Alba's raised eyebrows, she added lamely, "The priest delivered an uplifting sermon."

"And the man?"

She stared blankly at him. "What man?"

"You were speaking about a man when you walked through the door a moment ago."

"Oh...er...a rude vendor at the market." She urged him to sit and took her seat across from him. "Alba, pour us some ale. Silvio, where are you staying?"

Hurt by the question, he replied awkwardly, "I haven't made any arrangements. I thought you would invite me to stay here."

Isabetta cursed under her breath. There was no way Silvio could stay at her home while she slept in Cristofolo's bed. His unexpected presence in Venice greatly complicated matters. "Given that I'm living alone, it would be unseemly if I were to host you here."

Silvio looked pointedly at Alba, clearly implying that they would not be alone. Isabetta pretended not to notice as she sipped her ale. Conceding to her wishes, he said, "I would never risk tarnishing your good reputation, my dear. I'm happy to rent a room during my stay."

Relieved, she announced, "This calls for a celebration. Alba, fetch some of those tasty smoked sausages from the butcher, will you? Pick up a round of cheese from the market while you're out. Silvio, please excuse me while I go upstairs and change. I shall return in a moment."

Isabetta raced up to her bedchamber and locked herself inside. She donned a somber gown and scrubbed her face clean before descending the stairs.

"Much better," Silvio commented, his eyes following Isabetta throughout the kitchen. "You are naturally pretty and don't require artifice."

Placing a loaf of bread on the table, she quipped, "You are most kind. Are you hungry? Alba baked bread this morning so it's fresh. We also have some beef broth in the cauldron."

He stood and held out his hand. "Stop fussing, come here." Pulling her into his arms, he inquired, "Have you missed me?"

"Yes."

He captured her lips in a kiss and she instinctively opened her mouth to him as she would for Cristofolo. This realization made her stiffen within his embrace.

Pulling away, he asked, "What's wrong?"

"Nothing."

"Not a day passed that I didn't think of you."

"I thought of you too, especially after receiving news of the fever you had suffered in India. What happened?"

"At first, I became sick due to the food I had consumed. Then, I developed a terrible fever that kept me bedridden for days. I became so weak that I thought I would never see you again. God be praised, for I'm fortunate to be here today." Squeezing her tightly, he added, "I'm the luckiest man in the world right now."

His mouth came down on hers in a hungry kiss and she felt his desire against her thigh. She tried not to compare Silvio to Cristofolo, but it proved impossible. Alba's footsteps outside the door compelled her to push him away.

The servant began setting out a simple meal while the couple took their seats at the table.

Isabetta picked at the food whereas Silvio ate hungrily. She listened to his business plans with interest since, sooner or later, her life would be embroiled with his. After consuming most of the sausage and half the round of cheese, he reached across the table to hold her hand.

"I know life has been difficult for you, *my love*. I want to ease your financial predicament but I have yet to make my own fortune. My trip to India proved fruitful and I have acquired many things to sell. More importantly, I've made several contacts." At that, he pulled out a small leather book. "Each name and address is a step toward wealth. I promise to pay your debts once I begin making a profit."

Touched by his sincerity and generosity, she declared, "You're a good man."

"And you're a good woman, which is why I want to make you my wife as soon as possible. Marry me."

Alba glanced hopefully at her mistress.

Isabetta smiled at Silvio and chose her words carefully. "My affection for you grows daily. Nothing would make me happier than being your wife, but I need more time. I'm still in mourning over my mother, you see..."

Alba's face fell in disappointment and Silvio's did too.

"I understand, and I'm a patient man. It will take a few weeks for me to set things up in the warehouse. Also, I need to travel to Treviso and Genoa for business. I'll expect your readiness to wed once I am properly settled. I'm ambitious and eager to make my fortune in this world, and I need a woman like you at my side to help me succeed. Together, we'll forge a wonderful life. Of this, you can be sure." He stood and picked up his satchel. "There's a ship arriving from Spain this afternoon and I hope to purchase some of its cargo to resell. I met the captain during my quarantine and he liked my ideas."

"Are you leaving?"

"I am, but we'll see each other soon."

Isabetta walked him to the door and allowed him to give her lips a quick peck.

No sooner had she closed the door than Alba said, "That man

offered you a way out of your financial troubles and you're going to refuse him? Why not marry him now and be over with this sordid double life?"

"Didn't you hear what he said? He has yet to make his fortune. Silvio doesn't have any money."

"*Yet.* As his wife, you could help him achieve his goals. Lord knows you've amassed a tidy sum these last few months. Surely, you have enough to buy back the *Tramonto*."

"I do, but I need a bit more time to carry out my plan."

"What plan?"

Isabetta eyed Alba long and hard, then turned her back on the servant and went upstairs without another word. In the days that followed, she balanced her time precariously between two men. Living life on the point of a double-edged blade led to physical and mental exhaustion. Relief came when Silvio finally departed for Treviso, for it allowed her time to concentrate on formulating a plan to ruin her enemies.

Nestled within Cristofolo's arms, Isabetta noticed his forlorn face. They had made love throughout a rainy afternoon and were reluctant to leave the comfort of the warm bed. Studying his classic profile, she realized that some part of her nurtured affection for the man. Her body craved his. That didn't dissuade her from carrying out the revenge she had been meticulously planning for weeks.

She asked sweetly, "What ails you?"

Stroking her cheek, he replied, "Nothing."

"Have you already tired of me?"

"I could never tire of you."

"*Something* is worrying you," she pressed, hoping to glean some useful information.

"My niece has made several requests to see you."

"I'm flattered that a lady of her caliber would want to meet me. Why not send her an invitation to sup with us?" Isabetta suggested, knowing full well that Polonia would never accept.

"A respectable Venetian wife must not be seen consorting with a courtesan. You know that."

"I suppose we will never meet," she said, secretly relieved.

"Actually, she suggested you attend Holy Mass at *San Sebastiano* in the Dorsoduro on Monday morning. She wants to see you with her own eyes, nothing more." He took hold of her chin and forced her to meet his gaze. "Will you do that for me, Venerada?"

What if Polonia recognized her? She could easily ruin everything! Months of effort and compromising her innocence for nothing! "What if she doesn't approve of me?"

"Don't be silly. My niece is only curious because she loves me. Say yes, my darling."

Reluctantly, she nodded.

"Good girl," he whispered before kissing her temple.

On Monday morning, Isabetta donned a gray gown with high neckline and opted not to wear jewelry. She did her best to disguise her face with carefully applied cosmetics before covering her head with a black lace veil. She threw a cloak over her shoulders as she stepped into the cool humid morning.

Charcoal clouds eclipsed the sun and a fine drizzle began to fall as she picked her way to the church of *San Sebastiano.* Crossing the bridge to the other side of the Grand Canal, she uttered a silent prayer to God. Hopefully, He would listen to her desperate plea and render her unrecognizable to the woman who was out to destroy her life.

The church loomed before her and she hurried inside. A cluster of people gathered around the high altar at the front. Polonia, arrayed in a green velvet gown with matching cloak, stood out in stark contrast to the humbly clad parishioners.

Lowering the black lace veil over her face, Isabetta kept her eyes downcast as she neared the worshippers. She took a seat several rows away from them and felt her enemy's eyes on her throughout the entire service.

Polonia marched to where Isabetta stood at the conclusion of Holy Mass. Coming to a halt a few feet away, she said haughtily, "Venerada d'Oro?"

Averting her eyes, Isabetta nodded.

"My uncle deserves better," Polonia sneered before turning on her heel and storming off.

Isabetta watched the arrogant woman go with a calculated expression. Exiting the church, she rounded the first corner and headed toward an establishment where a wise woman who was known for effective remedies plied her trade.

A slight crone with blonde-white hair stood behind a table littered with mortars, pestles, and jars filled with unguents. Mismatched eyes roamed over Isabetta, one of them being clouded over with a milky film. "I don't rid maidens of unwanted babes since that would be blasphemous to God and against the law." A wink followed the staunch declaration.

"I'm not here for that."

"A love potion, then?"

Isabetta didn't know whether to focus on the crone's white eye or the brown one. "I want two people who are secretly in love to act upon their amorous inclinations."

"Ahhhh, you want an aphrodisiac."

Isabetta's face fell. "If you're going to sell me oysters or pomegranates, don't bother. I can procure those on my own."

The woman threw her head back and laughed. When she composed herself, she said, "Oh my child, I can do much better than that."

CHAPTER 20

Polonia paced the salon inside her uncle's home with agitated steps. Late-afternoon sunlight poured from the window to create a thick illuminated streak upon the floor. Cristofolo watched as she moved back and forth, her body repeatedly crossing from burnished gold to deep shadow. Dust motes danced above her head.

"I saw Venerada at the church this morning," she said, finally coming to a halt and facing him.

He offered a tentative smile as he tried to gauge his niece's mood. "I told you she would accommodate your request. You cannot deny that she is pretty."

"I could barely see her face beneath her veil, which I'm sure she wore in an attempt to appear modest." Rolling her eyes, she added disdainfully, "She's common."

His smile vanished. "She quotes Marcus Aurelius and foreign poets. I would hardly call that common."

"Ugly gown, plain cloak—she resembled a pauper."

"A fitting ensemble for Holy Mass," he countered in his beloved's defense. "You cannot expect Venerada to dress for church as if she were going to a banquet."

She laughed derisively. "No, *that* would require red velvet and fully exposed breasts."

"Must you be so petty?"

"Listen to yourself! Uncle, you are completely smitten."

Mustering every shred of his patience, he stood before his niece and took hold of her chin. "What is *truly* bothering you?"

Meeting his gaze, she replied, "I think you can do much better than a trollop."

"I've already told you, she has not been with any other man except me."

"And you believe her?" At his nod, she sighed in frustration. "Venerada is a whore after your money, and I'm astounded that you cannot perceive this obvious fact."

Studying her through narrowed eyes, he shook his head in denial. "I know you better than you know yourself, my dear. This tirade of yours has nothing to do with my mistress and everything to do with your possessive nature. You're envious of the attention I bestow upon her."

"Don't be absurd."

"You would hate any woman I love."

Stricken, she repeated incredulously, *"Love?"*

The word had slid off his tongue. Cursing himself silently, he pressed onward. "You heard correctly."

"You've never loved anyone except yourself."

Furious, she tried to storm off, but he gripped her upper arm. "How dare you speak to me like this?"

She whimpered. "You're hurting me."

Digging his fingers deeper into the soft flesh, he said, "These immature fits of anger were somewhat charming when you were a little girl, but they've long since become wearisome."

Never before had he spoken to her in such a callous manner. "This woman has bewitched you."

"Yes! I am utterly bewitched by Venerada's beauty and kindness. Her naiveté is refreshing—especially in a city as jaded as this one. Venice is only a step above Sodom and Gomorrah, and yet she stands out like a pure white lily amidst the vulgarity and immorality."

"She's a lowly courtesan!"

Cristofolo administered a sharp slap to his niece's face, causing her to stagger backward in shock.

Her hand flew to her stinging cheek. "How could you?"

"I've had my fill of your ill-tempered comportment. Go home to your husband and let him suffer your distasteful company."

"I cannot believe my ears. You're choosing a common slut over your own niece? Have you lost your wits?"

"No, I have only lost my patience. Forgive me for striking you, but it seems you have become obsessed with my lover."

"I care about your happiness."

"Then allow me to be happy."

She placed a hand on his chest. "Cristofolo *please—*"

Pushing her away, he snapped, "I'll have none of your manipulative wiles. Stop meddling in my personal affairs. From this moment onward, I forbid you from speaking of Venerada d'Oro. My love life is not your concern. Do you understand?"

"But—"

"No more!"

Polonia ran across the room and picked up the green Oriental vase—the same one in which he had hidden the necklace. In a fit of rage, she hurled it against the wall. Shards of porcelain rained down upon the floor after a verdant explosion.

Cristofolo caught up to his niece with long strides and gripped both of her shoulders. Shaking her roughly, he demanded, "What is wrong with you?"

Tears streamed down her cheeks and she went limp. A moment of heavy silence passed between the two as they stared at each other's mouths while breathing heavily.

She whispered faintly, "I love you."

Cristofolo's eyes widened with shock—*and something else.* "It's best if you leave now," he said huskily, pushing her away and going to the window.

Devastated by his rejection, she fled.

Isabetta, who had witnessed their exchange through a crack in the door of the adjoining room, quietly entered the salon.

Fate had bestowed a gift that day.

Cristofolo looked at her in surprise. "Venerada, I didn't know you were here."

"I noticed Signora Polonia's carriage outside when I arrived from the market and thought it best to wait until she left before announcing my presence. My intention was not to eavesdrop. I'm sorry you had to endure that on my account."

He rushed over to take her hands into his own. "It is I who am sorry, sweetheart."

"For what?"

Cocking his head to the side, he asked, "Are you not angry and offended by my niece's cruel words?"

"How can I be offended by the words of someone who doesn't know me?"

Touching her cheek, he smiled. "So young yet so wise."

"Obviously, your niece is worried about you. The passion she displayed, including breaking your vase, is derived from pure unselfish love. You see that, don't you?"

"I suppose you're right."

"You must be proud of Signora Polonia, for she is beautiful, sophisticated, and intelligent. I admire her immensely. You're a lucky man—*a lucky uncle*." She felt like rinsing her mouth out with rosewater after speaking those words.

"I *am* proud of her and I know she loves me."

"Don't be cross with your niece."

Those words sobered him. "She left here in a dreadful state. Do you think she'll come around?"

Isabetta shrugged with deliberate nonchalance. "If you continue to flaunt her feelings as you did today, she may keep her distance. I would hate for that to happen, my darling. I certainly don't want to create a wedge between you two."

Cristofolo wandered to the window again to stare blindly at the water. "Could I have been too harsh with her?"

Going over to the sideboard, Isabetta said, "You and Signora Polonia should mend the rift immediately. Wounds fester when left untended." Hidden in her cleavage was the tiny bottle of mysterious liquid she had purchased from the wise woman. Discreetly, she reached inside the top of her bodice as she inquired, "Would you like a bit of wine to calm you?"

"Yes, please," he replied, his eyes visually tracking the progress of a foreign galley sailing in the distance.

Isabetta dumped the potent aphrodisiac into a crystal decanter full of wine, then poured the ruby liquid into a chalice. "Here, drink this."

Turning around to accept the vessel, he smiled. "Thank you. Aren't you going to join me?"

She pretended to go to the sideboard to pour herself some wine, then stopped. "I almost forgot! I have an appointment with the seamstress in less than an hour. I'm afraid I must go."

"Hurry back."

Blinking, she said, "Veronica Franco asked me to dine with her this evening. Remember?"

"When did you tell me?"

"This morning," she lied. "You must have been distracted."

He appeared puzzled. "I don't recall."

"She hasn't been feeling well, and I cannot refuse my former mentor in her delicate condition." He took a sip of the wine and made a face, prompting her to add, "Is it not to your liking?"

"It tastes off, but not in a bad way." Frowning into the chalice, he said, "If it means that much to you, fine. Go and sup with her, but I want you in my bed before midnight."

Isabetta kissed his lips, then went downstairs without further ado. Glancing around, she opened and closed the front door to make it sound as though she had left the house. She then crept down the hallway and went out the back, leaving the servant entrance unlocked. The moment she arrived home, she put quill to sheet. She had seen her lover write enough letters to mimic his penmanship and signature.

My dearest Polonia,

Please accept my sincere apology. I cannot bear the thought of you thinking low of me because of my association with Venerada. I beg your patience, for I am a man with physical needs that must be met. Be assured that you possess the greatest claim over my affections. No other woman will ever take your place. Dine with your uncle tonight and let us make amends.

Your servant, C.

The second letter she wrote bore a feminine script.

Most beloved uncle,

Forgive me, I beg you. My conduct earlier was inexcusable. The love I bear for you clouds my reason. If Venerada makes you happy, then so be it. I only want the best for you. Please know that in my eyes you are above all men. I want to apologize in person tonight. Receive me as you always have.

Your loving niece, Polonia

Isabetta paid a messenger extra money to dispatch both letters as fast as humanly possible.

Alba, who had been silently observing her mistress for the last half hour, finally commented, "I don't know what you're up to, but the look on your face tells me it's no good."

Isabetta poured herself a tankard of ale, then took a long sip. "Tonight is very important. There is much at stake."

"Why?"

"Fate miraculously played into my hands today. If everything goes as I have planned, I will have my revenge on both Polonia *and* Cristofolo."

Resting her fists on her bony hips, Alba regarded her mistress with worry. "You must live with the consequences of your actions."

"I'm looking forward to it."

Isabetta ventured out into the deepening twilight in a black hooded cloak. Vendors were packing up their wares in the piazza, eager to go home. She caught sight of Viaro throwing the fish he hadn't sold into a basket. His wife would probably make a tasty stew with the leftovers.

Each anxious step took her closer to Cristofolo's home. Skirting the piazza, she clung to the deepening shadows in order not to be seen. Suspended in the violet twilight sky was a gleaming white crescent moon. Lurking in a narrow alley across the street from her lover's house, she waited patiently for Polonia's carriage to arrive. The instant she spied the vehicle turning onto the street, she crept toward the back of the palazzo. Thankfully, none of the servants had noticed the unlocked door. Without making a sound, she slipped inside.

***

Cristofolo sat in his study deep in thought while leafing through a book. Polonia's reconciliatory message had done wonders for his mood. The space contained mahogany furniture and the walls were painted pine green. A tapestry depicting a hunting scene hung beside a trio of wide bookcases. He paused to refill his chalice from the crystal decanter on the table beside him, then drank deeply.

Light female footsteps ascending the stairs prompted him to close the book and set it aside. He stood, catching his reflection in the darkening glass panes of the window. Slicked-back hair tied neatly at the nape and a crisp cravat afforded him a distinguished look. A servant opened the door to allow Polonia access into the room.

She flung herself at him the moment they were alone. "Oh my dear sweet uncle…"

Cristofolo staggered slightly as he wrapped his arms around her trembling form. Was she crying? In an attempt to sooth her, he said, "Don't worry, my pet. I'm not angry with you."

She gazed up at him. "I'm here to make amends."

"I know, I want that too."

"We should never quarrel."

"Agreed." He poured wine into a chalice and handed it to her before taking hold of his own vessel. "Let's drink to that."

After touching her rim to his, she drank deeply. "I don't think low of you, so erase the thought from your head."

"I never thought you did," he shot back, puzzled.

"I adore you, Uncle Cristofolo."

Tapping the tip of her nose playfully, he said, "And I, you. Am I truly above all men in your eyes?"

"You already know the answer."

"I want to hear it."

"Yes…and I'm not callous or stupid. I realize you're a man with certain *needs*."

Cocking a brow, he bristled at the invasive comment. "Indeed, as are most men."

"Indeed," she repeated, her face engulfed in flames. Wine had mellowed her senses and loosened her tongue. Iseppo rarely allowed her to drink undiluted wine.

"I'm glad you've come to your senses about Venerada."

Her eyes became two slits as she studied him intently. "What do you mean by that?"

"My happiness is important to you, is it not?"

"Yes, but…"

"I'm accepting your apology, Polonia."

It was her turn to bristle at his clipped tone. "I'm here to bestow forgiveness for your treatment of me earlier."

A mirthless male chuckle filled the room. "I wasn't the one screaming like a banshee and breaking things."

"You provoked my bad behavior when you confessed your undying love for a *whore*."

Cold steel crept into his eyes. "I don't recall using the word 'undying' on any occasion."

"You may as well have, the way you go on about her," she spat before gulping down some wine.

They stopped and stared at each other in the same challenging manner. Blue eye to blue eye, haughty stance to haughty stance—arrogance personified.

Exhaling a deep breath, Cristofolo turned his head to the side. "We're arguing again."

"It seems so," she agreed coolly.

"I can't afford your childish temper, my dear. That vase you destroyed was quite expensive."

"The only thing *destroyed* here is my hope that you would come to your senses."

"Now you're being melodramatic."

"And you're being stubborn. Listen to reason, *please*."

Refilling their vessels with more wine, he ventured, "I don't understand how you can judge another person after such a brief exchange. You saw her in a church for barely a moment."

"It doesn't require much time to sum up that woman. She can never love you in the manner you deserve."

"And what would you know about what I deserve?"

Swiping the chalice from the table, she took a long sip. Emboldened by the wine, she replied, "We may be related by blood, but first and foremost you are a man and I, a woman."

Incredulity colored his features. "My God, Polonia, you act like you're in love with me."

Tense silence filled the room as she went to the window and stared outside. Nocturnal Venice danced before her eyes as a strange feeling of lightness made her knees gelatinous. Peering into the chalice, she wondered where her uncle had procured such a potent vintage.

"Did you hear me?"

Tears prickling her eyes, she replied, “I did.”

“Do you have anything to say for yourself?”

Head swimming and muscles liquefying, she spun around to face him. “What if I am?”

He responded with a blank stare. “What if you’re *what*?”

“In love with you…” Her words were barely audible but the shock on his face meant that he had heard them. When he said nothing, she demanded, “Why is that so hard to fathom?”

He emptied the chalice and set it down firmly. “Of course you love me—I am your uncle—but you are not *in* love with me. There is a stark difference.”

“Is there?”

“You don’t know what you’re saying.”

“But I do, *Cristofolo.*”

Clenching his fists, he said, “Stop it.”

Boldly pushing aside the drapes, she pointed at their reflections in the dark glass panes. “Look at us. Beautiful, fierce, noble…we are perfectly matched.”

“Polonia—”

“I am not a child!”

Storming across the room, he removed the chalice from her hand and set it on the table. “I think you’ve had quite enough. This is why women should never drink undiluted wine.”

“I’m perfectly lucid, I assure you.”

“Don’t tease me, Polonia.”

The warning sounded like a feral growl. Fear and excitement made her throat tighten. “I’m not—”

“I’m in no mood for infantile games tonight. I’m speaking as a man and not your uncle.”

Moving in a slow circle, they measured up each other like a pair of jungle cats. Cristofolo’s hand darted out to seize her wrist. Pulling her into his arms, he debated for only a moment before lowering his head and plundering her mouth. She melted into the kiss without hesitation.

The sinful attraction between them had bloomed after her transformation from child to woman—neither of them could deny it. Society and religion had kept them from acting upon their dark, forbidden desires. *Until now.*

Attempting to preserve some semblance of propriety, Cristofolo reluctantly shoved her away. "I can't."

Pressing against him, she snaked her arms around his neck. "Don't deny me."

"We must stop," he murmured against her lips.

Her hand slithered down his chest like a serpent, past the hem of his doublet. "What if I don't want to stop?"

"Don't…" Her hand crept lower still and his breathing grew shallow. *"Oh God."*

"Do you want me?"

"I burn for you, Polonia…But this is wrong."

"Is it?"

Groaning from her sensual caress, his eyes fluttered shut.

Putting her lips to his ear, she whispered, "Take me."

No sooner had she uttered the words than he slammed her back against the wall. "Is this what you want?" His hands greedily groped her body as he pressed himself between her thighs. "Look what you've done…Do you feel *that*?"

"Yes," she breathed as he nuzzled her throat.

Leaning back to meet her gaze, his eyes glinted like ice. Cold. *Dangerous*. "God has already slated us both for Hell after what we've done. We may as well indulge in lust, for what's another mortal sin?"

"Quiet, you fool," she warned, her eyes darting to the door.

"I am a fool," he agreed, yanking at the fabric of her gown in order to devour her breast. After a moment, he continued, "Conspiring to murder—"

Clamping her hand over his mouth to silence him, she chided, "The servants may hear you." Retreating her hand, she yelped. "Ow! You bit me."

A devilish grin stretched across his face as she examined the mark of his teeth on the palm of her hand. "I'm going to do more than that to you, Polonia." Cupping her buttocks roughly, he ground out, "God might strike me dead, but not before I've had you, woman."

She gasped, relishing the animal she had always known

existed beneath her uncle's sophisticated veneer.

Cristofolo claimed Polonia in a savage manner, and she made no complaint. In fact, she fornicated with the same level of wantonness as the prostitutes in the dank alleys of the Castelletto. His seed came out in a hot rush and he prayed the sinful act would not result in pregnancy.

"Cristofolo," she murmured with closed eyes.

Surprisingly, the abhorrent yet satisfying copulation with his sensuous niece only reinforced his tender feelings for Venerada. His lover's sweet face shimmered into focus in his mind's eye as the last remnants of his climax raked through his body. Now more than ever, he loved his young mistress and could see himself as her lawful husband. Yes, Venerada would be his wife! Casting a glance at his niece, he imagined her as a child frolicking in the garden. Dear God, what had he done? Nausea swept over him.

Polonia opened her eyes, saw her uncle's expression, and faltered. Harsh reality served as a bucket of cold water to instantly douse the flames of passion.

Incapable of looking at each other, they panted within an obligatory embrace. Both realized in that moment that whatever special relationship they had fostered in the past was now dead. The playful flirtation, the easy banter, the afternoon outings, their friendship, the social events, the expensive gifts…

Gone forever.

Cristofolo and Polonia had partaken of the forbidden fruit and, like Adam and Eve, they would pay dearly for their sin.

***

Isabetta kept her ear pressed to the study's door. The entire scene had unfolded like a raunchy theatrical performance fit for peasants. Straightening, she squared her shoulders and took a deep breath. The hour of vindication had finally arrived and she shook with anticipation. Keeping the cloak's hood low to hide her face, she pushed open the door with dramatic flourish. Catching the sinful pair *en flagrante delicto*, she gasped loudly in feigned outrage.

Cristofolo's face blanched at the unexpected sight of his

lover. Untangling himself from his niece's embrace, he ran across the room while fumbling with the front of his breeches. "Venerada!"

Color rose in Polonia's cheeks as she cried petulantly, "Cristofolo, come back here."

Isabetta refrained from giggling at the tawdry spectacle as she forced a frown. "What is the meaning of this?"

Cristofolo reached for her hand. "I can explain—"

Recoiling, she cried, "I don't need an explanation for what my eyes behold. With your own niece? How utterly vile!"

Polonia's eyes flashed. "You're one to talk, you whore!"

"At least I am a *cortigiana onesta*. From where I am standing, madam, it is *you* who is the whore—and an incestuous one at that!"

Polonia's hands balled into fists. "How dare you? I will destroy you!" When Isabetta laughed at the threat, she looked to her uncle. "Say something, will you? How can you allow this prostitute to disrespect me in your home?"

Cristofolo positioned himself between the two women and ignored his niece. "I'm sorry, Venerada, I didn't mean for this to happen. I don't know what came over me."

Hearing this, Polonia fumed. "Do I mean nothing to you? I thought we loved each other…I gave myself—"

"Shut your mouth," he snapped irritably.

Isabetta's gaze slid from Polonia's distraught face to his pale one. "I believe you two deserve one another."

"Venerada, please."

Turning on her heel, Isabetta stormed out of the room and slammed the door behind her.

Cristofolo almost tripped in his pathetic attempt to chase her down. "My darling, wait!"

Two servants materialized in the hallway. One of them discreetly pointed to Polonia, who slouched against the wall in a disheveled dress with her breasts exposed. Cristofolo sped past them in a state of disarray, struggling to arrange his clothing while descending the stairs.

"Venerada, my love, come back!"

Ignoring his pleas, Isabetta exited the house and melted into the velvety night. Clouds had blown in from the North to obliterate the moon, casting the city in night shadows. She hid in a nearby alley to spy on Cristofolo, who stood in the doorway desperately calling her name. A few curious neighbors witnessed the commotion from their windows.

"Venerada!"

Running his hands through his hair in frustration, he began to pace. Thick strands came loose from the neat style and hung around his worried face. Polonia came out of the house and tried to persuade him to go back inside. He barely listened to her words as she stubbornly clung to him. At one point she took hold of his arm and pulled him toward the door. A struggle ensued and he broke free with a violent yank that almost caused her to fall backward. She stared at him in shock and anger.

Isabetta was too far away to hear the ensuing argument, but apparently the neighbors weren't since some of them threw open their shutters and leaned upon the window sill. She glimpsed smiles on a few faces as if the tragedy unfurling below was merely an act for their entertainment.

Afraid of being discovered, she left the scene and wove through a maze of streets with quick steps. Only when she had placed enough distance between herself and her enemies did she finally stop. Oddly, she didn't feel the great sense of satisfaction she had anticipated. Some part of her felt sorry for Cristofolo, whom she believed loved her in his own selfish way. Cursing under her breath, she made her way home with quick steps.

Chapter 21

The sordidness of last night's escapade with Cristofolo crashed down upon Polonia the instant she opened her eyes the next morning. Venerada's unexpected visit had only worsened matters. Her uncle had wept actual tears after his lover—*his whore*—had disappeared. She had never once seen him cry.

Groaning with regret, she burrowed her head beneath the covers to blot out the sunlight. Sleep had kept the demons at bay and she wanted nothing more than to return to oblivion. Her lady's maid entered the bedchamber, prompting her to throw off the covers with a resigned sigh. She held out her hand for the damp perfumed cloth. The servant handed it to her with an anxious, knowing look that failed to go unnoticed. "What did you hear, Goretta?"

A pair of brown eyes widened. "Pardon me?"

"Don't play the fool with me. I've known you long enough to recognize that expression. Something is afoot."

Goretta averted her gaze and shrugged.

Polonia panicked. "It's about me, isn't it?"

"I don't know, Signora."

"Dear God, now you're lying. It must be truly horrible. Hurry, help me get dressed." Under her breath, she muttered, "That good-for-nothing harlot has been spreading rumors."

How many people could Venerada have told in such a short period of time? There was only one way to find out.

"I'm going to church this morning and want to look my best. Take out the rose silk with gold embroidery."

Goretta performed her morning duties with ritualistic efficiency, but the firm set of her jaw signaled judgement and disapproval.

Polonia admired her maid's handiwork in the mirror with approval. "Fetch my cloak."

"Would you like me to accompany you, Signora?"

"When have I ever gone gallivanting through the city unaccompanied?"

"Last night."

Goretta's smart retort earned her a slap across the face. "You should learn when to keep your mouth shut."

"I'm sorry, Signora."

"Do you know how many women in Venice envy me? Nearly all of them. Beauty and wealth attracts resentment and covetousness. Remember that."

Goretta said nothing as she hastily readied herself to go out with her mistress.

No sooner did they exit the house than Polonia began drawing looks of disgust from both passersby and market vendors. Holding her head high, she paid them little heed and pressed on to the church.

"Perhaps we should go back," Goretta suggested.

"Be quiet."

"The women made their way down the nave, evoking whispers in their wake. Heads turned and parishioners stared accusingly at Polonia. They knew.

Everyone knew.

To Polonia's mortification, a single word floated down the nave until it reached her ears: *incest*. Gripping her maid's hand, she whispered through stiff pale lips, "Get me out of here."

The servant placed a steadying arm around her mistress's shoulders and guided her toward the exit.

Clutching her chest, Polonia could barely breathe as she stepped outside. She staggered blindly across the piazza with tearful eyes. Rather than go home, she went straight to her uncle's palazzo. It took several knocks to gain entrance.

Cristofolo received her in a black silk robe and long linen nightshirt. His legs and feet were bare. "Dear God, *already*? What time is it?"

Polonia's eyes glistened at the harsh rebuke. "Is that slut in your bed?"

He sighed. "You saw her leave last night, didn't you?"

Red-rimmed eyes and sallow complexion bespoke of his

misery. God curse Venerada! "Where is she?"

"I wish I knew," he replied softly, his voice on the verge of cracking with emotion.

"She really means this much to you?"

The venom in her voice made him cringe. "Yes, yes, and yes! How many times must I repeat myself?"

"Uncle—"

"Don't."

"Please, listen to me—"

A dismissive wave of his hand silenced her. "I need to get some rest because I haven't slept a wink."

Appalled by this, she demanded, "Tell me you didn't go searching for that woman…"

"Indeed I did, until five this morning and I still haven't found her. Leave me alone, will you?"

"I'm going to make her pay for her impertinence."

He rolled his eyes. "Polonia, please…my head throbs."

Balling her hands into fists she shouted, "I don't care!"

In a moment of blind rage Cristofolo raised his hand as if to strike her, then checked himself. Sighing wearily, he hung his head in defeat. "Just go."

Hurt by the violent gesture, she whimpered. "I thought you loved me…I thought I meant something to you. What we shared last night—"

Shoving his finger in her face, he said through clenched teeth, "*Don't!* Not another word."

A lump formed in her throat and her stomach sank. "How can you treat me like this?"

"As far as I'm concerned, last night was the biggest mistake of my life. Venerada is gone…*She's gone.*" Tears filled his eyes. "Damn you, Polonia."

Turning his back on her, he retreated into his private quarters without uttering another word.

Goretta, who had witnessed the volatile exchange, stood in the hallway fisting the fabric of her skirt in agitation.

Polonia shot her a contemptuous look. "You could have afforded us a shred of privacy, you stupid ninny!"

"I'm so sorry, Signora."

Goretta kept pace beside her furious mistress. The servant's eyes kept darting to Polonia's pale, distressed face. No words were exchanged between them as they rounded corners and hurried through the streets.

Polonia entered the house to find Iseppo in the corridor waiting for them. His eyes were pure ice, his face haggard. "Leave us, Goretta."

The maid scurried off as Iseppo urged his wife into his study and closed the door behind them.

Polonia took a deep breath. "Iseppo—"

His hand darted out and stopped inches from her face, silencing her instantly. Narrowing his eyes, he ground out, "Is it true what people are saying about you and Cristofolo?"

"Wh-what?"

"Is it true?"

"What are they saying, husband?"

Iseppo rounded his desk and sat down. "It seems the two of you have finally given in to your unnatural and mutual lust. You appear to be shocked."

"I don't know what you've heard—"

Upper lip curled in disgust, he snapped, "Oh stop it, Polonia. I'm neither blind nor stupid. Knowing Cristofolo's reputation, I'm surprised that rake didn't try to seduce you sooner."

She stood before her husband like someone facing a judge at a trial. "This is absurd."

"Is it? It's no secret that he finds you attractive. Lord knows he brags about his niece to every man in the city. As for you, the way you dote on your uncle—*openly flirt with him*—it's sick. I've turned a blind eye to it for many years."

Her body trembled. "People love to talk."

"Yes, but they usually have a reason to do so."

"Surely, you don't believe gossipmongers?"

Iseppo lifted a sheet of parchment. "This letter arrived while you and Goretta were out this morning."

She snatched it from his hand and read the words written in neat female script.

Signore Iseppo,

I regret to inform you of a distressing situation. You and I have both been betrayed by the people we love. I am referring to your wife, Signora Polonia, and her uncle who is also my lover, Cristofolo Trasontin. Last night, I caught the two of them engaged in the act of love. The memory will pain me forever...I believe you have the right to know the truth. I shall pray for you.

Venerada d'Oro

Polonia's rage caused her face to turn a purplish red. "That dirty scheming slut!"

Iseppo calmly stared at his wife's performance with disdain. Folding his hands on the desk, he demanded softly, "*Did you* or *did you not* fuck your uncle last night?"

Appalled by the question, she shook her head. "Please, Iseppo, let me explain."

Leaning across the desk, he roared like a lion, "Answer me!"

The entire household and possibly the neighbors had heard him, but he didn't care. Unable to withstand the pressure, Polonia collapsed into a chair and wept bitterly.

Taking this as evidence of her guilt, he recoiled in disgust. "Any other man and I would have understood. I may have even forgiven you...but Cristofolo Trasontin? Aside from him being your own kin, that man has been a thorn in my side for decades. Selfish, arrogant, snobbish—as vain and vile a creature as you."

"Husband, I beg you—"

"Pack your things at once." Reclaiming his seat, he took up a quill and set it to parchment. At the sight of her confused face, he added, "This is no longer your home."

She stared at him incredulously. "No..."

"Don't make me repeat myself."

Panicked, she demanded, "Where will I go?"

He stopped writing and looked up. "Stay with Cristofolo or the Devil. Either way, I don't care. I want you out of my house. I am now writing a letter to my solicitor, and the magistrate will be informed first thing in the morning. You will be charged with adultery and the courts will grant me a divorce."

"Divorce?" She blinked a few times as though she didn't

comprehend the words. "You're casting me out?"

"I am a generous man, so you may keep your clothes and jewels, but I will no longer support you. As of this moment you are cut off."

The blood rushed from her face and she gripped the back of the chair for support. "No, no…I'm sorry. Iseppo, I beg you, don't do this."

"Too late."

"I fell in a moment of weakness. We were drinking. He was drunk and we were arguing…and we…we got caught up in the moment. Before I realized it we were…" She broke off to wipe her eyes and gain some composure. "I swear to you, it will never happen again."

Regarding her icily, he said, "No, it won't. You've made a cuckold of me. I shall never forgive or forget, much less afford you another opportunity to repeat the offense."

Dropping to her knees, she begged, "Iseppo, *please...*"

Refusing to meet her gaze, he continued, "I am summoning the locksmith tomorrow morning to create a new mechanism for the door. By then, you will be on the other side of it."

***

Dark clouds scuttled across the sapphire evening sky by the time Polonia knocked on Cristofolo's door. Torches lit the piazza and all was quiet. A carriage full of packed trunks idled in front of his home. To her chagrin, one of the servants who had witnessed the fiasco last night came to the door. Pushing aside the lanky girl, she ran upstairs to see her uncle.

Cristofolo sighed irritably at the sight of his niece barging into the salon. "You simply cannot stay away from me."

Her face fell. "Iseppo cast me out."

Silence.

He walked over to his distraught niece but refrained from offering the comfort of his touch. She looked hideously pale and haggard. Her reddened eyes were swollen too. "Who told him?"

Bursting into a fit of tears, she replied between sobs, "Venerada sent him a letter…This is all her fault!"

Pinching the bridge of his nose, he took a moment to calm

himself lest he cause more damage with his anger. "*We* did this to ourselves, Polonia. For once in your spoiled miserable life you must assume responsibility for your actions and face the consequences."

She placed a tentative hand on his chest. "How can you side with her against me?"

"I'm not siding with anyone. I only ask that you put yourself in her place. How do you think Venerada feels right now?"

"I don't care!"

"Do you ever think of anyone but yourself?"

"Please hold me," she begged before succumbing to despair.

Against his better judgement, he pulled her into his arms and stroked her hair the way he had always done in the past. Memories from last night made him stiffen with regret. Sensing this, Polonia tightened her grip and tried to kiss him.

"No," he admonished.

"But you and me…"

Pushing her away, he ground out, "Don't you understand, Polonia? *There is no you and me*."

Emotions flitted across her features—pain, regret, love, humiliation—but rage is the one that contorted her face into a chilling mask. "I hate Venerada! May God curse that vile trollop and curse you too!"

Gripping her shoulders, he snapped, "Control yourself."

"I hate you! I hate you! *I hate you!*"

A sharp slap silenced her. Turning his face away, he muttered quietly, "Trust me, right now the feeling is mutual."

Polonia, overwrought to the point of exhaustion, had not touched food or drink throughout the day. Hearing his words, she fell into a dead faint at his feet.

Rather than personally tend to his niece, Cristofolo summoned his valet and instructed, "Put Signora Polonia to bed in one of the ground floor guest chambers and see that she gets some hot broth. Be sure to summon the physician if she doesn't come around soon. I don't want us to have an invalid on our hands."

"As you wish, my lord."

"Has the messenger arrived yet?"

A curt nod served as reply. "There is still no word, sir."

"I want the authorities alerted and the city searched. Money is not an issue. I want Venerada d'Oro found."

"Yes, sir."

Dismissing the servant with a flick of his wrist, Cristofolo reclaimed his seat by the fire and stared into the orange flames. He had spent the day searching for his lover while sending messages to his colleagues. Desperate to find his beloved, he had even knocked on Veronica Franco's door. The courtesan claimed she hadn't seen her former protégé in weeks. It's as if Venerada had vanished into thin air, leaving a surprisingly painful void in the center of his chest.

***

Alba procured a bucket of horse urine to bleach her mistress's hair. Veronica had suggested the stinky treatment in an attempt to restore Isabetta's original color. After several hours of saturating the strands and rinsing out the urine with cold water, they managed to transform the faded henna red to a warm gold hue.

Cocking her head to the side, the servant made a face. "Close enough, I suppose."

Isabetta examined the result in the mirror. "It's fine. The authorities are searching for a woman with red hair."

Alba shook her head in matronly disapproval. "I knew your relationship with that man would end badly."

"For him, not me." *Bad for Polonia too.*

"What of Signore Silvio?"

"He'll be none the wiser."

"Humph," the servant grunted while dragging a comb through damp locks. "Poor fellow believes—"

"Not another word!"

Isabetta had long reconciled herself to the positive and negative consequences of her decisions. Guilt had become a uniform she donned daily. Hopefully, in time, the nagging feeling would subside. She looked forward to having some stability in her life with Silvio, but would she ever attain peace?

There was also the matter of her approaching wedding night. Would she be able to fool her future husband? It would take more than shy blushes and chicken blood to fake virginity. A convincing performance would be required, which would be no small task after having been educated in the art of lovemaking by one of the city's greatest whoremongers.

Deep in thought, she eventually went downstairs and spent the remainder of the day working on accounting ledgers. She possessed more than enough money and could breathe easier. The *Tramonto* would soon be back in her possession and no one would ever take it away from her again. After retrieving her father's maps from the study, she began outlining the routes to Flanders and Holland. A knock on the door broke her concentration.

Alba peered out the window anxiously, then smiled in relief. "Signora Veronica."

Isabetta relaxed. "Let her in."

Veronica entered the room. "*Buona sera*. Ah, I see the horse urine worked."

"Just as you said it would," Isabetta said, patting her hair.

Alba interjected, "Signora Veronica, what will happen if Cristofolo Trasontin finds her?"

"Don't worry, I won't allow anything bad to happen to your mistress." Taking hold of Isabetta's hand, Veronica added, "I need to speak with you privately."

"Certainly." Isabetta said before leading the way upstairs.

Once they were alone, Veronica said in a serious tone, "Cristofolo has sent me several messages and has even presented himself in person at my door. As you know, the *vigili* are scouring the city."

Isabetta shrugged. "They'll get tired soon enough."

"I'm afraid it's not that simple. Cristofolo is determined to find you, and he has enlisted the help of the magistrate. You'll need to do more than color your hair to avoid him."

"What does he want?"

Throwing up her hands in exasperation, Veronica replied, "He wants Venerada!"

"Can't you invent something?"

Shaking her head, the courtesan replied crisply, "I have a reputation to maintain, remember? My protégé can't simply disappear without a feasible explanation."

"I'm sorry, I didn't realize…Forgive me, Veronica. How can I rectify the situation?"

Appeased, Veronica patted her friend's hand. "I told him that you went out of town due to a family illness. Sooner or later you must face him." Going over to the vanity, she toyed with some silk ribbons. "There's something else you should know."

Isabetta watched the colorful strips slide through Veronica's bejeweled fingers. "What is it?"

"Iseppo da Mosta has cast out his wife, denounced her as an adulteress, and is procuring a divorce."

"Are you joking?"

"No—and there's more. Cristofolo, wishing to put the incestuous incident behind him, refused to offer his niece refuge in his home." Veronica set down the ribbons and met her friend's intense gaze. "Polonia, who was already distraught at being tossed into the street like a peasant, became so upset by her uncle's rejection that she suffered an apoplexy. Half of her face and body went slack, so she slurs her words and hobbles with a cane. Unable to face the shame and humiliation of her current situation, she has cloistered herself inside a convent."

Heavy silence followed the account. Veronica studied her friend's face to see what kind of reaction her words had evoked. To her astonishment, Isabetta's face revealed nothing.

"And Cristofolo?"

Going to the window, the courtesan watched the busy world outside. "He is heartbroken, for he has lost both you and his niece at the same time."

"May I ask you a personal question? It's something I've been pondering ever since I became Cristofolo's lover."

"You may ask me anything."

"Do you hate men?" When Veronica glanced at her in confusion, she amended, "What I mean to say is, as a courtesan, has your contempt for men grown with time?"

"Are you asking me this because Cristofolo partook in the same sin as Polonia, but won't suffer the same consequences?"

"Partly, yes…My question applies to men in a more general sense, however."

"I see." Turning her attention back to the view outside, Veronica thought for a moment. "While I admit that being in this profession can be taxing to the mind and body, my answer is no. I don't hate men. On the contrary, I love them."

Isabetta flinched. "How can you feel that way? Men are violent, lustful, greedy—think of how many wars they've waged throughout the centuries. A man took my galley, a man killed my father and brother, a man inadvertently caused my mother's death, a man tried to seduce me, a man bought my virginity…I have grown to *hate* them."

A small eternity passed before Veronica said, "Imagine the cunning and precise calculation required to strategize a successful war campaign, or the courage to plunge a sword into an enemy's heart." She pointed out the window. "Behold that grand palazzo across the piazza and the gondola in the canal. Think of our beautiful public statues, the delicate glass chandeliers suspended from the ceilings of noble homes, our magnificent cathedral and its countless treasures fashioned from silver and gold. Men created these exquisite things with their hands! I could never loathe the beings capable of such skill and talent. *Such vision.* Men study hard to become doctors, scientists, navigators, builders, warriors, artists…even the simple farmers and fishermen feed us thanks to their knowledge of the land and sea. Better to try and *understand* rather than *hate* men." As an afterthought, she added, "Sometimes, I pity them."

"Why?"

"For all their physical strength and bravado, the vast majority are fragile. More than once I've heard a man whimper in the dark of night when he believed me to be asleep—powerful men who would never dare display such vulnerability in the light of day because their families and society expect them to be strong. *Invincible.* Heavy burdens are placed upon the shoulders of men, and they must carry that weight without complaint. Think on *that* the next time your heart leans toward loathing."

Isabetta lowered her head in defeat. "I concede to your many well-made points, Veronica. It's obvious that I have been too precipitous in my judgement."

"Wisdom comes with age, dear girl," Veronica offered with a friendly smile. "Before I go, there's one more thing you must do. Go and see Cristofolo."

"I'm sorry, but I can't do that."

The courtesan's mouth became a hard line. "At the very least send him a letter. Invent an excuse, but please don't leave things unresolved. Do it for my sake."

Isabetta nodded. "I will, I promise."

***

Alzo strolled up the path to his daughter's house on a fine spring morning in late May. Birds sang sweetly and wild baby rabbits scurried through the brush flanking his feet. Above his head, tree branches unfurled their tender green buds.

Cassandra greeted him at the door with an eager wave. "This is a wonderful surprise, Father. Is Mama with you?"

"Your mother is home resting."

"Is she ill?"

"Only a headache."

"I'm relieved to hear it." Glancing around nervously, she whispered, "I'm glad you came, for there is something I wish to tell you."

Upon closer inspection, he saw that his daughter's eyes were red and swollen. "Are you unwell?"

"Not here. Let's go inside."

Alzo tracked his daughter into the villa, his eyes falling upon the swell of her ever-growing hips. She would soon become corpulent if she wasn't careful. To his surprise, she led him to her private quarters. Once they had settled on a pair of chairs, he observed Cassandra's fidgeting hands. "You used to do that as a child whenever you were anxious about something."

"Oh, Father. I don't know what to do. I hate to disturb you with this matter but..."

"Out with it, girl. Tell me what's wrong."

"Donata needs to find a husband immediately."

Spreading out his hands, he retorted, "She's Petro's cousin. Let his family deal with the matchmaking."

Nervous hands repeatedly smoothed the brocade skirt over her rounded thighs. "You don't understand…She's pregnant."

He blinked. "Who is the father?" Given her matronly appearance, it wouldn't surprise him if Petro had impregnated his comely kin. His daughter's reluctance prompted him to add, "Come now, you must have some suspicion."

She stood and went to the door to make sure no one lingered in the corridor. Racing back to her father, she put her lips to his ear. *"My husband."*

His suspicion confirmed, Alzo hissed in irritation. "Does anyone else know?"

"I don't think so."

Gripping her shoulders, he instructed harshly, "Say nothing to no one, do you understand?"

Cassandra's eyes grew wide. "You're hurting me—"

"Do you understand?" Tears streamed down her cheeks as she nodded. Releasing his hold, he grimaced. "I must go."

"Don't go, please. Stay for the midday meal."

"There's no way I can face your husband knowing that he's placed my daughter in this compromising position." Softening in the face of her fresh tears, he cooed, "Don't cry, my darling. I shall fix this mess."

"How?"

"I'll figure something out."

Leaving Mestre with his stomach tied in knots, Alzo went straight to his workshop. Amid the clicking and clacking of looms, he recalled his appointment with Cristofolo Trasontin later that afternoon. They needed to discuss the details for the next journey. God willing, it would generate a fortune in profit to make up for the losses of the last two trips.

He set off for the nobleman's palazzo at a brisk pace. Clouds skidded across the sky to obliterate the sun, making Venice as somber as his current mood. How was he going to keep Petro's infidelity a secret? A bastard child, especially a son, would jeopardize Cassandra's position in the household. Petro could invent a reason to rid himself of his fat wife, legitimize his bastard, and marry his pretty cousin. The mere thought made him want to spit flames. After all, he had spent a fortune on that damn wedding!

Upon arriving at the nobleman's home, Alzo noticed a messenger leaving the premises. After giving his name to the valet, he was led upstairs to a finely furnished salon where Cristofolo stood by the hearth studying a sheet of parchment with a furrowed brow. Whatever news it contained had obviously upset him.

Alzo cleared his throat, then ventured, "Good afternoon, my lord. Have I come at a bad time?"

Casting a flickering glance at his guest, the nobleman replied distractedly, "Give me a moment, will you?" Indicating the sideboard, he added, "Help yourself to a drink."

While Alzo awkwardly poured himself some wine, Cristofolo silently reread the disturbing letter.

Dearest Cristofolo,

I am doing my best not to allow your sinful relationship with Polonia to sully the fond memories of our time together. That said, I cannot bring myself to face you. On a happier note, I'm to be married soon. My betrothed is a good man; a young and handsome Milanese. Farewell and God bless you.

—V

Maintaining composure for the sake of his guest, the proud nobleman kept the humiliating tears at bay.

Alzo neared his host hesitantly. "Shall I come back later?"

Cristofolo shook his head in response to the question while angrily crumpling the letter and tossing it into the flames. "What brings you here, Alzo?"

"We had an appointment, don't you remember? I need to know how many bolts of brocade and velvet you wish to order for the Flemish and Dutch distributors."

"Ah yes, that's right. Forgive me, I've been busy with another matter and forgot about our meeting. Please, sit."

Alzo selected a chair, then delved into a litany of numbers and figures. He had taken the liberty of lugging one of his accounting ledgers to the meeting, and he removed it from the satchel with a nervous laugh. "It's a bit heavy."

"I can imagine," murmured the nobleman.

Alzo delved into his ideas for the upcoming journey with great enthusiasm but Cristofolo appeared disinterested. The nobleman attempted to pay attention, but Venerada's hurtful words kept intruding upon his thoughts. He understood that she was hurt, but he couldn't accept her marriage to another man. Pain unlike anything he had ever known pierced his heart. A combination of jealousy, envy, and love…

"My lord, what do you think?" Alzo inquired at length.

"What?"

"About the inventory of supplies for the journey…?"

Rather than reply, Cristofolo stood and urged his guest across the salon. He had neither the stomach nor the mind to deal with business matters at the moment. "I beg your patience, my friend."

Puzzled, Alzo reluctantly shuffled toward the door. "Did I say something wrong?"

Shaking his head, Cristofolo turned the brass latch. "I don't feel well. Please come back tomorrow when my head is clear."

He then closed the door on Alzo's stunned face.

CHAPTER 22

Silvio returned to Venice at the end of May. His trips to Treviso and Genoa had proved fruitful and he had made valuable contacts. Eager to see Isabetta, he went straight to her home. She greeted him at the door with a smile.

"Isabetta, I've missed you." His eyes drifted from her pretty face to her hair. "Back to your natural color, I see."

"Yes," she said, leading him inside the house. She pushed him against the closed door and claimed his lips in a welcoming kiss.

"I take it Alba is not at home," he surmised with slight amusement when she pulled away.

"She's at the market," she replied before plying him with more kisses. "I'm happy you're home, Silvio."

"Me too, sweetheart." The urgency of her emotion and actions were not lost on him. "Did you think I would not come back?"

She held him tightly. "I appreciate you, that's all."

Gently pushing her away, he searched her face. "Are you all right? Did something happen?"

Shaking her head, she insisted on being within the circle of his arms. Sensing her need for comfort, he said nothing more as he held her close.

***

On the first of June, Isabetta donned her best gown and stepped into the warm morning air with a light heart. Tucked into her jeweled fist was a document worth more than gold.

Miro stood waiting for her at the top of the street. When she drew near, he grinned excitedly. "*Buongiorno*, Isabetta. Are you ready?"

"I've been dreaming of this day for months."

"You look pretty." He offered his arm. "Shall we?"

She accepted his arm and kept pace at his side in anxious

silence. Her heart fluttered within her ribcage like a trapped finch in a cage. She felt giddy from both joy and relief.

Miro inquired, "How is Signore Silvio?"

"He's fine, thank you."

"When is the wedding?"

"Next week."

A pair of boys in ratty clothing cut in front of them and Miro paused to make sure they weren't pickpockets. When the rambunctious children began teasing and chasing each other, he commenced walking.

Casting a side glance at Isabetta, he asked, "Why isn't your betrothed accompanying us this morning?"

"I didn't tell him."

He faltered. "He doesn't know?"

"I'll inform him later today that I've reclaimed the galley, but this morning is mine. *Only* mine."

"And mine since I am here with you," he reminded her with a playful wink.

"I trust you, Miro."

The unspoken question following her words hung in the air between them: *Don't you trust Silvio?*

Miro finally said, "I'll always try to live up to that honor."

She blushed. "I'll hold you to that."

"Fair enough."

The water sparkled in the sunshine and the sound of men shouting could be heard on the breeze. They cut through an alley and emerged onto the quay to witness a flurry of activity. Captain Rizo Santino stood on the deck of the *Tramonto* barking commands to the crewmen. Cristofolo sat upon his horse observing the scene in a costly outfit befitting his social status. She stared at her former lover with a blend of pity and resentment. As reluctant as she was to admit it, she no longer harbored hatred in her heart for him. How could she after the many nights of pleasurable lovemaking they had shared? His kisses, gifts, and endearments had melted away some of her bitterness. *Some*. Not all.

Alzo Cornetti stood beside Cristofolo's horse in a luxuriant cloak of red silk edged in silver embroidery. The confident tilt of her uncle's head caused her breath to quicken with anger.

"You've gone pale and your hands are like ice," Miro whispered in a concerned tone as he rubbed one of her hands between his own. "You can turn back right now and let me handle this situation on your behalf."

Retrieving her hand, she quipped, "And deprive myself of the pleasure? *Never.*"

Discreetly, she walked over to a pair of *vigili* who stood in the background supervising the loading. Holding up the certificate of ownership for the *Tramonto*, she said, "I want these men and their cargo off of *my* ship immediately."

One of the officers retrieved the legal document from her fingertips and read the neatly written words. Examining the official seal, he conferred briefly with his companion and then went over to Cristofolo. The latter studied the parchment sheet while seated upon the saddle, then dismounted with a frown.

Miro, who stood facing Isabetta, stared at a spot over her shoulder. "Cristofolo is behind you and he's coming this way."

"Does he look upset?"

"Furious."

"Splendid."

"What's the meaning of this?"

Cristofolo's voice held anger and outrage, which made Isabetta's heart race. She deliberately stood with her back to him until the very last moment. Turning around slowly, she replied, "I should ask you the same question, my lord."

Cristofolo froze at the sound of her voice. Recognition lit up his features, causing his indignation to melt into a mixture of relief and confusion. "*Venerada?* My love, what are you doing here? I've been looking for you. I received your message…"

When he reached for her hand, she recoiled. "Don't touch me! We are not acquainted, sir."

"What do you mean?"

Addressing the *vigili*, she demanded, "Who is this man?"

"Signore Cristofolo Trasontin, the gentleman who paid Zanetto Bastian's debt," the officer replied while looking from one to the other.

"Venerada, stop playing games," Cristofolo warned through clenched teeth as he reached for her hand once more.

Dodging him yet again, she snapped, "You are clearly mistaking me for someone else!"

The officer stepped between them. "This is Isabetta Bastian, my lord. Daughter of the late Zanetto Bastian. She holds the certificate of ownership for the galley."

"Impossible," Cristofolo said, surprised.

"And yet it's true. I paid off the debt *with interest* this morning." Pointing to Alzo, Isabetta added, "That man there is my uncle, Alzo Cornetti. He can vouch for my identity."

Cristofolo opened and closed his mouth twice like a freshly caught fish gasping for air. His puzzled expression transformed into one of realization as he hastily assembled the puzzle piece by piece. Pain, anger, and eventually begrudging admiration settled upon features. Narrowing his eyes, he nodded slowly in understanding. "Well played, Signorina Isabetta."

She said in a voice meant only for his ears, "I wanted to make you suffer as much as I have. Did I succeed, *my darling*?"

Glassy blue eyes stared at her and she spied pain in their depths. "Congratulations on your victory."

"I want the cargo hold emptied. *Now*."

Cristofolo was about to say something, then thought better of it when he noticed one of the officers watching him. Inclining his head at her, he turned on his heel and hastened to speak with his captain. Rizo's eyes darted to where Isabetta stood and his mouth twisted in anger.

Miro nudged Isabetta and whispered, "Your uncle seems intent on speaking with you too. Here he comes."

"Alzo needs to wait his turn."

Miro followed her gaze and saw Rizo stomping toward them. Scowling, the captain pointed a finger in Isabetta's face. "I've been promised this journey."

"Not by me," she reminded him coolly.

"I am owed wages."

She shrugged, unconcerned. "I am under no obligation to

pay you. Settle your account with the men who contracted you."

The captain cursed under his breath, prompting Miro to clear his throat in warning and step protectively in front of Isabetta. Staring each other down, neither man spoke for a long time. Rizo finally let loose and expletive and vacated the area.

"Isabetta, what is the meaning of this?"

Turning toward her uncle's voice, she feigned surprise. "Uncle Alzo, what are you doing here? Shouldn't you be home comforting Cassandra?" At his blank look, she added, "Donata is pregnant, is she not?"

His face blanched. "How do you know?"

"*Everyone* knows. People love to gossip and there's nothing better than a dirty scandal to set tongues wagging."

Alzo flickered a glance at Miro, then stated, "I would hardly call it a dirty scandal. Donata behaved like a trollop and is now reaping what she has sown."

Isabetta laughed again, only louder, drawing the gazes of many. "Your son-in-law is a rogue! Fornicating with his own cousin beneath your daughter's nose. Cassandra should leave Petro Vendramin at once."

"Keep your voice down, girl," Alzo snapped, his eyes darting left and right. "Your aunt has taken ill because of this."

"I am no *girl*, Uncle Alzo. I am a woman. Your days of dominating over me are over." She rearranged her face into a mask of pity and added, "As for Aunt Rosa, she spoke *so highly* of Petro before the wedding. How disillusioned she must feel right now. I never told anyone this, but your son-in-law once attempted to seduce me in the garden. Thankfully, I fought him off and fled. Donata must have lacked the will to do the same."

Alzo's face reddened. Staring pointedly at Isabetta's attire, he concluded, "Veronica Franco must pay you well if you can afford such fine gowns and jewelry."

"Don't you recognize your own fabric? This dress was one of Cassandra's cast-offs, which she substituted as payment for actual wages at your suggestion."

"An arm's length of Cornetti fabric is quite costly."

A saccharine smile settled upon her lips as she waved the

certificate in his face. "Yes, but one cannot pay a debt with fabric. I'm the owner of the *Tramonto* now."

Incredulous, he demanded, "How?"

"That's none of your concern."

Forcing a smile, he said, "Congratulations, dear niece. When do you plan to set sail, and where?"

"Silvio and I are planning to sail to Flanders, then Holland. We depart within a fortnight, after our wedding."

"Splendid news! Silvio Torres is a fine young man and I'm certain your parents are smiling from Heaven. Rocco too, of course. We shall make a fortune together."

"We?"

The smile faded from his lips. "I wouldn't dream of not splitting profits equally with you and Silvio."

Pursing her lips, she adjusted the gold bracelet on her wrist. "What about Cristofolo Trasontin and Iseppo da Mosta? I thought you were doing business with those men."

Red-cheeked, he replied sheepishly, "Obviously, the situation has changed. Now that the *Tramonto* is back in your hands, my loyalty is to my niece."

"Ah." Raising her eyes to meet his, she said icily, "The thing is, I've already made an agreement with the Bevilacqua family. Their beautiful fabrics will be in the cargo hold of my galley."

Bewildered, he blinked. "The Bevilacqua, you say? But they are my competitors."

"I'm well aware of that. In fact, they looked almost as surprised as you do right now when I arrived at their door with a contract in my hand and a solicitor at my side."

"You did what?"

"They've signed on with me for the next three years. The Bevilacqua stand to make a fortune on the deal."

"How can you conspire with the Bevilacqua behind my back? Have you no scruples? We are family!"

Cocking her head to the side, she feigned surprise. "I learned from you, Uncle Alzo. Did you not conspire behind my back? Were we not family then?"

"Your mother placed her trust in me, and I did business with your father for years. Who do you think you are consulting with solicitors? Making your own deals like some mad woman. You forget your place!"

She took a step closer and put her face near his. "You don't fool me, old man. Whatever relationship you fostered with my parents were advantageous to you, otherwise you wouldn't have wasted your time. Do you really believe I'm so stupid? I know what you did."

"You have no idea what you're saying."

"I beg to differ. Greed compelled you to aid Polonia and Cristofolo in undermining me. The *Tramonto* was the only thing I had left of Rocco and my father, and you took it away when I needed it most."

Panic crept into his eyes when he realized the extent of his niece's contempt for him. "You can't do this to me, Isabetta. My sales have dropped considerably these last few years. I rely on those profits to survive, to keep my business afloat."

Crossing her arms, she quipped, "How is that my problem?"

"Insolent girl! Your father would never choose the Bevilacqua over me." Covering his face with his hands, he whimpered. "Oh God, I'll be ruined…"

She waited for him to compose himself, then said, "My father would be devastated if he knew how you've treated me. As for your financial woes, perhaps your son-in-law can help you. There are plenty of galleys and ships seeking goods. Go and peddle your wares to them."

"What about your aunt and Cassandra? How do you think they'll feel when they learn about this?"

She shrugged, her face devoid of emotion. "I will show them the same level of concern they showed me when I was toiling away in Cassandra's home scrubbing floors and emptying slop buckets. Aunt Rosa can travel to Mestre each morning on the ferry and take my place if you fall on hard times."

Taken aback, Alzo sneered at her impertinence. "You ungrateful, rude, spoiled—"

Miro stepped in and pushed Alzo away from Isabetta.

Glaring at her uncle, she warned, "Be careful, dear uncle.

I've made many friends these last few months."

Alzo's hand lifted to strike his niece, but Miro clasped his wrist with surprising strength. "Best if you leave right now, Signore Alzo, before this gets ugly."

Regret and shame crept into Alzo's eyes. Shoulders sagging, he heaved a pained sigh. "I never meant for things to be like this...Forgive me, Isabetta."

He walked away a defeated man.

Cristofolo, who had witnessed the entire scene from a distance, stared at Isabetta with a mixture of awe and horror. She stared back at him levelly, her face devoid of expression. He averted his gaze, mounted his horse, and rode off without a backward glance.

CHAPTER 23
JUNE 1570

Isabetta never imagined such bliss could be possible. Marriage to Silvio proved a daily blessing. Handsome, kind, considerate—what wife could ask for more? Their wedding had been a simple affair in a local chapel with only Veronica, Alba, and Signora Paola present. Rosa had declined the invitation, as had Cassandra and Alzo.

Veronica had generously offered her home for the wedding supper, and everyone had enjoyed themselves immensely. The thoughtful courtesan had even hired a pair of minstrels to play music during the delicious meal.

Isabetta went through the trouble of procuring a bit of chicken blood from Alba in order to place a few drops on the bedsheet before Silvio entered her bedchamber. In the dim light of candles, they made love for the first time and she did her best to seem bashful and ignorant, gasping aloud in pain for good measure. If Silvio suspected anything out of the ordinary, he said nothing when they woke up the next morning.

Isabetta felt a mixture of relief and guilt at having duped her husband, but to tell him the truth would surely devastate the man. She experienced a tense moment a few days later when she and Silvio ventured out together. A familiar face from her days as Venerada d'Oro emerged from a palazzo. Keeping her head high, she pretended not to notice the richly dressed nobleman. Thankfully, he passed her without incident.

Smiling down at her, he asked, "Have I told you how much I love you today?"

They were leaving the church after Sunday Holy Mass, hand in hand, and smiling.

Isabetta peeked at him through her lashes. "Twice, I think."

"Let's make it three times, shall we? I love you."

"I love you too, Silvio."

They returned home to discover that Alba had baked apple tarts. The smell of cinnamon and cardamom filled the house, making Isabetta's mouth water. As they settled around the table to partake of the treats, a messenger arrived at the door.

Silvio snapped the letter's wax seal and then skimmed over the words. "It's from my contact in Genoa. He found a Dutchman who wishes to invest in our journey."

Isabetta's face glowed with excitement. "Really? That's wonderful news!"

"I should go and meet him, don't you think?"

"At once, yes!"

"I will be gone only one night." Reaching for her hand, he added, "I cannot believe our good luck. We'll soon be making more money than we can spend. I'll buy us a bigger house and you will have many pretty dresses. You deserve to live like a princess."

His words made her spirit soar. "I have no desire to sell my family home. Too many precious memories reside within these humble walls."

Silvio smiled. "As you wish, my dear."

They supped together that night and made love afterward. At dawn, Isabetta watched her husband go with a sad smile. He waved before turning down the street. Sighing contentedly, she closed the door and retreated into the kitchen.

Alba placed a pot to boil in the hearth, then commented, "Some of your husband's trunks are still stacked in the study. Should we unpack them?"

Husband. Isabetta preened at hearing the beloved word. "Oh? I thought he had unpacked everything after the wedding." She went into the study and placed her hands on her hips. "How did I not notice those?"

"You two have been inseparable since the wedding," Alba replied with a little smirk.

Isabetta's face warmed. "To be in love is a wonderful thing."

"Judging by the faraway look in your eyes, I believe you." The servant wandered to the doorway of the study and indicated the trunks. "Shall we take them upstairs to your bedchamber?"

Isabetta went over to the biggest trunk and peeked inside. "This one has clothing, so you can help me carry it up. The two small ones can remain here for now."

Together, they lugged the trunk to the bedchamber. Isabetta lifted the lid and was instantly engulfed by the scents of pepper, sandalwood, and the sea. The roomy receptacle contained a collection of tailored doublets, linen shirts, and a pair of leather boots. She felt proud to be married to a man of good taste.

After neatly storing the masculine items of clothing, Isabetta returned to the study and opened one of the small trunks. Journals of sea voyages, goose quills, thick ledgers, and an array of documents were stored within. "I can handle this chore by myself," she said to Alba. She preferred to go through Silvio's personal belongings alone rather than under the servant's curious gaze.

Alba retreated to the door and paused. "I'll be in the kitchen if you need anything."

Humming a merry tune, Isabetta went through the items and then opened the second trunk, which contained an assortment of leather gloves and an oiled cloak designed for inclement weather. The space seemed strangely shallow, however. She examined the outside of the receptacle, then peered inside and realized that only the top half contained the gloves and cloak. Tapping the bottom half, she discovered that it was hollow.

"That's odd," she mused aloud.

Removing the items, she discovered a thin piece of wood separating the top half of the trunk from the bottom. She went into the kitchen to obtain a knife, then slid the blade beneath the wood to pry out the divider. It came out easily and revealed a painted black box at the bottom. Unfortunately, it was locked. Shaking it gently, she heard a few items rattling within. One of them sounded heavy and clumsy, the others rustled like sheets of parchment.

"Alba!" The servant poked her head into the room and she continued, "Please fetch me a pin, will you?"

The servant left and returned a moment later with the requested item. Isabetta inserted the honed tip into the lock's opening and moved it around a bit, maneuvering the pin until the mechanism inside clicked open. Guilt accompanied this action, for Silvio had obviously wanted to keep the contents away from prying eyes. How would he feel about her betrayal? Besides, she was hiding plenty of secrets from him. She made to leave the room, then stopped.

What did he have to hide?

Like the mythical Pandora, she set aside her inhibition and flipped open the lid. A hiss of shock escaped her lips. Surely, her eyes deceived her! What other explanation could there be? She touched the dreaded thing with trembling fingers. There was no denying its veracity; this was no figment of her imagination. Slowly, she lifted up an ivory-handled pistol.

The ivory-handled pistol.

Horrified, she dropped the weapon and it fell to the floor with a loud clunk. Amid the meticulously carved vines adorning the handle were the letters A. T. *Alfonso Torres*. Only a rich man could afford such an exquisite piece. She didn't know much about pistols, but she did know their complicated wheel-lock mechanism allowed for only one shot. This explained the knife. The murderer had known all along that her father and brother would be together that night, thus the need for a second weapon. Silvio had aimed the pistol at Rocco figuring that it would be easier to stab an old man…

*No, no, no…*NO.

A sharp wail escaped her colorless lips. There must be a logical explanation. Maybe someone had stolen the gun, used it, and placed it back without Silvio's knowledge. Although the likelihood of that scenario seemed highly improbable, she preferred it to the devastating alternative.

Alba materialized in the doorway. "What ails you, Signora?"

Feeling nauseous, Isabetta squeezed her eyes shut. "Oh God, I'm going to be sick—" A dry heave cut off her words. When she had composed herself, she pointed to the floor. "That's the pistol that killed my father and Rocco."

The servant eyed the weapon warily. "Are you certain?"

"I would wager my soul on it."

"Holy Mary Mother of God." Alba crossed herself, then gingerly picked up the pistol from the floor and set in on the table. Peering into the box, she said, "There are some letters here. Maybe they can offer some information."

Isabetta's hand shot out. "Give them to me."

Blurred vision prevented her from reading the words, so she wiped the tears from her eyes with the back of her hand.

May 17, 1569

Signore Silvio,

I read your previous letter with disappointment. I realize that my proposal is dangerous, but removing the obstacles would bear profitable results for my uncle and our business partner. As I've stated before, you will be handsomely compensated for aiding us in our endeavor.

Sincerely, P.

Sickened, Isabetta could barely read the second letter.

June 22, 1569

Signore Silvio,

I'll remind you that we have a deal. You agreed to my terms and were given a handsome sum in advance. To hire an outsider would incur the risk of blackmail. Therefore, it must be YOU. If you do not fulfill your end of our agreed-upon bargain, there will be dire consequences.

Sincerely, P.

The business partner was undoubtedly Alzo Cornetti, and the "P" was Polonia. Her husband had done business with the Torres family for years, so she knew of Alfonso's illness and the ensuing row between the Torres brothers. The sly woman had pounced upon Silvio's misfortune by offering him an opportunity to make his fortune another way.

An illegal, immoral way.

Isabetta's blood chilled in her veins. She began pacing the room, her head throbbing with each step. Everything suddenly made perfect sense. Polonia had recruited Silvio to assassinate her father and brother. Through Cristofolo, she took over the *Tramonto* thus eliminating her husband's greatest competitor. Convincing her uncle to pay off the debt owed on the galley provided her with a means for raising more money to offset Iseppo's losses. Alzo's dire financial situation made it easy for him to continue working with the two conspirators. The sheer deviousness of the plan must have taken careful forethought on Polonia's part. A crippling apoplexy, public shame, and a cloistered life within a musty convent seemed too light a punishment for the vile woman.

How do you play into this scheme, Isabetta?

She checked the dates on the letters. Silvio had agreed to Polonia's plan *before* coming to Venice. Before Isabetta had met him. Had he not entertained any second thoughts once Zanetto invited him to stay in their home? Wouldn't Rocco's sincere friendship have altered his intention? How could Silvio have led her to believe that he cared for her while simultaneously plotting to murder her family members? While the second letter suggested he had experienced a change of heart, it didn't stop him from going through with the murderous plan. He was a monster.

A monster she still loved…

Seeing her mistress's face grow starkly white, Alba left the room and returned with some water.

Isabetta took a few sips and tried to calm herself, but the walls began to tilt. She gripped the corner of the desk and stared into space with steely eyes, her face an effigy of stone. The severe pain in her chest was most likely the result of her heart splintering into a thousand fragments.

"Shall I summon the *vigili*?" Alba inquired softly.

The question jolted Isabetta from her stupor. "No!"

"I don't understand. If Signore Silvio is guilty—"

"Hush! Don't breathe a word of this to anyone. The truth remains between us until I figure out what to do. No one must know about our discovery, do you understand? You are sworn to secrecy as of right now."

"But—"

"Swear to me, Alba!" Isabetta cried, her eyes wild.

Frightened, Alba nodded. "I won't tell a soul, I swear."

Isabetta slowly placed the damning items back into the black box with methodical precision and returned it to the bottom of the trunk.

The servant watched in fascinated terror as her mistress closed the trunk and then sank into a chair. "I'll brew a calming draught for you."

"No. I need to be lucid right now. I need to think. Leave me."

***

Silvio walked through the streets of the Cannaregio in the reddish hue of sunset. A mouthwatering aroma accosted him as he reached home.

Zanetto's house.

A pang of guilt accompanied the memory of the man and his son. The past could not be undone, no matter how much regret he carried in his heart. Deceiving his beloved pained him, but what other choice did he have? His sin would accompany him to the grave. Taking a deep breath, he went inside. Alba and his wife were in the kitchen preparing supper.

Isabetta glanced up, her eyes catlike. "Silvio."

After kissing her heartily on the mouth, he declared, "I've missed you, my love. It smells wonderful in here."

"I hope you're hungry."

"Famished." To Alba he added, "Hello."

The servant inclined her head while basting a perfectly roasted chicken. "Welcome home, sir."

Isabetta smiled sweetly at her husband. "Why don't you go up and refresh yourself while we set the table?"

"A fine idea."

Isabetta and Alba exchanged a meaningful look the moment Silvio vacated the room. The women's eyes trailed up to the ceiling as they heard him set down his satchel and mill about the bedchamber. They quickly set the table, then placed the succulent fowl in its center.

Isabetta lit only two candles and both were placed by her husband's dinner plate. "Remember the plan."

Alba nodded, solemn-faced.

Scrubbed clean and wearing a freshly laundered shirt, Silvio descended the stairs and took a seat at the table's head. "Alba, please light more candles. It's dark in here."

"Tell me about your trip," Isabetta prompted in order to distract him while Alba ignored his request.

Silvio began chatting animatedly while Alba poured the wine and served her master and mistress. Still and silent, Isabetta listened as he described the favorable deal he had struck with the Dutch investor. He stopped abruptly and eyed his wife's plate. "You're not eating much."

Pushing the food around with the tip of her knife, she shrugged. "I'm not hungry."

Setting his utensils aside, he frowned. "What's wrong?"

Something fell to the floor with a clatter and the couple turned their eyes to where Alba stood cleaning up a spill.

Isabetta stared at Silvio. "Tell me more about the Dutchman. What's his name?"

He commenced eating. "*Meneer Jakob*. He's an investor who wants to export textiles to Amsterdam, the same way Iseppo da Mosta exported them in Portugal."

"As did my father."

"That's right. Your father was a brilliant business man." He chewed a mouthful of food, then swallowed. "I told him my galley would set sail in less than a week, and he seemed quite satisfied."

Isabetta thought her heart would beat its way right out of her mouth. "Don't you mean *my* galley?"

"Huh?"

"You said the *Tramonto* was your galley."

"Mine, yours, ours—isn't it the same thing? We're married." When she failed to reply, he grew wary. "What ails you, my love?"

Her eyes flashed. "Am I your love?"

His face fell. "Isabetta, tell me why you're upset."

"Where were you the night my brother and father were murdered?"

"Treviso. Don't you remember, my darling?" He paused to arrange his face into a mask of empathy. "I wish I could have been here for you..."

Isabetta poured more wine for him. "I wish that too."

Lifting the chalice to his lips, he offered, "I'm sorry."

She watched him indulge in a long sip, then asked, "What does Polonia mean to you?"

He almost choked. "Who?"

"Iseppo da Mosta's wife."

The candles flickered and flared brightly, illuminating his distraught face in the darkness.

Silvio motioned to the servant, who watched the couple from the blackened corner of the kitchen. "Alba, make a posset, will you? Your mistress seems unwell tonight. Light some more candles too."

Alba neither moved nor spoke.

Isabetta continued in a flat tone, "Polonia convinced you to kill them."

Stunned, Silvio stared blankly at her. He then studied the food on his plate for a long time, his expression a combination of realization and panic. "What have you done, Isabetta?"

"I've confronted you with the truth. Be man enough to confess your crime," she replied, her voice cracking with emotion.

His eyes grew wide as he considered a terrifying possibility. Pushing himself away from the table, he gaped at the remains of his meal. "Dear Lord, what have you done? I'm innocent, I swear. I didn't kill anyone."

"Liar!"

He looked up to find Alba's eyes glittering in the dimness. Dragging his gaze back to Isabetta, he pleaded, "My love, you are overwrought…stop this madness."

Reaching beneath her chair, Isabetta extracted the ivory-handled pistol. "What about *this*?"

Anger colored his features for an instant. "You pry into my things, and then accuse me of committing atrocities without knowing the facts. This is unacceptable."

Isabetta stood. "I know for a fact that this is the pistol that killed my brother and my father."

"Don't be absurd!"

"I've read the letters."

The color drained from his face as they regarded at each other for what felt like a small eternity. Finally, he demanded, "Have you told anyone?"

Alba's gasp pierced the thick silence.

Isabetta's hand shook. "How could you, Silvio?!"

He licked his lips nervously. "Please…let me explain. Polonia sent me a letter shortly after she discovered that Fernando and I had parted ways. Iseppo must have told her of my dire predicament. Don't you see? She took advantage of my desperation. Iseppo's last journey to Portugal had not proved fruitful…Her solution would solve all of our problems."

"Kill the Bastian men, remove the competition, and seize their galley. Quite the brilliant plan, I'd say."

Silvio's face crumpled as tears filled his eyes. A burning pain in his stomach caused him to wince. "Please don't look at me like that..."

"How, *precisely*, should I gaze upon the man who murdered my father and brother?"

"God's teeth! My brother inherited everything. *Everything*! Don't you understand? I was left with nothing. I was only trying to make my fortune in this world."

"Even if it meant stooping to murder."

Spreading his hands in supplication, he admitted, "I wanted to back out of the plan the moment I entered your home, I swear. Had I known of your existence, I would never have agreed to such treachery. It was a moment of weakness—*of madness*. I went to see Polonia a few days after my arrival in Venice. I told her I couldn't go through with it. God knows I begged her to find another way and leave your family in peace."

Furious, Isabetta spat in his face.

His lip quivered as he wiped away the spittle. "They threatened me…they were going to kill me." At this, he broke down in tears.

"I wish they had killed you."

Pain made him cringe as his wife's vicious whisper reached his ears. "I'm sorry. Forgive me, please."

In that moment, she felt nothing but disgust. "Never."

"Isabetta, I beg you…I love you."

Eyeing her husband coldly, she said through clenched teeth, "Silvio Torres, you will make a full confession to the magistrate and hang for your crime."

"No…no, please." When begging didn't convince his wife, he grew angry. His features contorted frighteningly and he punched the wall. "I will *not* go to the gallows, do you hear me? I've come too far to have everything stripped away."

After exchanging a pointed look with Alba, Isabetta regarded him coolly. "Very well."

He nodded, satisfied. "That's better. If only you had left my things alone, none of this—" A loud explosion silenced him.

Lowering the pistol, she said, "*That* was for Zanetto…"

A second explosion was emitted from the pistol in Alba's hand. It had been easy enough to purchase the weapon yesterday in a tiny shop off the main square.

"And *that* was for Rocco," Isabetta declared.

Clutching his chest, Silvio sank to his knees. Two shots at close range meant he had little time left in this world. Bright red blood oozed between his fingers and stained the front of his linen shirt. Fighting to maintain consciousness, he slumped to the floor. "Please fetch…physician..."

She shook her head in response to his request as hot tears streamed down her cheeks.

"I love you," Silvio whispered before closing his eyes and heaving his last breath.

***

The rotting corpse of Silvio Torres was found several days later. Neighbors had alerted the *vigili* of a noxious odor, prompting them to investigate. Officers searched the house for clues but found none.

According to rumors, which were backed by the official report, the Bastian family's faithful servant had been away visiting a sick friend in a neighboring town when his death occurred. There was still no sign of Silvio's loving wife, Isabetta Bastian, who had gone to see her cousin, Beto, in

Treviso. Odder still, her clothing and jewels were neatly stored in the upstairs bedchamber. According to the servant, nothing had been touched or removed.

In time, Beto Bastian came forth to claim his inheritance. The young man, listed as "next of kin" in Silvio's recently amended will, was sole heir to the house and galley.

Silvio's death was eventually declared the result of a business deal gone wrong. The Portuguese merchant had made several purchases prior to his untimely demise. Some whispered that he had borrowed money from dubious sources who demanded high interest rates.

Isabetta's disappearance remained a mystery. Had she been kidnapped? Seduced by another man? No one knew for certain, and after a couple of weeks nobody cared. A destitute orphan and her commoner husband didn't provide enough fodder for gossipmongers. As a result, Isabetta and Silvio were soon forgotten.

***

Veronica Franco had already offered three masses and countless prayers to God and the Virgin Mary on behalf of Isabetta. That her friend would vanish without so much as a farewell seemed out of character, not to mention worrisome.

One fine morning, she paid Alba a visit in the hope of gleaning information. The door opened and the servant quickly waved the courtesan inside. "Signora Veronica, *buongiorno*. I had planned on going to your home later this afternoon."

Veronica's face lit up. "Have you heard from Isabetta?"

Ignoring the question, Alba fetched a letter from the sideboard. "My master instructed me to give you this."

"Your *master*?"

The servant's eyes gleamed with mischief.

Veronica studied the thick wax seal, which bore an imprint of the letter "B." She unfolded the sheet, instantly recognizing the neat script. Meeting Alba's insistent gaze, she grinned in complicit understanding.

Dear Signora Veronica,

My name is Beto Bastian and I hope you will consider this

letter an informal introduction. My cousin, Isabetta, spoke of you often and fondly, and I know the two of you fostered a healthy friendship. It is her trust in you and her respect for you that has provided the impetus for this missive.

I wish to present you with a profitable proposal. As you are well aware, the Bevilacqua looms produce the finest velvets and brocades in Venice. Dutch and Flemish nobility have developed a taste for these luxuriant fabrics, and I am currently exporting them on my commercial galley.

This venture is guaranteed to provide a handsome return on investment, and I am inviting you to partake of the opportunity. If any of your noble clients also desire to invest, I will gladly pay you a generous percentage for each referral.

I rarely step foot in Venice these days, so I have provided my servant, Alba, with a forwarding address should you be interested in my offer. Hopefully, our paths will cross someday soon. Until then, I wish you and yours good health and cheer.

Your Servant, B.

EPILOGUE
OCTOBER 1570

I stood at the helm of my ship admiring a rosy sky streaked with crimson and gold. According to my astrolabe, we were on a steady course. *Tramonto* meant sunset, my late father's favorite time of day. Zanetto Bastian had been a man of little words and great deeds. Rocco too. I, Beto Bastian, did my best to live my life in a manner that brought honor to their memory.

"Land!"

I stared at the man who had uttered that blessed word before extracting my telescope from my coat pocket. Sure enough, our feet would touch soil by dawn tomorrow.

Ervin, my first mate, approached me with his red felt cap twisted between his calloused hands. The name Ervin meant "warrior" or "friend" in his language and, since both were useful during a sea voyage, I hired him on the spot.

"Captain, the men are tired of eating eggs."

"Let them eat barley cakes," I retorted flatly, my eyes glued to the horizon.

The large Albanian shifted from one foot to the other in the hope that I would reconsider. "They're decent men…"

I smiled wryly. "Go on, slaughter the hens."

Ervin grinned before informing my crew that they would be dining on roasted chicken for supper. I would buy Dutch hens for the return journey.

The wind blew fiercely, tousling my shorn locks and filling the ship's sails until they resembled the ripe bellies of pregnant women. I kept my hair chin-length and had long exchanged my gowns for smartly tailored doublets and breeches. If my men suspected my secret, they wisely kept it to themselves and called me "Captain." They knew I wasn't afraid to use my weapon, which I wore on my person daily. It served as a silent warning to anyone who dared provoke me.

My fingers touched the ivory handled pistol that had killed both my brother and my father—*and Silvio.* Alba thought it macabre for me to keep it, but I disagreed. It served as a constant reminder of where I came from, and a talisman against the dangerous game of love. Maybe Fate would someday be kind and lead me into the arms of a good man. For now, I was content to be alone.

And free.

Footsteps prompted me to turn around.

Miro, my new business partner and longtime friend, offered me a conspiratorial grin as he closed the distance between us. "I wish I could capture the image of your face in this moment."

"Why do you say that?"

"I've never seen anyone look so happy. I think the sighting of land calls for a bit of wine. What say you?"

"A fine idea," I agreed before he went off to fetch some.

My gaze swept over the vast watery expanse of shimmering blue with renewed hope. This was my first time outside of Venice and I could barely contain my excitement. I planned on sailing to Portugal and Spain someday. Maybe India too. The thought of that faraway land brimming with vibrant colors and exotic spices lifted the corners of my lips. The future loomed before me, bright and full of possibilities. Donna Immacolata had been correct...*The most violent tempest can't keep the sun at bay forever.*

Did you enjoy this novel? The author would appreciate your review on Amazon. Thank you.

Turn the page to sample IMPOSTOR: A Novel Set in the Kingdom of Naples.

IMPOSTOR

A NOVEL SET IN THE KINGDOM OF NAPLES

C. DE MELO

ISBN 13 978-0-9997878-7-8 (C. De Melo)
ISBN-10 978-0-999787

PROLOGUE
KINGDOM OF NAPLES
JANUARY 1760

Celeste Carducci crept into the ancient chapel before hastily adjusting her starched white wimple. Sinking to her knees before the altar, she assumed the position of prayer with a racing heart. A Paternoster rushed from her swollen lips, the whispered words flowing like holy water over her tightly clasped hands.

His scent lingered on her fingers, his taste on her tongue...

Rusty iron hinges creaked as the esteemed Sister Assunta pushed open the heavy studded door. The nun genuflected and crossed herself, then rushed toward the altar with light steps.

"There you are, my child. I've been searching everywhere for you."

Crossing herself with a trembling hand, Celeste stood. "I've been here all morning, praying."

Sister Assunta took a step closer to her ward. A beam of early morning sunshine spilled from an open window, illuminating only half of her wrinkled face. Dust motes floated in the air between them. "I checked the chapel earlier and you were nowhere to be found."

"Oh," Celeste said, her mind racing to conjure another lie. "Ah...I did leave once to use the privy."

"Come along. Someone is here to see you."

"Valentina?" Sister Assunta slowly shook her head. The nun's pinched brow and worried eyes alarmed Celeste, who demanded, "Who is it?"

"Your uncle has sent a miniaturist to paint your likeness."

Celeste's face fell. "No..."

The matronly nun placed a comforting arm around the girl's shoulders. "Don't worry, my dear, we'll pray together on this matter. God will provide a way out. He always does."

CHAPTER 1
KINGDOM OF NAPLES
FEBRUARY 1760

Ferrante degli Spini checked his silver pocket watch for the second time. Exhaling an impatient breath, he scanned the lively sunlit square. Hearty vendors cried out to passerby while toothless old women selected their wares with meticulous care. To his left, a pair of servants bargained with a cloth merchant for a better deal on a measure of dyed linen. To his right, a boy peeked from behind the base of a statue. Ferrante watched with wry amusement as the lad darted from his hiding place, swiped an apple from a cart, and then vanished down an alley.

Across the piazza stood an outdoor tabernacle housing a painted statue of the Madonna. The amateur artist had selected garish colors in which to portray the Queen of Heaven. Draped in dried yellow roses and cheap green glass beads, the effigy gazed down at the Neapolitans in the square with a wan smile. Fresh posies tied with faded ribbons and flickering candles littered the base of the icon.

Clad in black from head to foot, an old woman paused to cross herself before the statue. She kissed her meaty palm and placed it over one of the Madonna's chipped feet, her lined lips moving in a silent prayer. The crone possessed only three teeth, and Ferrante couldn't help wondering if she had been a great beauty in her youth.

Someone nearby shouted a greeting, breaking his reverie. He noticed a dazed young man calling out to a pretty girl leaning from an open window. The enamored couple stared at each other as if they were the only two people in the city.

Young love.

Ferrante had never experienced such a frivolous emotion. A practical man, he focused his energy on running his small empire with an iron fist. Love was for peasants with nothing better to do with their time.

Speaking of time...

Checking his pocket watch again, he frowned and tapped his well-shod foot. His late father used to say that 'punctuality verged on sacred' and Ferrante strictly adhered to that concept. To be kept waiting—even if only for a few minutes—catapulted him into a foul mood. Resisting the urge to go home, he reminded himself that the outcome of this meeting could prove beneficial for both him and his daughter. Besides, he had already spent several months searching for a suitable girl and couldn't afford to waste any more time.

A ruddy-cheeked figure rushed across the square, his unadorned hand gripping the edge of a tricorn hat. Ferrante took in the shabbiness of the man's velvet coat and resoled leather shoes. Camillo Custozi had spent most of his sizeable inheritance on whores and gambling. The fool's fortunes were dwindling, which explained his desperation to strike a deal.

Camillo came to a halt with an apologetic smile hovering on his thin lips. "Signore Ferrante, please forgive my tardiness. The carriage wheel got stuck in—"

Ferrante lifted a jeweled finger. "*Don't.* There is a café over there where we can talk."

Camillo prudently refrained from speaking as he followed the nobleman.

Ferrante cursed under his breath. Once again, he failed to control his temper. He possessed a harsh personality, rendering him older than his thirty years. His intimidating persona served him well when dealing with rivals, but in social situations it proved disastrous. No wonder people gossiped about him.

They ducked into the cool shade of a portico and headed toward an elegant establishment brimming with gentlemen engaged in animated conversations. Some discussed politics, others art and finance. The rich aroma of freshly brewed coffee mingled with the sweet smoke of pipes in the crisp morning air. The men placed their order, then settled around a small table where they could privately discuss their business.

Casting aside the customary niceties of polite conversation, Ferrante inquired, "Have you notified your niece?"

Startled by the man's brusqueness, Camillo replied, "Not yet. I wanted to obtain confirmation from you before making an official announcement."

The firstborn men of the House of Spini were required to marry women of noble blood. This edict had been clearly stipulated in his late father's will under threat of forfeit of inheritance to his first cousin, Ruggero, who currently served as a bishop in Rome. Celeste Carducci was the only child of a duke, rendering her perfectly acceptable to the terms of the will.

"Tell me more about Celeste," Ferrante said.

Camillo spread out his hands. "My lord, I have told you everything about my niece in my letter. Did you not read the copies of the reports from the last five years?"

"Yes, but I want to hear it from your lips."

"My widowed sister died shortly after Celeste's fifth birthday. Fortunately, my late brother-in-law had already made provisions for his only child by endowing her with a handsome dowry. As Celeste's legal guardian and uncle, it is my responsibility to select a suitable husband."

While shamelessly profiting from the arrangement, Ferrante thought. "Why didn't you take her into your own household?"

Camillo emitted a deprecating laugh. "An old cantankerous bachelor like me raising a girl? I figured my niece would be better served by the nuns of Santa Patrizia."

"Do you visit her often?"

"Not exactly," he replied sheepishly.

"When was the last time you saw her?"

Camillo rubbed his chin in thought. "Five—no, I believe it was six years ago."

Ferrante regarded the man with skepticism. "Your letter offered a precise list of your niece's accomplishments and character. If my memory serves me well, you described her as domestic, submissive, and comely."

"According to the reports I've received from her chaperone, Celeste is all of those things and more. The respected nun has been her constant companion for the last twelve years and loves my niece as her own daughter."

"In those reports you forwarded to me, I noticed that Sister Assunta mentioned Celeste's 'delicate constitution' and 'frailty' on several occasions."

"My niece is healthy enough, I assure you."

Ferrante's eyes narrowed. "How can you be so sure when you haven't seen her in six years?"

Flustered, Camillo's face reddened. "Sister Assunta would have alerted me to any *serious* health problems. Remember, my lord, convents are drafty places and the nuns consume a sparse diet. A bit of rest and good nutrition will make Celeste truly robust." In an attempt at humor, he added, "I doubt she'll be accompanying you on the hunt any time soon, however."

Ferrante's face remained stoic. "I don't need her to hunt. I need her to run my household and, in time, give me a son."

"I understand perfectly. My personal physician will conduct a thorough examination to put your mind at ease."

"No. I'll send my own physician."

"As you prefer, my lord. May I ask you a personal question?" Camillo waited for Ferrante's nod to proceed. "Although my niece is of noble blood, she was raised among nuns. She has never attended parties or worn fancy dresses. I doubt she even knows how to dance."

"What is your question?"

"Celeste lacks sophistication and the feminine wiles expected from a lady of noble breeding. I daresay that she is innocent to a fault, and I fear that you may find her rather disappointing. Perhaps even dull. I would imagine that many noble ladies would eagerly avail themselves of your courtship. Are you sure you wish to marry my niece?"

Ferrante pinned the man with a hard stare. "My late wife was coddled and spoiled throughout her childhood. She grew into an exigent, frivolous, and arrogant woman. While I regret that God saw fit to take her in the prime of her life—for I wish ill upon no one—I am grateful for a second chance at a fortuitous marriage. This time, I want an obedient wife with a mild temperament. It's true that I have noblemen offering me huge dowries to marry their daughters, but I am not interested in another foolish woman. In answer to your question, yes, I am certain that I wish to marry your innocent, unspoiled niece."

Camillo begrudgingly admired the unconventional man. "In that case, I am confident that Celeste will not disappoint you."

"Assuming the nun's reports are indeed true, then your confidence is well warranted."

"You can rest assured, my lord. I will notify Celeste at once. When can she expect a visit from you?"

Ferrante cocked an eyebrow at the loathsome man. "I have no intention of paying her a visit."

"You wish to marry my niece without so much as meeting her beforehand?"

"Why bother? I have all the information I need."

Camillo found this odd but who was he to question the man's methods? Reaching into his pocket, he said, "I have taken the liberty of having a miniature painted so that you can appreciate her physical attributes."

Ferrante accepted the tiny oval portrait and brought it up to his face for closer inspection. A pale girl with a straight nose, rosebud mouth, and wide-set eyes stared back at him. "Pretty," he murmured before handing the trinket back to his companion.

Camillo shook his head. "Keep it. It's my gift to you."

Ferrante pocketed the tiny portrait. "Thank you."

"So, do we have a deal?"

"Marriage to Celeste will be contingent on her good health. The moment my physician sends me a full report, I will contact you. Only then will I transfer the land in your name."

"Fair enough," Camillo said, satisfied.

The men shook hands to seal their agreement.

***

Ferrante remained in the city to run some errands after his meeting with Camillo. Animals and people competed for space on the crowded streets, which were littered with dung and refuse. The endless noise and vile smells irritated him. To make matters worse, he ran into his aunt's acquaintances after exiting his solicitor's office. The tedious couple tried to ingratiate themselves through social invitations and banal conversation.

Ferrante sagged with relief in the saddle when he finally returned to his stately villa on the Vomero hillside. Late afternoon sunshine covered his home in a burnished gold veil. Two long rows of cypress trees created elongated shadows along the pebbled drive leading to the villa's entrance. Fortunately, he owned enough acres to enjoy the peace and tranquility of isolation, far from the vile smells and constant noise of the city below.

The stallion's hooves crunched along the pebbled path, lulling Ferrante into a thoughtful reverie. The mighty horse suddenly reared as it neared the imposing iron gates.

"Achille," he warned, pulling on the reins. Spotting the source of the animal's hesitation, he cried, "Berta! How many times have I told you to keep my daughter away from the gate? You know I don't like it when you take her outdoors."

The nursemaid scurried to fetch the adorable toddler, who stared at her father in terror. "Forgive me, Signore Ferrante. We were playing by the front door and she ran out here when she heard your horse."

"I should have you whipped for disobeying me."

"Nadia is getting too fast for me."

"If I catch my daughter playing by the gates again, I'll find a competent replacement for you. Am I clear?"

"Yes, my lord. Come, Nadia."

Nadia wailed as she was swept off her tiny feet and carried into the villa. Ferrante cursed under this breath while studying the retreating face of his daughter. The girl eyed him in the same level of contempt as one would an enemy. Given that his late wife's blood ran in her veins, it was no wonder.

"My lord!"

Ferrante turned toward the voice of his trusted valet, Sandro. He also noticed his aunt's carriage further up the drive. "If you have bad news, I don't want to hear it."

Sandro winced. "Your aunt is waiting for you in the library."

"So?"

"I'm afraid she already knows."

Ferrante dismounted as a stable boy ran over to take the horse's reins. "Did you tell her?

"Of course not, my lord."

Ferrante pinched the bridge of his nose. "Women are the source of men's woes. Remember that, Sandro."

"Yes, my lord."

Taking a deep breath, Ferrante entered the villa and veered toward the library.

Clad in one of her signature black gowns, Livia smiled a bit too sweetly when he entered the room. "Ferrino."

"You know I hate that nickname."

"Yet it suits you perfectly, my beloved nephew, for you are an unbending bit of iron. Even as a boy you were stubborn."

Ferrante kissed the severe woman's rouged cheek. "Hello Aunt Livia."

"What is this I hear about you seeking a nun for a bride?"

"She's not a nun. How do you know about her, anyway?"

"Donna Elvira heard it from Signora Teresa who personally knows Camillo Custozi. You're to wed his niece, Celeste."

Ferrante spread his hands in supplication. "Cristo Santo! It's only been a few hours since my meeting with Camillo and already people are gossiping about it? You women with your wagging tongues never cease to amaze me."

Livia quirked a black penciled eyebrow at him. "You're the topic of conversation in every salon and drawing room from Naples to Rome. Even now there are noblemen hoping to parade their daughters before your eyes."

"I'm not interested."

"Really, Ferrino. You shouldn't disregard—"

"I'll not have another spoiled creature defying me under my roof. Endless balls and dinner parties, vapid fops and frivolous women roaming about my home. Enough is enough."

"Calm down, my dear."

"Caterina cost me a fortune and provided me with nothing more than a useless mute daughter and countless headaches. What's more, she was a negligent mother who never cared a fig for Nadia. The only things that mattered to that selfish woman were her gowns and her stupid friends."

Livia puckered her vermillion lips as she watched her angry nephew pace the room like a caged animal. Several strands of shoulder-length black hair escaped the leather strap tied at his nape, affording him a wild appearance.

She ventured, "I'm here to convince you to reconsider."

"Too late."

"Ferrino—"

He stopped in his tracks. "Stop calling me that!"

"*Ferrante*, be reasonable."

"You're the one who is constantly pressuring me to remarry. Every week you remind me that my respectable period of mourning is over. I swear you've mentioned Ruggero's name at least one hundred times since Caterina's death. Now you're telling me not to wed?"

"You should marry but—"

"Nadia needs a mother *and* a brother."

Livia clicked open her fan. Eyeing her nephew above the curve of painted fabric, she inquired, "Have you met the girl?"

"No, but I know enough about her."

"Aside from the fact that she was Count Emilio Carducci's only child and raised in a convent, what can you possibly know about Celeste?"

"What's there to know about a seventeen year old girl who has spent the last twelve years of her life surrounded by nuns? She's *seen* nothing, *done* nothing. Her mind is a clean slate and I happen to find that quite appealing in a woman."

"What if she's hideous?"

Ferrante crossed the room while extracting the tiny oval portrait from his pocket. "She's not. See for yourself."

Livia examined the piece. "Hmm, attractive."

"More importantly, she is docile, obedient, and accustomed to the frugality of convent life. In other words, Celeste is the exact opposite of Caterina."

"Caterina was challenging, I admit..."

"Try insufferable, demanding, rude, and unfaithful."

"We can't prove the latter…" Ignoring her nephew's harsh glare, she continued, "Anyway, I agree that you were ill-matched the first time. You'll offend quite a lot of nobles if you marry this girl, however."

"I realize that selecting my bride from a convent will perhaps shock my peers, but I don't care. I refuse to be saddled with another Jezebel."

"May I accompany you to the convent?"

Confused, he said, "I'm not going to any convent."

She stared blankly at him. "Aren't you going to meet the girl before making a decision?"

"No need. I've already read all the reports."

"Reports?"

"One of the most highly respected nuns in the city sends Camillo an account of Celeste's health and accomplishments every six months. From what I've ascertained, the girl is perfectly suited to be my bride. There is only the matter of her frailty."

"Let me see if I've understood you correctly. You wish to marry a girl you've never met *and* she has health problems?"

"She doesn't have health problems. Camillo described his niece as fragile, which sums up most women."

Livia clucked her tongue in annoyance. "Don't listen to that old fool. What does Camillo know? He's a bachelor."

Going to the sideboard, Ferrante poured himself a drink. "You can put your fears to rest, Aunt Livia. I'm going to have my physician examine Celeste. My deal with Camillo is contingent on the health of his niece."

Livia went over to where he stood. "Don't trouble yourself, darling. I'll send my own physician, whom you know is very good. I'll even accompany Dr. Bernardo so that I can judge the girl for myself."

"I'm not sure I like that idea."

"Why not? You have so many things to worry about. Allow me to do this small task for you." She waved her hand to make a point. "One of us should meet Celeste Carducci before she becomes a part of this family."

"Very well, but don't try to scare her away."

"I daresay she'll want to bolt the moment she discovers the name of her betrothed."

Unamused, Ferrante said wryly, "Your faith in my abilities is always a source of encouragement."

"You know that I love you." Livia closed the fan and tapped the ivory spine against her palm while thoughtfully regarding her nephew. "Well, I've done my duty to my beloved late brother—your father. I've tried to talk sense into you but I see now that my attempts are futile."

"Don't be like that, Aunt Livia. All I want is an easy wife who will care for Nadia and bear me a son. I believe Celeste will fulfill those roles without any fuss."

Livia hesitated before asking the next question. "What about that other matter?"

"What other matter?"

She pinned him with a pointed look. "I'm referring to *her*."

"Nothing will change where she is concerned."

"Celeste may object."

"She'll learn to live with it." Livia was about to say something then stopped. Seeing this, Ferrante added, "Nothing you say will change my mind. We've already argued enough on the matter."

"I don't wish to argue with you."

"Good," he snapped.

"You know how I feel about it."

"I do, but can't you be happy for me?"

She sighed. "I'm tickled by the prospect of Celeste Carducci being your bride. *Better*?"

"Actually, yes."

"Good. Now, what's for dinner? I'm famished."

CHAPTER 2
MARCH 1760

The Countess of Saponara, Ippolita de Monti, lost three sons at the same time. The culprit? *Poison.* This alone must have been quite a tragic blow to the poor woman, but to discover that the murderer was none other than their uncle for reasons of inheritance…

I would have killed the man. Murdered him in cold blood. I would have severed his head from his neck in the same manner the biblical Judith decapitated Holofernes. Perhaps poisoning would have proven a better punishment.

A taste of his own medicine.

Rather than seek revenge, the noble Ippolita commissioned the great sculptor, Giovanni da Nola, to create a funerary monument unlike any other in Naples. She had insisted that her sons, each slain before the age of twenty, be depicted as they were in life—full of vitality and movement. Giovanni did not disappoint. The *Sepulchers of the brothers Filomarino* immortalized Ippolita's sons in the prime of life. Splendid work, indeed. Despite being created from marble, the handsome young noblemen seemed capable of jumping from their perches at any given moment. Their tomb served as a constant reminder of the fragility of life.

People milled about in the church after the conclusion of Holy Mass several minutes ago. To my left, a broad-shouldered man ushered his wife and small children toward a neighboring chapel. I discreetly lowered my gaze to admire his hard ankles and chiseled calves beneath the white stockings. As I studied his impressive form, I wondered what he looked like devoid of clothing. Curiosity of the male anatomy prompted the wicked thought, not lust. More than seeing men naked, I wanted to know what existed *inside* of them.

Last year, this burning desire had prompted me to sneak into the university and spy on the medical students. A professor spotted me while the young men were performing autopsies, forcing me to flee the scene. Two months ago, I popped into the morgue and saw two bloated men who had drowned in the bay.

Only one subject piqued my interest more than anatomy, and that was alchemy. Great debates were currently underway on the topic. Some argued that alchemy was a legitimate science while others branded it as quackery. The well-known chemist and physicist, Robert Boyle, insisted that alchemy and chemistry were two distinct subjects, defining the latter as a legitimate science. Some still believed in the process of alchemy for diagnostic tests while others disagreed. Having contemplated both sides, I still hadn't made up my mind on the issue. Not that my opinion mattered since these discussions were held among men, not insignificant girls like me.

My interest in science could be traced directly to my late father, who had worked as a chemist in an apothecary. He had fostered a deep respect for the mechanisms of our natural world and had often pointed out the chemical properties of things whenever we were together. Sometimes, he would prove his points in banal ways, like baking a perfect loaf of bread. The passion he had displayed for his work inspired me to read and reread his books.

I turned away from the exquisite chapel and headed down the nave toward the exit. The heels of my suede shoes clicked lightly against the impressive intarsia marble floor. I paused, as I always did, at the tomb of Belisario Corenzio. The Greek artist fell to his tragic death in 1646 while frescoing the marvelous ceiling of the church. To have died in such a terrible manner while creating something so splendid…

"Valentina!"

The gentle voice of my dearest friend, Celeste, prompted me to look up and smile in greeting. Every Sunday, after attending Holy Mass at the chapel of Santa Patrizia, she and her chaperone left the convent to stroll to the Church of San Severino in my parish. I waited for them each week with eager anticipation.

Alarmed by her pale face, I inquired, "What ails you?"

Placing a gentle hand on my arm, she whispered, "Valentina, I have much to tell you. You must come visit me soon."

"Perhaps this week—"

"You must come today, I beg you."

"Very well. First, I need to run an errand for my aunt. I'm sure she won't object if I slip out afterward."

"Thank you."

Sister Assunta greeted me with a nod before turning to her ward. "Have you told your friend?"

"Not yet," Celeste replied.

I looked from one to the other. "Told me what?"

Celeste urged me outside and Sister Assunta followed us. Once we had descended the steps to the street level, she said, "My uncle commissioned someone to paint my portrait."

"He's finally paying attention to you. How delightful."

She shook her head vehemently. "No!"

"Hush," the old nun admonished, her beady eyes darting toward a gaggle of old women exiting the church. "Keep your voices down. Lord protect us from gossipmongers."

I whispered, "I don't understand. Why are you so upset over a portrait?"

Sister Assunta sighed in irritation and took it upon herself to reply. "Don't you see, Valentina? This means that Camillo Custozi has found a potential husband for our dear Celeste."

"Oh. Who is it?"

The nun frowned. "Does it matter?"

I didn't particularly care for the shrewish old matron who coddled my friend, but I treated her respectfully nonetheless. "I am merely curious, Sister Assunta. I hope that Signore Camillo has chosen someone worthy of my honorable friend."

Celeste's eyes glistened with unshed tears. "My uncle did not reveal the man's name in his letter. He only stated that it would be a 'fortuitous marriage' for all parties involved. I haven't slept in days. I can't eat or think. It even hurts to breathe. I'm in desperate need of consolation."

"I'll come and see you as soon as I can," I promised, giving my friend's hand a reassuring squeeze.

"We'll be expecting you," Sister Assunta said with a nod.

The nun urged her ward forward and I watched their retreat with a mixture of concern and sorrow. Pulling my white lace head covering low over my brow, I headed home with heavy steps. People passed me on the street but I barely noticed them. I couldn't get Celeste's sad face out of my head.

"Mamma!"

A rosy-cheeked boy pointed at a sweet bun in a baker's window. His mother grinned indulgently before extracting a coin from her crocheted purse. The little boy's face lit up with the simple joy of anticipating a delicious treat.

For the majority of the city's inhabitants, Sundays were for thanksgiving and rest. *Church and food.* The sacred day involved attending Holy Mass, then roasting meats or fish, playing with children, and consuming wine. *Lots of wine*. Music and singing filled the air as people digested their meals.

My parents and younger brother had loved Sundays too. The three of them had perished within a week due to plague. I was only ten years old when it happened—too young to be on my own, too old to be adopted by a couple. The only place for an orphaned girl from a respectable family was a convent. I had been sent to the same one where Celeste Carducci resided, the Convent of Santa Patrizia. Being the same age, she and I instantly became the best of friends. I wept when my mother's sister had shown up a month later to claim me. Through a blur of tears, Celeste and I vowed to always be true to each other no matter what life doled out to us.

"Valentina!"

Craning my neck, I waved at the plump adolescent who watched me from the window high above. Guido and his parents lived in the building across from where I lived with my Aunt Gloria.

"You're looking quite comely today, Valentina."

At age twelve, Guido fancied himself in love with me.

I smiled at him. "Thank you, Guido."

"Will you marry me?"

Laughing, I shook my head and the boy appeared stricken.

Guido's mother ushered her ambitious son away from the window before I ducked into the butcher shop to make a quick purchase. A moment later, I walked into the apartment that I shared with Aunt Gloria. Cluttered with threadbare rugs, a pair of decent paintings, and a chaise longue in desperate need of reupholstering, the space felt both cozy and comfortable.

I set the parcel on the table. "Hello Aunt Gloria. Are you feeling better?"

"I am," she replied from her resting place on the chaise longue. "Did you go by the *macellaio*?"

"Yes," I replied while removing my lace head covering. "Natalino gave me the meatiest bone."

The best butcher in our quarter had a soft spot for my aunt, whom he fondly referred to as *Glorissima*.

Draping the lace over the back of a chair, I continued, "He asked after you, as always."

"That was kind of him," she said primly before taking a sip from the glass in her hand.

I unwrapped the bone and dropped it into a pot of water, which my aunt had already set to boil. "He's a good man."

Adjusting her linen mobcap, she said, "I know. Once upon a time, I was a beauty like you with flowing locks and a nice figure. You may not realize this, but I had more than my fair share of admirers."

Appealing to her vanity, I said, "I'm sure you did. You're still lovely, Aunt Gloria."

"You're a good girl, Valentina."

"When are you going to marry Natalino?" I teased while quickly chopping some carrots and celery to add to the broth.

She waved her hand dismissively. "What does he want with a sickly old woman like me?"

I smirked. "Shouldn't you be in bed?"

"I felt better after you left." Lifting the glass in her hand, she added, "This tonic that the apothecary prescribed is beneficial for my health."

Taking in Aunt Gloria's plump cheeks and florid

complexion, I wondered if she sometimes faked her bouts of illness to garner attention. To be fair, she often suffered headaches so severe that she was forced to take to her bed. She claimed that impurities blocked her nose to the point that she couldn't breathe. These symptoms usually became worse with the changing of the seasons, particularly in the spring and autumn. During these months, our home emitted the odors of camphor and peppermint oil.

I ventured, "Since you're feeling better, do you mind if I pay Celeste a visit?"

She pouted. "I hoped that you would read to me."

"I'll read to you once I return."

Tilting her head to the side, she sighed. "I suppose that will have to do. Perhaps you can brew me a bit of peppermint tea before you go?"

My spinster aunt thrived on being pampered. I had learned long ago how to navigate through the contrived petulance and melodrama in order to get my way. I set a small pot to boil before walking across the room to a sunlit window. A cluster of potted herbs sat on the maroon tile floor in a pool of sunshine. I tore a few leaves from a thriving peppermint plant.

I sighed loudly while tossing the fragrant leaves in the water. "Such a shame..."

"What is?"

"That a virile man like Natalino must live a lonely life. How long ago did his wife die?"

"Two years, I believe."

"A good woman is what he needs." I deliberately paused. "Donna Francesca recently lost her husband too. Do you recall how long ago?"

"Six months."

My eyes slid to where my aunt sat. "Did I mention that she was also there purchasing bones for broth?"

Alarmed, Aunt Gloria sat up straight and placed the glass of tonic on a nearby table. "You most certainly did not."

"Forgive me. My mind is on poor Celeste who looked so pale this morning."

"How did Donna Francesca seem to you?" When I feigned confusion, she clarified, "Did she look…attractive?"

"As a matter of fact, yes. I don't recall ever having seen her wearing that yellow silk—"

"Yellow silk?" She snorted in disdain. "The woman is barely out of mourning. What did she say?"

"Let's see," I said, tapping the side of my face as I pretended to recall something. "Oh yes. She sends warm greetings and wishes you a speedy recovery from your convalescence."

"Convalescence?"

I carried on nonchalantly despite her horrified expression. "I think Donna Francesca made a comment about illness being the bane of old age."

"The nerve! Francesca is older than me."

"Is she, really?"

"Yes! Besides, I'm not *that* sick. Knowing her, she'll tell the entire neighborhood that I'm on my deathbed." Gloria's expression went from anger to worry. "Did Natalino overhear this conversation?"

"I'm sure he did since he was right there and, as you know, the butcher shop is quite small."

"What did he say?"

I shrugged and made a face. "I think he said something about it being a pity that you're not doing well."

"Were those his exact words?"

"I believe so," I replied while pouring the tea into a tea cup. "Here you go, Aunt Gloria. I saved a bit in the pot. Shall I add camphor and make you a compress?"

She nodded distractedly before indulging in a careful sip of tea. I resisted the urge to smile as I dipped a soft cloth into the aromatic brew. She liked to apply the damp cloth to her face since she claimed that it helped her condition.

Stirring the simmering broth, I suggested, "Tomorrow I can get us a bit of beef liver to make a nice pie."

"No need, dear. I'll go and get it myself."

I did my best to maintain a straight face. "Are you sure? I mean, you've been sick. I don't mind..."

"As I said, I feel better. After applying the compress I'll be good as new. Besides, it's been a while since I've seen Natalino." Something occurred to her and she removed the mobcap. Patting her unruly hair, she inquired, *"Is it that time?"*

'That time' referred to her gray hair beginning to show. Peering at her head, I offered the same reply as always. "It wouldn't hurt."

At my solemn confirmation, she stood and rummaged through a cabinet. A moment later she began boiling walnut tree bark, which had been ground into a powder, along with the inner shell of the nut. Once it boiled, she added red beet seeds. My aunt would often apply this concoction to her hair before going to bed, then rinse it out in the morning. The result was a brownish pink color that nature never intended, but at least it hid the unsightly gray hair.

"Off you go to see Celeste," she said, for she didn't like me witnessing her beauty ablutions.

I scurried out the door before she changed her mind. Walking slowly, I admired the people on the street as I made my way toward the Convent of Santa Patrizia. A fancy lady on the arm of an elderly gentleman strolled past me. Cream brocade was a daring color to wear since it was so difficult to keep clean in a city crammed with people and animals.

Sidestepping a steaming heap of horse manure, I turned my attention back to the elegant woman. An ostrich feather adorned her powdered coiffure, and shiny topaz stones hung from her earlobes. An exquisite lace shawl served to cover her décolletage. I offered her a smile but she only regarded me with bland disdain.

Glancing down at my shabby linen dress, I wondered if I would ever own such a fine gown. It seemed unlikely, especially since my parents had left me a meager inheritance. We weren't poor but our limited finances forced us to live modestly. Last year, Aunt Gloria sold the last silver candlestick holder that had belonged to my grandmother.

I rounded a corner and the looming volcanic stone walls diverted my attention. The convents of Naples served as safe havens for orphaned girls of a certain social status. The Convent of Santa Patrizia was no exception. The seventh century saint, a chaste virgin and descendant of Constantine, was revered as a role model for nuns and novices alike.

Immense dark walls were rampant within the center of Naples because of the staggering number of women who chose religious vocations. Neapolitan streets were made according to Greek design, so they were quite narrow. The locally quarried black stone gave them a mysterious aura, especially at night under the burning flames of street lanterns. I used the heavy iron knocker at the gate to announce my presence. One of the nuns opened the viewing door and recognized me. After being granted access, I went straight to the tiny cell where my friend resided.

Celeste opened the door. "Thank you for coming."

I stepped into the modest space. A simple wooden crucifix adorned one of the cream plaster walls. "I hate seeing you upset like this."

"My heart is heavy, Valentina." She picked up a letter from the nightstand beside a narrow cot and waved it in the air. "To make matters worse, *this* arrived for me only a moment ago."

"What is it?"

"A letter informing me that a physician will be coming here tomorrow to perform an examination on me at the request of my betrothed."

I leaned forward to peek at the sheet of parchment. "Does it mention his name?"

"No."

"How odd. Why the secrecy, I wonder?"

"Isn't it obvious? He wants to make sure that I'm healthy enough to breed before sealing the deal and revealing his identity to the public." Crumbling the note in her hand, she added, "I've always known this day would come. At least I've had twelve years with Sister Assunta and the other nuns. My uncle could have married me off sooner, so I suppose I should be grateful."

"That's a positive outlook."

No sooner had I said this than her brave mask shattered. Tears welled up in her eyes and her lip quivered.

Desperately searching my brain for something to cheer my friend, I said, "You'll always have me, no matter what comes your way."

"I know that I can always count on you."

I touched her cheek. "Don't forget that."

She forced a smile. "Do you remember Chiara and Donatella?"

"The twins? Yes, of course I do."

"Their eldest brother found good husbands for both of them." Celeste rolled her eyes. "All they talk of now are gowns and parties. I can't bear to be around them anymore."

"I think it would be fun to own fine garments and host grand parties. Don't you?"

"I prefer the peacefulness of the convent. I enjoy working alongside Sister Assunta in the apothecary. Which reminds me…" She went to a shelf and grasped a small ceramic vessel. "I made some arnica unguent for your aunt."

Aunt Gloria often complained of aching hands and feet so I accepted the gift with a grateful smile. "I know she will appreciate this, thank you."

"Healing people is what I was meant to do. It's what *God* wants me to do, Valentina. Who am I to question Him?"

"God sanctioned marriage—it's a Holy Sacrament. Being a good wife is another way of serving Him. There's no reason why you can't continue brewing tonics and mixing curatives once you're married. I'm sure your future husband will find your skills most valuable."

A shadow settled upon Celeste's features. "While that may be true, it's not the same as being surrounded by my fellow sisters in the faith and living a cloistered life."

"I'm only trying to make you feel better. What does Sister Assunta say about this situation?"

"She puts on a brave face but I know she's as devastated as I am. Sister Assunta is the only mother I have ever known and it pains me to think that I'll soon be leaving her here alone."

Celeste had been orphaned at a much younger age than me. I remembered my parents with clarity whereas she did not.

Throwing up her hands, she continued, "I wish I could simply convince my uncle to desist in this matter."

I ventured, "You could send him a letter stating your feelings on the matter."

"I haven't seen him in several years. I barely know the man. I doubt he would take pity on me."

"Maybe Sister Assunta will be allowed to accompany you to your new home."

She shook her head. "My uncle will aim high. I'm a Carducci, remember? I can't imagine a nobleman tolerating an elderly nun glued to his wife's side."

"Your husband won't object to visits, I'm sure. In the meantime, you'll be living a comfortable life in accordance to your social status."

"What use will I have for comfort if I am unhappy?" Celeste shot back, indignant. "There is nothing that a rich man can provide me with that would compensate for the loss of Sister Assunta."

I imagined a jewelry box overflowing with sparkling gems, an armoire filled with lovely gowns, a table laden with succulent roasted fowl and tender beef. Sweetmeats galore. Finally, I imagined a library filled with books. *Dozens of books.*

"Having your own home, servants to command, a bountiful table—these are privileges that few people will ever enjoy in their lifetimes. Celeste, you must see the positive in this situation. Otherwise, you'll always be sad."

"I concede to your point, but what if he is unkind? Worse still, what if he's cruel?"

"Have you so little faith in your uncle?"

"It's not that…"

"I know he hasn't been a part of your life, but I doubt he would saddle his niece with a monster. You are the sweetest, kindest, most sincere person that I know. God will grant you a good Christian husband who will cherish you."

Celeste stared at me. "What if he's hideous?"

I made a face as I searched my mind for a suitable answer. "I don't know much about carnal matters, but I hear that men seek the beds of their wives in the dark so you'll be spared the sight of him."

At this, Celeste laughed. "Oh Valentina…"

"I'm trying to help you make the best of this terrible situation."

"I know, and I thank you for that. I've been asking the Madonna and Santa Patrizia for strength. I'm sure they'll help me when the time comes."

"There's something else you should consider."

"What's that?"

I shrugged. "You may fall in love with your husband."

Looking me straight in the eye, she said, "Never."

The vehement manner in which she said this puzzled me.

She continued, "Let's talk of pleasant things, shall we?"

"Yes."

Celeste extracted a deck of playing cards from a drawer and glanced at me. This was my devout friend's only vice. I nodded to her unspoken suggestion. We laid the subject of husbands to rest and enjoyed the remainder of our time together by playing a few rounds of card games.

I left the convent an hour later and returned home to find Aunt Gloria propped on the chaise longue eating sweetmeats. A cloth was wrapped around her hair like a Moorish turban.

"Celeste sends her warmest regards along with a gift," I said, handing her the ceramic vessel.

She opened the lid and took a whiff. "Bless her heart. I used up the last bit of arnica unguent a few weeks ago."

"The next time I go the convent, I'll ask her to teach me how to make it for you."

"How is Celeste? You mentioned that she wasn't well."

I sat in a chair and sighed. "She is extremely upset."

Aunt Gloria slathered the unguent on her hands. "Let me guess. Camillo Custozi has found a man for his niece to wed."

"How did you know?"

"A mere guess. Who is he?"

“We don’t know but he’s most likely rich. Celeste’s uncle commissioned a miniature, and she received notification that a physician will examine her tomorrow.”

Aunt Gloria’s eyes narrowed pensively. “Camillo Custozi is known for striking good bargains so I’m certain that it will be someone of importance. I realize this isn’t what your friend wants but she should consider herself a lucky girl.”

I toyed with a strand of my long dark hair as I pondered my own future. There would be no such advantageous arrangement made on my behalf since I had no male relatives—or an attractive dowry. As for my husband, he definitely wouldn’t be noble, wealthy, or powerful. I would be lucky to marry a chemist like my late father.

Aunt Gloria popped a piece of dried fruit into her mouth and held out the small plate. “Would you like one?”

I accepted a dried fig, relishing its flavor.

Seeing the serious look on my face, she said, “Don’t feel too bad for your friend, Valentina. Most girls in the city would trade their left eye for the chance at being a rich man’s wife.”

“Celeste isn’t like most girls.”

“Neither are you, but I’m sure you wouldn’t scoff in the face of such a good opportunity.”

She was right but I said, “Remember, Celeste is pious.”

Aunt Gloria’s eyebrow shot upward. “A bit *too* pious if you ask me.”

“What do you mean by that?”

She shrugged and selected another piece of fruit instead of answering my question.

CHAPTER 3

Furtive kisses tasted sweeter in the moonlight. Languid embraces and whispered words spoken beneath a blanket of twinkling stars held more value. At least this was what she believed to be true. Caressing his bearded cheek, she offered him a heartfelt smile. He smiled in return, then kissed her forehead before hastily rearranging his robe. The mere thought of these precious moments coming to an end filled her with tremendous grief. The exquisite pain in her chest caused her to heave a sad sigh.

He paused in his task. "Do not despair, my love."

"How can I not?"

"I will find a way, I promise."

She hugged him tightly. He meant more to her than anything on Earth or in Heaven. Surely, God couldn't find fault with an emotion as pure as true love? God created male and female, did He not? God instilled people with hearts and the capacity to fill that special organ to the point of bursting.

"I must go," he whispered.

She glanced over her shoulder at the quivering shadows of leaves disturbed by the wind. Every sound, every movement seemed amplified whenever they were together. Every fiber of her being felt wonderfully alive when he held her in his arms.

He continued, "Meet me tomorrow. Same time. I love you."

"I love you."

He scaled the wall as silently as a cat as she tiptoed back to her cell. Once inside, she fell upon the bed and wept in fear of their love coming to an end because of her damned uncle.

***

Livia's carriage came to a halt outside the walls of the convent. The footman aided her in alighting the vehicle, then turned his attention to the weathered man still within.

Shaking out the creases in her black satin gown, she said,

"Here we are, Dr. Bernardo."

The physician emerged from the carriage in a somber coat and knickers, gray stockings, and brown leather shoes. A black tricorn hat sat upon his balding head. "Lead the way, madam," he said, lugging a worn leather satchel full of implements and ointments—the tools of his trade.

Pulling a sheer dark veil over her face, Livia strutted to the main gate and made use of the iron knocker.

The viewing door slid open. "Yes?"

Livia said haughtily, "I am here to see Signorina Celeste Carducci. My personal physician will examine her today."

The plain featured nun opened the gate and stepped aside, granting access to the tall, gaunt woman. "Ah yes, we received your message. This way, my lady."

Livia's eyes darted right and left, taking in the manicured garden with its citrus trees and the cloister's frescoed walls. The convent seemed clean and well-maintained, which she took as a good omen. A few nuns sat on benches reading prayer books.

The nun led Livia down a hallway to a door. Three sharp raps later and a nondescript girl in a plain gray nun's habit appeared in the doorway. Livia studied the creature with an appraising eye and deduced that the miniaturist had obviously exaggerated Celeste's beauty.

"You have visitors, Signorina Celeste," the nun said before retracing her steps.

Celeste took in the stranger's fine gown and painted face but said nothing.

Livia frowned slightly at the girl's lack of good manners. "Celeste Carducci?"

"Yes?"

"I am Signora Livia, aunt of Ferrante degli Spini. Dr. Bernardo will be examining you today. You received my note, did you not?"

"Ferrante degli Spini?"

Livia hesitated. "Yes, the man you are destined to marry."

Celeste's face blanched in horror.

Afraid that the girl would swoon, Livia stepped into the cell and led Celeste to a stool. "Calm yourself, child."

Dr. Bernardo went directly to the pitcher on the table and poured some water into a ceramic cup. "Here, drink this."

Livia waited for the girl to take a sip. "I'm well aware of Ferrante's reputation, but I assure you that his bark is worse than his bite. The fact that you fear him tells me that you have some good sense in that head of yours."

Sister Assunta poked her head in her ward's room. Seeing the girl in such a panicked state, the old woman grew alarmed. "Celeste, are you all right?"

"I am to marry Ferrante degli Spini," Celeste replied in a trembling voice before tears ran down her cheeks.

Livia's brow knitted together in irritation. "Take a moment to calm yourself."

Placing a comforting hand on the girl's back, the nun whispered, "Don't be afraid, child. God never gives us more than we can bear." To Livia, she added, "I am Sister Assunta, her nurse and chaperone."

Livia inclined her head in greeting. "I am assuming that you have prepared Celeste for this day."

The nun gave a curt nod. "I was well aware of Signore Camillo's intentions when he dropped off his niece at the convent twelve years ago."

Livia glanced disdainfully at Celeste. "Good. I expect there will be no more of these theatrics in the future."

Celeste hastily wiped her face with her sleeve. "Forgive me, my lady. I meant no offense."

Sister Assunta added, "You must understand that Celeste is an innocent girl with a tender soul—a spiritual creature who has dedicated her life to God."

Livia's icy stare silenced the nun. "I'm glad to hear it. Now she will dedicate her life to my nephew and be a mother to his children. Each of us have our duties to fulfill in God's plans, wouldn't you agree?"

"Yes," Sister Assunta replied, albeit reluctantly.

Livia turned to the physician. "Shall we get on with the examination, Dr. Bernardo?"

The older women retreated to the opposite side of the room. They positioned themselves in a manner that allowed for Celeste's privacy, yet their sharp eyes missed nothing.

Dr. Bernardo opened his satchel and removed various devices, setting them in a neat row atop a nearby table. He checked Celeste's pulse, eyes, and ears, then proceeded to ask a list of questions before prodding the girl's firm flesh in various places.

Gently patting the sides of Celeste's throat, he said, "Stick out your tongue."

Celeste did as she was told, her eyes darting nervously to where the older women stood like a pair of sentinels.

The physician turned to Livia and said, "She seems to be in excellent health."

Livia's brow creased. "Are you sure?"

The physician nodded. "Hearty and hale, madam."

This information struck Livia as odd given that the reports Ferrante mentioned described Celeste as frail. Her eyes slid to Sister Assunta, the nun who had penned those fictitious reports. Livia suspected something foul afoot and, rather than confront the old woman, she thought it prudent to wait. Sooner or later, the puzzle pieces would fall into place.

Dr. Bernardo turned his attention back to Celeste. "Signorina, I need you to lay back on the cot."

Celeste's eyes were wide with fear as the physician lifted the hem of her habit. "Please don't." When the doctor persisted, she cried, "Stop, no!"

Sister Assunta's face melted into an expression of concern. "This is a common practice, my child. Men want to *know*." To Livia, she added, "Perhaps I should hold her hand…the poor thing must be terrified. She's never been touched by a man."

Livia gripped the nun's arm. "Leave her be. She'll need to get over her fear of men if she's to become Ferrante's wife."

Averting his gaze, the physician performed the examination as quickly and as gently as possible. He stood and wiped his hand afterward, his expression puzzled. Next, he collected his things.

Livia escorted him to the door and they shared a pointed look before the physician whispered something into her ear.

Livia's face blanched. She took a moment to compose herself, then said, "Please wait for me in the carriage, Dr. Bernardo. I'll be along in a moment." To the nun, she added, "I would like to have a word with Celeste in private."

Sister Assunta tossed an apologetic look at her ward before vacating the room.

Livia closed the door then wandered to the cell's tiny window. Gazing up at the sky, she said, "My nephew has been scouring the nunneries these last few months in the hope of finding a good wife. I was skeptical when he told me about you. For this reason, I insisted on accompanying Dr. Bernardo today. I wanted to see for myself what kind of woman my nephew has chosen for a bride. He believes you to be submissive, devout, obedient—"

"I *am* all of those things," Celeste interjected.

Garnets and sapphires flashed in a ray of sunlight as Livia's hand shot up in protest. "Ah, but not *chaste*."

Mortified, Celeste hung her head in shame.

Livia turned away from the window and pinned the girl with a cold stare. "Despite being cloistered and ignorant of the outside world, you have managed to find a way to play the harlot."

"It's not like that."

"Camillo Custozi would have you whipped and stripped of your good reputation if he were to discover the truth. More precisely, that old whoremonger would gamble away every penny of your dowry."

Celeste nervously wrung her hands. "My uncle can never know the truth. Please, I beg you."

"Who is he?"

"I'm sorry but I cannot tell you. I'm sworn to secrecy."

"May I remind you that you are in no position to bargain?"

"Please don't make me break my promise to him."

"I asked you a question and I expect an answer." When Celeste refused, Livia shrugged. "Very well. I shall notify your uncle at once that you've been playing the whore at his expense for years."

Celeste hesitated, then placed her head in her hands. "There is a monastery across the way…"

Livia gaped at the girl. "Your lover is a *monk*?"

"Luigi was forced into monastic life due to lack of inheritance. He's the only man I've ever known and I love him. I don't believe that constitutes being a whore."

"How far along are you?" At the girl's blank look, she demanded, "When did you last have your monthly?"

Confused, she performed the calculations in her head and whispered, "Six weeks ago."

Livia tapped her jeweled fingers on the table and mused aloud, "You are at the onset of your pregnancy. That's good."

A mixture of fear and bewilderment settled upon Celeste's features. *"I'm pregnant?"*

Livia froze, her fingers hovering above the wooden surface. "You didn't know? Santa Madonna. You are naïve, aren't you?"

Still in shock from learning about her condition, Celeste placed her hands on her belly. A hint of a smile touched her lips, then realization lit up her features. "Does this mean you will call off the wedding?"

Livia went back to the window, her mind racing with thoughts. She mused aloud, "A virgin who gave her maidenhead to a monk. Was he a virgin too?"

"Yes."

"I'll be surprised if the baby isn't born with a halo around its head," Livia murmured to herself.

"What did you say, madam?"

"Never mind. Who else knows about your illicit affair with Luigi?"

"No one."

"Not even the nun?"

Celeste shook her head.

Livia recalled Ferrante's pale face and hollowed eyes. Her nephew had spent three days in bed due to fever last winter. The fear of him dying without an heir had consumed her throughout the duration of his illness. Enough time had been wasted in finding Celeste. To tell Ferrante of the girl's folly meant searching for another suitable young woman. One who could be barren…Livia's gaze rested on Celeste. The girl was young, strong, and somewhat innocent despite the circumstances. Better that her late brother's legacy fall to a bastard raised as a Spini than to her sister's son, Ruggero. Her corrupt nephew was the embodiment of debauchery and decadence.

"You will tell no one of your pregnancy," Livia said at last.

Celeste gaped in disbelief. "You would have me marry your nephew while carrying another man's child? Forgive me, but I thought the whole purpose of Dr. Bernardo examining me *down there* was to determine if I was still a virgin."

"Ferrante has no doubt that you're a virgin. Dr. Bernardo examined you at my request. My nephew requires a healthy wife who will conceive and carry a child to full term. He desperately needs an heir. You should be grateful, Celeste. This means that you will have fulfilled your duty as a wife before the year is out—assuming the child is male, of course."

Celeste's brows knitted together in supplication. "Luigi and I wish to marry."

"Can he provide for you and the baby?"

Averting her gaze, Celeste replied, "Not yet, but we love each other and that's what matters."

Livia laughed derisively. "Do you think love will feed your hungry baby?"

"God will provide."

"As if God doesn't have better things to do than help a pair of fornicators. Wipe the foolish thought from your head this instant! You will bid Luigi farewell and that will be the end of it." The words propelled the distraught girl into a weeping fit, so Livia added in a gentler tone, "Think of your future and that of your child. Ferrante is determined to claim you as his bride, and when he sets his mind to something there is no stopping the man. He's tired of searching and wants to marry as soon as possible. This wedding will take place whether you like it or not, so I suggest that you start accepting your fate."

"I-I d-don't want t-to m-marry him. Please…"

Resisting the urge to strike the girl, Livia said, "Take comfort, child. Ferrante isn't a bad man. I won't vouch for my nephew's charming personality or easygoing nature, but at least he isn't stingy. Brash, moody, yes…but never cruel."

Celeste did her best to staunch her tears while nodding to the woman's words.

Livia continued, "I know you'll fall in love with Nadia."

"Who?"

"Ferrante's three year old daughter. She's a sweet little thing. Unfortunately, my grandniece is mute. God willing, she'll soon have a brother."

Celeste sniffed. "What will I tell Luigi?"

"You will explain to him that you have a duty to fulfill, then bid him farewell. Obviously, he knows nothing about the child growing inside of you and it should remain that way for everyone's sake. Afterward, you will get down on your knees and thank the Lord that you have been gifted a dignified way out of your current state of disgrace."

Celeste nodded distractedly at the woman's sobering words. "When is the wedding scheduled to take place?"

"On the first of April, so I suggest you pray for courage and tranquility of heart and mind. Ferrante won't take kindly to you moping about the house. You will be expected to perform your wifely duties with cheerfulness and efficiency. Do you understand what I'm telling you?"

"Yes, Signora Livia."

Livia regarded the girl with narrowed eyes. "Tell me, was it your idea or the nun's to send false health reports to Camillo?"

Celeste's shoulders sagged in defeat. "I begged Sister Assunta to pretend that my health wasn't good in order for my uncle to postpone his search for potential husbands."

Livia crossed her arms and studied the little schemer. At least she had the good sense to lower her head in shame. "Marriage has its benefits. In time, you'll learn to accept your fate and derive joy from motherhood."

"Is that what you did?"

"Unfortunately, no. I'm barren." *And everyone in Naples knows it too.*

"I'm sorry."

Livia's eyes turned hard. "At least that won't be the case for you, Celeste. We'll meet again on your wedding day and I hope to see an improvement in your spirits."

"When will I meet your nephew?"

Livia hesitated. "Ferrante is not coming here."

"Doesn't he want to meet me before making me his wife?"

Livia sympathized with the girl's bewilderment. "He's a *very* busy man, my dear, and he has placed his trust completely in your uncle."

"And you."

"And me, yes. You'll meet Ferrante on the first of April at the wedding. Until then, I suggest you pray for fortitude and begin reconciling yourself with what's to come."

"I'll do exactly as you say, Signora Livia."

"That's better. You'll see, everything will work out for the best. I promise."

Printed in Great Britain
by Amazon